THE UTTERLY SUBLIME
ADVENTURES OF
AVA ROBERTS

Lisa Frederickson

E-book first published September 2023
First paperback edition September 2023

Cover design by Sally-Anne Kerr
Edited by Adam Frederickson
Proofread by Kay Wilson

ISBN (ebook) 978-1-7393880-0-3
ISBN (paperback) 978-1-7393880-1-0

Published by Fred Rick Publishing
Fredrickpublishing@outlook.com
Fredrickpublishing.com

"And I'd choose you; in a hundred lifetimes, in a hundred worlds, in any version of reality, I'd find you and I'd choose you."

- Kiersten White, The Chaos of Stars

"Have enough courage to trust love one more time and always one more time."

- Maya Angelou

For my uncle David

CHAPTER ONE - LATEX LOVE

Delhi, India. January 2018

'Ok Miss, you may get dressed now,' the security official snaps. She is a thick-set woman in her early thirties with a distinctive monobrow, which puts me in mind of the Mexican artist Frida Kahlo; though this Frida's digits were not made for the noble art of painting, that's for sure. Two words spring to mind 'sausage fingers', or well-endowed in lesbian-speak. Suffice to say, this has not been a good day. It's 40 degrees and I've just been strip-searched in a backroom at Delhi International Airport. My parents would be proud.

The room is hot and stuffy as Frida removes the latex gloves and jettisons them into a scruffy tin bin by the door. Slam, dunk. This woman is the Michael Jordan of custom officials. Pretty impressive! Always good to focus on the bread when life serves you a shit sandwich, I find. I lock eyes with Frida, smiling politely in that British way, as if to acknowledge the unspeakable awkwardness of the situation.

'It's *soooo* hot!' I blurt, stating the blatantly obvious. Frida gives two slow nods, causing her chins to concertina like a French accordion. She is much friendlier than before, doubtless reassured that I'm not secreting narcotics in my front bottom. Or back one for that matter. It's funny, I'm the one who's just exposed my lady garden to a complete stranger, yet *I* feel the overwhelming need to apologise. Like I said, I'm very British.

The ordeal over, I hurriedly gather my undergarments from the table and start to dress. It's at moments like this that I wish I'd worn better knickers I muse, knowing full well that this is not the most important lesson to be drawn from the experience. Perhaps it's my way of coping...

Oh, listen to me babbling on!

Allow me to introduce myself. My name is Ava Roberts, I'm twenty-nine years old and, like I said, this has not been a good day. It started out well enough, with a glorious sunrise on my final morning at an ashram in Northern Goa, where I'd spent the last four weeks trying to cleanse body and mind of my ex. I'd taken a farewell stroll with my wonderful, new friend Indira, before savouring one last, life-affirming dip at the local beach.

The ashram had turned out to be quite the peaceful cocoon and my fare-well with the folks I'd met there was a bit of a choker. It's funny how close you get to people in a few weeks, especially if you're directly behind them when they're performing downward dog of a morning. Still, it was time to go, and Indira and I shared a last embrace.

'Ava my dear, you never leave a place you love, you always take a part of it with you,' she whispered, pressing me tight to her soft, doughy bosom. And so off to the airport I went with puffy eyes and a warm, fuzzy feeling in my belly, hungry for the next stage in my global adventure, Bangkok.

Everything went smoothly at first. I managed to cadge a lift to Dabo-lim Airport with some bendy back-packer lads I knew from my yoga group. 'Hop in with us, Ava!' they hollered, chivalrously pushing their Northface backpacks to one side. And into the dusty, white mini-van I leapt. They were sweet hippy boys. You know the type, mousey dreadlocks, Somerset accents and hugely fond of Bob Marley. Now I look back, I guess there was a hint of the 'Eau de Ganja' about them, but I didn't think much of it until a sniffer dog took a shine to me in Transit Zone A, Delhi International. I can only imagine the fumes had seeped into my clothing and, well, here I am getting frisked by Frida, who's straight in there without so much as a 'Hello love, can I buy you a shandy?'

I should say at this point that this isn't a usual occurrence for me. I don't generally get strip-searched by strange women unless A. They are very cute or B. See point A. No, this really is most out of character. I used to be a girl guide for God's sake. Had a sleeve full of badges and international drug mule wasn't one of them. So, to my earlier point, *what the actual fuck?* Truth be told, this unfortunate predicament can be traced back to an even more traumatic event, just four months ago in London….

One. Awful. Life. Changing. Night.

It was late summer and I was living the dream in a beautiful warehouse apartment in London's trendy Shoreditch; all loved up and settled down with my beautiful fiancée Scarlet. It was her dream home. Exposed brick walls, wooden floors – 'industrial' in estate agent speak or 'not very homely' to quote my nan. Don't get me wrong, it was a great place, I just find high ceilings give me a touch of vertigo, possibly because I grew up in a hobbit-sized bungalow with barely enough room to swing a hamster. Scarlet was everything I'd ever dreamt of: fun, beautiful and loyal. As it turned out, I was a bit off on the loyalty part, but, hey, two out of three ain't bad.

In short, life was pretty sweet and, as we all know, that's the perfect cue for some cataclysmic cluster-fuck to strike, in this case in the form of Carla De Vere, a big-breasted vamp from Chelsea. Carla was from the horsey set; a part-time Insta-model and full-time cow. She had one of those Monroe hour-glass figures, only in her case all the sand had got stuck in the top half, resulting in her tilting slightly forward when she walked, like she was going steadily downhill. Bit like my relationship when she started working at Scarlet's agency. Sometimes I kick myself for not seeing the signs, the working late, the constant texting. How could I not have spotted the iceberg that was about to sink our Titanic of a Love? At this point you should be picturing Kate Winslet (Scarlet) afloat a big wooden door, with Leonardo (me) freezing his knackers off in the icy waters below. I guess that I was blindsided. But that's the nature of love, it makes us blinkered to others' faults, oblivious to fatal flaws, or in layman's terms, love turns us into hopeless fools.

I can recall the night when everything fell apart like it was yesterday, rather than the two months, 19 days and six hours it really is. Approximately. Scarlet and I had just returned from a romantic trip to Rome where she had unexpectedly proposed. I'll never forget that night, sunset on the Piazza di Spagna, dining al fresco. Halfway through the meal, she had placed a small leather box on the table and sat back smiling. I remember how excited she looked – biting her bottom lip, not wholly confident. I didn't quite comprehend what was unfolding at first, I was so enamoured by my penne arrabbiata, but the longer she sat there, the more I realised that this was a moment that meant something, a moment that I needed to surrender to. So I laid down my fork, leant in and nervously opened the box.

'Sooooo, will you?' she asked. I felt euphoric. Giddy. Time stood still.

'Yes!' I whispered. 'Yes, Yes, Yes, YESSS!!'

It was the most wonderful night of my life and I couldn't stop smiling. Even weeks later I had this deranged perma-grin plastered across my face that made strangers wary enough not to sit next to me on the bus, which was an unexpected bonus. Like all smug fiancées, Scarlet and I decided to rub it in, I mean, *celebrate* the happy occasion with a big, fat engagement party – since renamed 'the most excruciating night of my life' bash.

Now I think back, she did seem uncharacteristically anxious that night, but I just put it down to excitement or too many espresso martinis on half a crisp-bread. God, she looked stunning, but then she always does. Scarlet is the kind of girl you don't look twice at, you look four or five times, then text your friends so they can have a look too. Blond, five foot nine, piercing blue eyes and cheek bones that cut glass. I always thought she looked like a young Charlize Theron. 'What, when she starred in that *Monster* film?' she'd laugh, pulling a woeful attempt at an ugly face, which of course is impossible with that DNA.

I remember watching as she applied a final coat of fire-red gloss, ominously named 'lady-killer rouge', to her gorgeous plump lips, flicking her hair off her bare shoulders. I felt so happy in that moment, gazing at her, tracing the contours of her body with my admiring eyes. Drinking her all in. Why is it that people always look their best right before they rip your heart out? Like the Love Gods are tormenting us, 'See this. You'll never have it again, loser.'

The buzz of the doorbell broke the spell as Scarlet promptly spun on her heels and pulled me close. 'You do know how much I love you, don't you Ave?'

'Dooooon't, you'll make my mascara run,' I grinned, kissing her full on the mouth. I see now that she was clearly feeling guilty about something, but I was far too distracted by the excitement of the big night, the thrill of having everyone I love together in one place, watching, witnessing…. my complete and utter humiliation.

It was a little after midnight when it happened.

The party was in full swing. My 70-year-old Aunty Beryl was break-dancing in the kitchen, cousin Maria was sobbing over her loser fiancé and Uncle George was hitting on the hot lesbians by the vol-au-vents. Pretty standard. Scarlet had gone AWOL and in my alcoholic daze I wandered off to find her, swaying through the merry hordes of well-wishers, dishing out kisses like Oprah hands out cars – 'You get a kiss! You get a kiss!'

The atmosphere was electric. 'Scarlet!' I called, searching for her face among the inebriated throng. 'Anyone seen Scarlet?' before catching sight of my brother tonguing one of my work friends, Psycho Sue from HR. *Slurp slurp.* That will not end well. 'Have you seen Scarlet?' I called again before running into my best friend Jen, entertaining a small group under the stairs. *Praise be! Sanity at last!* I tapped her on the shoulder and her eyes lit up like she hadn't seen me in years.

'H-h-heeeeeeeey. My bestest frienddddd!' she slurred, flinging her arms around me like an amorous koala. What a girl. Everyone needs a friend like Jen Jones. We've been inseparable since Uni, after I vommed in her sink on day two of freshers' week. She's as sharp as a butcher's blade and adept at unblocking plug-holes with just a Bic biro. We always used to joke we'd marry each other if we weren't hitched by 35. Looks like she's had a lucky escape.

The slur-fest continues.

'Hey Avaaa…You look *AMAZZZZZING, guuuurl!* That Schharlet's a lucky, lucky lady…isn't she, evy'one?' The group responded with a resounding 'Yaaaay!' which my cousin's fiancé followed up with an inappropriate 'I'd give her one!' resulting in a swift elbow to the ribs.

'Ignore him, bloody twat face. Never trust a man without a chin, I say!' Jen giggled, doing a ropey toad impersonation. 'Anyway…*this,* my friend, is a great party. Huuuuge congratulations on your engagement.'

'Awww. Thanks my love.'

Hearing her now, you wouldn't guess that she's a communications expert and head writer at the same media firm as me. Tonight, she has all the verbal dexterity of a slipper. I await her response, fearing my question might have been guzzled with the last tequila shot.

'So….? *Have* you seen her, then?'

'Shheen who?'

Small belch, hiccup, slow-slide-down-wall into hysterical heap

Patience prevails and I eventually decipher that Scarlet had gone to fetch some more Prosecco. *Bingo!* Target located, off I swayed, singing badly to Tay Tay's *"I knew you were trouble when you walked in"*. A few more kisses and 'heys' later, I arrived at the utility room, unaware that I was about to open the door not just to the room, but to a whole new destiny.

'Hello sexy fiancée. Come and give me a big, hot ki…'

My. Jaw. Hit. The. Floor.

There before my very eyes was my beautiful fiancée with Carla De Vere, half-dressed and fully going at it on the washer-dryer. It was like some dramatic Cluedo reveal: Miss Scarlet, in the utility room, with the Hotpoint! All that was missing was the true murder weapon – a dagger to the heart. Everything went into a weird slo-mo at that point and I just wanted to hurl. The image still haunts me now: Carla's perfect bottom, the mortified look on Scarlet's face and pathetic me, mouth agape in the doorway.

After what seemed like an eternity, I managed to muster a feeble 'How… how long has it been going on?'

They stared at me for a moment, before turning to one another, Carla blurting 'SIX MONTHS…' and Scarlet 'THE FIRST TIME!'

Awkward pause.

'Err. First time… in the utility room...' Scarlet clarified.

.

.

"Shame on me, now, now…."

CHAPTER TWO - WELCOME TO GOA.
NAMASTE IN BED

The ceiling fan whirs like a demented fly, jolting me back to reality in Frida's office.

'Won't be long now Miss Roberts,' she assures, pressing pen to paper on a stack of official-looking documents. 'Sorry. Computer is down, today.'

Course it is Frida. Course it is.

India is well known for its bureaucracy, so slow it might embarrass a glacier, so I resign myself to the wait, allowing my mind to drift back to happier times in Goa. Glorious life-changing days filled with sunset walks and laughter-fuelled evenings. Images of golden beaches wash over me like a warm, salty wave. What a difference 29 days make! What a transformation from the anxious, heartbroken wretch that stepped off that stuffy plane and onto Indian soil for the first time …

Goa, India. January 4th 2018.

Four weeks earlier.

The plane door opens and I'm struck by a wall of ferocious heat. I now know what a leg of lamb feels like at gas mark 7. Slap on some mint sauce and plate me up, mum! The air wobbles as I follow my fellow passengers out across the tarmac, which is decidedly tacky underfoot, like wading across the top of a giant sticky toffee pudding. If only it smelt as good. Instead, I get a whiff of B.O. from the red-faced man next to me, who inflates his cheeks and makes that *'Phewwwww!'* sound Brits make in temperatures above 18 degrees C. It must be close to 40 now and my eyeballs are fit to melt.

'Welcome to Goa!' he puffs like Thomas the Tank Engine. I nod and affix sunnies, Men in Black style.

So, this is India, my promised land of spiritual enlightenment. As I set foot inside Dabolim airport, it dawns on me that my knowledge of this place is like a Love Islander's bikini: skimpy. Aside from stories friends have shared, my only points of reference are *Slum-Dog Millionaire*, delicious curries and the legend that is Mahatma Ghandi. So yeah, this will be what you call a baptism of fire.

The airport is not what I expected. Modern, bright and most notably cow free. A far cry from the feral scene my cousin's fiancé described. *Bloody Marcus!* I should have known that he'd never been to India when he mentioned Chicken McNuggets at the Taj Mahal. #Twatface.

It is all rather chaotic and I wait in line for passport control for what feels like an eternity, before realising that I'm being steadily overtaken by a stream of mums, dads, grannies and kids. They glide past as if it's customary for locals to go to the front. Perhaps it is. They have the most wonderful smiles, so I'm powerless to do anything other than smile back and accept that I will be a barren spinster with chin hair by the time I leave here.

I finally reach the front and present my passport to the customs officer along with my best 'I'm not a fugitive' smile. Not sure what it is about airport officials that makes me feel so guilty and I actually start to wonder if I haven't inadvertently secreted those heroin bricks in my sponge bag after all. Crazy. He stares down at my photo, then back at me. Look, frown, repeat. It's not the best likeness to be fair. It was snapped on a particularly savage hangover, post Scarlet's 30th, and I look like that emoji you send people to tell them you have food poisoning. He stares at me one last time before giving a solid nod to proceed. 'Yesss. India here I come!' I proclaim, high-fiving the air, while my inner voice screams, 'OMG! I'm all alone with no one to help should I be bitten by a scorpion, king cobra or rabid dog'.

#RationalFears.

Baggage pick-up is a smooth affair and I set about my final mission, locating the ashram courtesy bus.

The car park is a lot. Hot and manic, with car horns, shouting, and yet more horns, and I'm instantly besieged by a swarm of pre-pubescent baggage handlers who buzz around me like bees around honey, all eager to carry my backpack for a few rupees. 'No, no thank you,' I politely decline before wrestling one skinny rake to the floor. 'Sorry!' I whisper, scurrying off only to be accosted by another.

This time it's a voluptuous older lady, immaculately dressed in a blue sari with the brightest smile. She grabs my backpack and we engage in a polite tug of war, pulling one way, then the other. Back and forth. 'Namaste!' she smiles. I'm not sure what that means, but I 'Namaste' her back, which she seems to appreciate. The bag-tugging and namaste-ing continues for a few more rounds, but it's not until I look down and see the sign for Rajem's ashram in her other hand that I twig.

'Ohhhh. Riiiiiight. You're from the ashram?'

'Yes, my dear. And you are Ava Roberts, isn't it?' she smiles.

Awkwardly hands over backpack

She draws me into her bosom like a long-lost aunt. 'I'm Indira, welcome!' she says, holding me there for what feels like an inordinate amount of time. I go to speak but, chin deep in cleavage, it comes out as a muffled '*Flubaawaabbaaaayoooo*', which does little to further relations. She eventually releases her grip, leaving me to contemplate the notion that she is the only person I know in India and, as such, is instantly elevated to best friend status. *You're welcome!* She has a wonderful lightness about her, and I watch as she smiles and chats to everyone en route, before leading us over to a white minivan, amidst a sea of other white mini-vans. 'Here we are,' she smiles, sliding the door back to reveal a shabby interior full of pasty faces that turn to greet me with varying levels of enthusiasm.

'Oh hello,' I say, clambering into the only vacant seat, second row, opposite a pale, red-headed girl. I give her a smile before attempting to crow bar myself into what is clearly a defective seat, which leaves me bent double and assuming crash position. *Excellent start!* Indira climbs up front with the driver and begins an introduction over a squeaky microphone with serious re-verb, which seems wholly unnecessary considering the size of the vehicle.

'Welcome! Welcome!' she smiles, drawing her hands together in the prayer pose. 'We are so happy to meet you all. My name is Indira and this is our driver, Sanjay.' Sanjay completely misses the cue as he is sparked out at the wheel – asleep or dead. The jury's out. She gives him a little prod and he opens his eyes and smiles, showing a formidable gap between his front teeth that you could happily park your bike in. 'Sanjay is just out of prison, so please forgive his driving, isn't it?' Indira says, completely poker-faced.

The remark elicits a dramatic gasp from the red-head opposite and I watch the blood drain from her face, which is near impossible as she's already semi-translucent. I fear she's about to lose it completely when Indira erupts into raucous laughter.

'Joking! I'm joking!' she howls, slapping her thigh. 'Ahhhh. Laughter is medicine for the soul. Medicine for the soul.'

And with that terrifying ice-breaker out of the way, the engine rattles to life and I resume battle with my seat. A few cranks and crunches later, Sanjay informs me that it is indeed 'buggered' and that I should sit in the back with the luggage. 'Very comfortable,' he assures, opening the rear hatch and ushering me in like the family labrador.

'Perfect!' I smile, feeling a buckle jab into my left buttock. *Just perfect.*

The gears crunch and we kangaroo off, blasting the horn and narrowly missing a family aboard a moped. *Beep Beep.* Indira wasn't kidding about the bad driving then. As I sink back into the bags, the realisation hits. *I'm in India. I'm actually bloody here!* It only seems like yesterday that I was crying on my bestie's sofa and now I'm halfway round the world about to check into a full-on spiritual retreat. *WTF!*

I'm not sure what to expect from the ashram – I don't have much experience of retreats, other than a pamper weekend at Champneys in 2017, when I picked up a nasty verruca. No, I have Jen to thank for this one. She'd stayed at an ashram after her father died a few years back and it had brought her some comfort, so who was I not to try it? Besides, I would have agreed to pretty much anything if it meant feeling less crap than I did. God, heartbreak sucks. It's akin to acute physical pain according to highly respected scholars on the subject. And Instagram.

The whole ashram plan had been hatched a few weeks after the fateful engagement party. Jen had kindly offered me a safe house at hers. 'Come and stay with me. It will be fun,' she assured, and boy was she right if by 'fun' you mean crying into a duvet 24-7 and consuming your body weight in wine. And so just like that, I left my warehouse love nest and took up residence on her IKEA couch and didn't move for a solid three weeks; stuck fast like a needy barnacle. And, in that time, Jen went above and beyond. She fed me, counselled me, rocked me to sleep, poked me awake and told me I was beautiful when I looked like Quasimodo's ugly sister. And in return for this kindness, I cursed Scarlet ad nauseum and blubbed into her nice floral cushions so much that the pattern got completely washed away.

And that was my routine. Cry. Binge. Repeat. Day in, day out for weeks. I was a lost cause, destined to forever dwell in the valley of the weeping vagina! I had become the very embodiment of everything I despised – the weak doormat, crying over a faithless lover who didn't deserve a single salty tear. But worse than that, it was the power Scarlet continued to wield over me I hated most. I still wanted her, but I wanted to get over her too and neither was happening.

Enough was enough; an idea was born.

An idea resulting in the purchase of a round-the-world ticket and the launch of 'Operation STD' – Scarlet Tennison Detox. An 80-day odyssey through four countries to mend my broken heart. Armed with my second-hand backpack from Oxfam and the requisite jabs, I set off from London Heathrow four weeks after my breakup, a courageous explorer standing on the precipice of a new reality. Utter lies. In truth, I was totally cacking myself.

BEEP. BEEEEEEP.

My inner musings are brought to an abrupt halt by another strike of the horn and a whimper from the girl opposite. I reach for my phone and snap a quick selfie entitled 'Jen, what have you done to me?' and hit send, as a voice addresses me from the 'first class' cabin.

'Good-eye-might. I'm Tom, from O'Straya.'

A tanned hand pokes through the backpacks. I give it a shake.

'Oh hi. *Straya?* Where's that?'

'O'Straya . You know, Oz…Down Under…' he laughs.

Penny drops

'Oh *Aus*-stralia! Sorry. Bit noisy back here.'

The guy is 100 per cent prime Aussie beef and I can think of a few of my friends who'd love to have a nibble. Blond, blue eyes – a kind of budget Chris Hemsworth.

'Feel bad you being back there, aye! Happy to swap.'

'Ah thanks, Tom. It's actually quite comfy!' I say it with such conviction that I almost believe it.

'Cool. Hey, don't suppose you could grab my headphones from that bag there?'

'This one?' I answer, as 20 condoms spill out along with a few packets of fruit-flavoured lube.

'Ah, yeah, nah. The other zip! Help yourself though.'

Not awkward at all.

I pass him the headphones and he settles back to snooze under his Rip-curl baseball cap, while I gaze out at the passing villages. They flash by, little glimpses of life: make-shift shelters, bright saris flapping like flags upon long washing lines, kids playing. It suddenly dawns on me that, despite everything that's happened, I really do have a lot to be thankful for – having small boobs being one of them. Lord, this van is a bone-shaker! No, aside from the crippling heartbreak, I really am a lucky bugger. I'm here on this incredible adventure, with new countries to explore, new friends to meet, and to crown it all I'm getting paid for the privilege. Yep, by some ridiculous stroke of luck that I still can't quite believe, I managed to land myself a paid sabbatical. I say 'I', it was more forced upon me really. It just so happens that THE Chief Creative guru at my office – a *Devil Wears Prada* type nicknamed 'Cruella De Grill' due to her love of putting people under intense heat – got wind of my 'situation' and felt my story would resonate with the company's target demographic. Or so she said when she cornered me in the kitchen the week before I left.

'Avaaaa daaarlink,' she purred, fanning her manicured hands wide like peacock feathers, 'I want you to share your truth'.

'Share my what?'

'Your truth, your reality, your *story,* daaaarlink! It has such power, such pathos!' Her eyes were practically rolling back in ecstasy.

I have to say I was a bit put out at first, I mean, *FML! Is there anyone in this bloody office that doesn't know my humiliating story?*

'This is going to be a beautiful voyage of healing…of empowerment, Ava. You rising like a phoenix from the flames and I want you to tell it, daarlink! Tell it to the world!' I nearly dropped my latte, it was so OTT.

Me, write a blog? Cruella must have hit the white stuff too hard this morning.

'Errr….I appreciate the offer, Lucrezia, but I'm really not much of a writer,' I protested, as she pressed her finger to my lips.

'Hush, darlink! Husssssshhhh! We are all writers… *in our souls.* Don't worry about the words, all we need are your stories, your adventures, your *journey.* I'll get Jen Jones to write it. You know Jen Jones, don't you daaaarlink? Huge talent. Benissimo! What a team you'll make!'

The whole exchange felt a little off. Cruella isn't exactly known for her generosity and I rather suspect that a heart-broken LGBTQ+ type travelling around the world ticked all her boxes: diversity, female empowerment and of course adventure. I was one of her KPIs. Guess I've been worse. I had all but decided to tell her to blog off, but any further objections were swiftly dismissed at lunch by Jen.

'All you have to do is feed me stories and I'll do the rest. This could be great for us both, Ave. I get to work on a juicy project, and you get paid to travel.' And when she put it like that, how could I refuse?

The deal was sealed with one important stipulation, I was to remain anonymous. 'But darlink! This is *your* truth, *your* story!' Cruella insisted. 'People must know it's you!' But I held strong – anonymous or no deal. And so with a manicured handshake, I became the inspiration behind Marshall Media's new online travel blog *Around the World in 80 Gays: A Journey Through Heartbreak.*

Pukes into mouth

So yeah, I'm not convinced myself, but I guess we'll see.

The journey to the ashram is set to the soundtrack of bhangra beats and car horns, *lots* of car horns. Barely a second goes by without one blasting out. The humble horn seems to have an altogether elevated function in India and is used, well, constantly. When overtaking – *beep!* When *being* overtaken – *beep beep!* And often for no apparent reason – *beeeeeeeep!* I watch Sanjay as he strikes the centre of the steering wheel almost like a tick. It's unsettling at first, but after a while I zone out, gazing out the window, taking in the unfamiliar landscape. Cows, roadside stalls and potholes so deep you could hide an *el-eph-UUUUUUUUCK!!*

There's an almighty jolt as the van veers sideways, flinging me boob-first against the window. ***SCRRRREEEEEEEEEEEEEEEECH!!*** Stomachs leap from mouths as a huge mega-truck thunders past, running us off the road where we smash through a stack of Pepsi crates before coming to a stunned standstill. *WTF!* A collective *'AHHHH!!!'* echoes around the van as I glance forward to catch our driver regaining consciousness.

'SANJAY!' Indira scolds, giving him a swift dig in the ribs. He raises his hands apologetically before pumping up the bhangra to drown out the whimpers of the red-head. The poor girl's sobbing for England now and desperately rubbing her St Christopher. Not sure he'll hold much sway here.

Well, that was fun, said nobody ever.

I'm on high alert for the rest of the journey, watching Sanjay like a hawk in the rear view mirror as he periodically douses his face with water to stay awake. *Splash, splash, beep, beep.* As soon as I suspect he's on the cusp of a snooze, I fake an almighty cough thereby causing him to throw more water and blast his horn a few more times. Perfect system. I look over to Indira, who is sucking away on a boiled sweet and nodding along to the music. She has remained remarkably zen during the whole experience. I get the impression this must be 'normal' driving in Goa, so I follow her lead and try to chill my chakras by distracting myself with my fellow passengers or 'ashramers', if that's a thing.

They're a mixed bunch, I have to say.

There's the pale red-head, Dawn I think her name is, who is much calmer now. I suspect she's cried herself to sleep like babies do. Poor thing! Behind her are two frizzy-haired women in head-to-toe tie-dye, nibbling on rice cakes. I presume they are French since they both bellowed 'MERDE!' very forcefully when Sanjay did his Vin Diesel slide across the highway. Across from them is a small Scottish guy whose head barely peeps above the headrest. He snored through most of the drama, so I'm guessing he's either very chilled/off his face/both. And finally, 'Aussie' Tom, King of the Condoms, who has taken to chanting '*Oooomm*' and sitting cross-legged post horror skid. All in all, we're a motley crew. Not sure we'll have much in common but hey, travelling is all about expanding your mind as my Aunty B told me before I left. She also said, 'Don't catch gonorrhea'. So yeah, sound advice all round really.

'My friends, we are almost there. I hope you are well rested,' Indira says with zero hint of irony. Most of us look like we've been on the rollercoaster ride from hell, which in a way we have. The van starts to slow as she points out an old colonial building to our left, framed by a small group of pointy trees. This must be the ashram.

'Beautiful, isn't it?'

I can hardly believe it. It's stunning; wonderfully majestic and ornate.

'Look at the architecture, the grand windows...each one hand carved.'

'Oh yes, lovely!' I say getting rather excited.

'Indeed. It is the finest example in Goa. The finest.'

'Wow, yesss.'

'Unfortunately, you are not staying there,' she laughs, as Sanjay takes a hard left into a tiny dirt road.

FML!

Dawn's face drops with the realisation that we are pretty much 'in the middle of bum-fuck nowhere' to quote Tom, who has ceased oooomm-ing by this point. Five minutes later, the engine stops and the door slides back. 'Shiiit, man!' Tom laughs, helping me out. 'If I didn't need my chakras sorted before, I bloody do now, aye.' He's got a point. Perhaps this is an ashram ploy to get everyone as wound up as possible, thus making the unwinding all the sweeter. Just a theory.

I have a good stretch and take in the building before me. It's a handsome white residence, not as grand as the palace Indira cruelly teased us with, but still lovely in its own modest way and set in the most gorgeous grounds, surrounded by tall trees and lush greenery. There are flowers in bloom everywhere, bright yellows and pinks. If appearances are anything to go by, I think I'm going to rather like ashram life.

We head up to the vaulted entrance and I catch sight of Dawn who looks like death.

'You ok there? I'm Ava, by the way.'

She looks up at me in that doe-eyed Princess Di way,

'Oh, hello, yes, I'm err…Dawn. Dawn Boldwood. Nice to meet you,' she replies in a crisp home counties accent as we make our way inside.

'Welcome everyone,' a voice calls out. 'I'm Gita. Please follow me.'

She is a petite, young woman with immaculately hennaed hands and a pristine yellow sari; she leads us to a table where we are handed hot towels and a glass of cold water with mint. *Ut oh! Ice alert!* I can just hear everybody back home now, 'Don't drink the ice. Don't drink the ice!' Gita clocks me eyeing the cubes and smiles. 'No ice for you, Miss?' I feel like an entitled princess, so promptly over-compensate by stuffing 20 cubes into my glass and sloshing them back in one. 'Yum!'

Please don't let me regret that!

Indira steps up to a long table and takes us through the ashram basics, rules and etiquette, before moving on to room allocations. Most people have their own, but I will be sharing with weepy Dawn. All good, I have my Kagool. Jokes aside, she's actually rather sweet and next to her, I feel positively brave – so every cloud. 'The ashram program will commence tomorrow,' we are told. This evening is chill time, which suits me fine as frankly I'm shattered after the 13 hour flight and terror van ride.

'Please come with me,' Gita calls as she takes us up a white, tiled staircase, all glossy and bright, and I get that excited feeling you experience when you arrive at a hotel. I always get that, even if it's a Travelodge off the M11. We arrive on the first floor. There are just three rooms; nice and intimate. The French women go into the corner one, Aussie Tom into the middle. 'And this is your room, Evie and Don,' Gita says, pushing back the heavy wooden door.

'Err …that's *Ava and Dawn.*'

'Sorry! Evie and Dons.'

She is so sweet that I don't have the heart to correct her again.

It's a very pleasant room with the faint scent of cinnamon. Two single beds with cane headboards are pushed against the wall and upon each sits a towel folded into what I hope is a swan, although might be a deformed penis.

'So, which bed do you want, Dawn?'

'Oh, the one nearest the bathroom would be ideal. I have chronic IBS'. *Oh great!*

'I'll go here then,' I say, flopping onto the bed nearest the balcony, which happens to overlook a charming, secluded garden. 'Oooh! Yes, this will do nicely. So, what do you think of it so far *Don*? Think I might call you that from now on! Don!'

She gives a little smile before bursting into tears again.

Oops! I suspect it's all been a bit much for her and she soon confesses that she had fully expected a paved high street with the Indian equivalent of Waitrose and Cafe Rouge. Possibly a Pret. 'But there are just cows,' she laments. 'Lots of bloody cows!'

'Awww, I'm sure it will get better, Dawn. It's just the initial culture shock. Why don't you have a lie down? It does wonders, you know.' I reassure her, before closing my eyes for a little pre-dinner power nap of my own.

Lord, this bed is comfortable.

.

.

Zzzzzzzzzzz

CHAPTER THREE - STICKY FINGERS, WARM HEART

'If you are going through hell. Keep going.'

- Winston Churchill

The thing about power naps is that they can go either way. You can wake up 20 minutes later thoroughly refreshed, or else full-on pass out only to discover you've overslept and missed your friend's bar mitzvah. August 2001. He never forgave me. This power nap fits into the latter category, and I awaken to hear Indira at the door singing Bob Dylan's "Knocking on heaven's door", which is all rather ominous.

'Good morning!' she calls, as bright as the lark.

'Sorry, what? *Morning? But…*'

'You girls were very tired, isn't it? Come. It's 5.30, the day beckons. Namaste!'

'Errrr. 5.30? A.M? *Nema-stay* in bed if it's all the same to you!' I quip, pulling a pillow over my head. *How did that happen? I barely got four winks, let alone the requisite 40!* I feel utterly cheated and lay like a defiant teen, while Indira has a good chuckle to herself. Dawn is more compliant and instantly leaps up and gets into her active wear.

'Ready!'

'Oh right! Actually, think I might just join you later by the pool,' I yawn. 'You can tell me all about it!'

Rolls over in bed and inserts ear plugs

Safe to say, I've never been the best of risers – 'don't wake me up unless it's for sex' is my usual mantra. I feel a little slap through the bedsheet indicating resistance is futile. 'Okaaayyy! Okaaaay!' I grumble, as Indira throws back the curtains thus ushering in the stark reality that this is not going to be the laze-about-the-place-watching-cat-videos kind of stay I envisaged.

Oh Jen! How could you?

The torture, err regime, commences bang on 6, and by lunchtime I'm out and out exhausted. I've been up for what feels like a week and I can already tick the following items off my 'Journey to Enlightenment' (My notes in italic.)

1. <u>Morning devotional chant – 'Satsang'</u>
Made funny noises as the sun rose through half-closed eyes. Felt stupid.

2. <u>Morning tea</u>
No Tetley. No Hobnobs. Disappointing.

3. <u>Asana yoga</u>
Hot, hurt and no, my legs do not wrap around my neck. Around someone else's maybe. Insert wink emoji.

4. <u>Vegetarian breakfast</u>
Pros: Good-sized portion. Cons: Cruelly catfished by a piece of tofu masquerading as chicken.

5. <u>Coaching class – Today's lesson: Relaxation</u>
Far from relaxing due to the Scottish guy snoring his head off for the duration. Thoughts: Perhaps more effective for people of Celtic persuasion?

And finally…

6. <u>Can.I.Go.Home.Now?</u>

By way of a reward, I sneak to the pool for some much needed me-time and to reflect upon my initial impressions of ashram life. On the plus side, it *has* taken my mind off the dreaded S-word, as I've only thought about her 67 times today. Most encouraging. Other pluses? Nice smelling towels.

Fact is, life here is not going to be easy breezy lemon squeezy and, as we learnt in this morning's coaching class, attendance is mandatory. 'No sneaking off for a ciggie behind the bike sheds, aye!' as Tom put it. I don't even smoke and I find myself gagging for a Marlboro Light. Forbidden fruit and all that.

My fellow newbies are positively embracing the experience, notably the French women, who I have discovered are sisters – the kind that finish one another's sentences. Dawn is another willing convert. She's 100 per cent giving it her all, notably when Aussie Tom is around. I get the impression she rather fancies a piece! Must keep an eye on that fledgling romance, could be good fodder for the blog. Faced with such overwhelming enthusiasm, I resolve to knuckle down and stick with it. Like my Aunty B says, 'Life's a bit like the hokey cokey. You only get out what you put in.'

The pool looks divine and I'm all poised to dive in when I hear a... 'So, tell me, what do you think of your first morning, my dear?'

So much for secret hiding places!

I look up, 'Oh, hi there, Indira! Ummm...I love it! Really ... err...fun.'

'Speak your truth, Ava!'

'Sorry?'

'You must speak your truth. What do you truly feel?'

'Oh, right, well in that case...I'm ravenous, my legs hurt and I think a stay at Guantanamo Bay might be less harrowing!' I grin, 'You *did* ask!'

She erupts with laughter, assuring me that this is all perfectly normal and that I will soon start to enjoy the routine. 'Life can only change when we do,' she smiles, 'And change begins with new habits. Wonderful new habits. You must just open your mind ...and hope nothing falls out, isn't it?'

She starts to laugh again, the kind of giggle that's infectious and I can't help but join in. This woman is a veritable burst of sunshine and she has the funniest turn of phrase, like she's speaking in motivational quotes. But far from being annoying, it's utterly endearing.

'Ava, my dear. How would you like to come to the market with me this afternoon? I need to buy supplies.'

'Ahhh, sounds great Indira, but think I'll just stay here by the pool, meditate a bit. Very important, you know.'

'Oh no, my dear, this afternoon there are more classes.'

'I'm sorry, what?'

'Lecture on spirituality, Karma yoga, chanting, group discussion, co...'

'Do you know what, the market sounds like a lovely idea, Indira. Do lead the way!'

FML!

If the schedule is this much of a punish, I won't have time to pee, let alone do that bloody blog thingamee! #ShortestSabbaticalEver. We head out and, before I can stress any further, the universe throws an altogether different curveball my way in the form of a big brown cow with the largest udder I've ever seen! Three words spring to mind: NHS. Breast. Reduction. She gives an enthusiastic moo and starts to trot over, dragging her udder in the dirt like one of those 1970s space hopper toys.

'*STAMPEEEEDE!*' I yell, '*STAMPEEEEDE!*' cowering beneath Indira's sari. She holds strong and next thing I know she's stretching out a hand to-wards the creature.

'Hello my Nandi! How are you, beautiful girl?'

The cow nuzzles into her armpit, clearly enjoying the head scratch, before transferring her affections to me and licking my legs with an awk-ward ardour.

'*Ooooh*! Stop stop!'

'She likes the salt, don't you Miss Nandi?' Indira laughs as the cow's great tongue enwraps my knees like a serpent, all wet and tickly. We give her a few more friendly pats before heading to the road where I'm half expecting to hop aboard Sanjay's van of terror, but instead, we stop beside a decrepit-look-ing moped by the hedge.

'Bloody hell, who owns this death trap?'

'I do!' she replies, handing me a scuffed-up helmet from the front bas-ket. I give the bike a once over, quickly concluding it's held together by rust and a prayer.

'This is Lady Miracle!'

'Lady *who*?'

'Lady Miracle. It's a miracle she works, isn't it?' Indira laughs as the side mirror drops to the floor. 'Quite right, my old friend,' she says, tossing it into the basket. 'We must never look back, only forward'.

And with that pearl of two-wheeler wisdom, we set off.

Chug. Chug. Chug!

I cling to Indira like a limpet, as we slalom around cars, vans, people plus the odd wandering cow. Standard. The traffic is just as insane as yesterday and I'm happy to report that horns are as popular too. The one on this bone-shaker sounds like a constipated duck, but that doesn't stop Indira blasting it hard and often. 'Fun isn't it?' she yells, swinging her head round to talk and narrowly missing a stray dog.

We must only be going for a few minutes when we happen upon the mother of all hold-ups. 'Whatever is this?' Indira asks, as I rubberneck from the back. She revs the engine impatiently a few times before I clock three elderly gentlemen, arm in arm, attempting to cross the road.

'Ahh, how sweet,' I gush. 'Nice to see men holding arms, showing affection. So much for toxic masculinity, hey?'

'Oh no, my dear. The men are blind.'

'*Blind?* Which one?'

'All of them.'

My heart instantly leaps up into my mouth as I watch them step out into the great unknown, only to be blasted by a chorus of almighty beeps which sends them scurrying back from whence they came. You couldn't make this up! Quite literally the blind, leading the blind, leading the blind. The men hazard a few more ill-fated attempts before Indira leaps off the bike and battles through the traffic to deposit them safely on the other side. 'Namaste,' she waves, before climbing back aboard to resume our journey.

The rest of the ride is less eventful, just bumpy, very, very bumpy and we bounce from pothole to pothole, which Indira finds hilarious, letting out little squeals of delight. I'm getting the impression she rather enjoys the excessive vibrating as she keeps giving extra revs at all the traffic lights.

Twenty minutes later, we pull up at the market. All in one piece. Aside from a bruised coccyx and minor road rage, I'm in relatively good shape and ready to experience my first ever Indian food market. What a place. And the size of it! Row upon row of stalls bursting with people, colour and the most intoxicating smells. We wander from one seller to the next, marveling at the spices piled into mountainous heaps: red chillies, yellow turmeric, green cardamon.

'Beautiful, isn't it? Like a rainbow has crashed down from the heavens,' Indira says rather poetically. 'Come, smell!'

She lifts some powder to my nostrils, triggering a flashback to a particularly fun night in Soho last November, before wiping some across her cheek.

'Look! We are the Spice Girls. "Tell me what you want, what you really, really want!"'

God, I love this woman!

This is exactly how I plan to be at 68. Full of life, the energy of a labradoodle. #SeniorGoals. Her zest for life is only surpassed by her flamboyant dress sense, electric blue hareem pants and green butterfly-print sarong, a migraine-sufferer's nightmare. I watch as she bounces from stall to stall, laughing and striking deals with a wag of the finger. 'Tut-tut' she smiles, holding firm until she gets her price. Her skill is such that we are soon laden down like a pair of mules, making me wonder how on earth we'll get everything back on that bloody moped!

'Not a problem, my dear. It is all about balance. Like life, isn't it?'

She's probably right; the things I've witnessed on the back of a moped so far is out and out headfuckery! Bales of hay, a fridge freezer, a small herd of goats…

We peruse a few more stalls before my tummy lets out the mother of all growls, and it occurs to me that I haven't eaten anything since breakfast, which is a lifetime ago now. Indira must hear as she immediately leads us to a little food stall at the back of the market where we are handed two plates of the most delicious smelling food. A rich brown curry, white fluffy rice and a chapati the size of Gorleston-on-Sea.

'Mmmmmm! This looks amazing!' I grin, searching the table for cutlery. Indira digs straight in, artfully scooping up the sauce with a spade of bread. I watch the sauce ooze between her fingers as she looks over at me and gives a little tut, shoving a piece of chapati into my hand. 'God gave you five forks, my dear! *Five!*' she says, wiggling her fingers in the air. 'When we eat with our hands, we nourish the soul, isn't it?'

I look about me and since everyone else is doing the same, I roll up my sleeves and tentatively poke in a finger. Then another. *Well, isn't today a day of firsts?* It feels a bit yucky at first, but since it tastes so bloody good, I soon get stuck in grabbing at the curry and scooping bigger and bigger blobs into my mouth, like a digger on a construction site.

'How do you like it?'

'It's delicious, thanks! Who needs utensils, hey?' I laugh, flicking another splodge of sauce into my hair, which doesn't bother me in the slightest.

'Ha! Very good. Very good,' she beams, like a proud mother. 'You know, my dear, you never forget the first time you eat curry with your fingers.'

'Really?'

'Never. Just like sex, isn't it!'

Ewww. Not quite the analogy I was expecting and I promptly swallow my embarrassment along with a mouthful of chapati. *Sex, like curry?* Not too sure about that, but as I gaze down at my sticky digits, I make a quick note to self: must wash fingers to avoid 'downstairs injuries' later. #FireInTheHole.

The meal is glorious and between mouthfuls we talk about life back in London, a little bit about Scarlet and then more about India.

'And have you always lived in Goa?' I ask, sucking my finger forks like a pro.

'No, I was born in Jodhpur. Like the trousers!' She stretches out the sides of her sari to mimic the distinctive shape. 'You know Jodhpur? The most beautiful city in Rajasthan. I came to live at the ashram in 1989.'

'Wow! Quite a long time ago, then. Did you come here alone?'

'No, I came with my son,' she smiles, playing with a necklace about her neck. A small, silver butterfly.

'Oh nice, and what's his name?'

'Sandip.' She flips her phone open to show me a picture. He looks just like her. Same eyes, same radiant smile.

'Oh yes, he's very handsome. Must be nice having him close by.'

She pauses for a moment, looking into her food.

'Sadly, Sandip passed away five years ago. He was a fine young man, a doctor.'

My fingers instinctively open, releasing the food back onto the plate.

'Oh, no. I'm so sorry.'

'Do not be sorry, my dear. Loss is but part of life. I have much to be grateful for, isn't it?' she smiles. 'You see, life can change in an instant, Ava. That is why we must enjoy every moment. Every. Single. Moment.'

The rest of our meal is consumed in thoughtful silence and the last mouthful gone, Indira pats her tummy and lets out the loudest burp, thus frightening a tiny bird that's feeding on the floor nearby.

'My dear. We have shared delicious food together. Next, I shall teach you how to cook it!' she enthuses, leaping up.

'Oh cool! Now?'

'Yes now! As I said, life can change in an instant and now you are going to change into a chef. Come, Gordon Ramsays!'

CHAPTER FOUR - AN INTERNATIONAL INCIDENT, SACRE BLEU!

Around the World in 80 Gays
"A better day"

Heartbreak. That most searing of pains. Merciless. Unyielding. As stinging as sunburn, as unrelenting as the sun upon the Goan sand...

There are one thousand, four hundred and forty minutes in a day and I have thought of her each of them.

Her - my ex-lover.

Her - the soul mate who shattered my heart.

London feels like a lifetime ago, another world, and as the golden sun sets over Mandolim beach, I feel at peace. Comforted by the rhythm of the tide. With every lap of the ocean, every whisper of the breeze comes the sense of a new day dawning. *A better day.*

It's just as Singrita said as we made naan this morning, 'the most beautiful thing about a sunset is knowing the sun will rise anew tomorrow'.

Namaste.

'So...what do you think?' Jen asks.

It's day four of my ashram sentence and our first official blog summit. Attendees: Me, Jen and new bestie Nandi the cow, who will act as today's focus group. I read that last line again, "the most beautiful thing about a sunset is knowing the sun will rise anew tomorrow".

'Err, it's...umm...greaaaat! Really great!'

'You're such a bad liar Ava Roberts,' Jen says, throwing her head into her hands. 'Urghhh! It was sounding so good, but then Cruella made me change it all, and now it's a whole heap of...'

'It's not that *baaaad*, Jen ...it's...'

'*DOG-SHIT*? You can say it.'

'Nooo! Well yes, maybe. There is a whiff of the canine turd about it, but that might not be a bad thing. I mean, dog turds have a habit of getting stuck to your shoe, hey? Maybe people will love it!'

We burst into hysterics.

'You know, it's actually quite charming in a way. A kind of poor man's *Eat, Pray, Love* double dipped in layers of very cheesy, cheese! Like mature Double Gloucester!'

'Well, you got that bit right! That's the brief, Ave... *Eat, Pray, Love* meets *Fifty Shades*! Cruella has, I quote "pulled the data" and reckons it will "resonate with ABCs and Gen Z". Pffft!'

'Well, if that's the brief, what can you do? What is it Cruella says, "BENISSSSIMOOO"!!! Anyway, more importantly Jennifer Jones, who the hell is *Singrita?*'

'Oh yeah, that's Indira! I had to change her name. All the names in fact! Legal reasons. Cruella loves Indira, the idea of a strong matriarchal figure, a spiritual guide. A...'

'*Naan maker?*'

'Yep. She's trying to create sponsorship opportunities, you know, product placement deals.'

Nandi is equally unimpressed by the cynical capitalism and lets out a disapproving *MOOOOOOOOOOOOOOOOOO* which takes Jen off guard.

'What the hell was *that*?'

'Oh, just my new best friend. She reminds me a lot of you actually,' I grin, twisting the screen so the two can meet. 'Jen... meet Nandi.'

Nandi has a quick lick of the phone and gives a contented snort.

'What the...? You're legit hanging out with a cow now! Still, guess you do have form – what with Scarlet and all,' she laughs. 'Sorry, couldn't resist! Bloody hell, the size of that udder though!'

'Who? Scarlet's or Nandi's?'

With that, Nandi ups and wanders off; not sure if she appreciates the comparison or the blog for that matter. I skim read the page to see if it gets any better.

'Bla bla... "naan bread"....bla bla..."sunsets".....Oh hang on.... "My first experience of eating with my fingers was a surprisingly sensual one. Like a sexual reawakening. The feel of the sauce between my fingers: sticky, warm, silky. It reminded me of her. Hot nights. Passionate days. I licked the sauce from my fingers, savouring every drop, remembering her taste".'

'EWWWWW!! NOOOOO!' I squirm. 'Jen...delete, delete! *Not happening!* We were in a market for God's sake. Not Amsterdam Sex Museum!'

'Like I said, *Fifty Shades*.'

'Of what, *cringe*? I mean, who even talks like that?'

'I know, I know! I was told to "sexify" it. Four years at uni to write this crap....'

'*Sexify*, is that even a word? And for the record, Scarlet does *not* taste like veggie tikka masala! Christ, my nan might read this,' I say utterly distraught.

'Your *nan*? You mean the lady who gave birth to your Aunty B? Remind me again, what was that story about her and the rugby team?'

'*Polo team* – it was a Polo Team. But point taken. Anyway, I'll never get laid again if this gets out!'

'It won't, Ave. Remember...it's anonymous, baby! *D.N.K.Y!*'

'*DNK what?*'

'**D.N.K.Y - *Doh! No one Knows it's You!***'

'Oh right! *Cleveeeeer!* Can tell you're a bloody writer! Now, clear off and write some more verbs and stuff, some of us have got spirit-cleansing meditations to attend!'

And just like that, the inaugural blog session concludes. Poor Jen. She looks utterly crestfallen. All aspirations of being the new Jane Austen have come crashing down, smashed upon the rocks of Lameville. Still, at least we managed to have a good laugh about the rechristening of the ashram group or 'cast list' as Cruella calls it. For future clarity, please note the following:

Indira = Singrita (named after Cruella's sitar tutor).

Dawn & Tom = Donna (abbrev. to Don) & Dan.

Amelie et Fleur = Claudette et Edith, 'the frenchies' (after the legendary Ms Piaf. Cruella is a passionate francophile and croissant enthusiast).

Big Gary = Big John. (Named after the cute IT guy Cruella shagged senseless last Xmas. Massive baubles. Allegedly.)

So, there you have it. *Benissimo!*
Now, where did I put my yoga pants?

*

'The secret to a happy life is not dwelling too much in the past' or so I learn in today's meditation session. *Shanti Shanti*. I only wish my brain would adhere to such wisdom, instead of drifting back into bad, old habits. Today's total Scarlet-based thoughts – 53. Still high, but heading in the right direction.

I have to say I'm only a week or so in, but I'm rather enjoying the meditations, along with the cooking classes, group discussions and beach walks during rare downtime. It's just as Indira had predicted, this spirited filly is slowly being broken in and I have a new-found joy in so many things, simple things like the smell of the morning air, the silver glow of first light. Lord, I'm starting to sound like that bloody blog now! I'm even enjoying yoga, God forbid. When I think of the times Scarlet and I would laugh at the hipsters along Shoreditch High St, posing with their designer yoga mats, and now here am I able to pull off a wobbly tree pose after just a few days!

In short, my mind is expanding, along with an appreciation of my new ashram buddies.

Bonding, or 'bondage' as Dawn put it, has successfully taken place. Not surprising when you're with the same people 24-7. Roomie Dawn already has a special place in my heart. She's an interesting creature – a walking, weeping paradox. Well-educated, yet apt to say the most ridiculous things, like 'Do French babies eat snails?' which amused the French sisters no end. The 'Frenchies' as we call them are equally good value. Amelie and Fleur Brouchon hail from the wine city of Bordeaux and are passionate debaters and champions of liberty and egality, thus making our evening discussions terrifying and entertaining in equal part. Other distinguishing features include a love of modern jazz and copious armpit hair. Then there's Aussie Tom who's an absolute delight. Light, fun and 'sooooo bloody hot' as Dawn keeps telling me. Tom is a meditation obsessive, earning him the new nick-name *T'ooooooooooom* in homage to his favourite chant. He does a killer Kylie impersonation, which

Big Gary finds hilarious, or at least I think he does, hard to tell since he speaks in such a thick Glaswegian accent that it's near impossible to understand him. Doubly so for non-British folks. 'Yeah, nah…he mighta confessed to heaps of murders and we'd be none the wiser!' as Tom put it as we walked back from a particularly satisfying yoga session one afternoon. It was day 11 and I was feeling super pumped as I'd almost pulled off a headstand but ended up pulling a hamstring. Aside from that, it was an afternoon to remember for a whole other reason…

'How are you, Gita?' I call, taking the shortcut through reception.

'I am well Avie, but I think your friend Don is very sad today.'

'You mean Daaaaawn?'

'Yes, yes, Don. Please give her this,' she smiles, handing me a freshly opened coconut.

I thank her and immediately take it up to the room, flinging open the door.

'All ok, Dawny?' I sing, only to discover the poor girl whimpering on the edge of her bed, her red hair glued to her head. I sit beside her, placing an empathetic hand upon hers. 'Whatever is it? Is it bad news from home?'

She makes a little snuffle sound and shakes her head.

'Is it your mozzie stings then?' I ask, looking down at her legs. The poor thing has been so bitten that her calves and ankles have merged to form thick cankles.

No response.

It's at this point that I notice her shorts are half unbuttoned and she is clutching a small hand mirror.

Well, this is awkward!

'Oh Ava!' she sniffles, her plumb voice warbling with emotion. 'I've got a...a...a...'

'*A?*'

'A…SWOLLEN FOO-FOO!' she blurts, yanking down her shorts. 'Look!'

Call me old-fashioned, but the last thing you want to do when you're nine days into friendship is to examine your new friend's vagina. Unless it's for romantic purposes. Ordinarily I would have refused, but the poor girl is so distraught that I do the honourable thing. I affix travel head-torch and get down to business.

Hmmmmm. So, what have we here?

Suffice to say, I've seen a few in my time and yet the huge variety of vaginas out there never ceases to astound me. *What diversity!* No two are ever the same. There are the perfect, neat ones, exquisitely formed like dainty pink macarons; there are the meatier ones where the 'burgers are bigger than the buns', or visa versa. There are those that resemble badly-rolled kebabs; and then there is *this* one….

Lord, it's an angry-looking beast!

Imagine layer upon layer of bright red pastrami, the kind you get in a New York ruben sandwich, though less appetising.

'Oh God! Am I going to die?' Dawn says, between sobs.

No Dawn, but I might.

Aside from the engorged appearance, what baffles me most is the curious aroma of mint emanating from the area.

'What do you think it is?' she says, all doe-eyed.

'Umm…'

I'm feeling about as useful as the letter 'g' in lasagna at this moment and then I smell it again, polo mints.

'Errr, don't suppose you've been over-doing it with the mint shower gel, have you?'

'What? Um, no, no,' she declares, rather flustered. 'Actually, it feels a lot better now I've got some air to it. Thanks, Ava.'

She abruptly fastens her shorts and walks over to the window.

'Errrr. You sure, Dawny?'

'Yes, all good. Really.'

She pops a couple of paracetamol and curls up for a bit of be-drest, leaving me to attend the remaining 368 classes of the day on my lonesome.

What a day!

Aside from the usual agonies, I'm actually rather concerned for my friend's foo-foo, so much so that I can barely concentrate during yoga. Thankfully by evening, she is looking a little brighter and even manages to eat her dinner, which is always a good barometer of health, vaginal or otherwise.

It's a lovely evening and the group retire for a spot of star-gazing in the secret garden. Every night is spent like this, chatting and sharing stories post-supper, which is always lovingly prepared by Indira.

'Is that Orion's belt up there?' Tom asks, pointing skyward.

'No, that's Saptarshi. And those are the seven great sages: Vashistha, Marichi, Pulastya, Pulaha, Atri, Angiras and Kratu. Do you see?'

And this is exactly why I enjoy our evenings in the garden so much. Always something to learn. Tonight, it's Hindu Mythology 101. When I first arrived, I was a bit closed in our group discussions, jammed up like a consti-pated clam, especially when we got into meatier topics. But I'm starting to find it all quite therapeutic now.

The conversation soon moves from the stars to more earthly pursuits.

'So, how is your blobby, Ava?' Indira asks.

'My *what*?'

She does a little typing mime with her fingers, 'Your bloggy…'

'Oh, you mean my *blog*! Yes, ha! Well, it's errrr….*going!*' I smile, not wishing to expand. 'I'm not writing it as such. It's my friend, not sure how she'll make my ramblings sound very interesting. But hey!'

'I wrote a blog once,' Dawn announces rather proudly.

'Oh, how lovely. About what, my dear?'

'Phosphorescent algae and plankton life at 86 metres.'

Crickets

'I had a decent readership too – well over 6…'

We lean in, poised to hear the word 'hundred' or 'thousand' even, but, alas, it never comes. Guess not all blogs are destined for greatness.

'So, come on Ave, what's your blog about?' Tom asks, stretching his arm so he can brush up against Dawn again.

'Oh, just travelling, heartbreak…you know…the regular stuff. We've only written a few entries.'

Indira stops me there. 'There is no *just* in life…' she says sternly. 'You either do or you do not, isn't it?'

'Oh… right…*I do,* then. I do!'

'Thank you,' she smiles before turning to address the group. 'My friends, do not limit your endeavours by fear and self-doubt. *What if I fall? What if I fail… but what if I fly!*'

Everyone instantly start nodding and I get the feeling that this is the lesson of the day.

'Well, I zink your blog sounds most interesting Ava,' Amelie says, fanning herself in the corner. 'You will read some to us, oui?'

'Nooo! Honestly, it's really not very interesting…'

Indira gives me another one of her looks and I reluctantly grab my phone and start to read from the latest entry, one that I'm not familiar with. *Untested material*, never a good idea. Ask any comedian.

'OK. Here goes then… "Everyone has a scent. A smell that is peculiar to them. There is a comfort in it – that's why the heart-broken embrace their loved one's shirt or a favourite scarf as they sleep. There's a soothing power in the smell of someone we love and, as I stretch out after my yoga class, I note that not all scents are created equal. Not everyone's smell brings joy and comfort. Some body odours are so potent that they make us want to retch…" '

I start to cringe, mindful that with every word I am digging myself a deeper hole.

'…"Claudette's scent is the worst. It reminds me of meat pies and school dinners and…"…'

Amelie and Fleur's faces drop. It doesn't take a genius to realise that, name changes aside, this is sounding suspiciously familiar.

'Oh no!' I say, breaking off mid-sentence. 'My phone has died, silly thing!' I quickly sit back and fold my arms as if to brace myself for the aftershock.

'Thank you for sharing that with us, Ava! Namaste,' Indira says, as the group follow suit, nodding and smiling in appreciation.

'Oui, oui. Merci. But Ava, what do you mean? Who 'az the terrible scent zat torments you so?' Amelie asks.

'Sorry, what?'

'Ze body odour in your story? Who are you talking of?'

'*NOOOOOO!* It's not real, Amelie. No no no! My friend added that bit in, to umm, spice it up…it's not *real* real! You know, poetic licence. So, yeah…'

I point to the sky, attempting to create a diversion.

'Oh, wow! Saptarshi again, how lovely!'

Indira is not so easily fooled.

'Ava. You must speak your truth.'

Develops sudden facial twitch

'Sorry, what?'

'Speak your truth, child. It is ok to say Amelie smells like Nandi the cow. For she is beautiful and her soul pure! Namaste.'

FML!

Talk about being thrown under the bus! Tom instantly erupts with laughter, badly disguising the outburst with a fake coughing fit which sends the French sisters into a blind panic.

'Fish bone! Fish bone!' Amelie gasps, 'He is choking on a fish bone!'

Big Gary instantly leaps into action, throwing Tom to the ground to perform a full-on Heimlich manoeuver.

'No! No! I'm good, mate. I'm good!' Tom shouts as Gary thrusts at him from behind, huffing and puffing like a scene from *Brokeback Mountain*.

'Come back to us Tom, come back!'

Poor Tom is going redder by the second as Gary gives a final thrust, before collapsing on top of him, thoroughly spent.

Sighs of relief all round.

'Bravo!' the sisters cheer, as Amelie leaps up to embrace Gary. 'Mon Dieu! What a 'ero!'

Gary is clearly loving the attention and is left with a grin even bigger than usual after he is proclaimed man of the night, with Tom relegated to his bitch for once.

Well at least it took the heat off the B.O. comment. #SmallMercies. The drama over, Indira concludes the evening with a rather insightful summary.

'An authentic life is what we must strive for, my friends. Many of us hide our true selves through fear of being ridiculed or rejected. But if we hide that truth, we eventually choke upon it like Tom.'

Everyone starts to nod as she adds a final coup de force.

'The only real failure is *not* being true to ourselves. It is only through honesty, and deodorant, that we can grow. Namaste.'

'Namaste.'

Despite feeling somewhat cleansed by tonight's truth session, I can't help thinking I haven't won any friends in the French camp, so I make a hasty retreat to my room, leaving Dawn and Tom to their romance and the French sisters to plot my demise.

Guillotine? Poison? I send Jen some notes from the day:

1. <u>Origins of the word 'foo-foo'</u>

Inspired by today's fannygate incident, I had a quick google. No concrete findings other than 'foo-foo' was Miss Piggy's pet poodle. Other amusing vagina euphemisms include: puff puff, nonny, twinkle, tuppence, front bottom, axe-wound, lady garden, cookie, foof, thingy, bajingo and my new favourite 'growler' as they say in New Zealand. LOL.

2. <u>Speak your truth</u>

Noble in principle. Excruciating in practice. French revolt imminent. I fear for my life. Tonight, mes amis, I will sleep with one eye open.

Around the World in 80 Gays
"Beware your words"

'There are few things that cut as deeply as angry words,' my nan once told me after a childhood spat with my brother. I was six. I called him a stinky slug-bum and he cried in his room for hours.

Flash forward twenty plus years and I'm feeling equally repentant about the body odour remark I made about my dear ashram friend. Lesson learnt. *Again.*

As an older, arguably wiser human, I appreciate that few things strike at the heart more savagely than words. *Few* things, but there are *some* things. Things like silence. Hard, cold, silence. I think that can strike more viciously, cause more suffering.

I recall arguments in my own relationship, when my ex would shut down, cut me out so I felt abandoned. Invisible. The confusion was agonising and would invariably lead to me over-thinking, then over-thinking some more. All those hours wasted, trying to imagine what she was feeling, what she was thinking. Terrified of what monsters might be lurking in that gaping chasm of silence.

Yes, no words can be as damaging as angry ones.

CHAPTER FIVE – BRIGHT EYED AND MINTY FRESH

'Morning Don! How's your foo-foo?'

A few days have passed since my foray into amateur gynaecology, and I'm not convinced that all is well 'downstairs at Dawn's'. She has missed a good few ashram sessions and, whenever she walks by, she has a look of mint-fumed anguish.

'Right. Are you going to tell me what's going on or what?' I say assertively. She doesn't respond, but I keep plugging away until she finally cracks.

'Oh, Ava, please don't think badly of me but, but…. *I must speak my truth*,' she declares, thus launching into a full-on confession that is both candid and heartfelt. And long. Very very long. In the interests of time and decency, I will attempt to summarise….

Feeling a little homesick and low of spirit, our Dawn decided to 'seek comfort' with her travel vibrator. However, discovering the batteries were flat, she reached for the next best thing, her electric toothbrush! Apparently, the pulse setting on the Oral B700 is akin to that of the Rampant Rabbit.

Minty mystery solved!

'You won't tell anyone, will you Ava?'

'Course not!' I assure, crossing my fingers behind my back. 'I won't say a word, Dawn. Not a word.'*

* I do, however, reserve the right to send a text containing aforementioned information to a certain writer in the UK. Real names withheld. Events might be dramatised for entertainment purposes. Always read the fine print. Terms and conditions apply.

Her soul bared, her truth spoken, I waste no time in ushering her towards the door and off to the local chemist.

'What, we're going *now*?' she objects, clinging onto the bedstead by her fingernails.

'Yes, *right now* or have you got something more pressing on your *vagenda* today?'

More grimacing. More groans.

'OK, OK. I give in! I can't take any more of your awful puns. I'll go!'

The walk to the village takes longer than anticipated since poor Dawn is walking like she has a watermelon between her thighs. Her words. Ten minutes later, we are at the pharmacy and feeling hopeful. 'Soon be sorted!'

It's a tiny place, thankfully quiet and we instantly default to standard chemist procrastination tactics – skulking about the aisles pretending to look at hair grips, shampoo and extra shiny lip gloss. In short, anything but what we have come here to buy. After five minutes and more audible grimacing from the patient, I initiate the uncomfortable conversation with the nice woman behind the counter. 'At least it's a lady', Dawn whispers as I give her a confident nod.

'Soooo…'

Not being fluent in the local language, I have no choice but to resort to my bestest charade skills, the kind usually reserved for family parties. I find myself smiling and pointing at Dawn's bits, mouthing 'VAGINAAAA! VAGIIIINAA!' with increasing volume. Point, shout, repeat. This method of conversing with other nationalities like they are deaf and/or stupid has been used by Brits for generations. With limited success, but luckily, the lady seems to catch my drift and beckons us into a small side-room where Dawn drops shorts and presents angry orifice.

'This is mortifying, Ave,' she quivers, looking like a sweaty radish as the lady starts the examination, prodding and humming a tune that sounds a bit like Neil Diamond's "Sweet Caroline".

A couple of minutes later, she stops and gives a solid nod.

'Well? What do you think?'

'Ooooh yes. Dear, dear. Very sore,' the pharmacist answers, as the pair of us gaze down at Dawn's lady-parts like art critics eyeing a Picasso.

'Yes, very sore. But you can give medicine, yes?'

The lady shakes her head.

'*Noooo?*' Dawn blurts. 'Is there no cure? No cure at all?'

The lady shakes her head again......'I do not know ... I do not work here!'

Jaws.

Drop.

I look over at poor Dawn who is seconds away from losing it when a balding man rushes into the room with a look of blind panic. '*Auntie!*' he scolds, 'Auntie. Get to your room now!' before switching language to admonish her with a string of what I assume are not very polite words. Poor auntie scurries out as he turns back to us apologising profusely. 'So sorry. So sorry,' he repeats before beginning the *real* examination.

Take two.

More prodding, more contemplation and finally, he gives a satisfied smile.

'I have just the thing,' he says, disappearing from the room.

'*See,* I told you it would be okay, Dawn. You'll soon be fixed up. Bet it will be good to get *little Dawny* back to normal – you know, now that Bigggg Tom might want to visit!' I tease, trying to lighten the mood. She nods and smiles as we sit and wait.

And wait.

Ten minutes pass. Fifteen maybe, before he finally reappears with another suited gentleman whom I presume is a specialist in the field.

'Oh, here we go,' I say, as the man kneels at our feet and proceeds to roll out a long sarong, onto which he places what I can only describe as, well, not what I expected.

A selection of dildos and butt plugs! WTF!

'NO, NO!' I object, but the dildo-dealer just shakes his head and grins.

'Lady, look! Much better than electric toothbrush,' he smiles, handing me the scariest looking double-ender that even Nandi would struggle to accommodate. 'Strong, yes?' he says pushing it against my forearm to demonstrate its immense power.

Needless to say, Dawn is dying of embarrassment at this point. All the girl wants is some bloody cream, but after saying 'no' more times than I care to mention, we lose the will to live and end up leaving the premises with one tube of steroidal ointment plus a 'double-delight' in neon orange.

#OnlyInIndia.

Dawn doesn't speak much on the way back, doubtless traumatized, and heads straight up to our room for a lie down upon our return. Now, I don't know if it's the cream, the toy or just the relief of being out of that pharmacy, but by the time we sit down for dinner she's a whole lot perkier and able to flirt up at storm with Tom over the tandoori kingfish.

It's a miracle!

'So, Ava…' Amelie says with a playful wink, 'I do 'ope you will be reading from your blog again zis evening?'

Nervous sweats

I have to say, the sisters have been surprisingly good about the 'misunderstanding' the other night; and the Anglo-French *entente cordiale* has been restored.

'No, no blog tonight! Think I'll have a break.' I smile, relieved to be out of la house de chien. 'But I'd love to hear more about your life in France.'

Amelie is delighted.

'Of course!' she smiles, promptly launching into a highly detailed depiction of the wine-making process in Bordeaux (using zero preservatives), a little about her family, before treating us to a potted lesson in French philosophy.

We start with the existentialists: Jean-Paul Sartre, Albert Camus, and Simone de Beauvoir, or *Bonebroth* as Tom hears it. It's all rather fascinating, if not a little depressing. Basic theory: it all starts with the *existential angst,* "a sense of dread, disorientation, or anxiety in the face of an apparently meaningless or absurd world".

'I get that most Monday mornings,' Dawn giggles. 'Right before work.'

The more Amelie speaks, the more I'm filled with A. Admiration for her aptitude to quote French philosophers like I quote Adele lyrics and B. Admiration for her ability to do so in another language! I mean, English is hardly the easiest, is it? Imagine looking at the word 'yacht' for example and not throwing in the towel there and then.

The philosophy talk goes from strength to cerebral strength and Amelie winds things up with a parting notion.

'As Jean-Paul Sartre said, "Everything has been figured out except how to live".'

Strong finish. One that Indira clearly approves of as she jumps to her feet to round off the night with her usual 'Namaste.'

Well, that was fun.

I head back to the room, feeling thoroughly learned, if not a little inadequate. Lots of meaty blog fodder here. Jen will be delighted.

1. <u>Travel and relationships</u>

Concept of time radically distorted when travelling. Bit like human vs. dog years situation. Case in point, Tom and Dawn who are getting very close in a disproportionately short amount of time. They are already doing the 'we' thing though they haven't even snogged yet.

Thoughts: isn't the honeymoon phase just wonderful? I think back to when Scarlet and I were first together, giddy in love! The excitement, the blushes, the butterflies. The bloom of new passion is beautiful – so, so beautiful. It's just the rest of it that's shit.

2. <u>'Speak your truth' and un change de heart</u>

Earlier concerns about the danger of honesty brought on by B.O./bloggate have been allayed. The sisters' buoyant mood, and subsequent use of deodorant, has led me to believe Indira might be right after all.

In short, 'Speak your truth' has real value. Must apply to everyday life.

I start to drop off with the words of JP Sartre trundling through my mind and, for some inexplicable reason, I think of that weekend in Italy with Scarlet. The weekend she proposed and the joy I felt in that moment.

Sartre was right about us not having life figured out, although in my case I'd like to amend that to 'Everything has been figured out except *LOVE*...'

Or rather, *how to love and let go.*

That's the thing I am most struggling with.

Bonne nuit!

CHAPTER SIX - NOT ALL HEROES
WEAR CAPES

'Time is a great teacher, but unfortunately, it
kills all its pupils.'

- Louis Hector Berlioz

'Is it me, or does time just fly here?' Dawn says one day after lunch. A big orange beetle buzzes past at that precise moment, making the observation all the more poetic.

She's not wrong. Time *does* fly here. It's day 19! A full 19 days of satsang, coaching, yoga, meditation, cooking classes, beach walks and group discussions have gone by in a flash, or a flush in Amelie's case. Menopause is no fun, especially in this heat.

Although there is something undeniably refreshing about being in a new place, particularly one as glorious as Goa, ashram life can feel a little, well, samey. I share the notion with Jen during today's blog summit and she thinks it might well have something to do with the nature of routine.

'I know it can feel a bit like that Ave, but I bet it's stopped you from thinking about Scarlet as much. Am I right?'

'Scarlet who?'

'Ha! Exactly. It's keeping your mind occupied. Just what you need!'

The conversation sparks a few ideas for the next blog entry, namely the power of routine, before she drops a little bombshell into the mix, 'Oh, good news. We're not getting fired this week after all!'

'Sorry, what? *Fired this week,* what do you mean? I wasn't aware we were getting fired, period.'

'Oh yeah. Ha! I didn't want to worry you. You know, ruffle your chakras! Anyway, we're not now, so all good.'

My head is in a spin right now. I feel like I've just had a last minute reprieve from death row without even knowing I was there in the first place.

After some gentle persuasion, i.e. crude words, Jen kindly enlightens me on the matter, namely that, following a rather worrying week of 'no growth' in our readership, the "Power of words" entry came through, attracting interest from Scrabble and the British Union of Librarians. Result: readership up by a solid 1470 per cent!

Word! Pardon the pun.

'So, in short, we're still employed and you're still getting paid,' Jen grins. 'So, like I said, what's not to love!'

And with that joyous revelation, we promptly sign off and I rush away to meet Indira for our usual afternoon stroll. Despite already being 15 minutes late, Dawn is keen to show me something 'truly splendid' on my way out. She thrusts her phone in my face with an enthusiastic 'Look!' and I glance down to behold the most beautiful spreadsheet I've ever seen, all colour coded with the finest fonts, **not a comic sans in sight.**

'Errr, very nice, Dawny. But ummm, *why?'*

'I'm glad you asked that Ave,' she grins. 'It might look like a normal spreadsheet, but this baby helps with the whole one-day-merging-into-another thing. Makes me more mindful. You know, more aware of my own existence.'

'Oh Lord, are you having an existentialist crisis? I blame the Frenchies for this!'

'Yes. Well, they did lend me a book on it. Maybe it's rubbed off.'

'Bit like your electric toothbrush.'

'Ha. Ha. Very funny. That's all cleared up now, by the way,' she smiles. 'Anyway, where was I?'

'Life-changing spreadsheets and please make it quick.'

'Oh yes. So, every day I pick three things that have stood out for me: something I have enjoyed, something I have learnt and something I'm grateful for. I then write them down in the appropriate columns. That way I can remember why every day was special. See?'

'Oh right! That's err ....'

'*Genius!* You can say it. I've been doing it since I got here. I'll do one for you if you want. It will help order your thoughts for your blog. You know, everything you need to remember all in one place.'

'Maybe.'

She is looking so chuffed about the damn thing that I feel I should indulge her further.

'OK, let's have another look at your one.'

I have a quick scan...

DAY	ENJOYED	LEARNT ABOUT
1	TOM	TOM
2	TOM	TOM
3	TOM	TOM
4	TOM	TOM
5	TOM	TOM
6	TOM	TOM
7	TOM	TOM
8	TOM	TOM
9	TOM	TOM
10	TOM	TOM

It runs all the way up to today, day 19, which is currently blank. The suspense is excruciating.

'So, what are you going to write in today's "Enjoyed column"?' I tease, 'Tom?'

'Yes! How did you know?'

'Just a feeling, Dawny! Just a feeling. So, in short, Tom is the best part of every single day here?'

'Yes! Oh, and you Ava, but that column is hidden. See?'

She promptly stretches the table out and there I am plain as day in the 'Grateful for' column, colour coded blue. Right next to Nandi the cow. Joint favourite. So that's nice…

*

It's a particularly hot day and my sprint to join Indira leaves me a bit flustered.

'Sorry I'm late,' I pant, promptly sharing the one-day-merging-into-another theory which doesn't land quite as well as expected.

'Tut, tut, tut,' she frowns, utterly unimpressed. 'But that is just an illusion, my dear! No day is ever the same, isn't it?'

'It isn't?'

'No, no, no! It's like this beach,' she says scooping up a handful of sand. 'Do you really presume it is the same one day to the next?

'Well…'

'Come now. It might look that way, but when we examine things closer, we see that so much is different. The sands have been blown flatter by the winds, the fronds on the palm trees are less green than yesterday, tilted in a new direction. Even the ocean is different. A new shade of blue.' She lets the sand escape through her fingers. 'Change is happening all the time, my dear. It's just that those changes are often very subtle.'

I can't resist but tease her.

'*Just* very subtle? *Just?*' I grin, telling her there is no such thing as 'just'. It either is or isn't. She gives me a little nudge, but I get the sense that she is secretly pleased that I've been paying attention in all those late night group discussions.

'Well, I'll tell you one thing that doesn't change, Indira – me thinking of Scarlet, so…'

'Such impatience, my child. Such impatience. Everything must happen in its own time. When we have loved so deeply, we cannot expect that love to simply disappear, isn't it? No, no, no.' She stops for a moment, unfolding a piece of paper from her pocket. 'Do you know the passage of the stonecutter?'

'I don't think so.'

She flattens the page on her leg and starts to read from it.

' "Look at the stonecutter hammering away at his rock, perhaps a hundred times without as much as a crack showing in it. Yet at the hundred-and-first blow it will split in two, and he knows it was not the last blow that did it, but all that had gone before." '

I think for a moment, 'Oh, I like that!'

'Good. Then you must keep it,' she says, pushing the paper into my hand. 'So, you see, we are all growing, my dear. Changing every second. Every day. Bit by bit! Though we might not know it.'

Every afternoon is spent this way. We come to the beach during rare free time to walk, talk, collect shells, before retiring to our palm tree therapy couch for an impromptu session. Most days I talk about Scarlet and most days it ends with me puffy-eyed and Indira's sari soggy about the shoulders. #NotAllHeroesWearCapesSomeWear Saris.

I can't believe how lucky I am to have met her. This lady has been a godsend, taking me under her wing when I was sad and broken. Sometimes I think I must have conjured her up, this fairy godmother-cum-therapist! I look over as she stoops to pick up a fallen coconut, placing it into my arms.

'So, you do not want to kick it today, David Beckhams?'

'Ha! No, not today!'

'Progress then,' she winks. 'Progress.'

The comment relates to one particularly angry afternoon when I'd kicked a fallen coconut and ended up stubbing my big toe. God, it stung! I hopped about on one leg, spitting and cursing while she just sat there laughing.

'Ava, you are as dense as that coconut! You are only damaging yourself, don't you see?' she said. 'Anger is like drinking poison and expecting the other person to die.'

I'd never thought of it like that – too damn angry, I guess! But she had a point.

It's funny, but despite all my cursing about my ex, Indira was never once unkind about Scarlet. She merely said she had some growing to do and sadly that growing had been at my expense.

'You see, every day a little change. You think of her less. You hurt a little less. And one day soon, you will be healed. But better than that,' she smiles, 'You will open your eyes to discover you have become a butterfly! A beautiful butterfly.'

She starts to laugh again, flapping her arms and running off down the beach. I chase after her, only to stumble upon the most glorious sight beside one of the fallen palms – Dawn snogging the face of Aussie Tom, tongues and all.

So, change really does happen.

CHAPTER SEVEN – GOAN, GOAN, GONE

Around the World in 80 Gays
"A farewell"

Glorious Goa! The land the Gods smiled upon. *Shanti!*
As I near the end of my time here, I am filled with a sense of gratitude. Profound gratitude for this glorious land; its people as warm as a mother's embrace. Nandi lies beside me as I sit in peaceful contemplation, and all is well.

The ocean is calm after last night's storm; her fury has subsided. Quelled like my own anger; washed away with the incoming tide.

It's just as Singrita said, I am now ready to speak my truth.

Namaste.

Day 28. My last day in glorious Goa and I awaken to a no-Dawn-at-dawn situation. I presume she has spent another night with Aussie Tom, the dirty dog! Not sure if that's quite within ashram rules, but hey.

Safe to say their relationship has heated up over these last few days which is rather cute, especially since he's infinitely more attractive than an electric toothbrush. Though not nearly as portable. He has even suggested that we meet up with him in Australia, so he must be keen. Dawn is overjoyed and convinced that their 'magical coupling' as she puts it, is all down to that spreadsheet of hers. 'It's called manifesting, Ave!' she explains. 'You just have to put it out there in the universe and trust.'

Inspired by her success, I have now added a few celebrity crushes to my own spreadsheet.

Watch this space!

It's a lovely morning and since it's our lucky last, class attendance is voluntary. *Vol.Un.Tary!* I have to pinch myself! Despite this much longed-for reprieve, I'm weirdly keen to get my downward dog on. #WhoAmIEven, so I grab my mat and head to the early yoga session, swinging by the front desk.

'Good morning, Gita,' I chirp.

'Good morning, Evie.'

Doh! I can't believe I've been answering to the wrong name for a whole bloody month. Must sign up for assertiveness training once I feel assertive enough. *Wink.*

Yoga is an absolute triumph and, for the first time ever, I manage to hold a headstand for a solid four seconds before collapsing into a quivering blob of jelly. No. Mean. Feat! Tom is beside himself. 'Good on ya, Ave! You'll be a Master soon, ay?' he smiles, inviting me to hang with him and Dawn for the afternoon. I politely decline, heading down to the pool to catch up on my messages.

Swipe. Swipe.

There are a good few.

One from cousin Maria about her upcoming nuptials, one from my mum and lots from Jen. *Lots and lots from Jen.* The girl is positively clogging my inbox, goddamit! Most of the messages start with 'Ave! You'll never believe it...' And guess what, I don't! Apparently, shock of shocks, the blog has gained lots more followers, although admittedly most of the comments are about Nandi the cow. *Way to crush a girl!*

I read on.

```
Cruella is optimistic about getting sponsorship from
livestock mag Bovine Weekly. LOL
```

LOL indeed!

'Are people actually reading this stuff?' I text, to which Jen replies something about gift horses and mouths. So that's me told.

I'm given strict instructions to obtain photos of Nandi for her new Insta profile, so I head outside to find my uddered beauty in her usual spot on the grassy knoll, getting a good ear scratch from Indira. I give them a little wave.

'Hello my dear! Please come join us.'

Nandi gives an encouraging moo and goes straight in for a leg lick. *Slurp slurp!*

'Nandiiiii!' I giggle, rubbing her long, velvety snout.

'Ha! She likes you very much, Ava! Very much!'

'Awww, I like her too and I'm not the only one. Do you know this lady has quite a fan club in my blog?' I laugh, snapping a few shots between leg licks.

'I'm not at all surprised. Just look at her!'

Nandi gives another moo.

'Doesn't she have the most beautiful eye lashes? Haven't noticed them before. Hey..' I giggle, ' "Maybe she's born with it, maybe it's Mooo-belline!" '

The joke is wasted on Indira who just stares at me like I've had too much sun.

'She needs those long lashes to protect her beautiful eyes. Cows have excellent vision, isn't it? Almost 360 degrees. They can see to the left, to the right and almost behind them, without even moving their heads. And yet they cannot see what is in front of their noses. Fancy that?'

Her eyes sit upon me for a moment and I can't help but think there's a lesson there. Scarlet, me – not seeing what was going on with Carla, right in front of *my* nose. Maybe there's a reason I love cows so much.

We bid farewell to Nandi and head down to the beach. It's quiet today, just a few fishermen mending nets and the usual local kids playing in the surf in their clothes. They bound over, all arms and legs, to collect their final consignment of Bic biros. Forget iPads and gadgets, if you want to make these kids smile, pens are where it's at! It's utterly humbling and I give the final red one to the cutest little lad with massive dimples, who rewards me with a soggy hug, before bolting off to show his friends.

'Awww. I'm going to miss all this,' I sigh, gazing out to sea. 'Especially you, Indira. What am I going to do without my spiritual guru?' I look down, putting my arm in hers.

'You'll do just fine, my dear. Just fine.'

She looks a little choked, so we move the conversation along,

'So, tonight…'

'Oh yes! Tonight! Tonight is a special one. Our last supper, like your Jesus, but without the betrayal, isn't it? I will cook something wonderful and you, Ava, you will help me. Would you like that?'

'I'd *love* that.'

*

7pm. Everybody has made a massive effort for this, our last night to-gether. The table is elegantly decorated with tea lights and happy yellow flowers, origami place settings (courtesy of T'ooooom) and what's more, we've all donned our Sunday best, aka any clothing that doesn't have a big curry stain down the front. Even Big Gary has gone all out with a new pair of fisherman pants. Can only imagine the old ones walked off by themselves.

We bring out the dishes for this feast of feasts.

'TA-DARRRR!'

Cue enthusiastic applause

'Ladies and gentlemen, we present tonight's menu: biriyani, khadi, dosa, tandoori kingfish and other fine delicacies from Rajasthan that I cannot pro-nounce – sorry Indira! Bon appetit!'

The table falls into a contented hush as we gorge ourselves silly for a solid ten minutes, barely coming up for air. 'Bloody tasty, mate' Tom says, inhaling his entire plateful in one go. 'Guess that's a compliment,' I smile as Dawn passes her beloved half her naan bread. Must be love!

The lovebirds are being particularly affectionate tonight and have now moved onto the 'matching outfits stage'. Jeez! I thought lesbians were fast! What's that joke again? Oh yes, what does a lesbian bring on a first date? *Her suitcase.*

The food demolished, appetites satiated, we roll into the enchanted gar-den as we have done for the past month or so. It's a ritual now, like wealthy Victorian gents retiring to the smoking room to discuss the issues of the day. It's a clear night and the mozzies are poised for one final attack, so Dawn pumps a massive squirt of Deet but misses, and it ends up inside my mouth, thus completely ruining the aftertaste of the tandoori kingfish.

'Thanks Don!'

'Ha! You're welcome, Evie!'

The chat returns to our wonderful dinner and then the stuffy evening heat before we sit back in silence. Delicious silence. It's funny, I always used to feel uncomfortable with lulls in conversation, like I had a duty to jump in and plug the gap. But I'm ok with them now. 'Not all silences need to be filled,' Amelie once told me, which cracked me up since you literally cannot shut the woman up! She's right though, silence *can* be golden, a shared one even more so. It's like an unspoken trust, a sign that you are comfortable enough with people not to have to speak.

The spell is broken by a familiar *moooo* and a brown freckled snout pushes through the dry hedge.

'Hello Nandi!' the group announce in unison and she pushes her snout even deeper.

'Ahh, you want to join us, Nandi?' Indira smiles, rubbing her nostrils. 'Oh yes, yes. You are most welcome. Do you know that a cow's nose is as unique as a human fingerprint?' We let out another collective 'Really?' followed by an embarrassed laugh.

'Oh Lord! We really have merged into one,' Dawn giggles, 'A shared consciousness.'

She's kind of right.

There has been a merging of sorts. It's as if, after all these nights of debate, we have finally gelled and what started out as a gathering of six very different individuals with their own stories and baggage, has now become a big awkward family. The kind you see in those embarrassing portraits online. You wouldn't put us together ordinarily, but somehow the recipe works. Every character brings their own unique flavour to the pot. Some are subtle, some more pungent (particularly post yoga). Some are instant crowd pleasers, like chocolate or ice-cream; while others are more of an acquired taste. But each one is no more or no less vital to the final dish. As I look about me, at the garden, my new friends, it suddenly hits. *I really am going to miss all this!*

Before I can dwell on the thought for too long, Indira starts chuckling to herself. It's a funny sound, like a vintage car starting up, and a sure sign that she's about to begin one of her legendary stories. The lady is a natural, so I immediately lean in as she starts to tell us about her early life in Rajasthan, and then about her beloved father.

'He was a very handsome chap, my poppa. And quite the ladies' man, you know. I remember one time he came back from a business trip and mommy chased him around the kitchen with a big wooden spoon. Round and round! He was terrified. "Rajid," mommy shouted, "So, you are wearing lipstick now, hey?" Poor mammy!' She chuckles to herself for a moment. 'And do you know what she used to call his lady friends?' She doesn't wait for a response. 'Pennies!' she blurts, slapping her thigh and rocking back and forth, the tears streaming down her cheeks.

Crickets

'Errr *pennies?*' Tom puzzles, daring to ask what we are all too polite to.

'Yes, pennies! Two-faced and in everyone's pants, isn't it?'

It takes a few seconds for the joke to land and then everyone explodes into raucous laughter, with Big Gary letting rip with an unscripted bottom burp. Probably the most sense he's made all month.

As amusing as it is, Indira's little anecdote inadvertently leads to a discussion about relationships and fidelity, with a capital F for 'Fuck, no!' It feels like a punch in the guts, an instant stinger, but, as brutal as it is, I feel that this is one discussion I need to hear. I take a deep breath, just as I've been taught in meditation classes, as Amelie opens the debate.

'Possession iz the grave of love!' she declares, pontificating rather theatrically. 'If you love someone, you have no right to own their body, non?'

It's a bold statement, made all the more dramatic by the light from tonight's full moon. Possession. Fidelity. Inevitably, thoughts of Scarlet invade my mind and swirl about like smoke…choking, pungent smoke. I feel sick. *How can I be so easily thrown off balance?* I want to up and leave, but something stops me. A need to understand perhaps.

'Well, I simply don't agree!' someone says. It's Dawn. 'I don't want to share my partner with *anyone*!'

I notice her reach for Tom's hand, almost seeking reassurance and he obliges with a little peck on the cheek, a display of solidarity.

Amelie is not easily put off.

'Oui, but do you *really* think such a love can sustain, uh? At first maybe, when ze fire burns bright. But after?' She shrugs and blows air though her pursed lips like the French do to show disapproval.

'Well, I just don't see it like that,' Dawn counters. 'I mean, there are lots of successful monogamous relationships out there… like….. like…'

'Beavers,' Indira interjects with no hint of a smile.

Her remark momentarily relieves the tension and I try to avoid Dawn's eye, not wanting to upset the flow of the debate.

'Yeaarr, nah. Lots of mammals are monogamous actually,' Tom chimes in. 'I've read about it – swans, wolves, water voles.'

'Well, my mother and father have been together for 20 years and they haven't so much as looked at another person.'

'But how do you know that? I mean how do you *really* know?'

I look around to see who has spoken out quite so cynically, only to realise it's me.

I sit back, annoyed by my outburst. Frustrated that I've somehow become *that* person. The person who scoffs at love. The person who snaps at their sweet, sweet friend. *Damn you, Scarlet! Damn you for making me so mistrustful!* Fortunately, nobody seems offended, in fact Indira almost looks happy, secretly pleased that I have found my voice perhaps. She places her hand upon mine.

'Ava makes a good point. Do we ever *really* know what happens in other people's affairs? Relationships are like icebergs, so much lies beneath the surface, out of sight.'

The analogy hits hard and I'm instantly besieged by a steady stream of memories, happy times with Scarlet. Holidays, mad nights out, lazy mornings in; hot, passionate moments that still make my tummy flutter and little intimacies that still hurt to remember. Yet in every one of those moments, I never really knew what was going on.

'Oui! Oui ! Exactement!' Fleur snaps, charging in. 'You know, zay say 70 percent of adults admit to cheating, so someone must be doing it, non? And what constitutes cheating anyway? Watching porn, sexting?'

'How about saying someone is attractive – is that cheating?' Tom scoffs, clearly triggered. 'I once had a girlfriend who bloody thought so. So, I reckon if you're getting the grief for it, you might as well do it, ay!'

Dawn gives him a look.

'Well, the way I see it is we're all human. Of course you are going to be attracted to other people. It's just about making a choice *not* to act on it, that's all,' she says defiantly.

At this point Big Gary becomes particularly vocal and, although nobody can understand him too well, we're able to get the gist: that it's 'different for men, a biological thing'. As you might imagine, the casual sexism does not land well.

'*BULLSHEET!* Fuck zat! Zat is just what we have been brainwashed to believe – zat men are born different. Merde, it is merde! You are just giving men a licence to cheat, non? We all have desires, women too! The need to fuck. Ava, Dawn – you like to fuck, yes?'

'Ummm…'

'Exactly, so fuck! *FUCK!* You English are so damn uptight, uh?'

'Not necessarily!' Dawn retorts. 'I once had sex in a shopping trolley actually. Marks and Spencers!'

'Oh, how lovely, my dear!' Indira smiles. 'And who are Mark and Spencer?'

'_'

We sit for a moment, quietly digesting what's been shared. Lord, this topic is a minefield! Like opening Pandora's box and watching all the opinions of the world tumbling out. The longer I sit, the more I feel the tide of vitriol rising up within me, higher and higher until I open my mouth and *whoosh,* out it pours.

'Well, I just don't know what I think anymore! I used to think it was possible to be with one person and for it to be enough, but now I'm not so sure. Perhaps sticking with one partner for life isn't possible. It's like everyone is disposable these days, like a smart phone. You love it for a while but then another model comes out, with a better camera or something, and everyone wants an upgrade.' I feel a lump in my throat. 'I dunno, it's like we all think we have this divine right to be happy and sod everyone else.'

Fleur smiles over at me, 'But Ava, zis is why you are angry, non? Why do you have to choose, you can keep both phones, non?'

Her statement throws le chat amongst the pigeons again, and Big Gary becomes a whole lot more confused, asking, 'Hang on, so which one has the best camera again?'

Point. Missed.

'Look, all I'm saying is that we dismiss one another too easily,' I continue. 'Even the way we date, swiping left and right on apps, rejecting someone because their face looks wrong or they're too short, too tall, too fat, too thin. Too, I dunno… *perfect!* The tragedy is we might be swiping away the love of our lives.'

I barely come up for breath.

It's like a giant dam has broken and I talk and talk, and just can't stop. I see Indira looking over at me, proud to see me so vocal. She gives a soft smile.

'Thank you for speaking your truth, everyone,' she says, casting her arms wide. 'If any of you wish to follow up on tonight's discussion, I can recommend a very enlightening talk by Esther Peres. She has some fascinating insights into monogamy and fidelity, believing that affairs are rarely about sex and all about desire. A desire to feel wanted, special. A desire to feel *alive* again. Affairs are not the rejection of a partner, but a rejection of the person we have become.'

'Mais oui! Oui!' Fleur enthuses, banging her hand on the arm of the chair. 'Zat is it! If you understand zat, you will be more happy, non? For me, it's ok to have many lovers. Jealousy serves no one. It is like guilt, a useless emotion, non? What are you jealous of?'

Her sister interjects, whipping her up into a heightened frenzy. 'Bravo! Say non to la jalousie! *Pah!'*

'Exactly!'

'Jealousy is like ze poison!'

'Poison! Yes, yes! It is like when I made love with my sister's boyfriend at college, nobody was angry...no one was jealous....'

Amelie's face drops, 'Pardon?'

'You remember, Jean-Pierre. We...'

'What? You made love with *Jean-Pierre?* My boyfriend Jean- Pierre*?'*

'Yes, when you had ze flu that weekend on Bastille Day ... you knew that, Amelie. Mais oui! *You knew*!'

I fear Amelie did not know and suddenly, she's up on her feet and yelling.

'Sacre Bleu! How could you? *Salope!* How could you? *Poufiasse*! *Boule de merde*!'

Well, that turned quickly.

The sisters are full-on balling at one another now – 'merde' this and 'salope' that. It's scarily entertaining, but after a couple of minutes Amelie storms off, closely followed by her equally irate sister.

'Well, that ended well,' Tom remarks, breaking the tension. 'Just goes to show, all good in theory, ay.'

'Hmmmm.'

At least we can all agree on something.

Around the World in 80 Gays
"Was I right?"

'The recipe for perpetual ignorance is to be satisfied with your opinions and content with your knowledge,' some wise soul once said. Well, after tonight, I'm all for perpetual ignorance!

The debate has me in a spin. Opinions this way, opinions the other. It gets me thinking about my own notions of fidelity.

Was I right to judge my ex so harshly? Was I right to leave like I did?

If I shared the views of some of the others, my life would be very different right now. I'd be back in London, enjoying a shiraz and hugging my girl silly.

Lord, this love game is hard! Littered with potholes, snares at every turn. I sometimes think being a human is too difficult and I'd be much happier being a cow like Nandi, wandering around, udder in dirt, content to get an ear scratch. My mind is still racing when I arrive back at my room.

Why did she do it? Why could I not forgive her?

Why, why, why?

However much I try to convince myself it's all behind me, the more I'm reminded that the past is never the past. We carry it with us every day.

CHAPTER EIGHT - THE WEISZ WOMAN

'Serendipity(noun.) Finding something good
without looking for it.'

Delhi International,
India, Jan 2018

'SHIT! BUGGER! FANNY FLAPS!' I curse, slaloming through the swathes of dilatory travellers at Delhi International. To call them snails, even snails on valium, would be doing our mollusc friends a disservice. It's hot and the unscheduled frisking has made me perilously late for my connecting flight. Everywhere I look, I see obstacles: humans, bags, pushchairs. And don't get me started on those wheely suitcase things for kids. As if travel wasn't stressful enough, 'I know, let's tow little Tarquin on his Trunkie!'

The panic is real.

I glance at my watch, two minutes until the gate closes.

FUCKETY FUCK!

I have to make that flight!

I can feel my chakras getting discombobulated, all the good work of the past few weeks in danger of unravelling. Head down, I sprint like a gazelle towards boarding gate 15. Do not pass go. Do not buy the stomach medicine I always buy when flying long-haul. Just in case. This kind of high-speed bolt always looks wildly exciting in the movies, but, in reality, it's anything but. I'm a sticky mess and in danger of swallowing my own tongue. Just a final few hurdles to negotiate: an Indian George Clooney look-a-like tying his Reeboks, two teens snogging the faces off each other, and the cutest little girl puking dhal pancakes over her baby brother. *Come on Ava!* I swerve them all with astounding accuracy, flash my boarding pass and leap up the final few steps.

YESSSS!

Plane erupts into spontaneous applause as sexy captain hands me a pina colada plus upgrade to First Class

In truth, nobody bats an eyelid except Sameer the cabin manager, who, far from impressed, looks like he'd like to administer a swift kick to my under-carriage. I'm curtly instructed to 'Sit down and belt up!'

Stellar start.

The important thing is I've made it and, as I flop down into seat 68B, my joy is almost post-coital. A quick scan of the cabin proves favourable, no crying babies and a vacant seat next to me, *the Economy traveller's nirvana!* I fasten my seatbelt and sit back in readiness for my next adventure, Thailand, the Land of Smiles.

Strange to say but I'm feeling surprisingly zen. If you'd have told me two months ago that I'd be relatively unfazed by a strip-search, I'd have laughed in your face. It's not that the ordeal hasn't rattled me, but rather that my new post-ashram calm has enabled me to process things different-ly. Less hysterically. Yes, I may have lost my fiancée, self-esteem and All Saints leather jacket (casualty of wardrobe custody battle) but I have found my inner peace. I flick through some photos of Indira and Nandi, random group shots in the garden, and one of Dawn mid-wobbly yoga pose with Tom pulling a face in the background. It gives me a warm, fuzzy feeling in my tummy.

Thank you, ashram fam! Thank you, Jen!

My phone buzzes; it's Dawn. She'll be joining me in Thailand as planned, excellent news. Can this trip get any bett...

'Excuse me,' a voice says. 'Can I squeeze by?'

It's a lovely voice. Well-spoken and husky, like the speaker is about to narrate a sultry chocolate commercial. I look up to see a statuesque brunette gesturing to the window seat beside me. She is gorgeous, the embodiment of calm and poise, despite having boarded later than me. Even cranky-pants Sa-meer is falling over himself to help, stuffing her bags into the overhead locker like a dinner lady stuffing the Christmas turkey. I start to rise and, forgetting I'm strapped in, jolt to an unceremonious halt.

'Ooops!' I laugh, unfastening my belt. 'The joys of cattle class, hey?' She gives a friendly smile. I try again, this time successfully rising, and she brushes past me with a whispered 'Thanks'. I catch a whiff of her scent. She smells delicious, like fresh linen and as I sit back down I'm aware that this must the first time I've ever been grateful for the cramped seating arrangement in Economy.

Her allure is such that I find myself wanting to look at her again. Like a magpie that's spied a shiny trinket, I lean forward as if to peer out of the window, while secretly surveying the real target in my peripherals. Easier said than done. The tricky focal battle results in me going boss-eyed, like I've had one too many scrumpy ciders. I persevere. She's wearing black skinny jeans and a fitted white vest, showing off a pair of magnificent square shoulders. *Model shoulders.* Some people like boobs or bums, I'm all about shoulders and eyes. Preferably two, but open to negotiation.

The more I stare at her, the more familiar she seems.

The dark wavy hair, heavy brows, those fabulous cheekbones. Then it comes to me. She has a look of the Oscar-nominated actor-cum-sex-goddess, Rachel Weisz!

My God, Dawn's spreadsheet really *does* work!

Falls to knees to praise heavens and Microsoft Office*

Oh Rachel! How I love thee!

Your films: The Favourite, The Mummy, Disobedience…apart from the spitting in Rachel McAdam's mouth. That was just plain dirty.

My euphoria is interrupted by a crackly tannoy announcement. 'Cabin crew, seats for take-off,' the captain instructs in a crisp upper-class accent as the engines roar to life. I feel my body tense and I reach for the security of the armrest, inadvertently brushing Rachel Weisz's forearm.

'I don't like take-off either,' she smiles, leaning into me.

'Yes! I'm …errr. I'm…..ummm…'

I'm totally incapable of speech! Reboot, reboot!

She breaks the awkwardness, extending an elegant hand.

'I'm Sara, by the way. Nice to meet you.'

'Oh, hi. I'm err, Ava. Ava.'

She holds my gaze for a moment, making me feel all shy and schoolgirly. If we were in a bar right now, I'd down a few shots and pluck up the courage to buy her a drink; but in the absence of such a luxury, I do the next best thing. I whip open my bag and offer something even better.

'Cheese and onion crisp?'

Sinks face in hands

Fortunately, Sara is wonderfully gracious and accepts the potato-based offering in the manner in which it is intended, as an icebreaker. *C-runch!*

The plane starts to climb and I tear myself away from her to perform my usual perfunctory in-flight checks, which consist of A. Staring at the crew's faces for signs of panic. B. Staring at the engines for signs of smoke and/or fire. Clear on both fronts. As the plane shakes itself silly, it occurs to me that this is the first person I've been attracted to since Scarlet and, for some ridiculous reason, I feel a pang of guilt. *Guilt! Pfft! Have a word, Ava!* I resolve to stop being so twattish and just enjoy the moment. That glorious feeling you get when in the company of someone new and exciting.

'So, Ava, how did you come to be in India? Holiday?' I like that she has remembered my name.

'Not sure I really want to bore you with that story. Torture at 30,000 feet!'

'Ha! Now I *am* intrigued,' she laughs, sipping on the slightly warm shiraz that Sameer has served up quick smart, clearly smitten. And with that unequivocal green light, I take a glug and leap into the sorry tale.

The more I share, the more I realise how insane it is that I'm telling a complete stranger my life story; how I wouldn't even be here had I not opened that door and walked in on Scarlet that night. But the fact is I *did* and, if that means I'm now talking to a beautiful stranger on a plane, I'm grateful.

I reach the end of a very potted version and, to my amazement, she is still awake. Not merely awake but smiling.

She lays her hand on mine.

'Oh! That's *brutal*. But there's nothing like travelling to get things in perspective. And India is the perfect place. There's something healing about it, especially an ashram. I've been a couple of times.'

'You have?'

'Yes, up in the north. It's so peaceful. Being surrounded by nature, the animals, the cows…'

'No way! A fellow cow-lover!' I grin, immediately sharing a few hundred pictures of Nandi in various poses: on the grassy knoll, next to Indira's moped and a particularly gorgeous one snapped from my balcony, after she'd broken into the garden and eaten all the frangipani. 'I totally get it,' I laugh. 'There are things I shared with Nandi that I wouldn't tell my bestie!'

'Ha! That's the thing about cows, they know how to keep a secret.' She raises her glass, 'To cows!'

'To cows!'

Now, I'm not sure if it's the plonk or the buzz of meeting my gorgeous travelling companion, but I'm feeling rather fuzzy and achy-jawed, probably because I've been chewing her ear off for the past 30 minutes. Poor woman! Before India I'd always been a 'stiff upper lip' kind of girl, tighter than one of my nan's Tupperware lids. But something has changed, a tap that had been tightly closed is now finally open and won't stop flowing. Flowing and flowing until I sound like… One. Big. Drip.

'God, listen to me over-sharing, I'm turning into my friend Dawn! The stories I could tell you about her! Not that I would. A cow…'

'…Knows how to keep a secret!' she laughs, finishing my sentence.

Gurgle gurgle.

My body lets out what I can only describe as an ungodly death knell and I pause for a moment to take stock, performing a quick internal M.O.T.

Heart? OK.

Chest? OK.

Guts? *Flobaawabaflaaaauuuaaaaoooobawabbbaaaaa!*

Confirmation. Definitely the guts.

I knew I should have bought that bloody *Dioacalm*!

I ignore the wailing from the depths, not wanting to ruin the moment, but my stomach lets out a second, more urgent growl. It's positively visceral, like an angry bear. She *must* have heard that one! I bet even the bloody Captain felt the tremors down at the pointy end.

BRRRRR-AAAAA-OOOOOOOO-RRRRR!

Code red, code red!

This must be every traveller's nightmare, being caught short aboard a packed aircraft. I make my excuses and start to survey the bathroom situation. Two toilets up front with a queue of five. Bad option. Two toilets behind, queue of four. Better option. I sidle along the aisle like an anxious crab, not wanting to make any sudden jolts. With every step I'm calculating my chances of a successful drop-off: four people in the queue at two minutes per person equals eight minutes.

I can do eight minutes. Eight minutes is fine. Absolute-

BRRRRR-AAAAA-OOOOOOOOOOOOOO-RRRRRRRR!

Perhaps not…

Ordinarily, '*Je ne regrette rien*', but right now je regrette that stale-looking samosa I gobbled down at the airport and today's wardrobe choices: baggy yoga pants and knackered knickers with failing elastic. In short, I'm questioning the structural integrity of my gusset right now! I stare fixedly at the toilet sign, willing the little red man to turn into a little green one. *Come on! Come on!* I resort to an on-the-spot shuffle wriggling like a demented worm and, after what seems like an eternity, red turns to green and the door opens.

Great! Only two more people ahead, four minutes to go. Doable. Very doable.

My shuffling gets ever more vigorous; I'm now jogging on the spot and have attracted the attention of a cute elderly couple who think I'm doing my inflight DVT exercises. 'Good idea, dear!' they smile, joining in. 'My ankles swell like beach balls at 30,000 feet, don't they Harold?' the lady says earnestly. Harold nods, confirming that her ankles do indeed swell like beach balls. Interesting as it all is, this is something I'd rather not get into right now, Harold and wife!

A further contraction.

FUUUUCK! IT'S HERE! THE CURRY BABY IS HERE!

The toilet gods must hear my prayers as suddenly, the door opens and I launch myself at it, pushing aside a small girl, who crashes head-first into Harold. 'SOORRYYY! EMEEEEERGENCY!' She instantly bursts into tears and I mutter another feeble 'sorry' and slam the door behind me. Trousers down, headphones on….

Hale-bloody-lujah!

.

.

There are few things in life as rewarding as averting a shit storm at 35,000 feet and I exit the cubicle a happier person than I entered it completely oblivious to what has transpired in my absence. Harold and wife (of famed beach ball ankles) seem to have been restrained by the air marshal!

WTF!

The poor things are strapped into the jump seats and Harold has one of those Hannibal Lecter masks strapped to his face. I give a confused smile and head back to my seat, eager to escape the bad juju and irate faces that seem to be looking my way. Most odd. Perhaps they are jealous of my fresh appearance? I've applied a bit of lip gloss and I've even had a squirt of the complimentary 'Eau d'airplane'. In short, I'm feeling fly. Pun intended.

Sara looks up from her magazine.

'You're looking revived,' she smiles, looking me up and down. 'Is there a secret beauty salon I should know about?'

'Absolutely and they're giving out free massages. Most invigorating,' I tease, flicking my hair. 'So, what did I miss?'

'Oh, just some commotion near the loos. Apparently, a man had a fit of air rage and pushed a little girl!'

'Oh, noooo. *Air rage*? Shit. Not cool,' I cringe, fearing I might have inadvertently instigated World War Three back there with poor Harold and wife taking the fall. I have a quick glance down the aisle only to be greeted by more filthy looks and one particularly rude guy who flicks me the bird.

'Air travel seems to bring out the worst in people,' Sara smiles. 'I was just chatting to the Cabin Manager about it.'

Sameer! Perfect opportunity to change the subject.

'I think he has a little crush on you, Sara. Play your cards right and you might get an upgrade.'

'What, and desert you, Ava? *Never!*' she winks, touching my hand for a micro-second. The tiny contact is enough to ignite every nerve in my forearm and a bolt of excitement shoots through my body. I haven't felt this sensation in months. It's like I'm finally coming round after a deep, deep sleep.

The rest of the flight continues in much the same way. We drink shiraz, eat pretzels and laugh...lots! She tells me about her work in Bangkok at a not-for-profit for children. *Kindness and beauty?*

'Surely you're hiding some fatal flaw?'

'Oh, plenty, believe me,' she smiles. Though for some reason I don't. Like Indira said, some people are just good to the core, no hidden traps.

'Well, you clearly enjoy your job. What is it they say, do something you love and you never work a day in your li…'

I feel a sudden heavy jolt and hear the roar of reverse thrust. 'Welcome to Bangkok!'

How did that happen? I've somehow missed all the messages about affixing seats belts and stowing my table. Oops!

Crackle crackle.

'It's 3pm local time. We apologise for the late arrival, this is due to an earlier incident aboard this aircraft.'

'What? *3pm?* Shit!' I blurt. 'My connection is at 3.30!'

I feel the blood rush to my head and my temples start to throb like someone's playing the bongos in my skull.

And breathe…

'Hey, don't worry. They'll just put you on a later flight. Happens all the time. Do you know, I think it might be fate!'

'Fate?'

'Yes! You can't come to Thailand without spending one night in Bangkok! It's sacrilege. You're welcome to stay at mine, no problem at all.'

'Oh no, I couldn't do that,' I say, secretly overjoyed that the air rage incident might have engineered this welcome change of plan.

'Think no more about it. It'll be fun. Besides, I enjoy showing people around. I secretly love the touristy bits!' she winks. 'Don't tell anyone,'

'Cow's honour!'

'So? Would you like to? Stay, I mean?'

'Errr…. yes! Yes, I'd love to!'

Around the World in 80 Gays
"Yes!"

If 'I love you' are the three most powerful words in the English language, then the three most powerful letters must be Y.E.S.

Yes to taking chances, to being open!

Yes to "throwing off the bowlines and sailing away from the safe harbour," as Mark Twain so eloquently put it.

There's a magic in a yes.

It can take us to places we never imagined, reward us with a life less ordinary, a whole new destiny even.

With so much potential in one tiny word, it's not surprising that yes can also be terrifying. It takes courage to utter those three little letters: to accept that unexpected dinner invitation, that fancy job offer or to stay at the house of a total stranger en route to a Thai paradise! But sometimes what's more dangerous than saying yes is *not saying yes.* Not daring to take a chance, not daring to venture out of your comfort zone.

As I climb aboard the taxi with my sexy stranger, I recall something Singrita said. 'The wind blows new opportunities every second. We are here to embrace them!'

I won't argue with that.

Especially when an opportunity looks as good as this one.

CHAPTER NINE – BREATHLESS IN BANGKOK

`'License my roving hands, and let them go`

`Before, behind, between, above, below.'`

`- John Donne`

Bangkok, Thailand. Feb 2018

Four fun Thai facts: 1. Thailand was once known as Siam, hence origin of Siamese cats – cute, skinny breed favoured by Marilyn Monroe and comedian Sue Perkins. Allegedly. 2. Population predominantly buddhist, thus jam-packed with opulent temples and people well versed in karma. 3. Super yummy cuisine. And most importantly of all, fun fact 4. Thailand is home to one of the most gorgeous women. On. The. Planet. *#SaraIsHot*

The cab clearly echoes my sentiments and the brakes shriek with delight as we pull up curbside at our destination. I peel my cheek from the window, checking for residual drool and trying to work out where on God's earth I am. A lively street, tuk-tuks buzzing like tiny mosquitoes and horns as regular as a heartbeat.

'Home sweet home,' Sara says, as we head up to a tall glass building nine or ten storeys high. It's hugely imposing with a Mondrian myriad of windows that reflect the sunlight into my face with the intensity of a laser beam. I shield my eyes and grimace.

'Oh no! I haven't brought Madame Vampiress home, have I?' she laughs, opening the door with a magic swipe.

'Guess you'll just have to ask me in and find out. A vampire must be invited over the threshold after all. Didn't you watch *Twilight?*'

She grins and ushers me in with a low bow, 'Ha! I can see I'll have to watch my neck with you around.'

Shit. Is it that obvious?

The foyer is equally dazzling, brilliant white walls with bursts of vivid orange provided by bunches of those gorgeous bird of paradise flowers, which instantly make me think of my Aunty B. She always has some back home. A touch of the exotic in Maidstone, Kent.

'So, how are you feeling now, Ava?'

'Pretty good, thanks. Be even better after a shower.'

'Oh, yes. I hear you. That's the best part about getting off a plane,' she smiles, running her hand through her hair. 'That and getting you into bed!'

'Sorry, what?'

'Getting into your own bed. It's the best feeling in the world, don't you think?'

'Oh, yes! Ha! Yes, it is!' I giggle, tickled by the combo of gluey plane ears and wishful thinking.

I find myself gazing at her again. Even daylight, the greatest leveller of them all, is unable to diminish this woman's beauty, not to mention the copious amounts of high-altitude plonk. Wish I could say the same for myself and, as we shuffle into the lift, I catch sight of my post-plane mop. Do by Thai *Hairways!* I've got some weird comb-over going on plus wispy side-burns. Hot! I smooth them down as the doors ping open and we head along a luxurious corridor with the bounciest carpet I've ever walked upon. It gives me a cocky spring to my step, utterly appropriate considering current cir-cumstances.

'This is us. Apartment 96,' she smiles, swinging open the heavy wooden door with a friendly, 'Come on in.'

I follow her into a rosy-coloured salon with white, bellowing cur-tains. It's surprisingly quiet up here, a little oasis of calm above the chaos of the street.

'Wow! It's lovely! Really lovely,' I gush, having a quick scan of the room, tell-tale yoga mat in the corner, plus a couple of hand weights. Suspicion confirmed. 'Mmmm, what's that smell?' I lift my nose to inhale the loveliest scent, a welcome treat after all that stale plane air.

'Oh, lotus flower. Do you like it? It's a sacred flower here. The symbol of rebirth.' She claps her hands decisively, 'Right, quick shower, then we can head out. If you can handle it, of course?' *Cheeky wink.*

The shower is a godsend and, as my body melts beneath the cascading water, I can't help but think of that scene in the *Psycho* movie. The one with Mr Stabby, aka Norman Bates and that poor blonde woman, and all the warnings about going home with strangers. *Oops!* Horse. Bolted. And all that. On the plus side, there is some comfort in the knowledge that should I be gruesomely butchered in the shower today, I will be discovered with my bestest body yet.

Flatter stomach – tick.

Traces of abs – traces are traces, I'm taking this as a win.

Even my bingo wings have flown the coop, though one more than the other. Most curious. In short, my post-India form is decidedly improved. Maybe there's something in this yoga malarkey after all. It certainly works for Sara. *Those arms! Those Legs! Those...*

Turns shower to cold

*

It's just past six when we step back onto the main street.

'Better?' Sara smiles.

'Yes! I feel so fres…'

Walks head-first into a giant wall of humidity.

She peels a strand of frizzy hair from my forehead, 'Just embrace it, Tina!'

'Tina?'

'Tina Turner!' she laughs, hailing a tuk-tuk with a casual flick of the wrist.

She looks great, every bit as hot as the Bangkok air, in white cotton shirt and jeans, and within seconds we are speeding into the city chaos. It's a veritable free-for-all as the driver bounces from lane to lane with little regard for The Highway Code or human life for that matter. In and out, blasting his horn. Anxious as I am, it feels exciting to be midst the madness, the ying after my ashram yang, and I cling on, masking my terror with a few playful 'whoops' and 'wooos'.

Ten minutes later, we arrive. Miraculously in one piece.

'Have fun girls,' the driver grins, giving a few impatient revs of the throttle. He has a cheeky glint in his eye and I can only imagine the hundreds of pleasure seekers he's dropped off at this very spot, all wide-eyed and full of expectation. After all, this is the tourists' playground, this is...

'The infamous Khao San Road,' Sara declares, stretching her arms out like a magician revealing her show-stopping trick. I struggle to take it all in.

Noise, smells, people. *Excitement!*

'This is a must-see on the one night in Bangkok tour,' she adds, her voice straining above the clamour. 'Mind you, my parents were absolutely terrified when I brought them here.'

I can see why. It's hardly a weekend away with the Richmond Rotary Club. Khao San is a lot. A lot of a lot.

A 400-metre strip paved with the lure of wild nights and bad decisions. Bars, stalls, cheap guest houses, nightclubs and then a few more even noisier bars in case you missed the first lot. As we walk, I am rapt by an overwhelming sense of déjà vu. Not surprising really. This street has been immortalised in countless Hollywood films: *The Hangover, The Beach, The Hungover Beach*. In fact, I can just picture a young Leonardo strolling past en route to his dystopian paradise. Nowadays of course, he's far too busy with global warming and hot models. Both worthy causes.

'Hey, let's have a drink here,' Sara grins, guiding me towards a cluster of plastic chairs a few metres along the road. It's one of those pop-up bars, filled with holidaying hipsters and locals high on the Khao San chaos. Sara heads straight to the bar while I grab us a table along the edge, perfect vantage point to indulge in some people watching. Particularly fun when overseas.

There's so much to see and my eyes dart back and forth like a pinball, right then left, left then right, before settling on a tailor's shop across the way, where a tiny man is yelling 'Suits for you, sir?' at the top of his lungs. It's one of those shops that can copy any design including '*Dolck and Gabbana*' and '*Versaze',* according to the neon pink sign. Next door, a group of lads spill out of a tattoo parlour, one of them looking decidedly green. I fear the inking has not gone to plan and will doubtless appear in Google's gallery of "Thai Tatt Fuck Ups*"* . He stops to expel the contents of his stomach against the wall, *Fifty Shades of 'Green'*. My guts give an empathetic gurgle as Sara reappears with a couple of beers and what looks suspiciously like cheeky shots.

'So, how do we feel about tequila?' she smiles, passing me a rather large measure of the devil's juice.

Now this *is* a bad idea. So bad that I reach out and grab it with both hands.

'Oooh. Dangerous! I've had many a good night on tequila.'

'And many a bad morning hugging the loo. Cheers!'

I down it and wince, biting hard on the wedge of lemon, as we stare at one another, awaiting the kick. 1…2…3….*whoooooosh!* It might just be the rush of the shot, but for the first time in a good while I feel, well, *alive*! Excited to simply feel something again.

'So how long have you lived here?'

'About a year or so. I came out for work, but it's like home now. It's not everybody's cup of tea, but I just love the energy. Plus, the people are the best.' She gives me the biggest smile which elicits a high to rival the tequila.

It's funny really, I know so little about this woman, but I just know that I like being around her. I'm not even sure if she's available, let alone if she sits on 'my side of the church'. Have to say, I do love all the euphemisms for being gay: a friend of Dorothy, light in the loafers, a wearer of comfortable shoes! Most of them are a delight apart from rug-muncher. Not a fan of that one. Truth be told, my gaydar is notoriously poor. It's quite the joke back home, even Rosie O'Donnell took me by surprise. Gay spotting is a whole lot harder these days of course. Sexuality comes in all shapes and sizes, a glorious rainbow spectrum. No need for labels. Though I do sometimes wish they'd invent some kind of Queer App that buzzes 'Gay' or 'Nay' with divisions inbetween. In fact, think I'll write to *New Scientist* magazine forthwith. In the interim, I'll just have to rely on old-fashioned female guile…

'So, did you come out here alone then?' I ask, casting my cunning lure.

'No. With my partner. I got offered the role and guess we fancied a change. You know, a bit of an adventure to bring the spark back.'

'Oh cool and did it?'

'Yes, absolutely! Until we broke up.'

'Oh no, sorry.'

'No, no! It's all good,' she reassures, touching my hand. 'It was months ago now, all very amicable. Sad, but my work is pretty full on, so guess it took its toll. Anyway...'

'Relationships, hey! Never easy, are they?'

'Ha! Nope. They're certainly not. When I was younger, I thought the hard part was finding someone, but now I think that's just the beginning, and the real challenge is keeping it going.'

Good point, well made. Might steal that for the blog.

All this ambiguity is killing me. I strike with the precision of a coiled Cobra.

'So, did they go back home then...your partner?'

She goes to answer and I watch her mouth open in a super slo-mo, like in the movies when some seismic plot twist is about to be revealed. Her lips start to form the first syllable. I lean in...

'Ssssshhhhheeeeeee ......'

There is it!

She said *'She!'*

Three small letters for woman, one giant leap for lezzakind!

The rest of the sentence is redundant, willingly surrendered to the noise of the street. All I want to do is rejoice, throw my shirt over my head like one of those over-paid Premier League footballers, but I resist, not wishing to expose my wares too early in the game.

'So...' she smiles, thrusting her beer into the air, 'Here's to strangers on a plane!'

'To strangers on a plane!'

Our bottles collide in a climactic chime and now, more than ever, I feel this might just be a good ni...

CRASSSSSSSSSHHHHHHH!!!

There's an almighty bang as our beers are unceremoniously knocked from our hands. I jump to my feet.

'What the hell was that...?' I quiz, grabbing at the bottles that are spinning like helicopter blades on the table. I look about me and my initial confusion is quickly replaced by an altogether higher level of bewilderment, when a small monkey hops onto the table and starts to drink from the frothy lake of beer.

'ELVIS!' a voice scolds. 'BAD BOY!'

I do a double take.

'Oh, wow! It's a …er…a …*M-O-N-K-E-Y*!' I stutter, as a handsome Thai guy steps forward in the brightest orange jacket known to humankind.

'So sorry,' he smiles. 'Don't worry, he is very friendly. His name is Elvis, like the King!' He orders the cheeky little lush off the table as Elvis curls his top lip and starts cackling like a lunatic.

'Oh right! H-h-hello Elvis, the err monkey,' I stammer, as if this is all perfectly normal which, if you're from Norfolk, it is not. The most exotic creature we can boast of is the badger. Possibly reed warbler.

Sara seems wholly unfazed by the incident, leading me to conclude that she must be in Elvis' circle of friends. Maybe not inner circle, but certainly Facebook variety. She throws a protective arm around my shoulder.

'He won't hurt you. But you have had a rabies shot, right?'

'Sorry, what?'

Health anxiety leaps to an eleven

I haven't been this scared since an alpaca nibbled my bumbag at Hackney City Farm. I was 26. Sara stares at me poker-faced and then I notice the sides of her mouth curling before she breaks into the biggest smile.

'Ahhhh, your face, Ava!' she laughs, pushing her head into my shoulder. 'He's a rescue monkey, he's had all the jabs. He's a bit of a face around here.'

'Oh yeah. Rabies – ha! Cool. I knew you were joking.'

Lies.

She glances down at her beer-speckled shirt. 'Think I need to clean up. I'll leave you guys to get acquainted. Won't be long.'

Elvis' chaperone instantly steps up, gallantly offering to replace our drinks.

'Ah. That's okay. I think we're about to leave. Thanks though.'

'Ok. You are on holiday, yes? Bangkok is the best city in the world,' he smiles. He is super friendly, with deep-set eyes. Kind eyes. 'My girlfriend came over and never left.'

'I can see why,' I grin, utterly enraptured by Elvis who is now dry humping a beer bottle to Britney's "Baby One More Time".

'You know, you look like her,' he adds. 'She is from Sweden. Like Abba.'

He goes to show me a photo before he's called away, leaving me to marvel at hairy Elvis again. *You know what, this little fella might just be the lucky charm I need. He has already gotten me a cuddle from Sara. Nice!* I have the sudden urge to contact Jen – fill her in. She'll be most heartened by news of my 'downstairs thawing.' She often compares my sexual organs to the polar ice caps, going as far as to say that when I do eventually defrost, I'll be responsible for a major global warming incident.

With that, my phone pings. *It's her!*

Hey super blogger! How's it going with Rachel W? So jel! Cruella is overjoyed with latest 80 Gays instalment. Loved monogamy debate. More. More! We might win the Pulitzer yet! LOL Xxx

It never ceases to amaze me when that happens.

You'll be thinking about someone and they suddenly text or call. Or even better, they walk into the bar with their new girlfriend looking all sexy and you spill red wine down your new white top. Babylon Bar, Shoreditch. Two months ago. *Bloody hilarious! Said no one ever.* But hey, must focus on the positive and the blog is one such positive. An unexpected one at that. *Cruella 'overjoyed'?* That's a first!

The text gets me thinking of life back home. My friends, family… what they're all doing, or more accurately, what *she* is doing. And just like that, she's back in my head like some hot inexorable menace. But that's Scarlet all over, the great disruptor. I remember the first time I saw her in that Soho bar. It was love at first sight for me and I chased her for what felt like an eternity. She was the queen of cool, madam of the 'make 'em wait' and boy did she know how to play it! I remember the angst every time I fired off a text. That agonising wait for the double tick.

Has she read it?

Was I too keen?

Too flippant?

Too serious? Not serious enough?

It's been 56 days.

56 days since I walked in on them.

56 days since the barrage of texts and calls I refused to take. Conversations I was simply too hurt to have. I wonder if she even thinks of me now, or if she's too busy making precious new memories with Ms De Vere? Urghhh! Even her name makes my stomach turn – it's about as real as her chest! Aside from the crippling loss you experience when a relationship ends, "it's the thought of being forgotten that really stings. Nobody wants to feel replaceable. Forgettable. Move-on-able." (*Around the World in 80 Gays.*)

I feel myself tumbling fanny-first down that rabbit hole again, imagining them together, in our home, *in our bed.* My chest tightens but instead of resisting, I allow myself to feel the pain. Something I learnt at the ashram – the importance of sitting with unpleasant feelings. Indira would always say 'Why do you girls drown your sadness in wine and the beds of strangers?' And I guess she was right, although sometimes it is just easier to avoid things.

'Hey there, daydreamer! Fancy heading off?' Sara says, all freshened up. 'There's another place I want to take you to, just down the way. We can grab some food.'

'Sure. Sounds like a plan.'

It's just past six and Khao San Road is even busier than before. Our walk alternates between a quick-step and a glacial waltz as we negotiate the ambling drunks, high on life and a bit more.

'Wow! *Smell that!* Cheap night out,' Sara laughs.

I smile back, promptly wafting the fumes away. That smell will forever remind me of Frida's gloved hand in an Indian backroom. #PTSD. We weave our way through all the souvenir stalls selling their ubiquitous Chang beer singlets and drink holders, others flogging fake uni degrees. Then there's the manicure stalls, massages with 'happy endings' and sizzling woks serving up Pad Thai. Lots of yummy Pad Thai. My tummy rumbles as we divert into a side road where we encounter a group of sloshed English girls, one of whom is being propped up by her friends. I raise an empathetic eyebrow as the drunk girl collapses like a ragdoll, exposing her knickers to the street. 'Oh Donna! You silly cow!' her friends curse, before dragging her into the nearest bar for a top-up.

'Here we are,' Sara declares, pointing at a roof bar above the main strip. It is positively buzzing. We begin our ascent. By the third step I'm terrified I might do a Donna and collapse with exhaustion, but I push on through, inspired by Beyonce's "Crazy in Love" and the shape of Sara's bottom in her trousers. She turns to look back at me, 'It's worth the climb.'

'Sure is!' I agree, but for altogether different reasons.

The summit reached, I pause to catch my breath, having a quick perusal of the establishment. It's a trendy place, very different vibe to the last bar, with the bartenders all dressed in crisp white shirts and presiding over the most luminescent bar, with row upon row of bottles arranged by colour, like a delicious liquor rainbow.

'So, what do you think of the tour so far? I'm giving you the whole V.I.P. experience, Ava, the platinum package!'

'Ha! I'd give you five stars for sure!' I gush, as we settle into our own private nook in the back corner. *Very cosy.* I feel spoilt to have her to myself in such a romantic setting. It's perfect. The table is lit by a tall candle which casts elongated shadows on the wall; and every time I lean in, it gives the impression that I'm lunging at her, which to be fair I might just do very soon.

Ravenous. On. Every. Level.

'They do the best food here,' she says, passing the menu.

'Oh cool! Anything will be great. Think all the beer and tequila are in need of more solid company!'

With that the waiter arrives and Sara orders us an assortment of Thai delights plus a round of espresso martinis, a little 'pick me up' after the gruelling hike. I watch her conversing in Thai which I have to confess makes me swoon just that little bit more, if that was even possible.

'Wow! Impressive that you speak the language.'

'I try. I'm a beginner really,' she says modestly. 'I have to speak a bit with work. Can't say it's been easy, but I'm getting there. How about you. Do you speak any other languages?'

'*Oui, oui* – a bit of French! I'm a little rusty, but I got to practice at the ashram with some French sisters.'

'Oooh. *French!* Now that's a lovely language,' she grins, raising an eyebrow.

'Isn't it? My first girlfriend was French actually. Giselle. I met her on an exchange programme. We mostly exchanged saliva and promises of love forever after,' I laugh. 'Wonder what happened to her?'

'Ahhhh. First love hey?'

'Kind of. Tongue like an eel, though! Sort of put me off for a while.'

'Hahhaha! Well, I'm sure you've had better experiences since,' she says with more than a soupçon de flirtation. 'So, tell me, besides brushing up on your French, what was your favourite thing about India?'

'Oooh, only one thing? That's not fair,' I protest.

'Yep. *One* thing. I have to be strict with this! Sorry. What's your *absolute, absolute* highlight?'

'Hmmm. That would have to be Indira, a lady I met there. She was like my fairy godmother. Put me straight about a lot of things. Guess she made me feel more hopeful about the situation. Oh wow...' I smile, distracted by the arrival of our food and drinks. 'That looks incredible!'

'Wait until you try it,' she smiles and I'm not sure if it's deliberate, but I feel her foot brush against mine. In shyness, I go to pull away, but stop myself. *No! I will not withdraw from this footsie encounter!* Instead, I inch my shoe closer. It's a bold move as I'm not sure I can handle rejection post-Scarlet. But hey, one night in Bangkok, what have I got to lose?

Our sandals meet.

She doesn't pull away.

'You have to try this, it's the best,' Sara says, offering up her fork of spicy noodles. I lean in and take the mouthful; half excited, half self-conscious at the intimacy.

'Oooh, yesss! That is *so* good! How do you say *delicious* in Thai?'

'*Aroi mak mak.*'

'*Aroyyy make make*,' I mimic, half-embarrassed. 'Is that right?'

'Perfect!'

This is all starting to feel rather romantic, I have to say. A shared mouthful. A shared moment. A shared… burning sensation on my lips! *Oh hang on!* The tingling rockets from zero to ring burn in a matter of seconds, and I reach for my espresso martini and glug the whole damn lot, coffee bean and all.

'Oh, sorry! Is it a bit spicy for you?' she laughs, passing me a napkin. I go to respond but I can only manage smoke signals at this moment. 'Ohhhh, ahhhhh,' I groan, fanning my tongue. Like that ever helps.

She sits there giggling and after a couple of minutes, I regain my composure.

'So, wooo…' I smile, clearing my throat. 'Nice! Tell me a bit more about your work.'

'Really?'

'Yes. I'm interested.'

'Well, it's a small charity. We look after Bangkok and some of the wider region, specialising in child education, health and development. It's funny really…'

* Room noise fades away. Crowds disappear. Swoon Swoon. *

I watch her as she talks, her whole face lighting up as I sink further and further under her magical spell, not blinking, barely breathing. At the risk of drooling, I shift back into my chair, inadvertently exposing my midriff. Her eyes fall upon me.

'Looks like you work out,' she says, gesturing to my tummy region.

I feel myself blush, 'Err…not really. I run for the bus sometimes!' I quip, at once flummoxed and flattered by the attention.

'You don't like compliments do you, Ava?'

'Not so much.'

The candle illuminates her face at that moment and I see her pupils suddenly dilate. My heart starts to race, my palms sweat and emboldened by the body language (and booze) I go to lean in, edging slowly forward, until I'm there, teetering on the cliff of rejection.

This is it, Ava! No turning back!

I commit to the move, tilting my head to one side, slightly opening my mou…

'Your bill ladies,' the waiter grins, placing the till roll on the table between us.

FUCKETY FUCK!

Great timing, mister. Great timing!

I glare at him. All I want to do right now is ram a satay stick up his nostril, but I maintain my dignity, coyly twiddling my hair while Sara smiles at me as if acknowledging the lost moment.

'So, Ms Roberts! One more for the road?'

'Sure, one night in Bangkok! Why not?'

We couldn't have timed it worse and, as soon as we step out onto the street, the heavens open. *Holy shit, it's heavy!* None of that half-hearted rain we get back home. This stuff is serious. Big fat splodges that cascade upon you, boring a hole in your skin.

'Welcome to Thailand!' Sara giggles as we stride out along the street. It starts to come down harder, so we break into a full-on jog, leaping over the newly formed puddles and weaving past all the equally drunk, wet people battling the Bangkok deluge.

'Quick! In here!' she says, pulling me into a narrow alleyway. We instantly break into hysterical giggles like a pair of schoolgirls. 'You ok?'

'Yep, just a little wet. I quite like it, actually. Kinda invigorating!' I assure, as a giant droplet tumbles off the end of my nose and bounces off my chest.

'Ha! Well, it won't last long…hopefully!'

The space is super tight, and Sara's body is pressed hard against mine. All I can feel is her breath on my cheek, warm and rhythmic, as her chest rises and falls in her damp, white shirt. We start to giggle again, all that pent-up excitement releasing itself, just like the rain. It's intense. Exciting.

We must stay like this for a good ten minutes before the cloudburst ceases as abruptly as it began. Sara looks at me. I look at her. Neither of us moves to pull apart.

Around the World in 80 Gays
"Breathless in Bangkok"

We stand motionless, locked in the moment. This sexy, wonderful moment.

This is hot, steamy hot.

A trickle of rain snakes down my chest as my breathing quickens. It's been months since I've felt such desire. Such intensity. Sensing my shyness, she turns my face to meet hers.

'I'm loving the wet look!' she smiles, brushing my cheek with her fingers. My heart leaps again.

'Thank you,' I mumble and then, at long last, she does it. She leans in and kisses me.

Softly at first, almost teasing – but then, as if aware of my impatience, she pushes her tongue into my mouth, moving her legs between mine. A hot, tingling sensation swells within me and I want nothing more than to rip her clothes off right here, right now, but she stops and grabs my hand.

'Let's go…' she whispers.

The journey home is a blur. A fast and furious blur.

Bright lights. Pumping music. Cascading rain.

'Well, you did want to get home quickly!' she smiles, as I alternate between feelings of wild excitement and paralysing nervousness. She kisses me again and suddenly I think of *her,* my ex, and an almighty wave of guilt crashes down upon me. It feels like, if I go through with this, I'm in some way disrespecting her. Disrespecting our relationship.

What the hell is wrong with me?

Before I can entertain any more ridiculous doubts, we are pulling up outside the apartment and I know exactly what I want.

Her.

Right.

Now.

We stumble into the lift, wet from the rain, giddy with excitement and I catch sight of our reflection in the mirrored walls – her body wrapped around mine, mine around hers and I can hardly breathe. Moments later, we are outside the apartment and she is opening the door and pushing me up against the wall, strong but gentle. 'I've been wanting to do this all day!' she whispers as my hands start to explore the contours of her back, her bum, her firm breasts. She moans louder, pulling me closer to her.

'Let's go to the bedroom!' I mumble, but she gives a little smile and pushes me onto the daybed.

'Here's good!'

I can't quite believe this is happening to me!

I pull away from her lips, my mouth slowly tracing its way down her soft neck. 'You're so hot!' she whispers 'So, so hot!' as our breathing becomes more rapid with every sensual kiss. Every. Beautiful. Touch.

She tugs at my vest, lifting it over my head and, before I can catch my breath, she is on me. Moving on top of me. Slowly. Passionately.

I lose all sense of anything other than the feeling of this beautiful woman's body on mine. Her soft skin, her hands delighting me with every touch.

'You're shaking,' she smiles, unfastening the buttons on my jeans. I don't reply, letting out a moan as her lips move down my body to my stomach. I feel the throb between my legs intensify as I pull her against me, rolling her onto her back and unfastening the clasp of her bra. Her body flinches as I reach down inside her thong.

She feels beautiful. Glorious.

My mouth moves further down her body, tasting every inch of her, as she lets out a breathy gasp.

'I want you so much...'

CHAPTER TEN – DIAMONDS ARE A GIRL'S BEST FRIEND

'It's not about the cards you're dealt, but how you play your hand.'

- Randy Pausch

'It was the best of times; it was the worst of hang-overs' to misquote Dickens and I awaken to the Nina Simone classic "Feeling Good". How ironic; I myself, am not. My head is pounding and it feels like the night goblin has taken a dump in my mouth. I peep out at the scene before me: an unfamiliar room, the scent of blue lotus, clothes scattered across the floor...jeans, bras, knickers...*MY KNICKERS?!*

I instantly thrust my hand beneath the covers.

SO, IT WASN'T A DREAM!! IT REALLY HAPPENED!

Salacious flashbacks to the night before: the Khao San Road, monkeys, rain, yummy pad thai, yummy Sara, her lips on mine, her body on mine. I squint towards a silhouetted figure standing in the doorway. *Oh crap! It's the Holy Mother Mary, the day of reckoning is upon us!* The haloed figure moves closer. One step, two steps.... then, *pheww*... all good, it's just Sara with two cups of coffee and a bumper pack of paracetamol.

The caffeine is as reviving as a slap in the chops.

'Mmmm, that tastes great,' I smile, savouring the first mouthful.

'Oh good. Wasn't sure how you take it.'

'I'd have preferred an intravenous drip if I'm honest, but this comes a close second!'

She strokes my hair back and my scalp tingles, like at the hairdressers when you're having a head massage and desperately trying to hide your hair-gasm face.

'So, last night was a lot of fun.'

'Wasn't it? Though I'm paying for it now!' My head delivers another reminder thump as I look her up at her. 'So how come you're up and dressed so early? I was hoping we'd have a nice...*lie in!*' I blush, surprised by my boldness.

'Aww, if only! Work just called. I have to go in for a few meetings.'

'Noooooo! What about our Bangkok tour? Dawn will be inconsolable. She was so excited to have a local as a guide.'

'Aww, I'm sorry!' she grins, planting the biggest, hottest kiss on my mouth. My lips tingle, like every nerve in my body is rebooting. 'Maybe this will make up for it.' She hands me a crisp white envelope.

'Ooh, what is it?'

'Two tickets for the Bangkok snake farm!'

'*Snake farm*? You're kidding!'

'Nope! We get them from work. It's all very ethical and pretty educational, actually. You girls might enjoy it.'

'Riiiight. So basically, I'm losing you and gaining a boa constrictor? Not the best of deals, is it? Still, maybe it'll get me over my phobia,' I laugh, leaning into her. 'And you're sure about Dawn staying? Don't want to put you out or anything.'

'Not at all, she sounds like fun.'

'She's that alright. Just don't let her near your toothbrush,' I mutter, pushing my head into her shirt. I nuzzle her neck and her breath starts to quicken. Again.

'Avaaa! You certainly aren't making this easy for me, are you?' She smiles, trying to limbo out of my over amorous octopus arms.

'Nooo! Can't you call in sick! *Pleeeasse!*'

'Ha! I really can't. I do have to head off.'

'*Really?*'

'Really! Have fun at the snake farm!'

'Ha! How could I not?'

The door slams and I throw myself back on the daybed, tossing the cushions into the air with a joy that borders on euphoria! *What bliss! What complete and utter bliss!* Last night was everything. A rebirth. The triumphant return of desire, of passion, *of life!* It's like Indira had predicted, 'The universe will send what we need – just trust!' Amen to that!

Sara is wonderful. A bright, glorious gift, not to mention a supremely trusting one. I don't know many people who'd leave a near stranger unsupervised in their home. I might well be stealing the family silver! But for now, I'll settle for a shower. My head is killing me.

The trek to the bathroom is an ordeal and I pace myself, stopping to look at all the photos in mismatching frames along the way. Portraits of family holidays, people on beaches with sun-scorched noses and several of Sara surrounded by smiling children with gaps in their teeth. It is a veritable wall of love and it gets me thinking of my own family back home. God, I miss them. I turn on the shower and wash away my hangover.

*

'EVIIIEEEE!'

'DONNN! Welcome to Bangkok!'

Dawn is unfashionably early as always. 'Punctuality is the politeness of kings' as she says. I have the feeling that might have been drilled into her at Cheltenham Ladies. She greets me with a long hug and a serious case of humidity hair, like she's had her fingers stuck in an electrical socket.

'I'm so excited I could pee!' *Giggle. Giggle.* 'So, tell me everything – how are you, Ava?'

'Hungover, my friend. But soooooo worth it,' I wink, taking her up in the lift.

'Ooooh, *really?*' She raises an eyebrow. 'Is there something you want to tell me, Ava Roberts?'

'Something I want to tell *you,* Dawny?* I wanna tell the whole bloody world! But a girl doesn't like to brag.' *Cheeky wink.* 'Anyway, how was your flight? Didn't run into a customs official with a monobrow, did you?'

'No! But I did meet a man who looked a bit like Ed Sheeran.'

'Oh right!'

The conversation soon shifts to her favourite topic, Tom.

'I won't lie, it's been hard without him, Ava. Very hard.'

'Oh no. How long has it been exactly?'

'Nine hours and three quarters. Thereabouts. He'll be in the air now, en route to Aus. Can't believe we'll be joining him there! Imagine that, all of us Down Under with the wannabies!'

'*Wannabies*?'

'Yes, they're like mini kangaroos.' She does an excited little hop. 'They're so cute. Like my Tom! He's splendid, don't you think? Utterly splendid!'

'Alright, calm down Jane Austen! Shit, I swear you're out of the 18th century sometimes,' I quip, opening the door to the apartment,

'Oh wow! This is nice,' she says, looking around. 'Sara clearly has taste, in some things at least!'

'Funny!'

It's a quick turnaround as Dawna the Explorer is keen to get out there and enjoy the many sights of Bangkok. 'I don't want to miss a thing, Ava!' and within minutes, we're out of the door and onto item one of her whistlestop tour.

The itinerary is a bold one, meticulously planned according to Tripadvisor and that man she met who looked like Ed Sheeran. He's lived here for years apparently and knows all the best places. I put myself in her capable hands as we work our way through the list item by item, line by line and, by early evening, we are done for.

Like. Really. Done. For.

'Well, I don't know about you, but I need a drink! A bloody big one!' Dawn declares, dragging me into the first bar we come to. It's kind of dark inside and, as our eyes adjust to the semi-light, I hear the familiar cackle of a monkey, thus triggering memories of little Elvis from last night. *It can't be, can it?* His lip curls in recognition as he leaps onto my shoulder, much to Dawn's horror.

'*OH MY GOD, IT'S A GREMLIN!*'

She lets out a blood-curdling scream that scares the hell out of everyone in the place.

'It's Elvis!!!!! Nothing to be afraid of, Dawn. We met him last night,' I say, trying to reassure her.

'Well, hello again,' a voice says and I turn to see his owner, Mr Orange Jacket approaching, which of course makes Dawn scream again. I cut her some slack. Today's adventures on the tourist trail have not gone quite to plan.

'It's been hellish!' she tells Mr Orange, who mentions that I look like his girlfriend. Again. I'm beginning to suspect it's just a chat-up line when she suddenly materialises and then I just feel bad.

'This is Nicole, she's working here today,' he says, as a tall brunette girl strides out in a red vest. 'And I'm Aroon!' He holds out a hand. The girl must be around my age, very attractive, so I suppose I should be flattered. I notice she has a bandage protruding out of her bra. 'Oh, don't mind that,' she shrugs nonchalantly. 'I had a bit of a motorbike smash in Samui. Ripped off half a nipple. It should grow back though!'

'Oh lovely!' Dawn says politely.

'You're here on holidays, yes? Bangkok is the best – just make sure you have a good guide. Lotta jerks here. Lotta jerks everywhere really!' Nicole winks, passing us a handful of drink tokens.

'Wow thanks, Nicole!'

'Yes thanks! We've had quite the day of it today. Quite the day!' Dawn sighs, before turning to the bartender to order double everything.

GLUUUUG!!!

It's not the most savoury of establishments. Still, any port in a storm, and Dawn and I retire to a table in the corner to dissect the day.

'But isn't that the point of travelling?' I ask her. 'The unpredictability, the adventure, the...'

'Losing your iPhone in the belly of a boa constrictor?'

Her bottom lip starts to quiver. *Oops!* Too early to move onto the 'let's laugh about it' stage, then!

I leave her to regain her composure, using the time to jot down some notes for the next blog entry entitled "Bangkok sightseeing tour" (my notes in italics). I feel this will be a good one…

1. Grand Palace and Wat Prakeaw
"Dazzling and spectacular" according to guidebook. Home of Thai kings since 1782. Famous for Emerald Buddha, most sacred buddhist temple in Thailand.

Lovely from outside. Upon approach, informed by friendly tuk-tuk driver that the palace was 'closed for cleaning'. We said, 'All day?'; he said 'Yes, it's very dirty.' Fair point. Driver kindly took us to his cousin's jewellery shop where we purchased rare gemstones at bargain prices! Dawn bought large diamond like the one in Titanic, the Heart of the Ocean. Driver then took us to another cousin's shop to buy Persian rugs (rare in Thailand). Dawn is having two shipped home with a laughing monkey corkscrew. What a helpful tuk-tuk driver!

2. Snake farm

Dawn (now a vegan like Tom) worried it might be unethical, so we googled it to check credentials. All legit, run by Animal Action. Used Sara's passes and got the full VIP treatment, including private show with king cobra. Cobra bit handler and was rushed to hospital. (Handler, not cobra.) Saw other snakes too. Dawn had a big yellow one round her neck that tried to asphyxiate her, resulting in her iPhone X getting swallowed in the kerfuffle. Phone not covered for snake damage. Dawn cried again. Not much better for me. Spent the whole two hours paralysed with fear, unable to speak.

3. Taling Chan floating market

To quote the website, "You will enjoy sightseeing the scenery of local community along canal…."

Sadly, we did not.

Pluses: Lovely people. Fun to eat from the little boats full of yummy food. Minuses: Dawn seasick, possibly due to overindulgence in papaya salad and/ or vegan spring rolls. Beginning to think she is jinxed. Did the sensible thing and headed to nearest bar to get shit-faced, as recommended by all good guidebooks.

'So, here's to more wild adventures in Bangkok,' I say, raising my glass tentatively.

'Cheers!'

Sniff sniff!

Thankfully, the espresso martinis soon work their magic and by the third the melancholic mist of the day is well and truly lifting. Dawn is even making jokes about her python-ingested iPhone. Most amusing was 'I'm well pissssssssssssed off' which I thought was a stellar effort considering the sssss-sircumstances.

'Still, at least I have this,' she sighs, producing the prized Titanic diamond from her shoulder bag. She lays it against her neck and throws her arm behind her head. 'Draw me like one of your French girls, Jack!'

We instantly crack up, attracting the attention of some men playing cards at the next table. I lower my voice. 'Do you know what Dawn, I think you might be the unluckiest person I've ever met. Actually, make that the second. I once knew a girl who reversed over her own foot.'

'I did that once, in my uncle's Renault Clio,' she hiccups. 'Tell you one thing I *am* lucky at though, Evie.' She gestures to the men at the next table again.

'What? *Cards?*' I say incredulously.

'Not just cards – *Poker*! I was house champ at school. They called me Snake Eyes.' She starts to crinkle her eyes into tiny slits.

'Honest to God, Dawn! You never cease to amaze me. So, now you're a card shark?'

'*Snake, Ava...snake!* Well, what else do you think uz girls got up to in the dorms at night?' she says, suddenly slurring her words.

I can think of a few things, Dawny, I can think of a few!

Her eyes widen. 'Lizzen to me, Ava! I reck'n I cud play a few hands, win just enough for a new phone and a nize dinner out. Whad'ya say?'

'Um, not sure that's a good idea. A, you're pissed and B, your luck has not been the best today, has it? What if you lose?'

She stares over at me, adjusting her demeanour like an actor getting into character.

'What if I lose, what if I fall?' she says in her best Indira voice. 'Ah, my dear, *but what if I fly!*' The impression is not the best, sounding more Welsh than Indian to be honest, but point taken. Nobody likes a Debbie downer and besides, I get the feeling I couldn't stop her now even if I tried.

What happens next is one of the most bizarre transformations I've ever witnessed. Forget Bruce Wayne to Batman or Peter Parker to Spidey, this is a whole new level of metamorphosis! This, ladies and gents, is *Wimpy Dawn* to *Poker-Don!* She rises from her seat and approaches the poker table with a weird swagger-cum-limp.

'Can a girl get in on this?' she says in an accent that's half Wild West, half West Hampstead. One of the players looks up, an older guy with a fluffy half-beard.

'You play?'

She squints at him, 'Sure. I play. What's the stake?'

'500 baht!'

'*In!*'

Snake Eyes pulls up a chair and starts to suck on a matchstick.

Who the hell is this person?

She peeps down at her cards. 'Raise you 100!'

The next thirty minutes have me terrified and transfixed in equal measure, as I watch them locked in psychological warfare around the table. There are four players: Dawn, the beardy guy, his Londoner sidekick (who keeps whispering to Mr Beardy) and another tourist, Texas Hank, who frankly looks more terrified than me.

The tension is palpable.

'Call!' Texas mumbles as Dawn fans her cards out on the table. 'Royal flush.'

Eighth win in a row. *Way to go Dawny!*

The Texan goes a deathly pale. 'I'm out,' he announces, dusting off his Stetson and heading for the door. Saw that coming – only room for one cowboy at this table and she's from Godalming, Surrey.

I breathe a sigh of relief, thinking his exit will spell the end of the game, but alas, another player appears. It's Nicole. She nods and smiles, taking a seat next to Dawn.

'Any objections if I join?'

And once again, there were four.

Eyes down. The cards are dealt.

There's a good bit of 'Raise you 200' and 'Raise you 500' going on and miraculously, old Snake Eyes does it again! She scoops the pot into her pile of notes, and I lean forward to whisper into her ear.

'You're on fire, girl! There's enough to buy a phone now. Call it a night, hey?'

She barely acknowledges me and Nicole shrugs as if to say, 'A girl's gotta do what a girl's gotta do' so I sit back down and buckle up. I fear this might be a bumpy ride.

Another hand, more raising, more squinting.

'Well?' the Londoner sneers. He's a flash-looking twenty-something, with *'Just did it'* splashed across his chest. Knock-off from the Khao San.

Dawn nods and goes all in, pushing her entire stack of notes into the centre of the table and I look away, feeling utterly sick.

'Fold,' Nicole says as Knock-Off Nike looks at his dealer buddy with a big grin, exposing a row of gold teeth. Now, what I know about poker you can fit into a thimble, but I sense all is not well. Dawn shows her hand next. A pair of tens.

'Sorry – Full House!' the older man says, 'You lose, lady!'

He scoops the pot from the table, leaving Dawn's fortune reduced to a... Big. Fat. Zero.

WTF!

'Don't worry, we give you chance to win back money,' the dealer says, and I look at Dawn as if to say 'Hell, no!' but to my horror, she lays her passport and credit card out on the table. '500,' she says. '500 ......pounds.'

'*Pounds?* Dawn! *Pounds!*'

It's a step too far for Nicole.

'I'm out,' she says, promptly retiring to the safety of the bar with Aroon and Elvis. *This shit is getting serious!* Serious enough that a small crowd of onlookers has now gathered around the table.

The dealer deals. Dawn stares down at her cards.

'Well?' He drums his bony fingers on the table and looks over at co-conspirator Knock-Off Nike.

Another shake of her red hair, and then Dawn throws in her hand.

'Lose again, lady! You lose!'

FML!

It's at this moment that I detect a distinct mood change. It's like a switch has been flicked and Knock-Off Nike starts to get a little handsy, trying to whisk Dawn off to the ATM.

'We get money now. Quick,' his friend barks and I fear poor Dawn is just a few moments away from meltdown, but instead of cracking, she does something I would have never predicted. Something wholly unexpected.

Poker Don rises to her feet and slams her hand down on the table with a defiant 'NO!'

All eyes fall upon her.

Everyone is awaiting her next move as she reaches into her shoulder bag and pulls out a small velvet pouch.

'I have better than cash,' she says, 'Look!'

Oh God. Not the Heart of the Ocean. I gasp as slowly, very slowly, she positions the big blue gemstone on the table. It's a scene of mythological intensity as the strip lights strike its mighty sides and I swear to god I actually see it glow! Like it's unleashing its magical powers.

The men look at the jewel. Bewitched. Mesmerised.

And then suddenly…they explode into fits of laughter. 'HAHAHAHAH-HAHHA! That's fake! Fake!'

'No, no! It's real! I have all the documentation!' Dawn says defiantly 'I know it's real….'

With that, Knock-Off Nike rises to his feet.

'Right, I'll test it ven!' he sneers, grabbing a big metal buddha from the bar and raising it above the glimmering gemstone.

'No, wait!' Dawn protests, as if stalling for time. 'You'll break the table!'

He doesn't take no for an answer. 'Move!' he thunders as the buddha slams down on top of the diamond. *THUD!*

Everyone stares as the stone holds firm, like Dawn's conviction. 'See! Buddha has spoken! It's *real!*' she beams, giving it an affectionate tap for dramatic effect, whereupon it promptly shatters into thousands of tiny pieces on the table.

'Oh.'

'HaHaHa! Fake. Fake. I knew it. Let's go!' Knock-Off snaps, 'Cash-point! *Now!*'

I bury my face in my hands, not daring to look and out of the corner of my eye, I see Nicole rising from her seat. Next thing I know, she's striding into the fray. 'Hey bud, don't push women!' she commands, shoving him back down. 'Not cool!'

Aroon nods in agreement, getting up to take his place beside her in a show of solidarity.

If they're going in, then so am I!

I take a deep breath and rise to my jelly legs, joining the resistance. 'Yeah! Don't push women!' my voice warbles.

There are a few more choice words, followed by a farcical scuffle, as Nicole and Aroon get the men into a headlock, with me pulling off a surprisingly effective thumbscrew on Knock-Off Nike.

'Right guys. Think we all need to play nicely here,' Nicole says, signalling to the back-up unit aka Elvis, who leaps down onto the table, curls his top lip before making a spectacular lunge at Knock-Off Nike's trouser pockets.

'Oi! Get that fuckin' rat off me!' he yells, spinning round and round in an attempt to throw Elvis off, but his monkey hands hold strong. It's almost comical: Elvis clinging on for dear life, Knock-Off twirling on the spot, and his mate getting irater by the second. This continues for a few more rotations before Elvis reaches into Knock-Off's pocket and, with a triumphant screech, extracts a set of cards – *Aces, Kings, Queens and Jacks!*

Gasps from the crowd, 'No way!' as the cards flutter back down onto the table, settling beside the golden buddha and shattered gemstone.

Now that's what you call the poetry of karma!

Dawn's whole demeanour suddenly changes as she proceeds to slap Knock-Off Nike about the ears with her knock-off sandals.

'Nobody cheats Snake Eyes!' she repeats, as he lets out some pathetic whimpers. A few sandal slaps later, the men drop the hard man act and make a desperate bolt towards the door.

'And where do you think you're going, Ace?' Nicole teases, as Aroon grabs the money and boots them out of the door right into the pathway of Sara.

'Oh, hello there. Did I miss anything?'

*

Suffice to say, today has been a day of surprises, *big surprises* and, as I look over at the bar, it strikes me that this really is the most unlikely bunch of superheroes. Nipples Nicole, Mr Shouty Shirt and a bloody monkey!

'Just goes to show, people never cease to surprise you,' Sara laughs.

She's not wrong there. People astound me all the time: Aunty B's appetite for younger men, Scarlet's cheating and now mild-mannered Dawn turning out to be a poker shark who's more than a bit handy in a crisis!

'Sorry about your diamond mate. Like I said, lotta jerks out there!'

Dawn gives a little shrug. 'Ahh, it's OK, Nicole. Besides, I kinda twigged it was fake.'

'What?' I say, shock layering upon shock. '*You were double bluffing!*'

She gives a devilish smile. 'Perhaps!'

'Shit, Dawn Boldwood. You really are a dark horse.'

'Snake, Ms Roberts. Dark snake.'

Around the World in 80 Gays
"Don't talk to strangers"

"Beware strange men with cute puppies and sweets." That's what I was taught as a child. Stranger danger. Mistrust.

Like all children, it was drilled into me and I'd lay awake at night, contemplating the unspeakable, being taken.

How quickly such childhood teachings evaporate when travelling. Doubly so when travelling alone, as frankly you have no choice but to trust. Trust your instincts, trust your gut and, most dangerous of all, *trust strangers.* But that's the joy of travelling, it not only opens the mind, but the heart too.

Sure, there are bad eggs out there, the con artists poised to devour unsuspecting tourists the moment they step off the plane. But there are the good people too. Those benevolent souls who are there to lend a hand, to do what's right.

Fact is, trusting another living soul is always going to be a gamble, as much with strangers as with those we love.

You roll the dice. You take your chance. A bit like today's poker game.

Fortunes change faster than the wind. Lady Luck can desert us at any time, like a faithless lover. All we can do is play the hand we are dealt. And, however daunting that might feel, I'm learning that life, like love, is better when you go all in.

CHAPTER ELEVEN - A FOND FAREWELL

'If you don't risk anything, you risk more.'

- Maya Angelou

'Stop! Dawn plays poker?' Jen laughs. '*Your* Dawn? Would never have guessed that.'

'Yep! Who knew, hey? Nicole and Aroon were a bit of a revelation too! Mad night, Jen. Mad night.'

'Hmm. Might be something in that.' She starts to type into her laptop. 'You never really know what people are made of, like Dawn's Heart of the Ocean.' *Tap. Tap.* 'Apply a bit of pressure and you discover some people are diamonds, while others crumble into a million pieces on the poker table of life.'

'Oh yes, YES! I love that, Jen. God you're good!'

'Yeah, I know,' she smiles. 'I know.'

It's 7am and we're ten minutes into a long overdue blog summit. Jen is seated at her desk at the London office, wedged in the usual spot between wilting pot plant and framed photo of Kate Winslet, munching on a snack. Jen, not Kate.

'Oh wow! Is that cheese on toast?' I gasp, my mouth instantly salivating.

'Yup, with Wurcester, Worcestar, Wocestershireshure sauce.... urgggh! That has to be one of the hardest things to say,' she grins, taking another bite. 'Does make you wonder though…'

'Wonder?'

'If anyone has ever lived long enough to buy a second bottle of Worcestershire sauce!'

C-RRRUNCH!

Oh, the mind of a writer….

She gives me a quick 360 of the office between munches. Everybody is looking decidedly glum, like they're just had an unsatisfactory poo. Not surprising really, most are pulling all-nighters, poor buggers. Can't say I miss deadline day.

'Right,' Jen enthuses, high on caffeine and vintage cheddar. 'Back to business.'

I sit up as she delivers the most encouraging blog report to date. 'Nandi the cow is resonating in Southeast Asia and "Speak your truth" is becoming a bit of a hashtag. Pretty cool hey?' She starts to get rather twitchy at this point; Cruella must be circling. *Please God, no!* She'll doubtless want to grill me about 'the next sublime instalment' for which I have minimal interest right now, especially as I'm playing second fiddle to a cow. Nandi is a big lure for our veggie readership apparently – her bountiful udder 'nourishing lost and broken souls'. I am the lost and broken soul in this scenario, for clarity.

A shiny, botoxed face suddenly lunges towards the screen.

'Avvvvaaaa! Daaaarlink! Tell me, how is Nandi?'

Like I said, second fiddle.

She doesn't wait for an answer, launching into a rapid-fire critique of the latest entries. 'I'm loving the Indiaaaaarrr content! So vibrant. The eating with fingers…dripping in sensuality! And the toothbrush…the symbol of female sexual empowerment! *Electrifying!*' She's so worked up now, that I think she might be having a toothbrush moment of her own. 'So yah, we're up 500 percent in engagement week-on-week. This blog has legs or should I say *udders*?'

Cue maniacal laughter

'I want more, Ava! More Bangkok glamour…'

'Riiiight, Lucrezia!'

'More alleyway sensuality – lips, I need lips, breasts! *Heeeeeaving* breasts!'

'Err, well I…'

'And you, darlink?' She tilts her head like a troubled cocker spaniel. 'Tell me about you. Are your chakras sorted now? I've been so very worried.'

'Well, yes, I think I'm feeling a bit bet…'

'Benissimo! Benissimo!' she snaps, instantly losing interest. 'Right, must run. I'm seeing Jean-Claude for a late night colonic. Lord, I need a purge!'

And *poof*, just like that, she's gone.

I flop back on the bed. 'Bloody hell! I feel violated after that,' I gasp. 'Still, she seems pretty happy with us though.'

'Yup! Enjoy it while it lasts. Can't wait to write up the latest Bangkok stuff. I don't know how you bloody do it, girl!'

'Err, I don't really *do* anything. It kinda just happens and…'

'OMG! Your romantic encounter…we need to talk! So come on… Sara sounds hot as.'

She is now speaking at such a volume that CFA (Cheryl from accounts) has dragged herself away from her spreadsheet to have a gander.

'Sssssh! She's in the next room,' I blush. 'It's not a forever thing, but she's great and hey, it's just nice to *feel* something again. Like, actual butterflies!'

'And the rest!' she winks. 'Anyway, so what if it's just a fling? Not all love stories are meant to be novels; some are short stories or sentences in my case! I'm just happy you've met someone you fancy!' She promptly breaks into impromptu song and robot dance. "Finally, it's happening to me, right in front of my face…" Another classic butchered. CFA is equally overcome, spilling a box of paperclips over the desk. If that's not a sexual metaphor, I don't know what is.

'So, what about you, Jen – any dates?'

'Well, the office dog's been humping my chair most days, so guess you could say we're going steady. His lipstick even came out today, rank!'

'Urghhh. Too much info, girl! Seriously though, have you met anyone?'

'I have been chatting to this one girl. She's a personal trainer, seems nice enough,' she says, just as Winston the office dog mounts her swivel chair. Some things cannot be unseen.

'Wow! He sure does like you, Jen!'

'What can I say, animal magnetism! OFF BOY, OFF!'

'So, how about the rest of the gang?' I ask, flagrantly aware that I might be inviting some Scarlet news into my world. But like a moth to the flame, or a fly to a turd, I can't resist.

'Yeah. We had Big John's birthday last weekend. He ended up vomming in a policeman's helmet…who turned out to be a stripper in fancy dress! So yeah, worked out well considering! Oh, and we bumped into…err…'

At this point, the screen freezes. *Bloody internet!*

I shake my phone but it's not until I spot CFA walking across the background that I realise Jen's faking it.

'*Jen Jones!* Stop bloody pretending, you nutter!'

She springs back to life, gasping for air, her big green eyes pleading '*Please don't ask me! Please don't ask me!*'

I show no mercy.

'Did you see Scarlet? You *can* say her name, you know. I won't burst into tears or anything.' Ironically, the moment I utter the words, that's *exactly* what I want to do. My chest tightens and a big lump forms in my throat.

'Errr, yeah, we kind of ran into her and, you know, Carla *De Venereal!* All the charm of a verruca, that one!' She gives a nervous laugh. Poor Jen. She's not very good at playing 'mean girl'.

'It's fine, honestly Jen. I'm going to have to get used to the idea at some point. Anyway, I'm well on the way to making a full recovery.'

In a few hundred years....

I sit for a moment staring at the screen, prolonging the agony. And then I do it. I ask the question I'm desperate to ask.

'So, did she... *mention me?*'

I instantly feel exposed.

If she didn't mention me, I'll be crushed. But if she *did,* I'll be encouraged. Neither is good.

'Yes, she did. Don't think Carla liked it much. She went all red and blotchy! Don't worry, Ave, I laid it on real thick! Told her what an *amazing* time you were having, how you were doing this really cool travel blog. I even told her about hot Rachel W. You should have seen her face! *Slapped arse!*'

'Wait, you told her about the blog?'

'Relax! There are hundreds of travel bloggers out there.' She gives me that smile that makes me feel everything is going to be OK. 'Listen, Scarlet is in the past. This is your time now, girl! *Your* time!'

The call ends abruptly after Winston gets a second wind, going in for round two. I lay back on the bed, feeling horribly unsettled. It's funny how things can throw you off. You're going along all 'ticked- boo' as my Aunty B says, high from a hot liaison with a Bangkok goddess, and then someone utters one little word and it all goes to crap!

Scarlet is that word for me. Two syllables, first one '*Scar*'. There's a clue there.

The scar that still itches. The scar that still stings.

Come on Ava! Pull yourself together.

I try to focus on the here and now, and that delightful aroma of bacon that's wafting in from the kitchen. Ah yesss! Now that's a smell. It gets me thinking of fry-ups back home and randomly some girl at primary school who had a morbid fear of baked beans. *Leguminophobia*, I think they call it. Most odd.

Speaking of odd, yesterday scored pretty high on that scale. Other descriptors might include shitshow, clusterfuck and right bloody Bangkok balls-up. Miraculously, we managed to salvage the day, ending on a Thai-high via a revitalising massage at Wat Pho temple with new besties Nicole, Aroon and Elvis. 'Never underestimate the power of someone standing on your back until your eyes pop out,' as Sara put it. The night went from strength to strength from there and culminated in a few drinks at a local bar followed by a discussion about travel, foam ear plugs and Buddhism. Apparently, shock 499 of the day, *Aroon trained to be a monk!* I thought I'd misheard at first, but turns out he studied for a few years and decided it wasn't for him. The whole story was fascinating. He took us through karma theory 101, the four noble truths of Buddhism and finally, *samsara*, rebirth. I have to say I quite like the idea of reincarnation, coming back to have a second go. Avoiding all the mistakes of the first time. Dawn, who'd had a few drinks at this point, was less enthusiastic and was convinced she'd come back as a sloth 'or something else with hairy toes'. A debate to be continued when compos mentis perhaps.

'Hey Ave! What you up to?'

I look up to see Dawn wandering into the bedroom. She's lost the swagger of last night, more walking dead today.

'Morning, Snake Eyes. Did you miss me or something?'

'A bit. But I'm missing Tom more,' she giggles. 'I can't believe I'll be seeing him in a day! Not that I'm wishing our time away. I've had the *best* time, Ava! The best! I mean, you know how much I love a spreadsheet, but I've kind of enjoyed the, well, *chaos* of this adventure!' She looks at me and smiles. 'Thank you.'

'For what?

'For making me appreciate spontaneity.'

'Awww! Careful Dawn! You'll be cancelling your Tripadvisor subscription next!'

She lays her head on my shoulder.

'It has been fun, hey?'

'Yep, and to think it all started with a gorgeous stranger aboard a plane!'

'There's a word for that, Ave...*Serendipity*. Unexpected good luck. Or in this case, *Sara-ndipity!* Ha!'

'Very good Dawn, very good!'

The last day of a trip is always a little weird, a kind of limbo. And, despite trying to enjoy your final hours, you invariably spend most of the time clock-watching, terrified you'll miss your flight. Not always a bad thing as we now know.

Sara appears with a massive tray of breakfast delights: smoked bacon, waffles and fresh fruit. I must blush or something as she gives me a look. 'Oh, hello! What are you girls talking about?'

'Oh, you know, just about fate and...'

'How great you are,' Dawn blurts. I give her a little kick and artfully change the subject.

'So, wow! Breakfast looks amazing!'

'Doesn't it just,' Dawn says, instantly tucking in. 'Thanks so much Sara. I'm gutted I can't eat the bacon. I'm a vegan now – like Mr Spock.'

'Isn't he a *Vulcan*?'

'Oh yes! Ha! Sorry Trekkies!'

We wolf down breakfast, going from starved to stuffed in a matter of minutes, before flopping back on the daybed like three deliriously stuffed ticks. Sara snuggles up behind me, the big spoon to my small. That's one of the things I miss about being in a relationship. The cozy intimacy of a good spoon.

'So, it's great that you're seeing Nicole and Aroon in Krabi. That ladyboy night they were talking about will be fun!'

'Yeah, sounds it. Would be even better if you were coming too,' I smile. 'Can't you get away?'

'I don't think my nerves could take it to be honest! Last night was bad enough! I have to say, Dawn, you really are full of surprises.'

'Isn't she just, bloody *card shark!*' I give her a poke.

'Oh really? Everybody plays poker in my family. It's a bit of a rite of passage. My grandpa said it's an essential part of a young person's education.'

'Oh, how so?'

'Well, poker is a lot like life. It's not so much about having the best cards, but playing what you do have well.'

Well, f*** me sideways with a rusty tuk-tuk!

That might just be the wisest thing that girl has ever said.

Around the World in 80 Gays
"A Goodbye"

Goodbyes. I always struggle to find the good in them. Even at birthday parties, I practice the 'ghost' exit, disappearing into a taxi, gone with the slam of a door. And yet here I am once again, saying goodbye. *Choke dee na.*

As I stand opposite my lady of Bangkok, our brief moments together flash before my eyes, like a pop video. 48 short hours! Just a drop in the Gulf of Siam perhaps, but then you can't measure the value a person brings to your life in hours or minutes. What is felt in just moments with one person, might not be experienced in a lifetime with another.

'Right!' I say, tugging at my backpack.

She gives a resigned look.

'Are you sure you don't want me to drive you to the airport? It's no bother.'

'What and miss out on another tuk-tuk terror ride?' I look down to the floor, suddenly feeling shy. 'Well, I've had an amazing time. I can't thank you enough. You've been, well... *aroi mak mak!*' I blush, embarrassed by the terrible pronunciation.

'Ha! I like that. I've had the best time too.' She lifts my chin. 'You really have been an unexpected adventure!'

We stare at one another for a minute, prolonging the inevitable before she leans in for a final kiss. My body tingles as I inhale her scent, lotus flower, and the taste of her lips. Trying to commit them to memory.

What sweet serendipity!

This stranger has given me the ultimate gift, a sensual reawakening. A jolt back to life, a shared moment in time. Life is nothing but moments. A long string of them and it's up to us to make each and every one as magical as it can be. It's moments like these that I plan to occupy my days with as an old lady in the retirement village. I can just imagine the smile creeping across my crumpled face as the nurse looks on.

'Are you ok, Ms Evie?' she'll say, wondering if I'm remembering some glorious moment from my past or if it's just indigestion.

'Oh yes dear,' I'll smile, 'Just fine.'

And in that one instant, I will be laughing once again on the Khao San Road, forever grateful for my *Weisz woman of Bangkok.*

CHAPTER TWELVE – THE 'L' IN MY LUCK

'No darkness lasts forever, and even then,
there are stars.'

— Ursula K Le Guin

Krabi, Thailand.

When I was 22, I almost choked on a BBQ Dorito resulting in a near death experience and some very deep soul-searching. I adopted a strict carpe diem approach for a while. 'Life is about doing the things you love and not wasting a single moment on the things you don't!' I declared, drawing up two lists to help me in my noble endeavour.

From memory, they went a bit like this:

1. Things I enjoy: sunset walks and ocean swims, the smell of leather and old cars, time with family and friends, a smile from a stranger, dogs, curry, dirty nights between crisp, clean sheets, IKEA meatballs and King Henry VIII (minus misogyny and 'off with their heads' bit).

2. Things I do not enjoy: rudeness, hangovers, people speaking loudly on phones, people who repeat themselves, bragging on social media, racism, sexism, people who repeat themselves and *night-time voyages aboard tiny boats in Krabi, Thailand!*

So, ok, I might have just added that last one, but fact is I'm close to having a nautical meltdown right now! It's 9pm and we're waiting to catch the boat from Ao Nang to Railay beach… *IN THE DARK*!
Breathe Ava, breathe.
'Don't worry Ave, it's actually better at night,' Dawn reassures. 'You can't see the sharks!'

So yeah, I'll be adding Dawn to the second list.

Thoughts of agonising death aside, it's a nice evening for it. Plump full moon, clear sky and the beers are doing wonders to take the edge off. I gaze out across the water, casting my eyes skyward in a moment of silent gratitude when I hear…

'Hey, 'xcuse me girls! Are youze catching the boat to Railay?'

I glance up to see the hottest Adonis standing before me, his man-bun perfectly illuminated by the moon.

'Oh hi! We sure are!'

Dawn doesn't utter a sound, *fannystruck* I believe the word is. I can see the appeal – rock-star looks, ripped shorts, and the most gorgeous lilting Irish accent. I can almost feel the 10% hetero stirring within, which hasn't happened since Cancun 2009. In a hammock. Shocking rope burns. A further once-over only adds to his allure, six foot tall and best of all, buoyant-looking. I'll be able to cling onto him in the event of a mid-sea disaster.

'I'm Alun,' he smiles, extending a tanned hand.

'Hi. I'm Ava and this is Dawn,' I say, as Dawn just sits there like a stuffed pepper. 'She's, umm, *tired* from the journey.'

She gives a little nod, eyeing him like a Greggs vegan sausage roll and leaving me to continue the conversation. 'So, have you been in Thailand long, Alun?' I ask. The traveller's equivalent of 'D'you come here often, luv?'

'A month or so, been at Railay for a week. Great craic!'

'*Crack?*' Dawn blurts, suddenly regaining motor functions. 'Oh no Alun, we're not here for Class A narcotics. Just a little R&R.'

Any awkwardness is short-lived as the boat guy comes bounding up from the shoreline. He's a skinny rake of a boy; all arms and legs, and young. Very. Very. Young. I place him somewhere between early twenties and early twelves.

'Going over to Railay beach?' he smiles. 'I take you. I am Kit, the captain!'

I watch as Dawn goes from *Dawn-the-Bold* to *Dawn-the-Bricking-It* in the space of a millisecond. He doesn't look very *captainy,* though, to be fair, my field of reference is limited to Captain Birdseye of fish finger fame and Jack Sparrow. Both of whom have facial hair – just saying.

Alun senses our nerves, offering a comforting 'Lovely night for it' as we make our way to the boat just a few metres out. It all looks rather romantic from here, the distinctive shape of the longtail boat with its colourful bunting bobbing up and down in the water, perfectly lit by an almost full moon. Picture perfect! Until we get closer and realise it's not so much bobbing, as rearing like a bucking bronco.

Alun and Captain Kit show no fear, leaping effortlessly aboard as I hitch up my sarong, can-can style, and wade out into the water.

'Come on, Ava! Throw a leg over!' Alun laughs but alas, my rhythm is woeful. Every time the boat rises up, I dip down, and every time the boat dips down, I rise up. It's like some God-awful teenage romp, with minimal satisfaction for either party. Thankfully a bigger wave rolls in and I propel myself from the water, flopping onto the deck with all the elegance of a freshly hooked salmon. *FFFLLOOOPPP!* Dawn gives a whoop of relief as we haul her aboard with minimal effort, since she is the weight of a small whippet.

'Please hol' tight,' the skipper bellows as the boat rears up, nose-in-air.

Railay beach, here we come!

The breakwater safely cleared, he throttles back and I find myself watching him. He looks pretty wired I have to say, like he's had too much pseudo-ephedrine. Either that or it's his first crossing.

'It's his first crossing,' Alun smiles and seeing our faces drop, instantly starts back pedaling. 'Err…his first crossing…*as a captain*! He's been working with his dad for years. Ever since I've been coming here. Oh look!' he says, pointing skyward. 'The stars! Look at the stars!' Utterly transparent, Mr Man Bun, but full marks for effort.

The diversion is rather effective and I'm soon swallowed up in the romance of the night sky, all twinkly with tiny studded diamonds.

'Magical, hey?'

'Well, it certainly beats my commute on the Piccadilly Line,' Dawn grins, looking surprisingly relaxed. London feels a million miles away as I stare out at the back of the boat, watching the water spewing up like a big rooster tail. Alun's right, it *is* magical.

'So, are you friends from back home?' he asks.

'No, we met in India.'

'In Goa and now I just can't get rid of her. We're partners in adventure, aren't we Ave? We've just been to Bangkok. We had a ball and Ava had sex at last, which was nice.'

'*DAWN*!' I scold, giving her a look.

'Oops! Sorry. I'm just excited for you,' she giggles. 'So, tell us about Krabi, Alun? It looks pretty splendid. We're staying at Sunrise Bungalows. 4.8 stars on Tripadvisor, scoring particularly highly in hygiene and bed linen.'

'Oh right. Yeah. My mate Gavin is staying there. I say 'mate', we've just met really. He's an interesting guy, eccentric English type.'

'Hmm, *eccentric English*,' I laugh, instantly picturing someone with big, wonky teeth playing lawn bowls. I do enjoy a national stereotype! In fact, the more time I spend away, the more I'm delighted by the global perceptions of other nations. Findings as follows:

Dutch – Pot-smoking, clog-wearers. Very liberal.

Germans – Famed for good cars, beer and overzealous placement of towels on sun loungers.

Americans – Come in two volume settings. LOUD and EXTRA LOUD! Trump wants to make them great again.

Italians – *Pasta-farians*. Love their mamas, nonnas and the Pope.

Swedish – IKEA, Abba, saunas.

Russians – Have vodka for blood. Don't smile much.

Thai – Smile lots. Excellent massages. Yummy food.

French – Sexy accent. Good at cheese and extra-marital affairs. And finally…

The Brits!

All rise for national anthem!

A nation famed for its stiff upper lip, obsession with the weather and tea. Lots of tea! By law, every British person must drink 10 cups per day. Three cups at breakfast. One at elevenses. Two with lunch and four at afternoon tea. Failure to comply will result in beheading.

'Not far now,' Kit says as we reach a choppier part of the water.

I look over at Dawn who has tightened her grip on the boat edge as we rise and drop, slapping down onto the water. Up. Down. *Slam!* As my stomach leaps in and out of my mouth, it strikes me that this is a rather good analogy for life. "There will be calm waters, the stormy waters, and no matter how much we are pounded, we have to push on through, like our little wooden boat." *(Around the World in 80 Gays).*

Next thing I know, I'm blurting, 'Ships don't sink because of the water around them, they sink because of the water that gets *into* them.'

'Bloody hell, girl! Is Indira on board this boat?' Dawn laughs. 'That's definitely something she'd say.'

'May-beeeee. Was just thin…'

BAM!

I'm suddenly propelled from my seat and slam dunked into Alun's lap! *FML.* Next thing I know, I'm feeling hands on the back of my head. *Oh no, oh no!*

'Oh *Avaaaa,*' he laughs, quickly scooping me up. 'I'm not that kind of boy!'

'Good. Because I'm *definitely* not that kind of girl!' I smile, giving him a look that communicates my dislike of Cumberland sausage.

'Oh *riiight*, gotcha! I wouldn't date men either. I've five brothers, so I should know!'

'Well, *I* like men!' Dawn suddenly blurts 'Very much so. I have a lovely boyfriend. He's Australian. From Australia. And his name is Tom.'

I worry she's about to add 'Do you know him?' but thankfully, we move onto other more global topics – tantalising tales of Thailand, like jungle trekking in Chang Mai, waterfall jumping, beach-hopping – and I start to feel more and more excited about our new adventure. 'The diving is awesome here too. Do you girls dive?'

There is of course a crude answer to that involving the word 'muff', but I refrain from going there so early in the friendship.

'I snorkel more.'

'Cool! A few of us are going out tomorrow. They take you to some great spots. And there's a beach picnic. It's fun. You should come.'

Dawn the Bold doesn't waste a second 'Absolutely!' she says decisively, 'Ava?'

I think for a second. This trip is all about finding myself, so why not find Nemo in the process?

'Errr, yes! Why not? I'm in!'

The lights of Railay soon twinkle into view and the skipper cuts the engine, allowing us to surf in on the waves, nice and controlled. I remain seated, wanting to get closer before dismounting in full view of the shoreline bars. Alas, the best laid plans....

'Ok, you jump now!' Captain Kit says.

'What, *now*? As in *now-now*?'

His eyes suddenly widen. '*We are too shallow. Too shallow!*'

I sense his panic as we get lifted onto the back of a particularly boisterous wave. *OMG! It's now or never!* Alun leads the charge, bravely leaping into the foaming breakwater. He makes a solid landing and I throw him the backpacks and step onto the side of the boat. I grab Dawn's hand.

'Come on, Dawny. One, two...'

SPLOOOOSH!

All aspirations of a Halle Berry-esque arrival à la James Bond go right out the starboard window when I do a spectacular belly flop, before getting bitch-slapped by an incoming wave. *Less 007, more double oh dear!*

I look round for Dawn who is still standing as rigid as a flagpole up on the deck.

'COME ON, JUUUMMMPPPPP!' we yell. '*JUUUMP!*'

A small crowd has now gathered on the sand, all anxiously awaiting Dawn's fate as she goes to leap but suddenly freezes. Failure to launch, they call it at NASA! The onlookers let out an exasperated gasp as the embattled craft drifts side-on into the path of an incoming roller. *Oh Lord! Oh Lord!* It's touch and go for a moment and then suddenly, as if guided by Poseidon himself, the young captain cranks the boat into gear and motors back over the angry breakwater, taking a terrified Dawn with him.

'AVAAA!'

'DAAWWWNN!'

'AVAAAAAAAAA!'

'TEXT MEEEEEE!'

'OOOOOKAAAAAYYYY!'

And just like that, she disappears into the blackness from whence she came.

'ALLLLLUNNNN! You bugger! Who have you kidnapped tonight?' a voice booms from the beach bar.

Alun raises a single eyebrow.

So *this* is the eccentric Brit I've been hearing about! His accent is distinctly cut-glass. Imagine the lovechild of Hugh Grant and Tom Higgeltybottom, the guy who dated Tay Tay and wore the bad wig in *The Avengers*. It's a voice that sounds strangely familiar. Alun gives him a wave before turning to me.

'Hey! Don't worry about your mate Dawn by the way. I know Kit. He and his dad run the snorkel trips. They're sound, those two.'

'Oh right. Good to know,' I say, suppressing all images of Dawn having a portside panic attack. 'Do you reckon she'll make it back over tonight?'

'More likely tomorrow. But hey, there's loads of places to stay over there. She'll be grand. Honestly.'

He leads us into the bar towards a group of people near the back, whereupon a chorus of whooping ensues before he begins the introductions.

'Everyone – this is Ava from London. Ava – this is… everyone!'

'Ava?' a voice interjects. 'Lovely Ava from Shoreditch?'

I instantly freeze.

It's that voice again, the boomy one, and I peer into the half light to see a chubby face grinning back at me. He looks familiar, but for the life of me I can't place him. The rosy cheeks, the slightly bucked teeth. Old school friend? Gynaecologist? Work mate? Then …*oh God, it's..it's…*

'It's me, GAVIN!' he beams, 'The Big G!'

I stand for a moment in complete disbelief. 'Gav-in?'

Wave of nausea rises up

He springs up from his seat and lunges at me, 'OMG! Avaaaa. How cool is this? I haven't seen you since your engage, engageme…'

He stops mid-sentence, too scared to complete the word.

'Hang on. Do you two know each other?' Alun says, his eyes bouncing frantically between us.

Gavin stares at me, I stare at Gavin. One of us smiling, the other looking like someone's pooped in her cornflakes.

'*Ab-so-bloody-lutely*! I adore the lovely Ava,' Gavin gushes. 'I'm friends with her ..her… ummm…err...'

The wait is excruciating. I rip off the Band Aid, '*My EX*! He's friends with my ex!'

I watch Alun's grin slide down his face, leaving him with an expression not unlike that of a stroke victim. *WTF!* I appear to have journeyed halfway across the world to escape my ex, only to run into her best work buddy! *So yeah, the 'L' in my luck has been replaced with a great, big 'F'!*

I look awkward, Alun looks awkward, everybody looks awkward, except for Gavin, who is positively beaming! The guy's like one of those trick birthday candles you can't extinguish, however hard you blow. You'd think he'd been reunited with a long lost friend, although, to be fair, we *did* used to get on well during our few nights out together. I say 'few' since Scarlet wasn't one to mix work and home. Perfectly understandable when you're shagging your co-worker.

He hugs me again, 'It's so *bloody* wonderful to see you, gorgeous girl.' In a strange way, it is quite nice to see him too. Gavin bloody Cooper. An awkward, affable papa bear. I mutter an embarrassed 'You too!' before he disappears to the bar to buy us a celebratory drink.

Make mine a big fuck-off pint of gin please…

The awkwardness of the situation is not lost on Alun.

'You OK, Ava? Not sure I'd like to run into my ex's mate! Jesus Christ!'

'Ha! Not ideal. But hey, I'm sure we can do the British thing and ignore the elephant in the room.'

'Or failing that, get absolutely wasted on *lao khao* – always a good plan. It's the local brew. *Lethal!*'

'Oh, did someone say lao khao?' Gavin sings, reappearing with a handful of drinks. 'I lost a whole weekend on that stuff in '98. Woke up with a stray dog and a tub of Vaseline…half empty,' he grimaces. 'Right then. *Chok dee everyone!*'

'Chok dee!'

The G&T, mostly 'G', goes down a treat and, after a few gulps, I readily embrace the fact that I will just have to roll with current predicament. Could be worse. At least there are enough people here to avoid a D and M with Gavin. *No water shall get into my hull tonight!*

I set about making small talk with anyone who makes eye contact. Luckily they are a friendly bunch... Jessica and George from L.A., an attractive couple in their early twenties. He's the strong, silent type whereas she must get paid by the word. Hind legs and donkeys. You get the picture! Then there's Jon and Inni, blond vikings from Norway, super smart and like all Scandi folk, fluent in most European languages plus conversational Swahili and a bit of Braille.

'So, Ava, where are you from?' Jessica asks, adjusting her perfect plaits.

'From the east of England - Norfolk, but I've been living in London for a while.'

'Oooh arrrrr, Naaarfolk!' Gavin interjects and sensing an impending six finger joke, I get in there first.

'Yep! Any more inbred and I'd be a sandwich!' I quip which everybody finds highly amusing, except for Jessica who sneers, 'I don't get it.'

'...'

'So, are you travelling alone?' she asks.

'No, with my friend but she accidentally got taken back on the boat.'

'Oh man. That sucks,' Jessica says dramatically. 'Still, I'm sure she'll be OK. There aren't too many homicides around here, more in Bangkok. Mind you...' Her boyfriend gives her a look and diplomatically steers the chat away from Thai murder statistics and onto life in Krabi. I'm given a potted guide to the best places to eat, drink and people to steer clear of – namely a Mancunian plumber who allegedly caught syphilis from a watermelon. Good to know.

I get the impression that Jessica is a bit *glass-half-empty* and I start to wish Dawn was here to balance the negativity. I check my phone. One message.

```
Ave, I'm alive!! Will stay over here tonight. Have
found a safe haven. I really am an adventurer now!
Dawn the Don xx
```

Pheww! Well, that's one piece of good news at least.

The drinks flow and flow, and by midnight I'm ready to drop, in other words know-it-all Jessica has given me a banging headache and I'm dangerously close to ramming her head in the leftover *pad see ew.*

'Right, I'm shattered,' I yawn. 'Think I'll head. Got to be fresh for tomorrow's snorkelling adventure. You guys all going?'

'Yep.'

'Not us,' the Nordic couple remark. 'Got to head back to Bangkok. Great to meet you though!'

'Yep, you too! Have fun!' I smile, gathering my bags.

'Hold up Ave! I'll walk over with you,' Gavin grins. 'A man needs his beauty sleep too! I don't just wake up looking this good!' He necks his pina colada and, before I can refuse, he's affixing head torch and leading the way along the path to Railay East.

Within minutes, we are at Sunrise Bungalows.

Check-in is mercifully quick and I'm about two steps from bed when Gavin casts his cunning lure, 'Why don't you come for a nightcap! We can have a catch up!'

I stand, key in door, on the threshold of another bad decision. I'm weary and my gin-soaked soul aches to hear news of Scarlet. I look at my door and then back to him… the door loses.

His room is tiny and I perch on the edge of a bed the width of a fish finger which pretty much fills the entire room, aside from a tiny nook containing a shower and loo, so closely positioned that you could manage a wash and wee at the same time.

'Don't you get claustro…claustr…err… Compact, isn't it?'

'Good things come in small packages, Ava my dear,' he says cracking his head against a poorly positioned shelf. 'Oops. No harm done!' he laughs, immediately cracking it again. 'They were actually full, you know. But I laid on the Big G charm, asked if they could squeeze in a little one.' He pats his rotund tummy and passes me a generous pour of his favourite malt whisky.

'Cheers!' I say, taking a small swig.

*Instant ugly whisky face. *

'So…'

We sit elbow to elbow, knee to knee on the bed like conjoined twins and pretty soon we're talking about life back home, work, family before the inevitable happens… the 'S word' rears its head! I brace myself for impact.

'Lizzen, I know Scarlet's been my friend for years and years and everything, but you know what I think?' he slurs.

'No. What do you think?'

'I think she's been an idiot! An out and out tit if I'm being honest. I know it's harsh, but I like to call a spade a spade…'

'And a tit a tit!'

'Exactly. I mean….*what* was she thinking?'

I look down into my glass.

That's something I've been asking myself for months.

What the hell was she thinking? Why did she do it? Why did she ask me to marry her in the most romantic city on earth and then cheat on me? Why, why, why?

Gavin doesn't let up. 'I mean, look at you, Ava! You're amazing. You're funny… hot…you are the *full package*!'

'Ahh, that's really sweet of you to say Gav,' I slur, a little embarrassed by the compliments which go on…

'Well, like I zaid, she's my good, good friend and I think she's great but…'

And on.

'I mean, I was just so scchocked. It was just so, well…scchocking, wasn't it?'

And on.

'Honestly, I was so sh…'

'*SHOCKED*?' I snap, a whisky rage surging from within. 'Yeah, you and me both Gavin! In fact, nobody was more shocked than me. Especially as I found out along with the rest of my guests at my own fucking engagement party!'

.

.

'Yeahhh. Brutal,' he mumbles, staring into space for a moment. 'And in the utility room too!' *Hiccup.*

I give him a death stare which goes completely unnoticed. He's right of course. *The utility room!* Of all places!

I mean, it's just not a room worthy of such a cataclysmic event. A bedroom would be more fitting, a kitchen even, where sharp knives are kept, but a bloody *utility room* full of spare tea bags and loo rolls! I feel myself getting more and more emotional, annoyed for coming to his room. Annoyed for talking about *her* and I make to leave.

'For what it's worth Ava, it won't last with that Carla,' he slurs, touching my hand. 'Scarlet knows she's stuffed up…and I *know* she knows she's stuffed up….. because…*hic*…because she told me!'

I freeze in my tracks.

'*What?* What do you mean she told you? When did you tell you?' I ask, giving him a nudge in the ribs, but he just keeps repeating 'Cos she told me, she told me'.

I nudge him again, 'But what did she say? Gavin! What did she say?'

Too late.

He's out cold and snoring like a warthog.

CHAPTER THIRTEEN – DEEP SEA CRAPUCCINOS AND DAWN THE PRAWN

'NOOOO! GET OFF ME, YOU FIANCE THIEVING WENCH!' I wail, punching the bejeebers out of my duck-down pillow.

Well, that was a nice dream! Said no one ever.

I was just in a full-on wrestling bout with Scarlet's floosie, complete with flesh-coloured bodysuits and guest commentator Gary Lineker, who munched on Walkers Crisps for the entirety. Carla had me in her signature 'titty clamp' hold as the crowd stomped and chanted 'Death by cleavage! Death by cleavage!'

What. A. Nightmare.

It's the first time I've dreamt of *her* in a while. 19 days to be precise.

I can only imagine last night's chat with her workmate stirred things up again.

A yellow light floods into the room, a sign from the universe to quit wallowing and get my shit together. I pop a hydrolyte, *plink plonk fizz*, as the dramas of the night before bubble right back up. Firstly, losing Dawn to marauding sea pirates (shameless ratings booster for next blog instalment) and then running into Gavin! You couldn't make this stuff up.

I have a sudden recollection of his comment about Scarlet 'regretting' things. *Regret. Regret.* The word circles round and round in my head. I try to push it down. "If you focus on the hurt you will continue to suffer, if you focus on the lesson you will...err..." Hungover brain can't quite recall, but something about feeling less crap.

Knock knock.

'Not today, thanks!'

'Charming,' a voice chirps. 'I know you missed me really.'

I leap up and swing the door back. '*DAWNY! YOU'RE ALIVE!* Bloody hell. I'm *soooo* happy you're OK,' I grin, checking for signs of bruising and/or trauma. 'What happened to you?'

'Err, you *are* kidding, right?'

I look at her blankly.

'You called me three times last night. We spoke at great length about Scarlet's friend? Drinking whisky in his tiny room? You even dialled your friend Jen in. *LOVE* her by the way!' She pauses. 'Tell me you remember, Ava?'

I give an unconvincing half-nod. 'Uh-huh!'

'And THEN it got really awks! You asked Jen's date, the personal trainer girl, if she took steroids! *Steroids!* I mean, you really were acting most peculiar! And then…'

'Please…no more, no more.' I throw myself back on the bed, hangxiety level at a solid eleven.

'Anyway, forget about all that. I, my friend, have been on quite the adventure! D'you know, I think it was fate getting left on the boat like that,' she smiles, looking rather pleased with herself. 'I was anxious at first, but I kept calm like you taught me and well, everything worked out splendidly. I ended up staying over with the boat captain's family. Lovely people. And, to cut a long story short, I think I might be engaged.'

'Sorry, what? Engaged to *who?*'

'To Kit, the captain! Keep up, Ave.'

'But, what, *how?* He's about twelve!'

'He's nineteen actually,' she says defensively. 'Anyway, that's beside the point. I…'

'Oh God, tell me you didn't…'

'Ewww! Of course not! I'm hopelessly devoted to Tom, silly! It's just a little misunderstanding, that's all.' She looks down at her watch. 'Ooh, damn! We need to get a shift on! We have precisely 29.5 minutes to get to that snorkelling boat, and frankly, you look awful!'

'Thanks, friend!' I grunt. 'Hey, I'm actually going to give the boat thing a miss today. Can't stomach it!' I throw the sheet over my head.

'*NO NO NO!*' she commands, pulling the sheet back down again. '*NOT AN OPTION!* Kit and his father are taking us and we can't disappoint them. What with them being so kind!'

'Dawny, Dawny. Life is full of disappointments – my A-level results being one of them. Now, run along and don't forget your sunscreen.'

She doesn't take no for an answer and within seconds I'm being dragged to the shower which she dials to *COLD* before pushing me straight under. *Utter savagery*! I shudder beneath the icy flow, and then, initial shock aside, it starts to feel quite soothing. I could stay here all day in fact, but, alas, Dawn the human alarm clock is soon at the door again.

'22 minutes, Ava. Chop chop!'

Resistance is futile. I turn off the taps and retreat back into the bedroom. Beaten.

It's a lovely place. I can't say I'd noticed much last night, other things on my mind. We're overlooking a lush figure of eight pool with hammocks casually slung beneath curving palm trees and I instantly think of Jen. We have this little joke that whenever we go to beautiful places, we just stand there and sigh 'Well, this is shit!' in our smug, in-joke way. So, in homage to that, I snap a photo, type 'Shit here, isn't it?' and hit send. She instantly responds with a shot of a grey London skyline saying 'Same.'

Gavin and Alun are already at the breakfast place. After a quick intro, we inhale two coffees and a few fruit pancakes. Always good to line the stomach. Gavin is taking the stomach lining thing to a whole new level and hoovers up a massive pile of shrimp noodles plus a side of omelette and bacon, extra crispy. He gives a satisfied burp, commanding 'Let's roll,' and leading the way to the boat.

I have to say he's disgustingly chipper this morning. Not even a sniff of a hangover. I, on the other hand, feel like I might die. On the plus side, he and Dawn are getting on like a house on fire, so I leave the new besties to it, coasting behind like the walking dead. #NeverAgain.

The squeak of sand under foot is the wake-up call I need and I look up to behold Railay beach in all its daylight glory! *What a sight!* Limestone cliffs looming above, mangrove forests so green and lush. *It's spectacular!* I peer up at two ant-like climbers dangling from a craggy cliff and instantly feel better knowing that, however ill-advised a boat trip on a stonking hangover might be, at least I'm. Not. Up. There.

It's a perfect day for an ocean safari. The water is as still as a bath and it laps at my legs, making them tingle as we wade out to the boat. I instantly recognise Kit from last night. He's flanked by an older man and woman, presumably his parents, and I watch their faces illuminate when they see Dawn approaching.

'Bloody hell, girl. It's like you're the second coming!'

'Ahh they're so sweet,' she grins, greeting them with a super smiley *sawadee*. 'I didn't know his mother was coming too! That's nice'.

'If you say so.'

I clamber aboard and clock Jessica and George at the front, hiding beneath their baseball caps.

'Morning guys. Lovely day for it!'

Mumble mumble.

Chatty Jessica is not living up to her nickname today. In fact, she's decidedly chat-less. 'Who's Miss Cranky pants?' Dawn whispers, and I give her a nudge before taking my seat and affixing travel sickness bands.

There are just six of us adventurers aboard today, plus Kit's family, making nine. Plenty of room to spread out then and I sit back on my wooden bench as the captain opens up the engine, thus evacuating an acrid stink of petrol. *Urgggh!*

I just pray the pancakes stay down.

We motor out to sea where the conversation turns to Gavin's flamboyant sub-aqua attire: *Finding Nemo* rash vest, yellow face mask with in-built snorkel and flippers that would stretch half a hockey field.

'What?' he says defensively. 'They make you swim faster!' He starts waving them in the air, almost taking out Jessica's eye.

'Hey!' she snaps. 'Watch it, dude!'

'Sorry Jess. You know me. All the gear…'

'*No idea!*' we sing out, which does nothing to dampen the guy's enthusiasm.

The cruise out to the first snorkelling spot is glorious: the blue Andaman Sea shimmering in the sunlight, green land masses randomly popping out of the ocean and that refreshing sea air everyone talks about. Restorative. Revitalising. Air that makes you sleep like a log for hours afterwards. I inhale a chestful and dangle my hand over the side catching little sparkles of water in my fingers. Dawn looks over at me.

'You OK, Ave?'

'Hideously hungover, but hanging in there,' I grin, desperately trying to focus on the horizon.

'No, I mean with Gavin being here. Must be weird.'

'Just a bit! It feels like every time I take the smallest step forward, up she pops again.'

' "Just when I thought I was out, they pull me back in". '

'Sorry, what?'

'Al Pacino in the *The Godfather Part II*,' she says in her best mafioso voice. 'One of the rare times a sequel has been superior to the first film.'

'Oh right. *Thanks Dawn Corleone!* No, it *is* odd though, don't you think? Like, I meet lovely Sara, start to feel marginally better…'

'Have hot sex.'

'Yep, thanks again and then *bam!* I run into Gavin. In fact, I'm getting the distinct feeling that the universe is fucking with me!'

'That's what the universe does, Ave. It's its job,' she grins. 'Do you know, I had a similar experience once. I was dating this guy, Martin St Claire. Rugby player, thighs like a Canadian pine, I'm talking chunky. Anyway, he kept dumping me. He must have dropped me once a week for a whole year! And every time it looked like I was moving on, he'd turn up again to win me back. Pathetic it was. Well, I was pathetic.'

'So, how did you break the pattern?'

She pauses for a moment, forming her fingers into a pistol shape. 'I had him taken out….*Godfather*-stylie'.

My face drops.

'Just kidding! Ha! I'm not really sure how it happened to be honest. I just know that one day I woke up and felt different. He'd somehow lost his appeal.' She sighs. 'It eats away at you, rejection. Begging for someone's attention. Any little sign that they might care. A text, a call. An 'I miss you'. Not that you're doing that of course. Anyway, guess what I'm trying to say is that you need to give it time.'

'Yeah, maybe. Thanks Dawny.'

She starts to wave over at her future mother-in-law again and I give her a look.

'Err, enough of my relationship woes. Don't you think you should have a chat with mummy dearest over there? I get the impression that she's a bit, well – *fixated*!'

'Noooo!

'Errr, yessssss.'

'Well, it's all very understandable really. She once had a dream that Kit would meet a porcelain-skinned, red-headed beauty and well, *tadarrr*!!'

'Oh God, so now it's a prophecy! This gets worse by the second!'

We drop anchor dead on 10 am and after a mandatory safety drill from Kit's dad, namely, don't touch the coral and don't get eaten (never did find that one funny), we don lifejackets and prepare for entry. I straddle the side, peering into the pristine waters beneath. It's crystal clear today and you can see right down to the reef, wobbling with all the colours of the rainbow.

'Right, last one in buys the first round tonight!' Gavin quips, flopping backwards and soaking the entire boat.

SPLAAASSSSSHHHH!

Alun is next, entering with an athletic backward roll, followed by yours truly, who leaps in with signature *Ava-flop*, which frankly should be an Olympic sport.

SLAAAAAAAAAAPP!

'Oooh! Way to ruin your sex life!' Alun laughs, as I land legs akimbo on a neon floaty noodle. I give the 'OK' sign, spit in my mask, and it's head down bum up as I paddle around with designated snorkel buddy, Dawn, who is so appalled by the spitting in the mask thing, that she is now refusing to wear one at all! This does not bode well. She is, however, wearing her snorkel *upside down*! My efforts to help get us nowhere, but luckily Jessica gallantly paddles over and sticks around like a proverbial limpet. Thus we are now in an aquatic throuple. *The joys!*

Jessica is back to her chatty self and is treating us to a wall-to- wall commentary, despite having a rubber pipe jammed in her gob. She sounds like a demented Dalek and I'm seconds away from shoving a finger in her breathing tube when she dramatically falls silent, clearly rendered speechless by the spectacle of the underwater kingdom.

The coral is almost other worldly: vivid reds, blues and the brightest yellows, all layered up into mini underwater castles. I watch Jessica's finger darting around, frantically pointing out every passing fish – long ones, flat ones, fat ones, some with balloon faces, others with bulging eyes that might indicate a thyroid disorder. All of them flitting about like multi-coloured confetti.

'LOOK!' I gurgle, barely able to contain my joy as the cutest puffer fish darts out, closely followed by little Dory. *DORY!! Now this is a good day*! I bob about like an elongated cork and after a while I forget all about my above surface troubles, relaxing to the sound of my own breath, the push and pull of the ocean and the mesmerising beauty around me. It's almost meditative. The warm water on my skin, the dull muffled sounds, and my mind thinking of nothing or no one. Simply surrendering to the moment.

I have no idea how long I've been submerged, but a glance at my prune fingers tells me it's time-to-get-out-o'clock. I clamber back aboard to join the others, including Dawn who I'm told lasted a solid three minutes sub-aqua. Gavin is not impressed.

'You've got no staying power you lot,' he gurgles, before splashing off in hot pursuit of George and a fleeing parrot fish. I sit back and remove my mask, putting my face into the sun. There's lots of chat about a stingray which I somehow missed, an angel fish (also missed) plus the flappy floppy McFish-Face. I wait for chatty Jessica to chime in and correct everyone, but she remains suspiciously quiet, huddled beneath her hoodie.

'You OK, Jess?'

'Not really, my stomach's a bit sore, but I just took something. I'll be fine soon. It's fast-acting apparently.'

'What did you take?'

'Just these,' she says, producing a half-empty box from her backpack. She hands Alun the packet.

'Stool softener?'

'What? *No!* Sea sickness tablets!' she snaps, snatching the box back.

'Umm, I'm pretty sure it's stool softener, Jess. How many did you take?'

'Just a couple.'

'Really?'

'Five!' she blurts. 'I took five, OK!'

Alun's eyes instantly widen as if having some apocalyptic premonition, as Jessica grows paler and clammier by the second. She starts to let out a series of drain-like belches, one after the other. Each one more disturbing than the last. *Lord! She wasn't kidding about the fast-acting bit.* Next thing I know, she's rocking back and forth on her seat, clutching her stomach. '*Oh God! Oh God*! *Oh fuck! GEORGE GEOOOOORGEEEEEE! WHERE THE HELL ARE YOU?*' And then it happens! The unthinkable! Beelzebub awakens in her bowels and she hurls herself into the water, letting rip with what one can only describe as an almighty *shart!*

It's like some kind of sub-aqua horror movie.

The water bubbles up around her like she's in a hot spring and we watch as a frothy layer of chocolate McFlurry starts to form on the surface, drifting right. Into. Gavin's. Path.

'No! God, no!' she winces as poor oblivious Gavin paddles straight into the brown zone, before resurfacing with what might be best described as a chocolate-coated face mask.

The boat falls deathly silent as scores of tiny fish appear from nowhere to partake of the all-you-can-eat buffet.

'Oh wow! *Look at this!*' he yells excitedly. 'Isn't it incredible?'

We reply with a slow nod. Nobody wanting to spoil his aquatic orgasm. He pops his head up again.

'Ahh. You guys are seriously missing out on this! *Come back in*!'

'Yeah, nah, you're ok…' I answer, trying not to catch Dawn's eye who is half giggling, half retching beside me.

Mercifully, the spectacle is soon over. Gavin and George jump back aboard, utterly buzzed and grateful to have the whole sun deck to themselves, since everyone else has moved to the opposite end of the boat. We pass them a muesli bar and say no more about it.

Part two of today's ocean safari (*"Delicious beach picnic on deserted beach"*), would ordinarily sound idyllic, but due to recent occurrences nobody has much of an appetite. Ho hum. Still, a schedule needs to be adhered to, so we up anchor and I throw my sarong over my face, allowing the ocean to rock me to sleep. Up and down, up and down. *Bliss!* It feels like I've only had my eyes closed for a matter of seconds when an excited Dawn sings into my ear.

'Wow! Look, Ava. I mean, *just look!*'

I open my eyes to behold a beautiful, secluded island covered with the whitest, most powdery sand I've ever seen, like icing sugar on a cake. It's dazzling, the kind of white you can barely look at. Within seconds, Kit has us moored up and we're stepping out onto the duvet-soft sand with a rhythmic *squeak, squeak, squeak.* We are modern-day Robinson Crusoes, no footprints but our own, and just a few palm trees to add a dash of colour to the starkness.

'Shit! It's like a Bounty Bar ad!' Gavin gushes, scooping the hot sand into his hands. The comment starts a debate about favourite chocolate bars and why Bounty bars are always the ones left in sweet tins after Christmas. 'I mean, that's got to hurt,' Gavin sighs, leading us to think he has perhaps contracted toxic poisoning after all.

We must only have been here for a matter of minutes when I look round to see Kit's mum cooking up a storm over an open fire, which is built and lit faster than I can turn on my gas hob. Oh, to have such talents! These are the kind of skills I wish I'd learnt at school, rather than Pythagoras and the descant recorder. No disrespect. I mean, I've lost count of the times I've resolved a tricky situation with a quick blast of "Three Blind Mice". *Toot toot!*

The deserted paradise beckons, so we head off for a bit of an explore, before the unrelenting heat gets the better of us and we scurry back to the shelter that Kit's dad has fashioned from fallen palm fronds. He's even created a special seat for Dawn. Right. Beside. Kit.

'That smells bloody epic!' Gavin grins, as we incline noses to inhale the delicious aromas of BBQ prawns, locally-caught white fish and lots of squid with freshly grated papaya salad. I can feel my appetite returning along with fears that Dawn is just a few crustaceans away from being officially betrothed. WTF! Kit is staring at her like she's on the menu too! *What is it with this girl? If it can happen, it will happen to Dawn.*

My suspicions are confirmed when another boat motors up to the shore-line, spilling forth a handful of smiling locals. Kit's extended family I'm told, and they join the circle to partake of the banquet. They're super friendly, and I can't help but notice that they keep looking over at Dawn, so I give her a little nudge. 'Um, Bridezilla. Now might be a good time to explain, hey?'

'I'm trying,' she says, as I watch her tell Kit 'I have a boyfriend! I have a boyfriend!' over and over. Unfortunately, it all gets rather confused and turns into a campfire sing-a-long, with everyone chanting 'I have a boyfriend, I have a boyfriend' like it's Bieber's latest download.

'What's the occasion?' Alun asks, intrigued by the impromptu celebrations.

'Don't ask,' I smirk, as Kit's cousin gives a big toothy grin and says 'Ra' or something like that, which is quickly translated by one of the smaller kids as 'Love.'

'Awwww, yes! I'll drink to that,' Gavin smiles. 'It's what makes the world go round. *To love!*' He raises his beer and starts to tuck into a humon-gous prawn that looks more like a lobster. 'Mmmm, try this!' he says, thrusting one Dawn's way.

'Oh no, I can't. I'm allergic to shellfish.'

'Oh shit! Sorry!'

'No, all good. They cooked them separately,' Dawn reassures as one of the kids runs up and plants a big kiss on her sun scorched cheek.

'Ahh, that's sweet. *Harpoon carp'* she replies, which the Thai folks of course find hilarious, giggling all the way through the part where she is presented with a special gift – a shark tooth necklace on a leather string. This is getting bad now, *really bad*, so I start mentioning Tom again, showing his photo to everyone in sight, but they just think it's Chris Hemsworth.

#NiceProblemToHave.

'This is harder than it looks,' I sigh.

'I told you! It's the whole language barrier thing.'

'Yep. But still needs to be sorted girl. It's not going to end well.'

'I know, but luckily I have a cunning plan. Nicole and Aroon are arriving later, so I can ask him to explain. Genius hey?'

'Let's hope so.'

'It'll be good to see them, hey? Such an interesting couple.'

'How so?'

'I mean you wouldn't necessarily put them together, would you? They were besties, before they got together, you know.'

'How on earth do you know all this?'

'Nicole told me at the massage place. Cute story, actually.' She grabs my hand. 'Ave, this could be a good angle for your blog! You know, the idea of love blossoming from the bedrock of friendship.'

'Cool! I'll call Jen and tell her you're taking over.'

'Ha! Well, we did kind of hit it off on the phone last night,' she grins. 'D'ya know, I think I'd quite fancy her, if I was gay I mean. I think she'd be my type. Oh, and if I wasn't with Tom.'

'That's a lot of *ifs,* Dawny! A lot of ifs.'

It's at this point that I notice something odd about her. There's a weird puffiness to her cheeks, that Hollywood 'pillow look' and her eyes look smaller than usual, as if they've been swallowed into her head.

'Err, you OK Dawn?'

'Yes fine, why?'

'Err, no reason,' I respond, not wanting to cause unnecessary panic.

'Actually, now you say it, I do feel a little warm.' She starts to rummage for her hand fan and when she looks back up again, I almost jump out of my skin.

'Shit, Dawn! *YOUR FACE!*'

Without meaning to sound rude, the poor girl looks like someone has shoved a bicycle pump up her bottom and given it a real good go! She runs her fingers over her red, inflated cheeks and lets out a little shriek, 'Oh no, it's the *prawns,* Ave! The prawns!'

'But you didn't eat any!'

'It must have been the kiss! From that little boy! Oh God, oh God! I'm like Jesus – betrayed by a kiss!'

She instantly goes into what I can only describe as survival mode, doing vigorous deep breathing exercises, like she's about to give birth. It's not long before all the kerfuffle and hyperventilating catches the attention of the kids, who take one look at her before bolting up the beach, bellowing 'SHREK! SHREK!' at the top of their lungs.

'Oh no, did they just call me Shrek? Do I look like Shrek, Ava?'

'No! Not at all!'

This is no time for honesty. This is a time for calm, for control and definitely not a time for Jessica to blurt, 'Shit Dawn! You look like somebody on that plastic surgery show, *Botched*! Hahahaahaha.'

Nice one, Jessica!

'Quick! My EpiPen! My EpiPen!' Dawn croaks, reaching for her bag with a hand that now resembles Nandi's udder. I grab it from her, removing the lid, and wielding it in the air like King Arthur pulling excalibur from the rock.

'What should I do? What should I do?'

'Stab her with it!' Gavin shouts.

'Where?'

'Here! On the beach!'

'No, you twat – *where* on her body?'

'Errr shit!' he bumbles, in a blind panic. 'Where did they do it in *Pulp Fiction*?'

'I dunno!'

'In her fanny!' Jessica blurts, 'Stab it in her fanny!'

'Give it to me,' Alun snaps, snatching the EpiPen from my sweaty hand, and with not a hint of nerves, he thrusts it into her thigh as the entire beach party look on in horror.

Dawn lets out a little wince and falls back on her palm frond mat. Motionless.

Oh God, Oh God!

My heart is thumping out of my chest. My poor friend is just lying there with a ridiculously large head, not breathing. My mind is flooded with all manner of terrifying thoughts: having to tell Tom what happened; worse still, her family! *OMG, what will I say to her family?*

And then…a visceral gasp, as she suddenly sits bolt upright again, like Frankenstein's monster.

'Dawn? Dawn? Are you OK?'

No response.

'Fuck! She might have brain damage,' Jessica sneers. 'It can happen. She might be a vegetable!'

I'm about to throttle the insensitive cow when I hear a familiar home counties voice say, '*Vegetable?* Hell no sister, *I am a vegan*!'

Cheers and jubilation all round

I lean over to embrace her, 'You're OK, you're OK! Shit, girl! You nearly gave us a heart attack!'

'So sorry Ave.' She smiles. 'Hey, don't suppose there's any food left? I'm starving.'

Around the World in 80 Gays
"Lost in translation"

As the sun sets on today's Krabi mad-venture, I reflect upon the other dramas of the last few days – bumping into my ex's bestie and Don finding herself betrothed to a boy she barely knows. An extreme case of 'lost in translation' perhaps. Yet such misunderstandings readily occur when people speak the *same* language!

It gets me thinking about the importance of communication. "Communication is to a relationship what breath is to life", I once read and, when I consider my own relationship, I fear we were gasping for air at some points, like poor Don on the beach today.

When love is new, it's just the opposite. We can't stop speaking to one another. Texting 24-7 from the bus or the shower, hungry for every drop of information, like it's some life-giving elixir. We delight in the most trivial of stories about our partner; the kind that leave everybody else atrophied with boredom and jabbing forks into their hands at the dinner table.

Sadly, that all changes as time goes on. The shine wears off and that thirst to know everything about our partner dries up. Until we no longer talk, we make assumptions. We don't ask, we presume.

That's when it all gets dangerous.

That's when you lose connection, when you lose faith.

That's when you walk in on your fiancée and their lover at your engagement party…

CHAPTER FOURTEEN – FULL MOON AND A FULL-ON SURPRISE

'The dildo of consequence is seldom lubricated.'

- James Howard Kunstler

The day begins with one hundred percent sunshine and zero percent hangover. Now that's a good ratio! Traumatized by yesterday's events, we slept right through dinner and a minor storm that resulted in a tree crashing through the middle of our perfect figure of eight pool! #Crushed. It's now more of a figure of two wonky threes.

Dawn has fully recovered from her ordeal and we rise early, ashram o'clock as we like to call it, and head off for more touristy adventures with Gavin and co. The day runs as follows. (My notes in italics.)

1. Phra Nang beach and 'surprise' local grotto

Right on our doorstep, thus rude not to. Beach utterly beautiful. Grotto, however, was a load of cock – literally! Turned out to be a legit shrine to the penis! They were everywhere, hundreds of the bloody things. Big cocks, small cocks, black, white and green. Some with small pink heads, others with giant red ones like Mexican sombreros. All carved from wood and adorned with flowers. Offerings to Phra Nang, the female spirit of fertility, we were informed. Due respect aside, had great fun making up inappropriate jokes like 'Do you come here often?' and, my particular favourite, 'Is this a boner-fide shrine?' Utterly juvenile. You're welcome.

2. Sea tunnels at Talu cave

"Be amazed by the spectacular stalactites and beautiful cave structures…"

Just a short hop aboard a longtailed boat (now like the tube to us locals) and we were there. Stalactites galore! They were almost alien-like in appearance, hanging down like wobbly, grey icicles. Shocked to hear they take around 100 years to grow just 1cm! A lesson in patience for us all. On way back, had quick swim whereupon Jessica was stung by a jelly fish. Ouch! Karma perhaps for yesterday's Botched surgery jibe. Dawn found the revenge particularly sweet, sharing the following quote with us, "The dildo of consequence is seldom lubricated."

3. Beach chills and massage

Rest of afternoon spent lounging around and having my legs pulled every which way during invasive massage. Had flashback to particularly unpleasant scissoring experience from my youth. Note to self: is there such a thing as 'successful scissoring'? Must conduct survey amongst lezbiana community.

It's a little after 8 pm when we congregate on East Railay's shoreside for a pre-party snifter. Tonight is special. Tonight is our last night in Krabi and we plan to tick two gargantuan items off our 'Thai-Do' list. Firstly, Full Moon party: messy rave-type affair characterised by excessive alcohol consumption, neon body paint, and likely death. Secondly, and most exciting of all, Ladyboy show! This particular one is *the* best in Thailand, possibly the world, according to Aroon and Google. Five stars do not lie. Cannot. Wait.

Dawn is beside herself.

'This is just the *best* Ave! One last blowout before we head Down Under.'

I give her a little squeeze before she bounces out of my arms and starts waving frantically across the bar.

'OH! OH! NICOLE! AROON! *OVER HERE*!!!!'

I swing round to see our Bangkok buddies striding on over: Nicole in signature tight ribbed vest (*Why not, with those shoulders?*); Aroon in zebra print trousers and tiger striped T (*Why? Just why*). Seeing them makes me feel happy. Always nice meeting someone you vaguely know when you're far from home, unless that someone is Jessica of course. There's something about that girl that puts me on edge. You never know what's going to come out of her mouth, or bottom for that matter. Thankfully, she will not be joining us for pre-drinks tonight as she's still feeling unwell. 'They'll meet us over there later,' Alun tells me.

Nicole is on characteristically good form and throws her long arms around my neck with a 'Heyyy, girl! What's been happening?'

'Oh, you know. The usual life in paradise stuff, snorkelling, beach and...'

'My head almost exploding!' Dawn interjects, showing a quick snap of her oversized noggin.

'Oh, shit! That looks bad. Anaphylactic shock?'

'No, BBQ prawns! I'm allergic,' she responds, as Gavin arrives with a tray laden with drinks which he almost drops upon beholding Aroon, a fellow fashion rebel.

'Oh, yessss mate,' he beams. 'A man with style, like my good self! I'm Gavin. Nice to meet you.'

'Ha! Hello, Gavin!' Aroon smiles, looking him up and down.

The competition is stiff tonight. Aroon in jungle chic and Gavin in *Kanye-meets-Kumbaya* aka purple fisherman pants, green day-glo T, plus wooden tribal beads of various sizes.

'So, I hear you rescued these two from card sharks the other night,' Alun smiles, joining in the intros.

'Ha! Nicole did really. I was backup,' Aroon says modestly.

'Yeah, he's a lover not a fighter, aren't you Roon?' Nicole winks, giving him a big sloppy kiss which from anyone else would make me feel queasy.

'It was such a fun night,' Dawn beams with her new-found appreciation for chaos 'Things just seem to happen with these two around. *Crazy things.*' I don't have the heart to tell her that *she* is perhaps the bringer of drama to this little set-up.

'Well, I'll drink to that. To new friends and crazy nights! Cheers!'

We clink glasses and Gavin necks his pina colada (pint of) before letting out a satisfied hiccup. Alun gives him a look, 'Wooo! Slow down, big fella.'

'I'll slow down when I'm dead, matey,' he retorts, throwing his head back and letting rip with an off-key howl. 'It's full moon - *OWWWWWWWWWW!*'

And now I'm just scared!

Nicole wisely calls it after a couple more rounds and we wander down to the shore to catch our ride. Forget longtails, it's a fancy red speedboat tonight and the moment we set foot on the sand it roars up, its engine deep and throaty like it has a summer cold.

'So, your fiancé's not taking us over, Dawn?' Alun teases. 'Or is he not into hardcore prawn?'

'Ha ha! Very funny. Oh, that reminds me – *Arooooon!* I might need your help with something later, a little translation job.'

The boat arrives and we stand aside to allow the previous group of ravers to disembark. I don't know whether to laugh or cry as I watch them limp past in puke-stained T's and neon paint splashed across faces, buttocks and boobs. In a word, carnage!

'Oh God, that's not blood, is it? Tell me that's not blood,' Dawn whispers as one hobbles by with saline drip peeping out of backpack.

'Don't you worry about a thing,' Gavin reassures, leaping aboard. 'This ain't my first rodeo, you know! Did Bestival back in 2015. Survived the whole weekend on Red Bull and half a Twix. Plus, a little help from my friends *M D and A!* Hahahha! Let's do this, my friends.'

The boat ride to neighbouring Phi-Phi Island is exhilarating. The setting sun on our faces, salty wind in our hair and we arrive an hour later with that tousled beach look popular in all the hair ads. Gavin is first man off, quickly explaining he has actually misread the Insta page, and this is not *THE* Full Moon party everyone talks about, but a smaller, more select affair. Suits us fine since nobody wants to die tonight.

I look about me. It might not be the real deal, but Jeez, it's a lot! We're instantly met by an army of sticky neon bodies dancing to 90's rave classics. Average age 19, maybe younger. #Dinosaurs.

'Now this is what I'm talking about,' Gavin beams as we strut past a line of charred fire-eaters and head straight to the main bar.

'Right! What are we having, partay people?'

'Try the local brew! It's wicked,' a rosy-cheeked man slurs. 'That's what that lot are on.'

He gestures to a pair of teens who are having a massive spat, which ends with the girl throwing a drink over her boyf, before snogging his mate and vomming over her espadrilles.

'Looks great. I'm in,' Gavin grins.

'Yeahhh! Wickid, dude! Love it!' Mr Drunk says, giving him a forceful nudge in the ribs. 'I've been on the stuff for years. It's the fountain of youth, ya know! Guess how old I am?'

Dangerous game this one, especially when the enquirer looks like Keith Richards after a big night.

'Umm, dunno mate,' Gavin answers politely.

'Go on, man. *Guess*!' he says, angling his face into the light.

'Well, clearly very young,'

'*Maaaate! How young*?'

'Dunno?'

'Come on, have a guess for fuck's sake!'

'*FIFTY*?'

Mr Drunk slams drink down on bar

'FUCK BRO! I'M TWENTY-EIGHT! What the hell's up with you?' he barks, before giving Gavin a solid thump on the nose.

THUD!

'Well, that was a good start,' Alun laughs, as we lead a bloody-nosed Gavin away with a few buckets of Zombie Apocalypse, plus some bright green shot that looks like it might have been brewed in Chernobyl. We knock it back and after a quick dance, we follow Aroon to the much anticipated ladyboy show just a few metres away.

'This is it,' he smiles. 'You are gonna love it.'

'I already do,' I grin, as we make our way into a fabulous rainbow-festooned tent which looks decidedly out of place here. Far too glam. 'It's a full moon special,' the woman at the door tells us. 'You very lucky.' Won't argue with that. Not that I could, since my face is completely numb post green shot.

The tent is heaving. Packed with the most gorgeous women I've ever seen, some of them are the ladyboys or *kathoey* as Aroon calls them. Another new word I've learnt today. #CunningLinguist.

'There's an amateur competition on tonight,' Nicole says, guiding us into a small gap at the front of the stage. 'They're always fun.'

I give an enthusiastic nod and within seconds the lights go down and an almighty cheer goes up.

"All the single ladies, all the single ladies All the single ladies, all the single ladies…"

The crowd start to stamp and cheer, and the next thing I know the sexiest Glamazonian comes strutting out onto the stage, throwing down pure Beyonce magic from the dizzy heights of her six inch heels. 'I'm Anna Philactic,' she sings. 'Prepare to be *SHOCKEDDDDD*!' The crowd instantly respond with a 'Shock us Anna, shock us!' at which she unsheathes a glitter gun strapped to her thigh and starts shooting into the adoring crowd.

'*Woooohoooooo!* Party, bitches! Partaaay!'

Everyone goes completely nuts at this point, as a net full of coloured balloons descend from above.

'OMG! Anna Philactic, I heart her,' a familiar voice says. I look round. It's Jessica and George.

'Sorry we're late guys,' George says, as Jessica makes a lunge at me.

'Yay! Jess is in the house, girlfriend! The party has begun!' she yells, evidently back to her cocky self.

'Yaaaay! That's great news!'

I turn back to hostess Anna who is now whipping off her jacket to reveal the skimpiest leotard known to humankind.

'I don't know where she hides it all,' Jessica says bluntly. I see her point. You couldn't hide a dill pickle in those knickers! I'm soon onto cocktail bucket number three and I don't know whether it's the heat or whatever's in this bloody drink, but I start to get the spinnies.

'Hey. Think I'll head to the loo, Dawny.'

'You OK? Want me to come?'

'Nah, all good,' I reassure, making my way through a sea of sweaty torsos to join the queue of hotties snaking down the side.

'Wow! Is this the line?'

The beauty in front of me nods, mumbling something about 'Good luck!' and I respond with a drunken smile. Thankfully the line starts to quicken and I follow the others down a little tented corridor where I see an opening. Excellent! Nearly at the loo! Will be much quicker than I thought. The lady in front holds the flap open and I walk into the brightest lights I've ever encountered in a bathroom. *Jeez! That's some serious wattage!* The music is thumping too and there's even a disco ball hanging from the ceiling. *What kind of loo is this*? Suddenly I feel an arm round my waist and, still a little dazed, it takes a moment to realise that a microphone is being shoved in my face and that I am not in the loo at all, but standing on the stage with a host of other hopefuls!

WTF!

'Welcome to the show!' Anna Philactic smiles, guiding me into the full glare of the spotlight. 'And who are you, sweet cheeks?'

'Ummm. *Lost?*' I stammer.

Uproarious laughter from the crowd

'Well, you've certainly lost something tonight! *Your titties!*' she laughs. 'Did you leave them in the tuk-tuk, girlfriend?'

More laughter. 'Errr…'

She makes another joke about giving me her surgeon's number and I reluctantly play along. Next thing I know, I'm being voted through to the next round!

'You go girl!' a voice shouts and I look down to see Dawn fan-girling with the rest of the gang in the front row.

How embarrassing is this?

Anna moves onto the next contestant, so I seize the opportunity to sneak back through the curtain from whence I came.

'Hey, lady!' the bouncer smiles, 'You are lost again, silly' thus redirecting me… Right. Back. To. The. Stage.

Oh God! This cannot be happening.

Anna seizes me once again.

'OK, sexies. How are we all feeeeeeling?' she croons, whipping the crowd into a heightened frenzy. 'Next round is the dance-off!'

'Dance-off, dance-off,' they chant, stamping their feet, clapping their hands.

'Round one is Honey Girl versus Lost Titties! Let's go!'

Honey Girl instantly springs to her feet and gets right into it. She's a six foot powerhouse, feet like surf boards and lips like those inflatable cushions favoured by haemorrhoid sufferers. Shit, can she move! She's flinging herself this way then that, shaking her booty and singing 'I'm bringing sexy back!', while I'm just standing here, bringing absolutely nothing back.

Nothing but shame and humiliation.

I must be in this state of paralysis for a good half minute when, for some reason, I think of Cruella and that chat we had in the kitchen before I left. Her rousing 'phoenix from the flames' speech circles my mind and then, just like that, I rise up and start busting out the kind of moves usually reserved for the privacy of my own bedroom. This Norfolk girl is not just bringing sexy back, she's filling the shopping trolley, changing the lightbulb, before seamlessly moving into crescendo move, *the worm!* It's painful. Quite literally as I gyrate my way across stage, throwing out a disc with every thrust.

Surely this agony is over now.

'TWERK! TWERK!' the crowd call. 'TWERK! TWERK! TWERK!

Apparently not…

Two silver poles magically descend upon the smoke-filled stage, taking the competition to a whole new level of erotic athleticism. Honey Girl is not in the least bit intimidated, and she leaps aboard, spinning from the top to the bottom with an enthusiasm that makes my eyes water. She's licking that pole, caressing it and frankly I don't know where to put myself. I can hear Dawn chanting my name again. 'Do it, Ave!' she yells, 'Just do it!', which is all the incentive I need and, just like that, I'm coiling myself around that pole like a python and joyfully sliding my way down until I end up in a big, tipsy heap at the bottom.

More cheers! More laughter!

'LOST TITTIES! LOST TITTIES!' they chant and, unable to bear it any longer, I seize the mic and bellow.

' *"ARE YOU NOT ENTERTAINED? ARE YOU NOT ENTERTAINED!!!!"* '

This theatrical move must appeal to the Russell Crowe fans in the house and, after what seems like an infinite number of dance-offs, I'm awarded third prize and bundled off stage with a bottle of finest Thai bubbles.

'Let's hear it for Lost Titties! *Wohoooooo!'*

Needless to say, the relief is immense and I step down from the stage, half-traumatised and fully over it, with my number one fan lying in wait…

'Do. Not. Say. A. Word. Dawny!'

'What?'

'Not. A. Word!'

'But Ave, it's not every day you come second in a ladyboy competition!'

'Third. I came third. Though to be fair, I do think I was robbed. Bloody *Lost Titties*! The cheek!'

'Well, I thought you were the best,' she beams. 'By far the most convincing!' *Cheeky wink.* 'So, c'mon. What did you win?' She grabs the envelope from my sticky hands and has a read. 'Oh no…'

'What?'

'Two tickets for the Bangkok snake farm!'

'You're kidding?'

'Nope,' she giggles. 'Think you're right, Ave. The universe really is fucking with you.'

It turns out that two more Zombie Apocalypses are the perfect remedy for post stage trauma and, after a few big slurps, I start to see the funny side. *Oh, the wonder of booze, the answer to all of life's ills…*

Breakup? *Have a drink.*

Lost your job? *Have a drink.*

Giving up drink? *Have a drink!*

Dawn and I rejoin the others for a quick debrief about recent stage shenanigans, whereupon everyone tells me how great I was. Everyone except for Jessica, of course.

'OMG! How embarrassing was that Ava! Like, no offence!'

Gavin gallantly leaps to my defence. 'What? Noooo! I think she did well,' a bloodied tissue still rammed up his nostril. 'You're a natural, girl.'

'Thanks.'

'Look, I reckon we should all get out there and throw some shapes. Get the vibe back. Wha'd you say?'

'Nah. Think I'll sit this one out, thanks,' I smile, escaping for some solo time plus much needed phone distraction. *Swipe swipe*. Two unread messages. One from mum about bloody cousin Maria's Cape Town wedding again. And the other from Jen.

```
How goes it, girl? THE BLOG IS KILLING IT! Cruella
wants to FaceTime next week. She's got ideas. Dread
to think what. LOL. P.S. U ok? U got really pissy with
my date the other night! xx
```

Good news re blog. Bad news re being a drunk twat!

I'm halfway through a grovelling apology text when Gavin returns all sweaty and shirtless.

'Avvaaaaaa! What you doing? Let's partayyyy!' he grins, staggering around like a giant tree that's about to be felled.

'You alright there, Gav?'

'I, my friend, am grrrrrrrreat!' he answers, collapsing in a big heap right on top of me. 'Oops! Sorry!' He starts to randomly jabber on about the origins of rave music and then how cool Aroon is. How *really* cool he is. 'He's a buddha, you know!'

'Think you mean a buddhist.'

'Wha? Oh yeah! Ha! Ahh mate! Isn't this the best night? THE BEST! I do love you,' he grins, planting a big, wet kiss on my cheek.

'Ahhh. Someone's drunk,' I laugh, trying to push his sweaty face away.

'It's true. I really do! Really love you, Ave! Hey, lizzen...' He lays his hand on mine. 'I just wan'ed to say I'm zorry about the other night. You know, bringing Scarlet up! Proba'ly the last perzon you want to hear about, *hic.*'

The irony is not wasted on him as he instantly follows it up with a 'Shit! I've done it again, haven't I?' before flagellating himself with a glow stick.

'It's OK. All good, Gav.'

'Really?'

'Really.'

'Yesssss!' he grins, punching the air and somehow missing. 'I just feel... well, like a piggy in the middle, I guess. I love zou both!' *Hic!*

I can't help myself; I'm drunk, he's here. I go there.

'So, what did you mean, when you said about Scarlet regretting stuff?'

'She told me she'd fucked up, that zhe still loves you. She wantz to speak to you.'

That's a lot of information. A lot of information that makes me feel a lot of sick.

'What? She knows I'm here with you?'

'Yes, no. Maybe. Can't rem'ber,' he hiccups, snapping another glow stick onto my wrist. 'You know what, Ave,' he says, fixated on the bright pink hue. 'People are a bit like glow sticks, if you think abou'it.'

'They are?'

'Yeahhhhh. It's like, sometimes we gotta break to shine.'

With that wisdom imparted, he flops back, instantly falling into a coma.

.

.

ZZZZZZZZZZ

The Full Moon debauchery is a welcome distraction from the Scarlet news. It's all happening now. Teens stumbling about, too drunk to stand and I watch one young girl topple backwards into a bush. FLOPPPPP!

She's about as messed up as my love life.

I take another swig from my bucket, when Dawn comes bounding over with Aroon.

'There you are, Ave' she grins. 'I'm about to have that chat with Kit. Aroon's going to help.'

'Oh, right. Be gentle with him.'

'I will. He's just over there with his family. Will you come too?'

'Errr, I'll stand behind, Dawny. Think getting dumped in front of an army of people might be a bit overkill, hey?'

'Yeah, you're right. Always thinking of others.'

We head over and I hang back a bit, doing an awkward on the spot shuffle dance. I'm full of anxiety at this moment. *Poor Kit!* He's about to get dumped by someone he's not even dating. Now that really sucks. I see Dawn whispering into his ear and then five minutes later Aroon is throwing a brotherly arm over his shoulder. I dance a little closer. There's a fair bit of nodding, leaning in and I get the feeling the 'Dear John' chat is going better than anticipated. Much better. No sign of tears. I'd call that a result. I give Dawn a little thumbs up and, next thing I know, she steps into Kit for what I think must be the final goodbye. That final 'I wish you well' moment.

I'm just about in earshot at this point, so I'm able to half listen, half lip-read the conversation.

Dawn: 'I'm so sorry Kit. So very sorry. I do hope I haven't hurt you or your lovely family.'

Kit: 'No problem!'

Dawn: 'Thank you for being so understanding. It's OK to be sad. Men can cry, you know! In fact, they should cry.'

(She pulls him to her bosom. He smiles. A lot.)

Dawn: 'And although it won't be me, I just know there is a girl out there for you, more your rage' *(think I misheard that bit).*

Kit: 'Yes I know.'

Dawn: 'A girl who will make you very happy, so very happy.'

(Dawn touches Kit's hand.)

Kit: 'Yes.....I have found her!'

Dawn: 'A girl who will love you and....*what?* Wait! *You've found her?*'

Kit: 'Yes!'

Dawn: '*Already?*'

Kit starts to nod enthusiastically at this point, reaching over to a skinny, pale red-headed lady, Dawn 2.0! She must be 50 if she's a day.

Jaw. Drops*

Kit: 'See! Much prettier too! Goodbye Dawn.' (*Dawn smiles and walks away.)*

This unexpected plot twist in Dawn's non-love affair is a stark reminder that we are all replaceable. Every one of us. Funny really. We spend our lives thinking that we are special to someone, that we are 'the one', only to discover we are perhaps just '*one* of the ones'. Does 'the one' even exist, I wonder? Is that whole thing just an illusion? Some kind of fallacy invented to keep us searching.

These are the thoughts that go through your mind when you're covered in paint and high as a kite on dodgy cocktails at a Full Moon party. Dawn thinks I have a point and, the deed done, we wander back to join Gav and the others. I flop down, relieved.

'All sorted?' Alun smiles. 'With Kit, I mean?'

'Yes. Worked out well, actually.' Dawn smiles. 'Really well. He has a new girlfriend – well, not that I was the old one!'

Jessica doesn't miss a beat.

'*What already*? Jeez! You must feel special! Ha!' I shoot her a look, but she continues anyway.

'Man, you guys sure do suck at this stuff. Maybe it's an English thing?'

'Sorry?'

'The whole not being able to express emotions thing. I mean, it's all about the stiff upper lip with you, right? No offence. My grandma is English, so ...'

'Well, that's a bit of a generalisation, don't you think?' Nicole says. 'Stereotypes are never very useful.'

'Whatever! Just saying it as I see it, Nic. What do you think, Aroon? Everyone tells me you're the wise one.'

Aroon looks a little embarrassed. He thinks for a moment before answering.

'I think people are different, Jessica. Everyone has their own way of dealing with things. At their own speed.'

'Oh yeah, geddit! Are you, like, some kind of guru?'

'We don't have gurus in Thailand. That's Hinduism!'

'Oh. Like, yeah! Cool. Cool. Like no offence, right.'

I think the painful conversation is over, but alas Jessica pipes up again, like Chucky back from the dead.

'All I can say is life's short and I ain't got time for bullshit. You gotta be honest, right? Tell people like it is. Like your captain guy.'

'Kit?'

'Yeah, right! I'd have sorted that shit straight away.'

'I'm sure Dawn tried,' Nicole explains. 'But it's not that easy. Especially in another language. Besides, you don't want to hurt people.'

' Sure. I get it. I just dig honesty. Like, isn't that one of the principles of Buddhism, Aroon?'

'Yes, along with compassion, kindness, moderat..' he answers before being rudely interrupted. Again.

'For real! I mean, like, I dig Buddhism. I chant every day. *Love that shit!* I'm kinda into a few faiths at the mo. Bit of Christianity, Hinduism, Vishnu and the elephant one. She's the coolest! I guess I'm poly-religious, right?'

Oh my God(s)! Shoot me now!

Dawn looks a little irritated at this point.

'Well, honesty is all very well, but it needs to be tempered, don't you think? I don't believe in being careless with people's feelings. I was always taught you should pass everything you say through three gateways: Is it kind? Is it necessary? And, is it true?'

'That's beautiful,' Nicole smiles. 'Really beautiful.'

Jessica sits in thought and I start to think that Dawn is actually getting through to her when more crap comes pouring out.

'Nah, think I'll just pass it through one gateway, the *Jessica gateway*! HA! I don't like to waste time. You fuck me over, you're dead to me,' she slurs. 'If you're piss me off. I'll kick you to the curb!'

Gavin's phone starts to go off at this point, adding to the drunken theological angst. I give him a nudge, but he is spark out, face down on the sand.

'Anyway.'

Jessica continues to chime on and on, as does the phone.

Ring ring. Ring ring.

'Like, it's simple. If you have a problem, tell me. You don't wanna be with me, have the balls to say it. That's how cheating happens. Right? People not being honest with each other.'

I feel my chest tighten. This is all starting to feel like that night in the ashram garden, the great monogamy debate. I buckle up.

'And what would you do if George came to you and said he'd cheated?'

'Break his balls,' she says matter-of-factly.

'And that's your choice Jessica,' Nicole answers. 'It's like Aroon said, people are just different.'

'*Fools* more like!'

I look down into my drink.

'Oh, I dunno.' Alun says. 'Don't think you can be black and white about it. We've all made mistakes. I know I have!'

'Whatevs!'

I find myself staring at her, annoyed by every little word that is coming out of her entitled little mouth. I can hold myself back no longer.

'So, if someone is annoying you, you believe in telling them?'

'Hell, yeah!'

Ring ring!

'You'd just come right out with it, say it, regardless of hurting their feelings?'

'Damn straight!' she says, sounding more and more like a bad Macklemore song by the second. 'I have respect for that shit. Simple'

Ring ring!

With that, I take a deep breath.

'OK then. Jessica, *you're annoying the crap out of me*! Please shut the fuck up!' I snap, before having a big slurp on my empty bucket.

She looks a little taken aback at first, but then strangely respectful that I have some starch in my spine after all.

'And I'll tell you another thing that's annoying me, *that bloody phone*!' I grab it from Gavin's limp hand and swipe it to life. 'Hello!' I say, in my poshest phone voice. 'I'm sorry but Gavin is orrff his face and cannot come to the phone at the moment! May I take a message?'

'Oh, right! Sounds like him.' The voice on the other end says. 'Can you tell him I called. It's... *crackle crackle...*'

'Sorry, who?' I'm straining to hear against the techno bass and Jessica who is now yelling at George, accusing him of cheating. 'Who shall I say called?'

'Scarlet. Tell him Scarlet called.'

Around the World in 80 Gays
"EpiPen"

'People come into our lives as a lesson or a love,' my aunty once said. 'Every interaction leaves an imprint on us. Like footprints in sand. Some footprints are quickly washed away, while others stay with us forever.'

I think she was right about that.

Some people bring us the good stuff like wisdom and kindness, new ways of thinking. They inspire us to be our best selves. Others do the opposite, showing us who we do *not* wish to be. They stir us up, summoning chaotic tides within, raising them so high that we end up answering a call we shouldn't have, hearing a voice we wish we hadn't, and lying awake thinking about the one person in the world we wish we could forget.

As I leave Thailand, I'm reminded of a simple truth. Life is unpredictable. We must expect the unexpected – the seafood allergies, the upset tummies aboard longtail boats and exes. Always exes.

Fact is, life can lob a custard pie in our faces at any moment and the best thing we can do is to embrace it, prepare to be surprised. Oh, and always carry an EpiPen.

CHAPTER FIFTEEN – MAKING A SPLASH DOWN UNDER

'I'm so excited, I could poop glitter!'

– Donnie D

Sydney Australia, March 2018
DAY OF MARDI GRAS!

'Strewth! It's hotter than a dingo's dongle!' said no Australian ever, but that won't stop me from adopting this as my fave antipodean expression, with "You're terrible Muriel" coming a close second. We've just touched down in the land down under and I'm stoked, though not as stoked as Dawn who's bouncing about like Skippy on poppers.

'So, this is it, Dawny. Just one flight away from seeing T'oooooooooom.'

'Oh Ave, I'm so excited. I do hope he's missed me.'

'How could he not? You're a catch Dawn Boldwood, a bloody catch! I can't believe how much you've changed from that frightened girl I met in Goa. Look at you.'

'Aww thanks, Ave' she blushes. 'Do you know, I feel a bit like the lion in *The Wizard of Oz*. You know, the one who was afraid of everything.'

She starts to paw the air and make an odd growling sound. 'Errr, where are we going with this, Simba?'

'Well, it might sound silly, but it's like I've finally found my courage! And...' she reaches for my hand. 'It's all because of you, Ava.'

My bottom lip starts to quiver and she holds my gaze. 'I've never had a friend like you before.'

'Awwww, Dawny! You've helped me too, more than you'll ever know.'

'Truly, Ava?'

'Truly.'

'Well, that's just splendid then. Splendid. Plus, it's not over yet. You'll be coming to join us in Byron Bay. Yippee! The Adventures of Evie and Don continue. 'She glances down at her watch, '*OH SHIT TITS!!* Better run! Have fun and don't forget to call Tom's friend. She's happy to show you around Sydney.'

'Yep. Maybe.'

'Have you got her number?'

'Yes mum! Oh, and Dawn...'

'Yes?'

'No prawns on the barby, hey?'

Eye-roll

I bounce towards Arrivals, giddy on Dawn's words. It's like they say, the best way to make yourself feel better is to help someone else. Even in the smallest of ways: carrying their groceries, holding the door, cheeky snog aboard the night bus. Christmas 2016, too much eggnog. It all counts. But more than that, I just feel blessed to have made such a good friend in Dawn.

The airport is rammed. 'Busier than a one-legged man in an arse-kicking contest,' as one local put it and I take my place in the snaking Customs queue. I love how they do that at airports – coil the line to provide the appearance, though not the reality, of movement. On the plus side, such a set-up means you come face to face with the same people at every turn, hearing snippets of their conversations. Today is no exception and I've already been privy to such scandals as: 'Shaniqua can go f*** herself!' and 'I'm not doing it like that again, Mark. It hurts!'

The mind boggles.

Earwigging complete, I reacquaint myself with my Sydney to do list. 'Failure to plan is planning to fail' as Dawn always says.

My Aus-genda goes as follows:

1. Sydney Mardi Gras. No. Explanation. Required. Goals: (A) Have fun; and (B) Become besties with Kylie. #IShouldBeSoLucky.

2. Cultural attractions. Opera House and Harbour Bridge – possible climb depending on knees and/or hangover.

3. Bondi. Most famous beach in world. Swim, have photo with Bondi Rescue crew. Try not to get eaten by a shark.

4. Marsupial experience. Kangaroo or koala. Any pouch will do. And finally…

5. Cheeky pash. Aussie for snog. Ideally with a hot local.*

More of a nice-to-have than an essential.

I'm soon nearing the front of the queue, only to discover that I'm stuck behind a man with two dead lizards and half a tree in his carry-on. Rookie error. Customs are not impressed. Luckily, I've left my reptiles at home, so I'm ushered straight through along with the most fabulous hottie, rocking a rainbow vest and tight glitter shorts. 'G'day darl. Happy Gay Xmas!'

'Oh G'day. Same to you,' I reply, effortlessly slipping into the lingo.

'I'm so excited I could poop glitter,' he giggles. 'Where you heading to, girl?'

'Errr, to Bondi.'

'Shut up! Me too. Let's be Uber BFFs.'

The 30 minute journey with new bestie Donnie D is a revelation. He tells me all about his boyf (former 90's boyband star with major drug habit), the best Botox joints in Sydney, followed by a brief education on the joys of rimming. Tom's right. Aussies really are the friendliest! By the end of it, I feel thoroughly enlightened, if not a little queasy. I wave him off and head to my Airbnb.

It's just perfect!

A cosy little studio in the heart of fabulous Bondi. Air con, small galley kitchen and balcony the size of a dachshund. I look onto the sun-drenched street below and want to pinch myself. *I'm here! I'm actually in Sydney bloody Australia! WTF!* This is a dream come true for me. I've been a massive Aussie-phile from an early age. Ever since I started crushing on Natalie Imbruglia. I played "Torn" that many times that my family renamed it "Yawn". *Flamin' cheek!* My addiction got more serious from there and I was soon on two Aussie soaps a day along with movie classics like *Priscilla Queen of the Desert* for which I blame my very real fear of ping pong balls. *If you know, you know.*

Despite being knackered from the triple dose of 'F's (Flight, Full Moon party and 'Fuck, I accidentally spoke to my ex'), I shower and head straight out. It's a steaming hot morning and everything instantly feels so familiar – the street signs, the shop fronts and the bare-footed hotties with surf boards tucked under their arms like newspapers. All those years of *Home and Away* research are finally paying off.

Everywhere I look, there are signs of Mardi Gras. Rainbows here, bunting there, and a good few bars that are already heaving with shirtless hunks dancing their nipples off! I'm gagging to join, but first things first, my inaugural dip at Bondi Beach. Item three on to do list.

I'm there within minutes, along with the rest of the world it would seem. Lord it's packed! You can barely see sand for bodies, row upon row of humans sizzling atop fluffy towels. Guys in budgie smugglers, babes in the teeniest, weeniest bum flossers and a good few scorched lobsters to boot. That's gonna sting later!

Have to say, Bondi feels bigger than on the TV; bleached white sand hugging the blue ocean, all beautifully framed by a rocky headland. I remove my flip-flops and like the intrepid explorer I am, set a first foot upon the famous sand. HOT sand!! *HISSSSSSSSSSS!*

Instantly launches into hot sand shuffle, whilst making high-pitched whooping sounds

My ridiculous mating dance attracts the attention of a surfer girl who's waxing her board a few metres away and she shoots over a "G'Day!" with the loveliest smile.

'Oh. G'day,' I blush, before whooping my way over to a quieter part of the beach. This will do nicely. I spread out my sarong and, feeling the overwhelming urge to gloat, I grab my phone and, before you can say 'time difference', I'm dialling Jen's number and she's picking up.

'Hey gorge. I'm in Sydneeeeeey!'

'Hey gorge. I'm *in beeeed*!'

'Oh shiiiiiit! Totally forgot the time, Jen. I'll call back later.'

'Well, I'm awake now, ya flamin' galah,' she chides. 'So…' ***Big yawn***
'How is it? Have you run into Hugh Jackman yet? He's a legend. Oh, and have you recovered from the Full Moon party?'

'Pretty much, aside from the ladyboy comp.'

'Yeah, that was impressive. Can just see the headlines now, "Blogger finds new career as erotic dancer"!

'Well, it's better than "Blogger caught in lewd sex act down Bangkok alleyway", dig dig! Yes, I read that bloody instalment Jen! Filth! *Hot* filth, but filth all the same.'

'Ha! What can I say? Cruella strikes again. We had a massive spike in readers after your Bangkok bonk. And as a result, drum roll, we are now proudly sponsored by *Fruity Friends Lube*. I've got free samples coming out of all my orifices! And that's not all.' Her voice suddenly becomes more reverential. 'Get this. *Around the World in 80 Gays* is now number 22 in Google travel blogs.'

'What?'

'Yup! *Number 22!* Can you believe it? Cruella wants to get some merchandise produced: Captain Kit cuddly toys, Indira motivational quote app, Nandi milkshakes! Oh, and better still, since that alleyway was such a hit, she wants you to…errr…'

'She wants me to what?'

'She wants you to….*have more sex basically!* 'She explodes with laughter.

'Are you kidding?'

'Nope.'

'What kind of sex?'

'She didn't specify. Just *more* of it. She didn't give an actual figure but she did say that given the blog's title, 80 might be poetic.'

'*Poetic?* Syphilitic more like! Jeez! The woman is deranged, Jen. Deranged.'

'Don't shoot the messenger. Still, it's nice to have a goal in life and if it distracts you from you know who. Still can't believe you spoke to her. Shit, Ave. Was fate you picking up that phone.'

'Fate? It was bloody Jessica! God, it was awful. Hearing her voice like that. Urrgghhh. Can you imagine the shock?'

'Nope. Thank God, she didn't know it was you.'

'I know. I was doing my best Claire Foy from *The Crown* voice.'

'Thank fuck for the Foy, hey! So, any other news from your lovely ex?

'Oh, just that she still loves me.'
Silence.

.

.

'So that's why she cheated on you, is it?' She snaps, dropping her phone. 'Sorry Ave. Don't mean to go off. She just makes me mad! Just remember who you are, Ms Super Blogger. *Number 22, Ave*! Number 22!'

'I'll try. Anyway,' I quickly flick to FaceTime. 'Check this place out. It. Is. Incredible!'

I give her a quick 360 of the magnificent Bondi backdrop.

'My God. It's sooo bright there,' she squeals. 'Oh, wait – AND. WHO. IS. THAT?'

'*Who?*' I turn to catch the hot surfer chick from before jogging past.

Cue Baywatch music and sexy slo-mo.

'Oh yeah. I saw her earlier,' I smile, completely distracted.

'Err, hello? Earth to Ava. Are you still there, girl?'

'Oh right, yes! Still here. Err, where were we?'

'Going back to sleep,' she yawns. 'I'm shattered. Oh, don't forget to follow the new *80 Gays* Insta account. We need to go Top 20.'

'Will do. Is that before or after my next 79 sexual conquests?'

'After is cool. Catch ya later, lover girl!'

The ocean is glorious, infinitely warmer than the North Sea, so I wade straight in, allowing my charred toes to snuggle in the cool seabed. I give them a wiggle. 'Number 22, hey?' That feels kinda good. A quick splash of water around my shoulders and I'm in, resurfacing near the surfer girl who's dropping in on a wave. I watch her glide along its fluffy white crest. Jeez, she makes it look easy! It puts me in mind of that time Scarlet and I went surfing in Cornwall. I got hypothermia and she knocked out a tooth. Good times!

I swim out a bit further, deeper into the glorious Australian ocean, the ocean full of Australian beasts with big Australian teeth! And then, I hear them. Those two notes that haunt every Brit who ventures beyond knee deep in foreign waters.

DERR NERR. DERR NERR!

I look about me to evaluate current G.W.D. (Great White Danger).

Quick glance left, quick glance right…no sign of incoming dorsals. I scan for nearby swimmers, always good to have someone further out than you. *Bingo.* There's a couple of meaty specimens just a few metres away. Perfect *amuse bouche* for any passing shark. Sufficiently spooked, I decide to breaststroke back to shore. One stroke, two strokes, three, then four. Strange. I don't seem to be getting anywhere! I switch to front crawl with turbo boost leg kick. Used to win medals with this one back in my swimming club days. Still getting nowhere. Then it hits me…

I'm in a rip current!

Fuckety flamin' fuuuuuuck!

This is the kind of twattery I've witnessed on *Bondi Rescue* so often that I have memorised the dictionary definition: "Rip: a fast-flowing area of water that can pull people or objects away from the land*"*.

I am 'people' in this scenario.

I start to chastise myself, expending even more valuable energy with minimal result. *Why didn't I swim between the bloody flags?* I'm really starting to tire now as a set of bigger waves roll in, knocking me over and I tumble arse over tit, over and over in the water.

This is it. Farewell cruel world! Farewell!

Images of my life flash before me. Family holidays, my first bike, first kiss, Scarlet's proposal, Jen. Then suddenly, I feel a sharp tug on my arm and, hallelujah, I'm back above the surface!

'Grab onto the board,' a voice says as I gulp the biggest, most glorious breath of air into my lungs – instant *airgasm*!

I'm alive! I'm alive!

I gaze up at my rescuer through half-open salty eyes. *It's her!* The surfer girl from earlier! She smiles down at me like some omnipotent sea goddess and I look back at her like a drowned beaver. I would be mortified, but frankly I'm so happy to be alive that I don't care about the snot that's ballooning from my nostrils at this precise moment.

Thank you universe! Thank you surfer girl! Thank you! Thank you! Thank you!

I throw a spent arm over the board as she paddles us into the shallows. 'How are you going now? There's quite a rip out there today,' she says, helping me to my feet.

'Ahhh! Thank (breath) you (breath) so (breath) much! Oh my God, I'm sorry.'

'And I'm Hannah,' she smiles, holding out a hand.

'Oh, yes, ha! I'm Ava. Lord! Am I glad you were here, Hannah! I can't thank you enough!' I pant, utterly inadequate before this antipodean Wonder Woman.

'All good. Happens all the time.'

'Yes. But I'm so sorry.'

'Ha! You're English, hey?' she says with the biggest grin.

'Yes!' I puff. 'My accent?'

'No, you keep apologising!'

'Oh, right. Sorry.'

Instantly covers mouth with hand

She laughs again, revealing the cutest set of dimples. 'Well, Ms Sorry, welcome to Bondi.'

'Thanks,' I laugh. 'It was very nearly the shortest visit ever. I only arrived this morning!'

'Well, you're certainly cramming it in. Though think drowning is a bit much. Hold on, did you say your name's Ava?'

'Yeah?'

'Not Tom's friend *Ava*?'

'Yee-ees-sss,' I say, eyeing her incredulously. 'Hang on…'

'I'm Hannah! He said you'd be getting in contact. I was expecting a text – guess this is more original.'

Penny.

.

.

Drops.

'*Hannah?* OMG! Yesss, yesss! No way! What are the chances?' I laugh. 'Well, shit, it's doubly good to meet you then!'

'*Doubly* good to meet you too!'

I like this girl already.

There are few things finer than *not* drowning at Bondi beach on your first day down under, and I sprawl out across my sarong, contemplating the fragility of life and the complete fucking awesomeness of coincidence! 'Well, isn't this just nuts!' I keep repeating to myself. 'Of all the people in all the world. It was her!'

The words whirl around in my head and I must doze off or something as next thing I know, Hannah the hero is leaning over me again. 'Hey, Ms Sorry,' she smiles. 'You wanna head up, grab a coffee or something?'

'Oh sure. Cool,' I quickly scramble for my things, 'A ripper coffee! My treat. It's the least I can do.'

She explodes with laughter. '*Ripper coffee?* Tom said you were funny!'

'He did? Oh right!'

Now, I'm not sure if that's a good or bad thing, but judging by her smile, I'm leaning towards the former. We begin to walk up and I'm all nervous for some reason and start dropping the contents of my bag everywhere. Lip gloss, phone, sunnies…

'Here, let me help,' she says, handing me a super size tampon that's just tumbled onto the sand. *Smooth, Ava, smooth!*

'So, it's nice to hear Tom's loved up at last,' she smiles. 'What's Dawn like?'

'Ahh, she's the best. They make a great couple. Has he been single for a while then?'

'Yep. Ever since he got his heart broken. He might look tough, but he's a right softie, that one. He certainly seems to like your friend though.'

'Well, that's good to hear – cos she's mad about him – like *really* mad!' I grin as we embark on a Bondi beach mini tour via a skate park and the coolest graffiti walls, adorned with murals of surfers and beautiful indigenous works (plus some strange looking birds that appear almost prehistoric).

'Wow, just love this place! Must be hell living here!' I grin, snapping a few choice shots for the new Insta blog.

'Ha! It is pretty cool, hey? Mind you, can't say I'm not jealous of all your travels. Sounds like you guys have been having a ball.'

'Yes, it's been pretty fun. India, Thailand and I'm off to Cape Town next for a wedding. Not that I like the groom much – bit of a twat! Well, a lot of a twat really!' I giggle, instantly feeling like a tragic oversharer.

'Well at least it's in South Africa. I love that part of the world. My dad is African, from Zimbabwe. I was born there.'

'Oh right! Zimbabwe. I'd love to go. Victoria Falls is on my list – looks spectacular!'

'It is. Mind you, with your track record with water, I'd stay well clear!' she winks as we head into a café bar just off the main strip. It's already heaving, despite being just before noon and we stop at the long, wooden bar right beside a DJ in full drag.

'Welcome to Mardi Gras! Hope it's not too manic for you?'

'*WHAT?*' I shout, pretending not to hear her over the music.

'Ha! I know I said we'd grab a coffee, but it *is* a special day!' she grins, handing me an ice cold beer or *schooner* as they say in Aus. Less than a pint, more than a half. Just right, Goldilocks!

'Cheers!'

She has the loveliest soft accent and that Aussie way of talking, when they go up at the end of the sentence as if they're asking a question, when actually they're not.

'So, Hannah. What do you do when you're not saving tourists?'

'Err, I save animals!' she laughs.

'You're kidding? You're a vet?'

The revelation is all too much and before I know it I'm blurting, 'I have a thing for women with stethoscopes!' #FootInMouth.

'Really? Sadly I left mine at home, didn't want to get sand in the earpiece. And what about you, Tom says you're a graphic designer?'

'Yes. In London.'

'Oh cool, sounds fun. I'm always envious of creative people, it's a lovely thing…' Her phone starts to ring, 'Oh, sorry! I need to take this. It's about a job.'

She wanders outside, so I use the time to snap some more shots and have a snoop at the *80 Gays* Insta account Jen was talking about. *Scroll, scroll. Tap tap.* Shit, it looks professional! Gorgeous shots of Goa: golden beaches, spice markets, a few of Nandi (with Indira's sari sleeve just cut out), Krabi snorkelling trip and Bangkok. There's even one of *that* alleyway! *Blushes slightly.* Strange to say, but all these photos are making me feel envious of my own life! How is that even possible? The power of social media.

I quickly flick onto Jen's account: shots of a night out, Jen looking merry, another one of her looking even merrier and then one of her and that personal trainer girl, both in active wear. I zoom in closer. Wow! She looks fitter already! Honestly, you leave someone for a couple of months expecting them to go into a state of mourning and eat their body weight in donuts, and they have the audacity to bloody improve themselves!

'Oh, who are you stalking?' Hannah laughs.

'Oh hi! Just a friend. She's been getting disgustingly fit in my absence,' I turn the phone screen towards her.

'Oh yes. Very fit! Is that her girlfriend? They look loved up.'

'Oh right, yeah.'

'So, more importantly, what are your plans for Mardi Gras? I'm meeting some friends in Oxford Street later. You should come along. Watch the parade. It's mandatory for Mardi Gras virgins!'

'That's really kind but you've more than excelled in your babysitting duties today. You don't have to invite me along,' I laugh.

'What? Tom would never forgive me! Come! It'll be fun.'

'Well, in that case, I'd love to!'

CHAPTER SIXTEEN –MARDI GRAS AND THE PEEPING TIT

'Life is either a daring adventure or
nothing at all.'

- Helen Keller

I sneak a cheeky nana nap before the main event, waking up fully clothed on a bed of Tim Tam wrappers. Classy. Tim Tams are the stuff of legends over here, Aussie biscuit royalty that taste like our Penguins (chocolate bar, not the cute flightless bird).

My afternoon snooze was fitful and frankly bizarre.

I dreamt I was discussing fate and coincidence with Greek philosopher Aristotle and randomly, Dolly Parton, clearly triggered by near-drowning incident with Tom's friend as unlikely rescuer. The debate was most enlightening. Aristotle kept banging on about free will, Dolly was in the 'it was fate' camp, while all I could do was grin and suggest a quick chorus of "Jolene".

I'm still not sure where I sit on the whole destiny versus coincidence debate if I'm honest. In some ways, I'm a big believer in fate – walking in on Scarlet that night, meeting Sara on the flight. I have a sense of 'it was meant to be', but then again, I hate the idea that this game of life is pre-destined. Rigged, like some dodgy boxing match. Fact is, whatever forces were at play today, I'm just grateful that I'm alive and ready to dance my bits off at item one on my Ausgenda, *Mardi Gras!*

It's around 5 pm when Hannah rocks up. She looks every inch the cool Sydneysider in cut-off dungarees with strap seductively dangling off one shoulder. Her long, spiral curls are still damp and I catch a whiff of her scent – mmm, fresh fruit cocktail. 'You look great!' she says, leaning in for a hug and before I can say 'Wonder if she'll count as one of my five-a-day' we're in and out of the Uber, and being swept along in the tide of Mardi Gras massif.

The streets are rammed, like the whole world and its gay dog has turned out. Tipsy teens giddy on alcopops, grandads high fiving drag kings and hip, young parents pushing baby strollers like battering rams and wishing they had used contraceptives. 'It's not Mardi Gras, it's *Partiii* Gras!' a fabulous drag queen yells. She is rocking a mahoosive pink wig you could happily secrete a pony inside, and she leans down from her eight inch heels to flirt with a passing nipple-pierced hunk, who promptly falls backwards into a hedge.

#PeakedTooEarly.

We go with the flow, eventually spilling out onto the gay golden mile, aka Oxford Street, where we stop outside a smart, glass-fronted bar. 'Here we are,' Hannah says. 'Follow me.' There's a ginormous queue, but since the bar is owned by her ex, we strut on past like regular gay-listers. I feel a tad guilty, I must confess, but as it's a special occasion, I ditch the self-reproach and embrace the universal truth that it's not what you know, it's who you've had.

'HANNAAAAH!' a voice sings out. 'Over here!'

We head straight over to join a group by the bar, whereupon a heart-warming hug fest ensues. Embraces here, kisses there. Lots of whooping. I'm hit by a pang of homesickness, and I think of my own gang back in London and how great it would be if they were here right now, throwing back shots and having their tourist visas revoked. Turkey 2014. Embarrassing incident involving a jet ski and a bowl of calamari.

'Hey there! I'm Nicky,' a pretty brunette says. 'Happy Mardi Gras!' She hands me a welcome shot and before you can say 'bad idea', I'm knocking it back and getting introduced to the rest of Hannah's friends. There are a lot of them…

Takes deep breath

Rach, Yaz, Lisa and Abs, Nat, Jo, Laura, Lauren, Kate, another Lisa, an Ori or Dori (not sure which, since she's had a few), Colleen, Alex, Una, Sarah and Jess.

'Oh, hello everyo…'

'And that's Shelley, H, Toni, Ash, Ally B, Rachelle, Charlotte, oh and Dei…' she grins as the Dei girl comes bounding over, her curls bouncing on her head like golden springs. 'Hi! Don't worry, I don't know half their names and I've known them for years!' she laughs. She's Irish and very smiley. We get to talking about life down under and how I came to know Hannah, which Dei declares a 'wonderful coincidence', before our conversation is halted by the arrival of a striking blonde. I suspect she might be the infamous ex, *Emma T,* as she is strutting around like she owns the place, probably because she does.

She makes an instant beeline for Hannah, giving her a massive hug. It's an embrace intended to mark territory, like a dog peeing up a lamppost. Now, I'm no body language expert, but I suspect Ms T might be looking for a reconciliation and she seems less than thrilled to meet me, promptly launching into a game of one-upmanship. Every time I say something, she betters it. I mention India, she's been eight times. We talk about languages, she speaks ten. If I said I had syphilis, she'd say she'd had it twice! In short, I feel about as welcome as a fart in a spacesuit, and I turn back to the bar for a welcome reprieve.

OMG! What is it with exes?

Gay, straight, bi, queer, black, white, green…they're all a right royal pain in the bum! And what's worse, you can bet your Aussie bottom dollar that if you're on a fun night out with your friends, you'll run slap bang into yours! Fact. This is doubly true in the lezbiana community since the gene pool is shallower than a puddle in dry season. I glance around the room at all the smiling faces, concluding that everybody here must be somebody's ex. The 'one-who-got-away' ex, the 'it-was-bad-timing' ex, the 'what-was-I-thinking?' ex and, most dreaded of all, the 'bunny-boiler' ex. Particularly heinous for pet lovers. Point is, no one is without baggage and dating anyone over the age of twenty is a bit like buying a second-hand car. Namely, you just have to jump aboard and pray the wheels don't fall off.

Hannah's tête-à-tête with her ex is cut short by the bar manager, who summons Ms T to sort out a broken cash till. She wanders back over, a tad shell-shocked.

'You look like you need a drink,' I smile, passing her a tall G&T.

'Thanks. Yeah, it's all a bit fresh.'

'So I see. Well, you know what they say Hannah, the world is full of exes and a whole lot of Y's. As in, "Y did I go out with them in the first place?" '

Lame joke it might be, but she cracks a smile. I get the impression that she wants to forget about that part of her life tonight and hey, I can *so* relate, so we quaff another shot and say no more about it.

'15 minutes 'til the 40th Sydney Mardi Gras parade, people! Get your party on!' the DJ announces, so we spill out onto the balcony to join Hannah's gang. It's the perfect vantage point and she manoeuvres me into pole position, front row, by the banister.

'How's the Mardi Gras virgin going?'

'Amazing, thanks. I can't feel my cheeks!' I giggle, looking down onto the crowded road below. The whole of Oxford Street is aflutter with rainbow flags and happy, smiling faces ten rows deep in some places. People are standing on bus shelters, milk crates, friends' shoulders, friends of friends' shoulders. All desperate to secure the best view.

Hannah's friend Dei suddenly appears looking like she's about to burst.

'There you are, Han! Hey, how do you fancy joining the parade?'

'Seriously? Are there places?'

'Yeah. Dykes on Bikes. Couple of last minute replacements needed.' She turns to me, 'They're legendary, Ava. They always lead the parade. You guys should do it.'

'Oh…. Right…'

A stare-fest ensues, with them glaring at me as if to say 'Let's do this' and me glaring back as if to say 'Nah, let's not!' I'm far too shy to be parading myself in front of the whole of Sydney, thank you very much. Hannah and Dei have other ideas and, before I can protest any further, we're pushing through the crowds, limboing under cordons and I'm throwing my leg over a Kawasaki 850.

'Welcome aboard, darl!' my driver says. 'I'm Penni. Good to meet ya.'

She's a youthful, fab-at-fifty type dressed to impress, with day-glo here, feather boa there and glitter every bloody where! GLITTER! I *HATE* GLITTER, GODDAMMIT! I'll be finding it in my knickers at my 80th. I flick another piece off my arm and glance over to Hannah, who's looking like a cover girl for *Vintage Bikes Weekly*.

'What do you think?' she grins astride a beautiful old Harley.

'It suits you,' I wink before casting an admiring glance over my biker sisters. There must be a hundred or more: cowgirls, leather queens, unicorns and silver-winged angels, plus a good few bravehearts who are letting it all hang out in rainbow nipple tassels. Now *that* takes some front!

Suffice to say the boob count is high today. All shapes and sizes! Something for everyone. It's funny, but when you're little, you think boobs are boobs. Not so. There's a big ole booby chocolate box out there people, and you never know what you're gonna get, from the low hangers with headlights permanently dipped, to the light, bright perky ones that greet you with the enthusiasm of a golden retriever. I'm feeling woefully underdressed at this point, so Penni chivalrously hands me her feather boa and some rainbow stickers. 'There you go, darl!' The rider next to me gives a whoop of approval, lifting her pink cowboy hat just as a young twink shimmies past, tossing a little package into my hands.

'Rock up and frock up, gurllls!' he sings as I peep inside.

NIPPLE TASSELS!

'Err… that's hardly a *frock!*' I say, utterly horrified.

The lady in the pink cowboy hat shoots me a look, 'Life's short, darl! Buy the shoes, eat the cake, wear the tassels!' I glance over at Hannah for back up, but she's too busy having a rummage in her T-shirt. Oh, hang on…

She's not?

She can't be!

Oh Lord. She's wearing the bloody tassels!

'Come on party girl,' she laughs. 'What are you waiting for?'

'Errrr, my boobs to grow!'

The engines rev with anticipation and I feel myself teetering on the edge of a terrifying titty precipice. *To tassel or not to tassel? That is the question*! I'm here at the biggest Pride event under the sun, I know only one person and so, in an act of wild abandon, I affix the tassels and *whoosh* the puppies are unleashed!

'Wohoooooo!' I laugh. 'I can't believe I'm doing this!'

Beep! Beep!

There's an almighty chorus of horns as our biker cavalcade starts to move off. I still can't quite believe I'm here with this army of Glamazonians leading the bloody Sydney Mardi Gras parade. *Holy Fuck!* I've never felt such a buzz. The whole street is reverberating with excitement, people whooping their hearts out, rubbernecking to see all the fantastical floats and marchers. Burly bears beside burlesque babes, sporting legends next to firefighters, trolley-dollies, bankers, artists. You name it, they're all here. Then there's the LGBTQ+ service people in full-on military regalia, waving 'Love is Love' flags high in the air. I'm already pretty choked, when I see a pair of elderly ladies sharing a kiss and my heart just explodes.

What changes they must have seen in their lifetime!

I'm suddenly overcome by an enormous sense of gratitude for those courageous souls who have gone before us, the trailblazers who fought for our freedoms, marched for our rights. As I ride down Oxford Street, boobs out and head held high, I feel the proudest I've felt in my 29 years. Even the presence of an Australian TV crew doesn't faze me. Instead, I look straight down the lens, shake my tassels and bellow 'Happy Mardi Gras, Sydney!'

This uncharacteristic peacocking is seen as a green light by the TV folk and, next thing I know, I'm having a microphone thrust in my face by queer comedy porn legend Angel Delight.

'Looking hawt, girl,' she sings. 'So, how's your Mardi Gras going? You enjoying the parade, darl?'

'Oh wow! It's AMAZING, Angel. Amazing. This is my first Mardi Gras,' I gush like some teenage fangirl.

'Love it, girl. Living your best life!'

'God yes,' I whoop, turning to camera for an off the scale cringeworthy 'Hello mum, dad and Aunty B'.

And from that moment, there's no stopping me. I am a woman possessed, barely coming up for air.

'Oh Angel - I did love you in *Sticky Fingers 3*. That film changed my life!'

I go on...

And on...

And on. I can see the producer telling Angel to wrap things up with the overexcited English idiot, but alas, this idiot is buzzing with no sign of a slowdown. I'm soon in full overshare mode. 'I'm on a world trip to get over my ex, Angel. She's been a bit of a cow...well, not a cow. I actually like cows! Do you like cows?'

Someone shoot me now!

Angel looks more and more awkward, but I'm now so worked up that my titty tassels are swooshing in all directions and, next thing I know, they've lassoed the microphone wire and we are bound together in some awkward S&M clinch!

'You're just getting clingy now, darl!' Angel quips, trying to maintain a semblance of professionalism. I tug and I pull, but all attempts to extricate myself fail miserably. Then just when I think it can't get any worse, some random launches himself at us, doing a full-frontal to camera! 'Happy Mardi Gras bitches!'

Jiggle, jiggle, jiggle.

I don't know where to look as he starts wielding his appendage about like an elephant swinging its trunk! To the left, to the right! Up and down. Angel suddenly ducks, thus yanking the microphone cord and *TA DARR!* my puppies are spectacularly exposed to all in TV land!

FML!

I'm seconds away from a breakdown, when a kindly camera assistant swoops in to cover my modesty with his clipboard and, just like that, Angel moves on to talk to the guy next to me. 'Hi there, big boy? Enjoying the day?'

The rest of the parade is no less exhilarating. I'm waving to the adoring crowds, high-fiving fellow marchers, desperately trying to savour every beautiful moment. It's like being wrapped in a fluffy blanket of love and then, just like that, it's over.

The three miles of boob flashing.

The thousands of marchers.

The 40 minutes of full-on euphoria... all gone in the blink of an eye and yet I get the feeling that this is one day that will stay with me forever. I turn to Hannah.

'Thank you so much. This is one of the best days of my life!' I plant a big kiss full on her lips, 'Oh! Err. Sorry!' I blush, quickly pulling away.

'Don't be,' she smiles.

Part two of our Mardi Gras night is no less of a buzz as we are promptly whisked off to the Official Afterparty by our biker friends, who drop us outside with a few triumphant toots of the horn.

'Thanks Penni. Thanks everyone,' I beam, peeling myself off the back of the bike and striding towards the club.

'Look at this place! It's amazing!'

Four giant rooms across two levels with big name DJs, laser stages, girls in body paint, performers dangling from high wires and more topless men than you could shake a big gay stick at. Hannah takes my hand and leads me deeper into the crowd, shimmying past Ru Paul lookalikes and the most gorgeous boy in silver shorts, who is snogging the face off another boy who looks exactly like him. #Doppelbanger. 'I'm in *heaven,*' I beam, running face-first into a six foot-four nun with hands the size of dinner plates.

'I'm Sister Ophelia Tits,' she sings, spinning me round like a ragdoll.

'Oh right. Good to meet you sister'.

Gotta love Mardi Gras. It's one of the few times in life you get to bump and grind with a sister of the cloth without anyone batting an eyelid. I catch sight of a cute older couple who are busting out the old skool moves with such gusto that I can't help but join in. After a solid half hour of hardcore raving plus minor hamstring injury, we leave the dance floor ready to collapse.

'I am officially knackered,' I laugh, melting into a big sofa just beneath the air con. Perfect spot! Hannah leans her head on my shoulder, her warm breath tickling my neck. Instant goosebumps. It's all going rather well when *Fred and Gingivitis,* the middle-aged ravers from the dance floor, flop down opposite.

Great timing guys!

It doesn't take long before the woman engages us in conversation. 'Having a good Mardi Grardi, darl?' she smiles revealing an unfortunate tooth to gum ratio. 'I'm Carole King. Nice to meet you.'

'Hi. I'm Ava and this is Hannah. Likewise.'

I'm keen to just snuggle up to Hannah but alas, the lady is *very* chatty and within a couple of minutes we're sharing her life story along with a chilled bottle of Moët. 'Always better shared, darl!' she smiles, dabbing her tomato-red face with a tissue. She is clearly the boss in the relationship. A real force of nature; not to mention open, very, very open. So, by our second drink, we know the name of her first pet (Smokey), favourite boy band (NSYNC) plus full medical history, including recent battles with nits and uterine polyps. Her partner is a Welshman. A bit more reserved, but still up for a chat.

'I'm Steve,' he grins. 'People sometimes say I sound like Tom Jones, you know.'

'Oh, really?'

'Well, *It's not unusual!*'

Carole practically wets herself at is and is all but rolling on the floor and howling like a banshee. Now that's true love for you. Hearing the same gag over and over and still finding it funny, or at least caring enough to pretend. #CoupleGoals. There's no stopping these two and, after 30 minutes, we've covered most major topics including politics, religion (always a risk), plus best places to visit in Australia.

'We love Byron Bay, don't we buttercup? Beautiful spot it is,' Steve says. 'Talking of which, we really should be going. We're off to a conference there the day after tomorrow. Those cases won't pack themselves, will they my love?'

Carole is having none of it. 'Oh, calm your farm, Steve King. Honestly girls, his arse is so tight, only dogs can hear him fart!'

BAHAHAHAHAHAAAA!

I almost spurt out my Moët, as poor Steve scurries off trying to gather Carole's belongings, which have been discarded en route from the dance floor. Sequinned handbag, killer stilettos, lipgloss and pocket-sized vibrator.

'Oh wow, Byron Bay,' I say, rather excited. 'I'm going to visit some friends up there soon.'

'No way, darl! Well, isn't that a coincidence! Isn't it a coincidence, Steve?'

'It sure is my angel plum hairy fairy.'

'Well, that settles it,' Carole declares. 'You girls should get a lift up with us. Plenty of room in the Nissan.'

'Oh no, we couldn't possibly.'

Hannah stares at me with her big champagne eyes, giving one of those drunken 'Why not?' shrugs and, just like that, the plan is sealed with a clinking of glasses and an exchange of numbers.

'Until Thursday then! Don't do *anyone* I wouldn't girls,' Carole laughs, before tumbling fanny first into the next table.

#WinningExits

The rest of the night is a haze – a wonderful, delirious haze. There are more drinks, more dancing, more chats with randoms and we finally call it a night when Hannah's friend Nicky charges the stage and climbs into a giant champagne glass, thus getting us all ejected. Respect!

The ride back to Bondi is magically fast, courtesy of the Uber fairies, and we fall out of the cab outside my Airbnb just before sunrise.

'Well, that was *the* best night ever,' I hiccup. 'Fancy a…cup of tea?'

'*A cup of tea?*' she grins 'Yeah, sounds great.'

We stumble inside and before I can say 'one lump or two' Hannah is pulling me to her and kissing me so hard that I forget all about my Tetley with two sugars.

Around the World in 80 Gays
"Explorations in love"

Exploration is the best part of travelling.

The joy of discovery. The thrill of a new land. A new person.

As I trace the contours of her body, I have the feeling of an adventurer in a new place. There is a familiarity about it. It's somewhere I've visited with other lovers and yet it is never entirely the same.

A variance in touch. A sigh. A look.

Every encounter as unique as a fingerprint.

Her legs curl around me, her breath quickening as I lean in to kiss her again. She tastes wonderful, an intoxicating mix of warm champagne and salty ocean.

'I'm so glad I nearly drowned today.'

'Me too!' she smiles. 'Me too!'

CHAPTER SEVENTEEN – PLAYING THE TOURIST WITH HANNAH

'Stop worrying about the potholes in the road and enjoy the trip.'

– Babs Hoffman

There are officially four types of kissers in the romantic universe according to uber talented blogger Jen Jones. They are:

1. **The Anaconda tonguers.** A group characterised by overzealous use of the tongue with little warm-up and/or skill. This technique of using the tongue as if it were a fencing foil tends to stimulate the gag reflex, rather than the sexy bits. Never pleasant. People have been beheaded for less.

2. **The Rhythm right-off'ers.** Like bad rhythm on the dance floor, woeful rhythm in the snogging arena is *kiss-a-strophic*. You go right, they go left; you go left, they go, well, home frankly! Invariably ends up with the clashing of teeth and colossal dental bills. Case in point, work friend Cheryl from accounts who had a full set of veneers fitted after passionate run-in with a Brazilian landscaper.

3. **The Tight-lippers.** This group have a tendency to not open their mouths much, leading one to think they have contracted sudden onset lockjaw. Potential trust issues/PTSD from previous anaconda tonguer encounter?

And last but not least, my personal favourites:

4. **The Angel-lippers.** The Rolls-Royce of kissers, guaranteeing a more than satisfactory ride. Het, hem. 100 percent would recommend.

And there you have it!

I'm happy to report that Hannah is a fully paid-up member of group four and, as a result, this Norfolk girl is more than a little bit happy this morning.

What a night! What an incredible night!

Mardi Gras did not disappoint and, aside from vague memory of exposing myself on national TV, I have no regrets. I take that back, I have one. Agreeing to go on Hannah's Sydney sightseeing tour this morning. *Kill me now*! I do not wish to adult today. In fact, I don't wish to *human* today! I just wish to be a cat lying in the sun, quietly licking my own paws. Fortunately, the tourist agenda is a stripped back one, a post Mardi Gras special, and we agree to proceed with caution after a strong cup of coffee down at Bondi.

'So, have you heard from your mate Angel Delight today?' Hannah teases, as we settle at our table.

'Nooo, not yet. But hey, I'm sure she had more exciting incidents to contend with than my...'

Buzz Buzz.

Not again!

My phone is blowing up this morning. Cannot. Deal.

I switch it to silent, directing both functioning brain cells to the important task of breathing. In and out. Nice and easy. Nope, still feel sick and I get the feeling I'm not alone. There are a good few fellow zombies about today, brushing shoulders with the Bondi babes and hipsters with immaculately styled facial hair. The beard game is strong here; every other man has one. Have to say, facial hair is a bit of a gamechanger, with beards doing for the face what push-up bras did for the flat-chested! I often wonder what will happen when the trend passes and those poor women who went to bed with Jason Momoa wake up with a chinless wonder. Not a problem I have to worry about, thankfully.

I'm still feeling a little off, but the coffee aroma wafts under my nose and I start to revive. I'm loving the brew down under. Every cup is served with such artistry that you don't know whether to drink it or hang it on the wall. Since my arrival, I've been treated to a fine array of images painted into my latte foam: love hearts, roses and, on one occasion, the face of our Lord, but might have been Richard Branson. Sadly, such creativity is wasted on me today, as *I JUST WANT MY BLOODY COFFEE, PLEASE, MR BEARDY MAN!* Thankfully the barista gets the hint and serves my flat white quick smart along with a complimentary slice of banana bread, as I'm looking 'a little dusty, mate' quote, unquote.

Slurp, slurp. Normal service starts to resume.

'So, Byron Bay will be fun,' I smile. 'I'm so glad you're coming.'

'Oh crap, I forgot about that!'

'You hadn't!' I say with a look of horror.

'Just kidding. Will be great. I've applied for a job up there actually, so perfect timing. Let's just hope the lift pans out, hey? Carole and err...'

'Sean? No, Steve? I still can't believe we agreed to go with them. What is it they say about accepting lifts from strangers?'

'Ha! Well, they're certainly keen,' she says looking at her phone. 'They've texted me twice already today.'

'Wow! Well, they seemed nice enough. Mind you, Jeffrey Dahmer probably seemed OK after a few shandies. I'm not sure if drunk me is the best judge of character...'

'Whereas *sober* you is faultless?' she smiles, leaning in to give me the nicest warm coffee kiss.

Hannah's hungover tour, here we come! (My notes in italic.)

1. Sydney Opera House

"Sydney Opera House is an architectural marvel, a historically significant landmark and home to some of the city's best culture and theatre."

Breathtaking! Looks like a set of billowing, white sails. Or could be dorsal fins? Jury's out. Apparently, the project went over budget and everybody fell out. Bit like my engagement party. #NotBitter. Hannah treated me to lunch at the Opera Bar café overlooking the harbour. Oysters, champagne and big pile of chips. Ran into Hannah's friends. Apparently, her ex is fuming. Please God, don't let me be murdered today.

2. Harbour Bridge and climb

"The Harbour Bridge has been likened to the Golden Gate Bridge of San Francisco. It earned the nickname 'the coat hanger' due to its unique shape and metal frame structure."

Nicest looking coat hanger I've ever seen, though might struggle to fit in my IKEA Malm wardrobe. Just saying. Hannah persuaded me to join her on the climb. Thus we ascended the 1332 steps on a hangover and half a bottle of Vimto. Wanted to give up, but was spurred on by 92 year old who said I was 'holding him up.' View from top incredible, even through closed eyes.

And finally…

3. Australian Museum

Saw beautiful dot paintings by local indigenous artists. LOVED! LOVED! LOVED! Visit to other sections of museum aborted due to legs seizing up after 1332 sodding steps up that sodding bridge. #IBlameHannah.

Headed home for pizza and highly recommended sexploring of our own. No map required. *Wink emoji.*

CHAPTER EIGHTEEN –THE KINGS OF THE SWINGERS AND AN OUTING

'One minute you're young and wild, and the next you're buying air fryers.'

- Carole Jane King

When I was a little girl full of hopes and dreams, as opposed to a big one full of gin and regret, I had a particular fondness for a tea towel that hung beneath my Aunty B's sink. It was the colour of sunshine, with big swirly writing that said:

Instructions for Living a Life...
Pay attention
Be astonished
Tell about it.

For some inexplicable reason, that tea towel fluttered into my mind this morning and now I can't stop thinking about how those words I loved as a child have become a kind of prophecy. How, over these past few weeks of global adventuring, I have been living by those three commandments, albeit subconsciously.

Too much sun perhaps? But please indulge me for just a moment.

I have dutifully: (1) 'Paid attention'. Living in the now, as per Indira and ashram teachings. I have thus learnt lots, namely the importance of openness, self-worth and the dangers of masturbating with electrical appliances. (2) 'Been astonished'. Often and greatly. Be that by poker sharks or the kindness of strangers. #AlleywayToHappiness. And finally, in the wake of such mind-expanding adventures, I have learnt to: (3) 'Tell about it'. Yep, by some literary miracle, this non-writer has started to forge a whole new career in, well, blogging! Kudos to the uber-talented Jen, the Rumpelstiltskin of Microsoft Word who manages to spin my ramblings into solid gold.

What a team!

Consequently, we have risen to number 17 in the Google blog chart thingamajig, as reported in last night's text update! Not a bad turn-around considering I was a blubbering wreck just two months ago.

So, like I said, a prophecy indeed and a story I'll be sharing with Aunty B at the upcoming nuptials in South Africa. Can't say I'm looking forward to it much. Not only because the groom is a git, but since I'll have to face all those awkward Scarlet comments such as, 'What a shame it didn't work out, dear', 'Wasn't she pretty?' and most annoying of all, 'Is that behaviour normal with the lezzbians?' A question my Aunt Agatha invariably asks regardless of the situation.

Still, must not be bitter. Must focus on the good. Namely, the awesome Cape Town location and safari. *Gratitude, gratitude!*

*

'Almost ready?' Hannah asks, slurping on her flat white.

It's just before 8 am and we are all set for Steve and Carole's 'Ripper road trip'. Their words. There's a little *toot toot* from the street and we head out to their freshly valeted Nissan Dualis with 'leather dash and alloy wheels' to quote Steve. I don't know what's more shocking – the fact that we agreed to go on a trip with random strangers or that the random strangers showed up! Both minor miracles and I shall be petitioning the Catholic church forthwith.

'G'day girls.' Carole sings, in the lowest-cut top known to mankind. 'Throw your junk in the trunk and get your sweet arses in here.'

'Thanks,' I gush, trying to mirror our hosts' ebullient mood while Hannah just about manages a grunt from beneath her Ray-Bans. The curse of a two day hangover. We climb aboard. Mirror, signal, manoeuvre and we're off. Destination, Byron Bay.

I have to say, I'm pretty excited. Not only do I get to hang with Dawn and Tom, I also get to explore a cool, new place. Win win! Byron is a must-see by all accounts, "picturesque beaches, epic surf", plus it's a favourite spot amongst the fabulously famous. Namely one Chris Hemsworth, who I have strict instructions to 'locate and befriend, darlink' so as to add star quality to blog. *Bloody Cruella!* I swear those colonics fill her with more shit than they remove.

I sink into my seat, sun on skin and big grin on face, and everything feels good. Really good.

'It's so great of you to drive us, Carole and Steve.'

'Not at all, pet. The more the merrier,' Steve sings in his undulating Welsh lilt.

'Oh yes, we love company, darl. Just love it!' Carole gushes. 'So, wasn't Mardi Gras a blast? I was only saying to my Steve earlier, how much I love the gays, wasn't I Steve?' She looks over to him for corroboration.

'Yes, my little buttercup. You do love the gays. Especially Elton John.'

'Oh yes, Sir Elton...'

They promptly launch into an off-key rendition of "Sacrifice" before Carole resumes the Mardi Gras chat.

'What a night. I slept like a baby. Terrible wind though. Must have been that champers. Makes me gassy. Does it make you gassy, girls?'

I'm not sure where to go from here, but luckily Hannah has an idea.

'So, er...is it a work conference you're going to in Byron?'

Steve gives a little chuckle. '*Work?* Oh no, no! It's our annual bond...'

'*Bonds*, shares, investments...' Carole interjects, 'Financial conference for the over 55's, darl. Boring really, but we know lots of folks there as we go every year.' She swiftly changes the subject, 'Oh, look at those trees over there!'

It's funny how different people seem in the cold light of day, when you're not as battered as a saveloy. Carole is older than I recall, slightly heavier and her nose is pink and bulbous, like a proboscis monkey; and Steve looks, well, hairier! In fact, I suspect he's wearing a toupee as his fringe keeps lifting up in the wind like a pigeon's wing.

It doesn't take long before our hostess starts to dish out the in-car snacks, Tim Tams! *Chocolate heaven!* I devour mine in one.

'Do you know, you can tell a lot about a person by the way they eat a Tim Tam?'

'Really, Steve?'

'Oh yes,' he pontificates. 'My Carole loves to lick hers until it's all sticky and moist, and then she swallows it whole. Don't you, my love? No gag reflex you see.'

Carole erupts into a fit of giggles, banging her hand up and down on the dashboard. Well, that turned awkward fast.

'Oh, Steve King. You are a devil. You'll have to excuse him girls. He's a little *perky* today.' She gives him a sloppy, open-mouthed kiss and I feel my Tim Tam do an unplanned U-turn.

Please no, Lord! Not on a hangover!

'So, umm…how long have you guys been together?'

'Fourteen wonderful years,' Steve announces rather proudly. 'I know what you're thinking – you get less time for murder!' He gives Carole a playful nudge.

'*Fourteen years?* Wow! You wouldn't know it. What's the secret?' I ask, immediately wishing I hadn't.

'Well, let's just say we know how to keep it *Jalfrezi*!' they say in unison, as Carole gives me a little wink in the passenger mirror. I presume jalfrezi is their cutesy way of saying spicy. She holds eye contact with me for longer than is comfortable, so I quickly turn to look out the window. 'Oh wow! It really is beautiful, isn't it?'

I'm not lying. The Australian bush is breathtaking. We're only a couple of hours out of Sydney and it already feels so vast. Acres upon acres of lush bushland and green fields bordering the road like thick carpet. It's all very hypnotic. The Eucalyptus trees rushing past, the warm sun on my face and I feel my eyelids getting heavier and heavier. This is what I love about road trips; the purr of the engine, the motion of the car. It takes me back to childhood holidays, dozing in the back of our VW camper van en route to some English seaside town. Of course, in those days, our journeys were punctuated by scheduled 'vom stops', whereupon my brother and I would take turns to bring up our HARIBO Starmix into a plastic bucket. *Happy days!*

Hannah starts to wriggle about in her seat and next thing I know, she's lifting a butt cheek and dangling something pink and fluffy before my eyes.

'*Handcuffs?*'

Carole swiftly snatches them away. 'Oopsie daisy,' she snorts, her bingo wings wobbling from the exertion. *Cough cough.* 'Oh, girls, isn't this wonderful? The open road, the great escape!' she enthuses, barely coming up for a breath. 'Do you know, Steve and I have been reading the most wonderful travel blog, haven't we Steve?'

'We certainly have, buttercup. It's a smashing read, absolutely smashing. It's all about life, love, adventure. All sorts of things really. It's called *Around the World with 80 Gays.*'

My heart skips a beat. *Did he just say what I think he did?*

'No darl, *80 Gays around the Globe...Universe...Globiverse.* Well, something like that. Anyway girls, you should have a read. It's written by a lovely English girl and she's travelling to heal her broken heart, the poor darl. She goes meditating in India, partying in Thailand. Oh, *such* adventures!'

'And now she's coming here! To Australia! Oh it's wonderful, you know. Makes you laugh, it does. Laugh *and* cry.'

'Poor Steve finds it very emotional, don't you Steve?' She places her hand on his knee. 'He's an empath. Takes it all to heart, bless him.'

'I won't lie. I do get upset. I just feel for the girl, you see. Mind, I rather enjoy her sexy encounters too!' he says, with a sudden flush of the cheeks. 'She even inspired a little *alleyway adventure* for us, didn't she, buttercup?'

Alleyway adventures? Ewww. Noooo!

The thought of Steve and Carole storing me in the wank bank is not something I wish to think about, thank you very much. Sexy encounters aside, it feels utterly surreal to hear people discussing my life. Well, a 'pimped up' version of my life. Both mortifying and thrilling in equal measure.

'Tell you one thing, girls. Her ex sounds like a piece of work,' Carole sneers. 'I'm terrified she's going to try to win her back.'

Steve instantly goes to comfort her. 'There, there, my love. I've told you before, you don't need to worry about that. I don't think she loves the ex anymore.'

Now this really *is* getting interesting. Like some perverse therapy session, minus the big bill. I lean in.

'*Really,* Steve? You don't think she loves her ex anymore?'

'No, I do not, Ava! I don't think she realises it yet, but I have a theory that it's the other one she loves, the...'

BEEEEEEEEEEEEEEEPPP!

With that, something big and hairy leaps out in front of the car and we screech to a violent halt.

'Well stone the crows! Is everybody OK?' Steve asks, surveilling all passengers for signs of injury. I glance towards the bonnet to see a massive kangaroo standing there. *WTF!* He's a big'un. Unlike us, Mr Roo looks wholly unfazed by the near-death encounter, and he wriggles his nose, scratches his dangly bits and bounces back into the bush.

'Well, at least you got to see one in the wild, Ava!' Hannah smiles, 'Not the most relaxing of encounters, but hey.'

'I can't believe it! It was so close too. I love kangaroos. They are so beautiful.'

'They certainly are...' quips Steve '...*on a barbie with onions*!' Carole starts to snort with laughter again. 'Oh, you're terrible Mr King!'

I myself am not nearly so impressed. I prefer my roos uncooked, thanks. Mercifully, Carole is able to dispel any awkwardness with the perfect follow-up fact.

'Female kangaroos have three vaginas, you know!' She starts pointing at her own crotch rather excitedly.

Tumbleweed

We sit for a moment, contemplating the possible benefits of owning three vaginas, before Carole reaches into the glovebox and pulls out a deformed scrap of paper.

'Look! Steve does oregano you know – Japanese paper folding. Can you see what it is?'

'Errr...ummm...'

'Come on, darl! It's obvious...' she beams, making the grey blob do a weird little dance on my knee. 'BOING, BOING, BOING! It's... it's ...a ...*KOALA*!'

'Oh yes. I see it now. A koala! They're another must-see on my list.'

'No way! Well, that settles it. Aunty Carole is here to make your dreams come true! Oh, daddykins,' she says in a high-pitched baby voice, 'Can we stop at the koala sanctuary? Show Ava and Hannah my fur babies? Oh, can we daddykins? Puuuurlease!'

My tummy does a little flip and, after a short conflab with Steve, we veer off down a side road. Thirty minutes later, we're pulling up outside the New South Wales Koala Sanctuary.

First a kangaroo, now this! Can this day get any better?

Suffice to say, I am more than a bit excited, although not as excited as Carole, who is 'frothing at the bung hole' as Steve puts it. It's a joy I've not witnessed since Christmas '03, when Aunty B got her phone stuck on vibrate. "O Come, All Ye Faithful" took on a whole new meaning that year.

'Right, girls. Can we synchronize watches?' Steve says officiously. 'We have precisely...*beep beep*...1 hour 15 minutes until we reboard the vehicle, including restroom visit and perusal of gift shop. All major credit cards accepted. Now, are you going to be able to do that, girls?'

'Affirmative Steve, affirmative!'

We give a cheeky salute and stick like glue to Carole, who evidently knows the place like the back of her hand. The sanctuary is gorgeous. A large wood-clad building nestled in the heart of the bush and, after a quick safety drill, Carole leads us to a small enclosure near the entrance, and that's where it happens. That's where I meet my first koala!

'This is Rose!' Carole coos. 'Isn't she a doll?'

I peer inside to behold the cutest mass of grey fur buried in the dense eucalyptus forest. She looks at me, I look at her. *It's love at first sight!*

'Oh wow, she's beautiful! Just beautiful!' I swoon, before Rose promptly turns her back and starts stuffing her furry face with foliage. *Munch munch.* Lord, she has an appetite! It's magical to come face to face with your childhood animal idol, a creature you've watched on countless BBC nature docs. She looks different to how I'd imagined. Her head is larger and she's slow, sooo very slow, like she might just flop over and start snoring at any moment.

'They sleep up to 20 hours a day,' Carole tells me. 'Lucky larakins.'

'Really?' I incline my face adoringly towards Rose before quickly inclining it away again. *Abort, abort! The smell!*

'Oh yeah! Quite some fragrance, isn't it darl?'

'I'll say!'

Less rose-scented, more wee-wee and cough drops!

'Koalas eat *a lot* of eucalyptus. That's why they smell like that. It's like Chanel No.5 to me,' she beams, inhaling a huge lungful. 'Breathe it in, girls! That's it, all the way in!'

Carole proves herself to be quite the koala aficionado. Full of fascinating facts and on first name terms with every creature in the place, humans included. We soon get introduced to the 'koala mums', as she calls them, the ladies who run the sanctuary. There's Brenda, Lottie, Little Ann, who's just had her hips done, and Big Kylie who works in the Fat Possum Café. Kylie clearly has a penchant for donuts as she has a ring of sugar around her mouth and a very sticky handshake.

'Nice to meet you,' we call, moving on to meet Carole's favourite koala resident, a regal looking male called Master Willy. He's the most handsome of chaps, I must say. 'Willy is a lifer,' she explains. 'Poor li'l fella won't ever be released back into the wild. Terrible case of the chlamydias, you see. He's riddled with it, riddled! Can't risk him spreading it in the wild population.'

'*Chlamydia?*' I blurt, just as Master Willy squirts a hefty dose of revenge pee my way. It ricochets off the side of a tree and splashes down the front of my new Ripcurl T-shirt. Hannah passes me a tissue.

'Ewww. Don't think he appreciated the STD judgement Ava.'

'Clearly not!' I say, dry retching into my mouth.

Lord it's pungent! Pungent and, like most smells, highly evocative. I'm instantly transported back to Glastonbury 2012, when a drunk Scarlet hydroplaned on a pool of urine and brought down an entire row of Portaloos. Down they went, like dominoes. *Thud, thud, thud!* One of the best weekends we ever had.

I'm brought back to the present by a panic-stricken Steve, who is now flicking water at me like a priest anointing a new-born.

'Don't worry, pet. I've got you.' *Splish splash.* 'You have to watch out with that urine, you know. Don't want you catching chlamydia.'

More splashing.

'From koala pee?' Hannah puzzles. 'Highly unlikely, Steve!'

'Oh yes, my lovely! No word of a lie. My Carole got infected a few years ago, didn't you Carole? Terrible business.'

'What's that, darl? Oh yes, errr the chlamydias. I umm caught it from a koala here,' she stammers. 'Anyway, come over here girls! Quick, quick!'

She can't get away fast enough and hurries us over to the highlight of the NSW Koala Sanctuary, a viewing platform two hundred metres up in the treetops. *Vertigo central!* We follow her up and start picking out the little grey fur balls nestling in the trees. We count fourteen before Carole has a funny turn and has to be escorted to the Fat Possum Café where she is fed half a donut by Kylie in the backroom. Now I don't know what's in those jammy donuts, but let's just say she emerges 15 minutes later looking a whole lot perkier. As does Kylie.

*

'Well, that was pretty amazing, Carole!' Hannah grins, as we clamber back aboard, thoroughly buzzed and just a little bit smelly.

'Pleasure treasures! D'ya know, I never get bored of that place. It's a little piece of heaven.' She smiles, reapplying her pink lipstick in the mirror. In the absence of Steve (who has gone to 'strain the weasel') I perform a quick change out of my pee-shirt and, call me paranoid, but I swear I catch Carole peeping. I pull my top down as Steve leaps back aboard.

'Right. All set then?' He checks his watch. '1 hour 15 minutes on the dot! You can come again girls! Hahahha!'

And just like that, the Nissan Dualis roars to life and we're back on the road.

I have a little stretch and check my phone. *Swipe swipe. 60 new messages! WTF!*

The first ten are from my mum.

Instant traveller's anxiety including paranoid thoughts of family death, divorce and/or both

I click on the first:

Ava, dear. Emily Johnson-Smythe from the Rotary Club saw you on TV at Sydney Mardi Gras. Apparently, you had your booby-doos out next to a gentleman with a large flaccid member. Have you had a breakdown? Call home immediately. Love mum x

WTF? I quickly open the next:

Ava! Aunt Mary has seen it too. She had to withdraw from the W.I.'s bake-off comp on Sunday, she was so ashamed. What a waste of flapjacks. Call me asap. Your mother x

I read the next.

And the next.

Each one progressively worse than the last. Text six is positively coronary inducing:

Ava! I don'.t know what you are up to young lady - your chest has gone virals! You're on the front page of *The Norfolk Gazette* and all over the world wide web. Father is beside himself and the dog has diarrhoea. I think it's the shock. Mother x

'SHITTTT! SHITTTT! SHITTTT!' I blurt, rocking back and forth with my head in my hands.

'What on earth is it?' Hannah asks, as the car falls into a state of tense hush.

'Oh Lord…'

'What?'

'Oh God!'

'Say it, Ava!'

'Oh *Fuuuuuck!*'

'For pity's sake, spit it out, pet! I've got asthma!' Steve rasps, sucking on his blue inhaler.

'My…my…my boobs appear to be an international incident!' I declare.

Silence. Followed by eruption of hysterical laughter

'Your boobs are *what?*'

'It's not funny, Han! I've been on TV…and the internet. It's that bloody Mardi Gras parade! The interview with Angel is trending all the way back to Gorleston-on-Sea!'

'Oh, I say! *Was that you, darl?*' Carole guffaws. 'With the man with the flaccid penis?' She gives Steve a nudge. 'It was her Steve. *It was her!*'

'Well I'll be blown!' he answers, mouth fully agape. 'And wasn't he a big boy?'

Hannah is about to lose it, but seeing my bottom lip quiver, leans over to give me a consolatory hug.

'Come on, Ava! It's not that bad. It will soon blow over!'

'Blow over? No, it won't. It's gonna linger… like that bloody koala pee!' I whimper, 'In fact, I can still smell it on me! Somebody open a window….PLEASE!'

'Well, I *love* koala pee,' Carole says defensively. 'Let's have a sniff!'

She promptly pokes her head through the seats to have a snort of my midriff.

'Carole! NO! PLEASE, NOOOO!'

'Just one sniff!'

'Ladies, ladies! I think we all need to calm down here,' Steve interjects. 'Everything will be fine, Ava. Just fine. I always think it's good to look on the bright side in such matters. I mean, worst case, this could launch a whole new career for you…on *RedTube*.'

'What?'

'RedTube. The erotic adult entertainment site. There are some lovely girls on there. We like the small-breasted hairy armpit category, but they have all sorts – naughty nymphos, buxom Bavarians…'

'Yeah, OK Steve. Think we get the picture!' Hannah snaps.

I sit in silence for a moment, catastrophizing that all this will somehow lead back to the blog. That I'll be unceremoniously outed and labelled a raging nympho, who does it down Bangkok alleyways and exposes themself on TV!

Breathe, Ava, breathe!

The paranoia is all too much. I start scrolling through Facebook, WhatsApp and Insta, each swipe soliciting another flurry of messages from colleagues, friends, relatives. Even one from the smelly girl from primary school, Rachel Matthews.

WTF!

Mercifully, Hannah is able to administer a mild sedative, one usually prescribed for Yorkshire terriers. It does the trick and within minutes I'm feeling all warm and fuzzy and resolving not to worry about *'things I cannot control'*, ashram teachings 101.

I switch off my phone.

All I need to do is have a good chat with Jen. She'll put my mind at ease. She always does.

Yes, that's what I'll do. Great plan. Feeling better already.

Much bet…. Zzzzzzzzzzzzzzz

I must nod off as next thing I know, Carole is yelling 'STEEEEEEVE!' at the top of her lungs and we are hurtling across the highway, narrowly missing a 'Fatigue Kills' sign. The irony.

'Right, I think it's time for a break,' Hannah says decisively.

'Good idea, darl. I mean, I would drive, but I've got terrible bunions. *Look*!'

Deformed sweaty foot suddenly lands on my lap

'OK! Yes. I believe you.'

After a quick confab, everyone agrees that it would be best all round if we stop off overnight, not to mention safer. As luck would have it, Steve knows just the place, a little motel down the way. Within minutes, we are pulling into the Happy View Hideaway which, for the record, has a view that makes me not the slightest bit happy. Next to the bins. Overlooking noisy highway.

Still, *gratitude, gratitude.*

'Aren't we the lucky duckies?' Carole giggles, bouncing back from reception with two sets of keys. 'We've got the last rooms, adjoining ones too. Nice to be close *neighbour!*' She hands me fob number seven. 'Lucky, lucky, lucky!'

We part ways, arranging to rendezvous in their room later for 'drinkies and finger foods'. It's the last thing I need, but Hannah says it will take my mind off things. So, after a quick shower, we're knocking at their door dead on 7.30 pm.

'Willy-comen, bienvenue, well-come!' Carole sings, ushering us inside. I instantly feel underdressed. The woman is togged up to the nines in a tight leather skirt and an almost see-through top with plunging neckline. A little OTT for corn chips and salsa.

'Oh, wow. You look…err nice!'

'Oh, this ole thing?' She playfully flicks her hair back over her shoulders. 'I bought it online. It's from Paris, you know.'

'Oh, tres bien!' I quip, trying to make the best of things. Carole explodes with laughter.

'Oh si, si! You are funny, darl! Isn't she funny, Steve?'

Snort snort.

The room is semi-lit and we can't help but admire the buffet selection they've somehow knocked up from nowhere. 'Always good to be prepared,' Carole blushes, clearly enjoying the flattery. They really are pulling out all the stops tonight: French brie, cracked pepper crackers and bubbles. Reserved only for 'special people' Steve tells us.

'Cheers everyone! Here's to fun adventures with new friends!'

We clink glasses and Hannah and I take our seats on the matching floral side chairs as Steve leans into me. 'Well, isn't this pleasant?'

'Yes, very.' I smile, suddenly having a hot flush. 'Pheww! Bit warm in here, isn't it?'

'Is it darl? Warm in here, is it?'

I put my hand up to the aircon vent to discover it's pumping out hot air. In the middle of summer.

'Yeah, nah, not sure what's wrong with it,' Carole puzzles, giving the box a solid thump. 'Bloody thing! Ha!'

Downs champagne

It's not long before the conversation turns to my new-found internet fame.

'So, how are you feeling now, darl? You do look stressed. Is it because you've exposed yourself on national television and fear you'll never get another girlfriend?'

'Ummm…'

Hannah leaps in, 'I don't think it's quite that bad, Carole.'

'No darl. Probably not. Ignore me! Ha! I'm such a worry wart! But she does look stressed, doesn't she?' She turns to her husband. 'Steve, doesn't poor Ava look stressed?'

'Oh yes, very!'

Carole is now standing directly behind me and giving my shoulders a little squeeze. 'Oh… yes, you're *very* tense. Let me see if Aunty C can help with that.' Her voice is now sounding like a stage hypnotist. Slow and deep. 'Relaaaaax… Relaaaaax. Oh Ava… you do feel hot my dear. Why don't you take off a layer? I can really get into those knots then'.

I catch Hannah's eye; she is desperately trying not to laugh as Steve turns up the music and starts swaying to Celine Dion, Live from Las Vegas.

"Near, far. Wherever you are…!"

'Oh, yes! I do *love* seven time Grammy winner Celine, don't you? *"My heart must go o-o-n",'* he warbles as his sway turns into a lazy hip thrust.

WTF!

Carole is still kneading my shoulders despite my protestations and, as she presses closer, I feel her breasts poking into my back like puppy dog snouts. Oh Lord! I'm feeling more and more uncomfortable by the second as she starts to regale us with tales of her massage days aboard the cruise ships. 'These hands were the toast of the fleet. Very much in demand. Just don't ask me for a happy ending though!' she shrieks, in such a way as to imply that's *exactly* what she wants me to do.

How is this happening?

It's getting even hotter, so much so that Steve's toupee is starting to curl up at the edges. I shoot Hannah a terrified glance.

'Well, this has been lovely, but I am sooo tired! Awwwww!' she says, feigning a colossal yawn. 'Think I might need to sleep!'

It's a performance worthy of Meryl Streep, but alas, no match for Steve.

'Noooo… don't be silly, pet. Have some more champagne, soon perk you up!'

'And a brie cracker,' Carole smiles. 'It's French you know – from France!' as Hannah gives a defeated giggle and tucks into her fifteenth.

Escape thwarted.

'So….err, HASN'T IT BEEN THE BEST DAY? SEEING THE KO-ALAS,' Hannah shouts, straining against the music. Celine gets turned down a notch.

'Oh, yes! Wonderful, darl. Do you know, I've been visiting that sanctuary since 2016 and I never tire of it. Just love my koala babies!' Carole gushes.

'Don't you mean 2015, my love?'

'No, definitely 2016. It was my 50th birthday, remember? I know I don't look it,' she giggles. 'Oh, girls, it was magical. I adopted a beautiful male that day, Barrington Javier his name was. Such a handsome chap! That was my very first encounter. *You never forget your first time, do you?*' she winks.

Hannah swallows another brie fancy and Steve looks more confused by the second.

'No, no…that can't be right my love. You caught the chlamydia in *2015* from Barrington Javier, remember?'

Carole looks awkward, leaping up with the bottle of bubbly, 'More champagne, anyone? Nice isn't it? Not too gassy!'

The man will not let it lie, 'It's nothing to be ashamed of, buttercup! It's not your fault is it, Hannah? Not Carole's fault she caught the chlamydia from a koala?'

'Um well…'

'Come on! You're a veterinarian. It can happen to anyone, can't it? If they get koala urine on them?'

'Well, it's err…'

The pressure is too much for Hannah and I can see she is struggling to hold it together. She sips more champagne and he asks her again, then again, and then, *whoosh*, she explodes,

'NO, Steve! It can't happen to anyone. It can't happen as it's pretty much impossible for a human to catch chlamydia from koala pee!'

Jaws. Drop.

.

.

'Brie cracker, anyone?'

Carole is now the colour of the beetroot dip and Steve is blubbing his little Welsh heart out, accusing his wife of all sorts of things.

'Steve, darl! Don't be silly! You know I only have eyes for you.'

'Rubbish! It was *Kylie...Big Kylie... wasn't it?* I knew it wasn't just about the donuts! Jesus Christ, Carole! The woman's got breath like a labrador!'

'But darl! Please!'

Steve is beside himself. Huffing and puffing on his inhaler as Carole rebuffs accusation after accusation. 'No' this and 'Never' that, but he will not let up,

'*Denial* – it's not just a river in Egypt!' he proclaims, dramatically ripping off his toupee and stamping on it like a hairy cowpat.

I look at Hannah, she looks at me and Steve just looks like an angry boiled egg, whimpering in the middle of the room.

'HARLOT!'

'No, my love!'

'JEZEBEL!'

'But Daddykins!'

'FLOOSIE!!!'

.

.

'Think we all need to calm down,' Hannah says.

'CALM DOWN?' Steve barks, 'I'll show you calm!' He marches over to a suitcase, reaches inside and proceeds to toss a pair of pink furry handcuffs at his wife. It strikes her on the nose which doesn't go down well and pretty soon she's retaliating and lobbing a dildo the size of a rocket launcher his way!

'Take that, you bastard! Take that!'

Next comes a neon green butt plug, a second dildo plus fluffy whip which whistles past my head, bouncing off the wardrobe and knocking over the plate of French brie fancies!

'Not the brie!' Carole yelps. 'Anything but the brie! You heartless monster!'

It's all starting to feel like we've outstayed our welcome to be honest – abuse being hurled, weapons of mass-turbation flying everywhere. So I give Hannah my 'Let's roll, troops' signal and we make a furtive slide towards the door.

'Umm. Thanks for the lift, guys!'

Door squeaks

'Yeah, really kind of you,' I whisper, before being cruelly struck in the boob by a low-flying gimp mask.

'Ouch!'

Around the World in 80 Gays
"Birds do it. Bees do it…"

We all fall in love. Sometimes from such dizzy heights that we end up a big, sticky mess of roadkill. Never pretty.

As we flee the *Kings of the Swingers* under the cloak of darkness, I find myself ruminating on the complexities of relationships. So many types out there, like cheese in a French supermarket. Brie or Roquefort? Comté or Camembert? Everyone must pick their flavour.

There is no right or wrong with matters of the heart. No 'one size fits all'. Swingers, monogamists, polygamists… What works for one, might be disastrous for another. While some relationships thrive on exclusivity, others flourish on openness, the sharing of sexual partners only strengthening the bond.

I'm reminded of something Singrita told me at the ashram, 'Love is like a fine curry, it requires balance,' she smiled. 'No single ingredient should dominate, every flavour should have its moment to shine. And you cannot just throw everything into the pot and hope it will come out perfectly. That is just folly! It must be

tended and stirred. Loved and indulged. Too much heat, it dries out. Too little, it doesn't become its finest self.'

I think of the couples I know – friends, co-workers, even the Sydney Swingers (who ended up kissing and making up over the Corby trouser press). And I conclude that the relationships that work the best are those where both people feel heard. That magical blend where both flavours can be tasted.

When I think about life with my ex, I question that equilibrium. I always felt I was the keener one, the puppy dog to her cat.

'Everything in balance' Singrita smiled. 'Nature, food and love. Most of all love.'

CHAPTER NINETEEN – GIFT HORSES, MOUTHS AND COOKIE MONSTERS

`'Choose to be optimistic. It feels better.'`

`- Dalai Lama`

Byron Bay, Australia.

'Cheer up, slow down, chill out' reads the iconic sign at Ewingsdale Rd, Byron Bay. Sound advice. Could almost have been written for me. It's nearly daybreak and, after a daring escape from the middle-aged swingers, we arrive shaken but not stirred, like a good martini.

'I feel like Thelma and Louise,' I declare theatrically.

'What? On the run in a Toyota Yaris hire car? Very Tarantino!'

I have to say, I am rather relieved to be here.

The last 12 hours have been BIG on many levels. Shock upon shock. Revelation upon revelation. Not to mention almost being concussed by a flying dildo! Never a good look. As we sweep along Byron's beautiful coast road, I try to blank it all out, allowing myself to be seduced by the view.

'Come on, you need to see this,' Hannah says, as we park up at the main beach for my first Byron Bay sunrise.

It's wonderfully serene at this hour, just a handful of local surfers and joggers as we take front row seats on the cool, white sand. An orange hue appears on the horizon and then up she rises! The sun! She peeps her head up, illuminating the sky in pastel pinks and oranges. *Now, this is a good start to the day!* I open my lungs to inhale the first air of morning, every breath full of the promise of a new start. All worries relegated to the backburner, although I'm praying they don't burn down the whole damn house.

'That's Cape Byron Lighthouse up there,' Hannah says, pointing up to the cliff above. 'The most easterly point in Australia.'

It's rather imposing. Tall and white, proudly standing guard over the beach below, which is now alive with nattering gulls and tiny crabs going about their business. I watch one scurry past in characteristic sideways fashion, wielding its big boy pincers, full of crabby attitude. *Oh, to trade places!* Bet crabs don't stress about ex-girlfriends and viral bloody videos! And, even if they did, nature has gifted them a good, solid shell to absorb the blows. Lucky blighters. Never thought I'd be envious of a crustacean, I giggle to myself.

'What's funny?'

'Oh, nothing. I was just thinking.'

'Oh yeah! Sunrises can do that. Were you contemplating the wonder of creation? The meaning of life?'

'Nah. Just totting up Carole and Steve's butt plug collection! I mean, Jeez! How many do you need?'

'Hahaha! That whole trip was sooo awks! I nearly died when she started massaging you.'

'*You* nearly died! You didn't have her nipples digging into your vertebrae! Honestly! I'm just terrified they'll bloody track us down. Pop up somewhere unexpected like in the shower.'

'Ooooh, yes. I can just imagine those pink, fluffy cuffs dangling over the curtain!'

'Dooooon't! They could be right bloody nutters for all we know. In fact, I did notice that when I yawned, Carole didn't. Textbook psychopath. Read it on Facebook.'

'Ha! Must be true then.'

We look out to sea for a while, contemplating life further.

'Have to say, Han, I don't think swinging is for me – far too jealous. Though I guess it's quite nice in a way. You know, to find someone who really gets you, however strange everyone else might think you are.'

'So true. Have you been reading that *80 Gays* blog as well?' she laughs.

Nervous giggle

It's close to 7 am and we chance our luck at a mega early check-in at the Balinese Villa Escape, aka the accommodation we booked at stupid o'clock last night. Only four hours early then! We have officially turned into those nightmare guests who rock up way ahead of schedule demanding extra tea-bags and an ocean view. Fortunately, the owner has a less rigid view of time and greets us with a radiant smile.

'I'm Moon. Namaste,' she says, her voice as smooth as honey.

'Hi. We're Ava and Hannah. Sorry we're so early.'

'All cool, girls. I'm always up with the sun. It's a magical time of the day, don't you think?' She tilts her chin skyward, as if communing with the powers above. She's an attractive hippy-looking woman, with masses of grey curls and an armful of jangling bangles. Oh and no shoes. Seems to be de rigueur down under. No shoes and no worries. 'I'm just out look-ing for Gerald actually,' she says, peering under one of the villas. 'Ger-ald... hey boy!'

'Is Gerald your cat?' I enquire, joining the search under a nearby bush.

'Oh no, our python. He swallowed a wombat earlier. Think he might have indigestion, poor boy! He thinks he's bigger than he is, that one.'

'Oh riiiiiight. And how big is, err, Gerald exactly?'

'Just five foot or so. Geeeeeraaaaald!'

Little bit of wee comes out

We leave Moon to the great snake hunt and skip off to villa 3 down the back, throwing open the door.

It's a lovely room. Dark timber interiors and one of those colonial style nets hanging over a four poster bed. We even have our own little zen garden with wooden deck and outside shower.

'Wow! I can't believe our luck,' I say, leaping onto a bed the size of a ten-nis court. 'Jen would love it here.' I snap a few shots, type the usual 'Shit here, isn't it?' and hit send. Next thing I know, her face is lighting up my screen. Per-fect timing! She'll soon put my mind a rest about all this titty tassel malarkey.

'Oh, there you are, Ms Porn Star! Thought you'd got too famous to speak to me.'

Or maybe not.

'Oh God. You've seen the bloody video then?' I say, plunging my head into my hands. 'How bad is it, Jen? Honestly?'

'It's not bad.'

'Really?'

'Noooo. Well, yeaaaaaah. It's kinda bad, but *funny* bad! I mean, it's not every day someone gets their tassels caught round Angel Delight's mic on live TV! You're quite the internet sensation, girl! As is your mate with the big, flaccid...'

'Oh, don't *you* start with that!'

'Well, it *was* rather impressive! Cruella is trying to make it a hashtag! Or should I say 'flashtag'! Hey, on the plus side, the blog has literally gone through the roof. We've got over 50,000 new subscribers!'

'*What?* Tell me you didn't put the titty tassel bit in the blog?'

'Ummm, deeeerrrrr, of course not. I wouldn't do that to you, would I? DNKY code of honour and all that! No, think people are just really loving the whole Mardi Gras thing. Cruella is convinced we'll get a book deal out of this. Maybe a movie. Oooohh, I wonder who will play me? Gemma Arterton?'

'Gemma from TOWIE, more like. Shit, girl! All this is making me uneasy. People can't know the blog is me...I'd die!'

'It'll be fine, Ave. Promise. The tassel thing and the blog are totally separate, no one will link them. Just try and enjoy your trip, hey? Byron looks magical by the way!'

'Yeah it's pretty co...'

I'm rudely interrupted by the sound of giggling in the background.

'Who's that?' I ask.

'Natasha. She's been staying with me. Her flat is being redecorated.'

'Oh right, nice! So, has she like *moved in* then?'

'Well, *STOP! STOP!*' she giggles 'Oh sorry not you, Ave. It's Tash, she's bloody tickling me! *STOOOOOP!*' More giggling. More tickling. 'Sorry. I'm gonna have to go,' she squeals. 'No more worrying. Everything is under control, OK?'

Giggle giggle. Hangs up

I fling myself back on the bed feeling a little deflated. Titty tassels trending everywhere? Flaccid penis hashtags? And to top it all, my bestie has shacked up with a gym bunny with a tickle fetish! That's all a bit fast, have to say. And what's with the tickling anyway? Jen *hates* being tickled.

I start flicking through my phone – more new messages, more *UR-RRGHHHHH!* I opt to ignore them, as per Jen's advice and concentrate on the now. Mindfulness, mindfulness. Shouldn't be too difficult in such a gorgeous place, with equally gorgeous companion.

Hannah wanders back into the bedroom.

'That shower is amazing.' She smells incredible, like she's been rolling around in the fruit aisle at Tesco's. 'All OK, Ava?

'Yeah, been chatting to Jen.'

'Oh cool. Hey, Tom just texted. They want to meet in an hour or so.' She flops onto the bed beside me and I run my hands over her soft, brown skin and nuzzle into her neck, feeling weirdly vulnerable.

'Sure you're OK?'

'Uh huh,' I say pulling her into me.

She kisses me hard and just like that my woes are all but forgotten.

*

Sexy time + Vitamin Sea = Happy Ava and I emerge from my post-sex-ercise dip at the beach a whole lot perkier. I'm beginning to think there might be something in this healing power of the ocean malarkey. I feel infinitely more relaxed, although might just be the three orgasms. #Hat-TrickHeaven.

'EVIIIIEEEEEE! HELLOOOOOOO!'

I look up to see that unmistakable mop of red hair cascading from a floppy straw hat, walking beside the mountainous figure of Tom.

'DONNNN! I'm so glad you're here!' I give them a big, salty beach hug. Always awkward when you're half naked.

'Ahh, us too!' Dawn smiles, doing her little *Happy Feet* dance while Tom looks on admiringly.

'How's it goin' Ave? Loving it down under?'

'Ah, Tom! Good eye might! Pretty fair dinkum y'eeear!'

'Yeah, nah – so that accent is no better. Thought Hannah would have helped, aye?' he laughs, pulling her in for a cuddle. 'How you goin', Han? Have you been out today?' instantly launching into surfer talk.

'Yeah, briefly. I'm trying to get Ava on a board, but she's got an unnatural fear of sharks.'

'Errr, it's called *galeophobia* and there's nothing unnatural about it. In fact, I'd argue it's more unnatural *not* to be afraid of a big, toothy fish that might chew off your feet! Am I right, Dawny?'

'Ha! Absolutely, Ava! I said the same thing to Tom earlier. Did you know, six of the 10 most dangerous animals on the planet live in Australia? Plus 20 out of the 25 most venomous snakes! Incredible, isn't it?'

'Yeah, OK *Rain Man*. Way to kill the vibe.'

'Oops, sorry! Animals are my passion. A bit like you, Hannah! Tom tells me you're a vet?' she giggles. 'It really is the noblest of professions – second to pilots and paediatric nurses. I'm Dawn, by the way.'

'Good to meet you. I've heard lots about you,' Hannah smiles, going in for a hug.

'Aww, really? Well, just so you know, the electric toothbrush was a one-off. In fact, I've gone manual now.'

'No, umm, all good Dawn. I didn't mention the toothbrush thing,' I interject, narrowly averting a colossal overshare. 'Right, so what's been happening? Tell me everything.'

We flop down onto the sand and don't come up for a good hour or so. All the major issues are covered including travels down under, Dawn's new vegan diet (high in peanuts hence boobs now one bra size bigger) and then the ashram or 'shram' as Tom calls it. Aussies do love an abbreviation.

'Talking of India, I've got something for you, Ava.' He smiles, passing me a large rectangular package.

'Oooh, what is it?'

'It's a gift, hand delivered from Madame Butterfly herself!'

'Really? *From Indira?*'

I can barely contain myself and start ripping at the paper with all the vigour of a teething puppy. 'I was only thinking about her earlier, saw an old Yamaha down the way.' I laugh, pulling a beautiful leather-bound book from the wrapping paper. 'Oh wow! Look at this!'

'Actually Ave, Indira left the ashram a couple of days after you did,' Tom continues. 'I heard she flew back up to Jodhpur. Not sure of the deets.'

'She went home? Oh right. I've been emailing her, but she's not too good on the ole interwebs, is she? Might have better luck with carrier pigeon.'

'Ha! Or a phone number. She wrote it in the book,' he smiles as I pull at the little bow on a second smaller package, *Rip rip.*

Jaw. Drops.

.

.

'Awww, that's beautiful,' Hannah smiles as I hold the silver butterfly necklace up against the sun. The same one I've seen hanging around Indira's neck every day in Goa.

'It's her favourite. Can't believe she's sent it to me.'

'Well you always were her favourite,' Dawn says, which makes me blush a bit.

The gifts couldn't have come at a better time; they serve as a gentle reminder that all is not completely crap. I open the leather book and begin flicking through the petal-textured pages. Some adorned with photos, others with little poems scribbled willy-nilly down margins. There are some funny drawings of Nandi the cow (with giant udder) and a good few recipes too, like dahl pancakes and roti, in fact all the dishes we cooked together. It's wonderful. The kind of gift people don't really give anymore. Thoughtful. Irreplaceable. One of the few keepsakes you'd race into a burning building to save. I hold it to my chest.

Ahh, I do miss that lady!

She'd have something to say about all this boob-gate nonsense, I'm sure. I can almost hear her now, 'Tut tut, Ava! Worrying only zaps today of its joy.'

I close the book. Who am I to argue with that?

Byron Bay is putting on quite a show. This place doesn't just excel in the beach-and-chill department, the tucker is pretty damn bonza too. So we head into town for a spot of lunch. The main street is buzzing, full of quirky little cafes, gift stores and boho boutiques selling handmade clothes and jewellery. It feels so relaxed here and I'm happily embracing the laid-back vibe, even giving the shoeless thing a go for all of three minutes, before I step in something slimy and retreat into the safety of my flip-flops. 'Yeah, nah. Good effort!' Tom laughs as he plants another little kiss on Dawn's cheek.

The lovebirds literally cannot keep their hands off each another and I secretly delight in all their loved up interactions: the giggling, the coy looks and knowing smiles. They are walking, talking exemplars of the 'honeymoon period', that most revered stage in the relationship cycle that typically lasts two years, three if you're lucky. You can spot couples in the honeymoon phase a mile off. They have that blissed out look, a dizzy delirium that nothing or no one can spoil. Not missing the train or getting soaked in the rain; not even a long wait at Starbucks for their mocha-choca-latte of a Monday morning.

Dawn has that look.

She is positively blooming. Her once hunched shoulders are now firmly pulled back, giving rise to new power boobs. 'I can't lie, Ava. It's the love of a good man,' she tells me as we sit down to eat. Not before time. I am famished.

'This is one of my favourite places in Byron. They use locally sourced ingredients. You have to try the dahl, it's almost as good as Indira's,' Tom smiles. *Fighting talk indeed.*

'Sold!' I declare, slamming the menu shut.

It's a lovely place, 'Karkalla' it's called. Rustic vibe with nice plump cushions you could easily fall asleep on. This has to be one of the best things about travelling – sampling the local cuisine. I sit back, relishing the look of unbridled joy on the faces of my fellow diners as they devour their first delicious mouthfuls. *Food euphoria!* Eating is so much more than a survival thing; it's a pleasure, a glorious indulgence that like most things in life is best shared. Be it an *amuse-bouche* at a fancy bistro or a slice of pepperoni pizza. A shared meal just tastes better. It can forge relationships, bury anger, provoke laughter. My tummy elicits a gurgle of approval as I tuck into the famous dahl plus lots of other yummy dishes: saltbush, lemon myrtle and karkalla, a native succulent 'used as medicine too' our waitress says. Big tick. Gobbles double portion.

'So, what do you think of my hometown, Ava? Can't wait to hear what you're gonna write in your blog,' Tom asks, clearing his plate.

Hannah instantly looks up, 'Oh, I didn't know *you* were writing a blog.'

'Oh, didn't you?' I say with feigned innocence. 'Thought I said…'

'Yeah, nah, it's pretty popular Han,' Tom gushes. 'My sisters are all over it. We're up to the Mardi Gras bit. So funny. *Around the World in 80...* '

'Noooo! Not that *80 Gays* one, the one Carole was on about?'

'Err, maybeeee!'

I feel myself blush as Dawn piles in on the admiration session. 'Ave has got lots of followers, you know! Of course, she's far too modest to talk about it. Always hiding her light under her bush.'

'So I see. Well, I'm defo checking it out now! Wonder if we'll make the cut?' Hannah winks.

Cue flashback to mermaid sex scene, salty kisses and 'final thrusts of carnal elation'. Cringe. Cringe

The embarrassment must be written all over my face as Dawn leans in and whispers, 'You OK, Ave?'

'Urghh, just a bit worried, you know, that more and more people are going to find out the blog is me, that's all.'

'Oh, right. Well, we won't tell anyone else, pinky promise! You're not angry Tom mentioned it to Hannah, are you?

'No, course not... Hannah's cool. It's just, well, I'd hate Scarlet or anyone back home to know it's me. There's lots of personal things in that blog and everything's still pretty raw.'

At this point, Dawn takes me off to the ladies toilet for a stern talking to. Don't cry over spilt cream and something about bolting donkeys is the gist of it, followed by a much more effective piece of advice.

'Well, you know what Indira always says, "Don't stress the *What-ifs.*" '

Good point, well made and after a quick hug we head back to the table in time for some wonderfully distracting news.

'Oh, guys. I've been offered a job here in Byron,' Hannah says excitedly. 'Looks like you can't get rid of me quite yet Tom!'

'Really! *You got the job!* Amazing!'

'Yeah, they just mailed me now. It's only a small practice, which will be perfect.....Shit! They want me to start next week!'

'Wow, that's fast.'

'Not fast enough if you're a sick wombat,' Dawn adds earnestly. The joyous news is to be celebrated with a G&T back at our villa. Rude not to.

It's a decent walk, so Dawn gets to quiz Hannah on all things animals, namely the duration of pig orgasms. 40 minutes, she read on Google. Hannah cannot confirm, but we concur that anything in that ballpark would be most agreeable.

Upon arrival, Tom and Hannah head to the garden to talk Aussie, while the poms descend upon the delicious-looking plate of biscuits sitting on the breakfast bench, labelled 'Eat me!'.

'Ooooh! Vegan *and* gluten free,' Dawn grins as I read the accompanying note. ' "Love from Moon. Kiss kiss.*"* Awww, that's sweet of her!'

She passes me the plate and we're soon tucking into one, two, then five when Hannah and Tom wander back in, pink from the heat.

'Hannah, Tom! You have to try these cookies! They are splendid,' Dawn grins, reaching for another.

'Oh wait,' Hannah says. 'Not the ones Moon left?'

'Yep…'

'She said to go easy on them, guys. They're pretty trippy.'

'Really? They taste normal to me,' I say, as my eyeballs start to throb. 'Do they taste normal to you, Dawny?'

'Oh yes! Perfectly normal! Perfectly normal indeed.'

.

.

45 MINUTES LATER…

'Oooh! Aren't fingers *cooooooooool*?' Dawn grins, completely mesmerized by her own hand. 'And toes! Toes are cool too.'

Throws off flip-flops. Wiggles feet in air

Around the World in 80 Gays
"Tripping the light flan-tastic"

'Yummy cookies, yummy, yummy cookies!'
Bahhahahahahaha!
What happens next can only be described as a scene straight from *Alice in Down-Under-Land*. Our peaceful little zen garden

starts to transform magically into a full-on enchanted forest. Lime green vines curling their way to life like mythical serpents, while the once slumbering buds explode into bloom, sprouting petals every colour of the rainbow.

'Wow! It's just like *Avataaaaaaaaar*!'

'Yeah, but without the funny blue people!' Donna gasps, pointing excitedly into the space behind me. 'Look, look!'

I spin round to behold one of the cane chairs magically rising from the floor, its long, curved back splitting into two to form giant psychedelic wings. Butterfly wings and then, *POP*, a human head!

'*Singrita!* Is that you?' I beam, mesmerized by the familiar red bindi on her forehead.

The creature inclines its head. 'Namaste,' she says. 'Oh, wow! Namaste to you too. I've missed you, my friend. I've missed you so much.'

She gives an elegant nod and *WHOOSH,* two other butterflies appear by her side, both equally radiant and looking scarily like my aunty and my mother. *OMG!*

Singrita beats her great wings, 'Come! It is time to rise up! Liberate yourselves from the shackles of self-doubt!'

Powerless to resist, we follow the formidable matriarchs onto the main street which has miraculously transmuted into a full-on Dali painting. The grey concrete buildings are now fabulous cakes – bright, fluffy sponges five or six stories high, flapjacks as wide as lorries, even a giant Jaffa Cake soaked in the finest French cognac.

I take a lick, 'Ooh yum,' as we skip over to the most spectacular waterfall I've ever seen (the kid's fountain on main beach) and then to the Ocean of Rainbows (rock pool, next to the 7-Eleven).

'WOW! Just wow!' Donna marvels, as we curtsey before the Mermaid Queen sitting atop a gleaming emerald throne. 'Your Majesty!' she whispers.

The Queen gives a flick of her tail before turning directly to me, 'Beware the colour red and an unexpected message.' I give another little curtsey before we take our leave and swim out to a huge floating toothbrush a few miles out. Donna gives a smile of recognition and courageously mounts the thing with a masterful,

'Floss me, floss me harder.' The ecstasy is real, but alas short-lived and two seconds later she is spectacularly thrown off and we are back once again on the cool, wet shoreline. 'Fuuuuuck! That was some trip!' *BOING BOING BOING!*

'Oh, what now? No more flossing... I'm red raw!'

We sit bolt upright, squinting at the horizon as a wobbly pink blob starts to take shape.

BOING BOING!

It bounces closer and closer, getting larger by the second, until Donna lets out an almighty gasp,

'IT'S A... IT'S A...'

BOIIIIIIINGGGGGGGGGGGGGGGGG!

'GREAT. BIG. TIT!'

WTF!

I look to my left to behold a second boob, even bigger than the first bounding over, 10 feet tall, DD for danger!

'Look out, Don!' I shriek, throwing her to the floor as the giant mammaries bounce over our heads in a carefully coordinated attack. *BOING BOING!* We brace ourselves for a second wave and before I can say 'big, erect penis'... *BOOM,* one appears!

Donna's eyes all but pop out of her head.

'Holy shit! That's a big one,' she guffaws as the B.E.P looms over us, like a drunk one-eyed monster. I wrap my arms around its mighty girth.

'Get back, get back you beast! *IT'S TOO BIG! IT'S JUST TOO BIG!'* I strain, knowing I'm but seconds away from being spectacularly cock-crushed, and then...

'DAR DAR DAR DAR DAAAR, DAR DAR DAR DAR DAAAR....'

The rousing theme of "Ride of the Valkyries"! It's Singrita and her winged sisters!

They align themselves in perfect battle formation. 'Stand aside girls!' Aunty commands. 'Singrita! Sis! You take the tits, leave that cock to me!'

She gives a little wink, leaping upon the beast legs akimbo, while Singrita and my mum pelt the giant boobs with a bumper bag of M&M's.

SPLAT! SPLAT! POW!

What valour. What utter gung-ho'ery!

They swoop in again and again, unleashing their chocolate bombs...and then after four or five attempts, they land a perfect hit.

BOOOOOM!

'They're going down!' Singrita cries, as the great tits spectacularly tumble to earth like a pair of mighty redwoods.

KABOOOOM! KABOOOOM!

We can barely contain our joy.

'Ding dong the tits are dead!' we chant as Singrita hovers above the doomed penis which is wobbling and teetering, and wobbling some more, and then KABOOM... it too flops to the ground.

Hoorah!

I gaze up at the winged heroes as Singrita smiles down at me.

'Always remember, you are mightier than your fears, my child!' she grins. Then *whoosh,* just like that, all three vanish and we flop back on the wet, sticky sand utterly spent.

CHAPTER TWENTY – BIG NEWS AND SCAR TISSUE

'Travel doesn't become adventure until you leave yourself behind.'

– Marty Rubin

"Dreams are constructed from the residue of yesterday" or so clever Mr Freud said and, although he didn't mention hash-cookie 'dreams' per se, I'd wager they're also constructed from same said same "residue of yesterday". In other words, our brains are a bit like sofas. All the crap that gets dropped down the back has a nasty habit of coming back to haunt us – things we've done, things we've said, exes, trauma. It all gets moulded into one big snowball of head-fuckery, only to be lobbed in our faces when we least expect it.

'Are you alive?' a voice says. 'It's nearly 9.30.'

'Oh right, I've slept in.' I yawn.

'Yeah, 9.30 am on *Wednesday*!'

SORRY WHAT? WHAT THE HELL HAPPENED TO TUESDAY?

FML! A whole day has come and gone with zero participation from this girl! Good to know the world keeps on turning without me. #ExistentialistCrisis.

I go to get up, inducing a sharp pain in my hip area.

'Owwww! I feel like I've run a bloody marathon,' I wince, catching sight of a few random bruises, tell-tale signs of a good night, plus a handful of glittery stickers stuck to my person. I peel one off my forearm. 'Err, question. Why am I covered in kids' stickers?'

'That would be the mark of the, let me get this right, *mermaid tribe*,' Hannah laughs, handing me a glass of water.

'Huh?'

'The mermaid tribe! Don't you remember? Led by the beautiful and valiant Queen Miranda. You had quite the conversation with her!'

Cue flashback of mermaids, humungous sponge cakes and giant appendages

'Oh God, no! *The cookies*!! Was I a twat?' I cringe. 'Please tell me Dawn was too. I really need to not be the biggest twat in this story!'

She smiles and shows me a photo of Dawn in a white neck brace. 'Shiiiiit! What happened?'

'She got into a tussle with a pool noodle and lost. We took her to ER. But don't worry, it looks worse than it is.'

'That's awful,' I say, staring at the photo. 'So come on, anything else I should know? Any murders? Beheadings?'

'Well, there is one more thing…'

I hide my head beneath the covers.

'No more, please! I can't take it!'

'This is quite serious actually,' she says, her face dropping.

Dramatic pause

'I read your blog.'

'Oh. Right. I thought you might. And?'

A bead of sweat snakes down my forehead as she just sits there staring. The longer she stares, the more I get the idea that she's mad. Incensed even. Then she's… breaking into a Great. Big. Smile.

'Bloody hell Hannah, that was cruel,' I laugh. 'I was terrified!'

'Sorry.'

'So, did you, well, like it?'

'Like it? *I LOVED IT?* It feels really…I don't know…authentic I guess.'

'Really? And you read all the Sydney bit. Even the … you know…'

'Oh yeah, what was it? "Salty kisses and carnal thrusts?"'

'Oh don't! I don't write all that smutty stuff. It's our big editor. Sex sells and all that.'

'Ha! I thought it was kinda hot. Was thinking we could write some more scenes later,' she winks. 'Seriously though, you should be really proud. You and your friend have created something people are really connecting with. That's pretty special.'

'Aww thanks Han. That mean a lot.'

'I have to say one thing though. It strikes me as a bit odd that someone who speaks so much about personal growth and honesty would want to hide their identity. What is it you say – *speak your truth*?'

'Yeah but, come on. Would you want your mum to read all that sexy stuff. Yuk!'

'Mums are people too! Probably got up to far worse, partying in the 1970s.'

'Ewww, don't.'

'It's true. Besides, you can't live for other people. I'm with Dawn on this – don't hide your light under your bush,' she winks.

I sit for a moment.

'Guess so. Now, can we please get the hell out of this room? I've got bed sores!'

Inhaling one's own gases for 24 hours is not the healthiest thing, but fortunately Hannah has the perfect remedy, a post-trip trip to the famous Cape Byron Lighthouse! 'A bit of cardio will blow the cobwebs away,' she assures and, despite mild neck injury, Dawn and Tom come along too, albeit at snail's pace.

Poor Dawn! She has that forlorn look dogs have when forced to wear a post-op neck cone.

'I can't see my feet, Ave. I'm not sure I like it.'

'I know Dawny. I know.'

I have to say, it's a strange thing to see your friend in a big white neck brace. Alarming, yet also just a teensy-weensy bit, well, HILARIOUS... especially when they have a name scrawled across the front of it, like when you break your leg at school.

'Errr, who the hell is Barry Gleeson. And why has he signed your collar?'

'Oh, funny story, Ave! Really funny! After I got out of ER, Tom took me for ice cream to cheer me up and we ran into Matt Damon.'

'No way! *Matt Damon*? Maybe Cruella will get her star content after all!'

'Yes. He's got a place here, beautiful house. Anyway, he was lovely. Much taller than I imagined. Bigger chin. I asked him to sign my collar like you do and, well, turns out it wasn't him after all. It was some guy called Barry

Gleeson! A builder or butcher, something beginning with b…' she ponders. 'Oh, those cookies, Ava, those *cookies*!'

The views from Cape Byron Lighthouse are worth all the pain. Breathtaking vistas over the rocky coastline and white sands snuggling up to the turquoise ocean. Perfect photo opportunity for the *80 Gays Insta blog*. I snap away while a pensive Dawn gazes out to sea.

'You OK?'

She turns stiffly towards me,

'Yes, was just thinking…who's your lighthouse?'

'Sorry, my what?'

'Your lighthouse. Everybody needs one,' she says rather philosophically. 'Someone to watch over you. It's comforting really. Tom's mine now. He looks out for me. Keeps me away from the rocks.'

I'm starting to think she might have had too much codeine, but as I stand beside her, watching the waves crash upon the jagged coastline, I can't help but appreciate the analogy. The idea of someone standing guard for you. Having your back.

'So, come on. Who is *your* lighthouse?'

I think for a moment, 'Oh, Jen, I guess. Or maybe you.'

The day is a bit of a go-slow and, after some much needed chill time at the beach, we head back to the villa. Just what the vet ordered, particularly for Dawn who is so bushed that she falls asleep in the hummus dip. Tom and Hannah head for an afternoon surf, so I use the opportunity to catch up on some blog notes. I'm running perilously behind at the mo, #ACrocodileAte-MyHomework.

As I put pen to paper, it hits me that my arrival down under has somehow triggered a shift in the cosmos. It's like a giant cog has started to turn and now everything feels a little, well, off kilter. Boob-gate, the swingers. I lay on the daybed, flicking through Indira's leather book. It's just beautiful. The feel of the handmade paper, all textured with crushed rose petals. I trace my fingers across her handwriting, feeling the indentations of the page. What is it about a person's writing? It's as if you're getting a glimpse into their soul. I follow the flourishes of her pen strokes, the big playful loops as energetic as her personality and I can almost hear her laugh. That big, contagious laugh. I turn to the inscription at the front:

'Everything will be alright in the end. If it's not alright, then it's not the end'.

John Lennon

I flick to her phone number and start dialling.

Ring ring, ring ring.

It clicks into one of those old school answer machines.

'Please leave a message after the beeping,' she says and I leap right into it.

'Indira! It's Ava, your favourite English girl! How are you? Thank you sooo much for the gifts. They are just beautiful. Can't believe you gave me your favourite necklace! I'm wearing it as we speak, well as I speak – you're not speaking. Ha! Anyway. Yeah. I hear you've left Nandi and the ashram. Hope all is OK. I'll try you again later. Big hugs.'

I hang up and my phone instantly chirps, like a hungry chick wanting a feed.

Probably more boob-gate nonsense. I have a quick scroll, only 75 new messages! Excellent! Things must be dying down. I flick to the latest ones – a couple from mum, and one from an unknown number. Might be a scam. Might be important. I take a chance and scroll to the name at the bottom.

.

.

Love Scarlet xx

CHAPTER TWENTY-ONE - 'S' IS FOR SCARLET. 'C' IS FOR COW

`'Wabi-sabi(noun.) Finding peace in imperfection.'`

A shark can detect a drop of blood from a quarter of a mile away, eagles can spot a rabbit at two; add to that list, exes – who can sense vulnerability across the other side of the planet. My finger hovers over her message and, poised to press, I remember something my Aunty B says, 'You don't have to show up to every argument you're invited to'. I put my phone down. Not today, Satan. Not today.

It's our last day as a cosy foursome in beautiful Byron and I fully intend to make the best of it. The morning starts well, refreshing swim followed by breakfast at a beach bar with pastel blue shutters overlooking the ocean. Dawn is much more chipper today. Her neck is loosening up and she's no longer walking like R2-D2 with piles. She gives us a quick demo.

'Look, guys! I can move it all the way to here now,' she says, eliciting a blood-curdling *cccc-runch* sound, which puts me right off my avo on toast. I nod and turn to Hannah.

'So, first day in the new job tomorrow. Exciting, hey?'

'Yup. Can't believe it's come round so fast. Was kind of getting used to a life of leisure,' she laughs.

'Ooh. I wonder what the first day is like for an Australian vet? Kangaroo surgery? Wombat whisker removal?'

'Err, try two sick cats. Oh, and I'm delivering a calf apparently.'

'No way! I love cows.'

'Ha! Good to know. And what about you guys?' Hannah says, turning to Tom. 'Off to the Blue Mountains? That'll be nice.'

'Yeah, reckon it will be good for Dawn to get some mountain air. Aids recovery,' he smiles.

'Awww, you're so caring but I'm fine, honestly,' Dawn insists, eliciting a second blood-curdling c-rrrrunch, which makes Hannah visibly wince.

'Make sure you go easy with that neck, Dawn. Lots of rest, hey?'

'Guide's honour doc!'

'Good! You know, it's a shame you guys are leaving. I have a little treat planned for Ava,' she winks. 'Would be fun for you to witness.'

'*Witness*? That doesn't sound good,' I quip, instantly terrified. 'What on earth is it?'

She goes to answer but is interrupted by Tom who explodes with laughter across the table.

'Sorry guys… Just been sent something about an incident at Byron's local swingers convention! So funny!'

'*Swingers convention?* What, here in Byron?'

'Yup. It's an annual event, apparently. All those years wasted,' he teases. 'Anyway, says here that some kinky couple got themselves stuck in an S&M entanglement with a waiter at a local hotel. 'He looks down at his phone again. 'They couldn't get out of the cuffs!'

I sit there waiting for the punchline.

'Is this a joke, Tom?'

'Yeah, nah. Swear to God. It's all here, look!'

He hands me his phone and I start reading aloud.

' "A Sydney couple were caught in a kinky frisson with a 32 year old employee of a popular Byron hotel …bla bla…After an ordeal that lasted over 28 hours, they were finally liberated when worried employers raised the alarm. Steve and Carole King of the Northern Beaches"…'

'OMG! Hannah! It's Carole and Steve…' I guffaw, showing her the phone. *'It's them!'*

'WHAT? Noo, it can't be!'

I read on, barely taking a breath.

' "The couple were found in surprisingly good spirits, explaining they managed to keep up morale by playing *I spy* and sharing stories from popular travel blog, *Around the World in 80 Gays*. Carole King *(39) commented, "We knew we could get through if we could just keep ourselves entertained!" The blog is currently number 10 in the Google travel chart and is written by a*

London woman whose identity is becoming a matter of great speculation. Current suspects include award-winning comedian Phoebe Waller-Bridge and TV presenter Holly Willoughby".'

No. Words.

'Shit, Ave! You don't get better advertising than that, ay?' Tom laughs, 'Bloody hell!'

'It's insane! I can't believe they actually gave us a plug.'

'*Butt plug* more like,' Dawn giggles. 'Sorry!'

I would laugh, but frankly this is all starting to get a bit real now. I feel like I'm being suffocated, like Gerald the python swallowing that poor wombat when we first arrived. I try to breathe, nice and slow in and out, and enjoy the rest of my coffee.

*

'That's it, keep pushing, girl!' Hannah shouts, elbow deep in a cow's birthing canal. That's not something you say very often. This afternoon's calving activity is not quite what I had in mind today. I was thinking more of a nice chill in our zen garden counting pebbles, but alas, best laid plans and all.

It's 32 degrees and we are at a small farm half an hour south of town. Hannah's new job has started unexpectedly early, rather like Bessie's labour pains. Evidently cows have little regard for HR contracts. Better still, the farmer has gone down with a nasty case of gastro, hence I have been promoted to emergency birthing assistant.

Poor cow!

The learning curve is steep.

The only thing I've ever delivered is a pepperoni pizza (thin crust) and then Jen had to help when I got lost in the one-way system. Bessie senses my nerves and looks on disapprovingly, 'Moooooooooo! Mooooooo!' I want to reassure her, tell her I'm a big hit in the cow community *just ask cousin Nandi*, but now doesn't seem like a good time. Not with a seven inch dilated cervix.

Mother-to-be is tethered to a fence and I'm down the 'exciting end' with Hannah, wishing I'd paid more attention in biology A level. Popping out a human sprog looks hard enough, but a 90 pound calf *with hooves*? Now, that's going to sting! Bessie lets out a second *mooooo* and it all starts to get very real, very fast. I peep through a semi-open eye to see one leg emerging.

'That's it…come on, girl! You're doing really well.'

'Thanks, Han!' I smile, buoyed by the much-needed encouragement.

'I was talking to Bessie!'

'Oh. Yes.'

Bessie lets out another maniacal 'Moooo!' while Hannah loops a rope around one hoof and takes up the slack. 'Moooo! *MOOOO!*'

'Right, Ava! Grab hold!' I take the rope between my sweaty palms and together, we give it a big old heave. A couple more inches of hoof appear.

'Oh God! Oh God!' I stammer as Hannah loops the other leg.

'And again, Ava! Pull….Pull.'

SWOOOOOSH!

Bessie promptly slaps me square in the nose with her tail. Think she wants this over with even more than I do.

'Right, let's try this,' Hannah says, producing what looks like a medieval torture implement from her medical bag. I instinctively cross my legs. 'Almost there, girl! Almost there!'

A few more moos and twists later, and then…*PLOSSSHHH!*

'Oh my God. *It's here! It's a cow baby! It's a…*'

THUD!

Faints face-first into big, fruity cowpat

*

In life, there are good afternoons and there are bad ones. This will most definitely be filed under *f'ing exceptional*, despite having cow dung up my nostril. *What an experience!* Today I got to witness the miracle of life and it only seems fitting that we partake of a celebratory drink to wet the cow baby's head.

'Cheers!' Hannah says, clinking my glass. 'We'll make a vet of you yet.'

'Ha! Thanks. D'you know, that has to be one of *the* best experiences of my life! Not the fainting bit – that sucked. But, seriously, Han. WOW! *Just… WOW!'*

'Awww. Glad you enjoyed it.'

'I wouldn't say *enjoyed* exactly! But I mean, you were, well, amazing. You brought a new life into the world,' I start to get a bit choked. 'Imagine that, a brand-new life. A blank sheet, untainted by stupid mistakes and…' I stop speaking, feeling like a bit of a fool.

'You OK, Ava?'

'Yeah, ignore me. Just things playing on my mind. *Urghhhh! Silly cow!* Scarlet, I mean, not Bessie!'

Hannah leans across the table, bringing her hands together like she is about to say something profound. 'OK. Here's a question for you. If you could go back and undo things with Scarlet, never have met her. Would you?'

Like I said, something profound.

My mind is instantly flooded with all things Scarlet. Her piercing blue eyes. Her cute lip curl. Sunday morning lie-ins. Drunken nights dancing around the lounge in our undies. Happy times.

'Oh, I've thought about it, believe me. When we first broke up, I thought of nothing else. I used to fantasize about not walking into that bar that first night. Not laying eyes on her. But now…' I pause.

'Now?'

'Well, if I undid the whole Scarlet thing, I'd undo all the good stuff too. This incredible travelling adventure, the amazing people I've met, even the blog! None of it would exist without her. Not one wonderful, crazy moment. Mad, hey?'

'It is a bit. I guess it's like birth in that way. If you take away the excruciating pain, you take away the joy too.'

Dawn and Tom rock up a bit later, eager to hear the ins and outs of our birthing experience and, after a few minutes of forensic-style description, Dawn goes a deathly pale, rather like she did on the minibus the first time I met her. We quickly change the topic.

'So, did you get hold of Indira?' Tom asks.

I flick through my texts again, 'Nah, not yet. I left another message, so fingers crossed.'

Have to say I'm having a rather strange relationship with my phone at present. You might say we're 'on a break'. I've switched it to mute and have mastered the art of selectively peeping at messages. It's a bit like a game of Russian roulette; I only check the ones I think are safe.

The afternoon runs away with us and pretty soon it's sunset and we're heading down a decadent path of seafood, champagne and shots. I willingly go unto my fate. 'One tequila, two tequila, three tequila, floor!' the barman laughs, overfilling our glasses again.

'Bet he's used that line before,' Hannah quips as we bob down to bar level to syphon up the overspill. Everyone except Dawn that is, who due to neck brace situation has fashioned herself a giant straw so as not to miss out. *Slurp slurp!*

'So....relationshits, I mean relationships...' I slur, waggling my index finger in the air.

'No. You were right the first time,' Hannah laughs.

Massive outburst of giggles*

'Yeah. No, what is it with them? I mean, it's never easy is it? Never. Like, you can have the two most compatible, lovely people, who fall hopelessly in love and then after a few months or years ...*boom!* It all goes to crap. Present company excluded of course,' I say looking at Tom and Dawn. 'You guys are just making us look bad.'

'Sorry! Not sorry,' Dawn laughs, hugging her man.

'Actually, maybe it's just me who's cursed. Even my bestie seems to be all ...*cosy cosy* with her new lady. Think I might be a bit, well, relationship defective!'

'Nah, I don't think so. No relationship is perfect, Ava. And that's OK. What's it called – wabi-sabi'

'Wasabi?' Dawn quizzes. 'Don't you have that with sushi?' *Hic!*

'Noooo! *Wabi-sabi.* the joy in imperfections. Think it's a Zen Buddhist thing.' Tom smiles. 'We learnt about it at school.'

'Wow, cool school! We just learnt about Winston Churchill and the life cycle of a frog!' I laugh.

'Ha! Well, I reckon it all comes down to compatibility,' Hannah says profoundly. 'Choosing the best fit. Not the most fit.'

'Ooooh, I like that, Han. Might use it in the blog.'

BEEP! BEEP!

Phone alert.

'Oh cool, maybe it's Indira.' I squint to read the words that are bouncing around the screen like a drunk aunt at a wedding. The letters gradually settle. Notification: 1 new email.

From: Scarlet Tennison.
Subject: Hello.

#BulletInTheChamber.
I stare down at her name shamelessly sitting there in my inbox. Unsolicited. Uninvited.

Scarlet Tennison.
Scarlet Tennison.

The letters start to leap out of the screen, jumbling and reforming before my drunken eyes, rearranging themselves into new words, anagrams like *'Careless' 'Inconstant'*. Amazing what's hidden in a name. Red flags, warnings; they were there all along. I close my eyes and next thing I know, I'm doing it. I'm clicking on it and opening Pandora's box...

Dear Ava,

I imagine I'm the last person you wanted to hear from, but truth is, I couldn't live with myself if I didn't try one more time.

The last few months have been a whirlwind, but now I'm waking up from the mess I've created and realising what I've done. I've made a terrible mistake and I've broken it off with Carla. It's over.

I just want an opportunity to talk to you. Please believe me when I say that I've regretted my actions ever since that awful night. I've been a fool. An absolute fool.

I miss you. I miss us. More than that, I love you and I never stopped.

Scarlet xxx

CHAPTER TWENTY-TWO –
HER ROYAL HIGHNESS

'Sometimes a change of perspective is all that
is needed to see the light.'

– Dan Brown

"Tis an ill wind that bloweth no good" as the proverb goes and I awaken to an upbeat voicemail from my mum on this, the last day of my Byron Bay adventure. The message is overflowing with 'dears' and 'darlings' and there's even a nod to me being her favourite child, which hasn't happened since 2002 when my brother graffitied a giant phallus on the local chip shop wall.

In a bizarre twist of fate, the Mardi Gras incident has given my mum unexpected street cred at her book club, and Ms Emmanuelle Salisbury OBE, founder member and celebrated local gay, has asked her to become club secretary! 'Imagine that Ava. Me being asked by an OBE! An O-B-E, no less!'

Perhaps Jen was right, things are soon forgotten, well, most things. The other gargantuan item on my worry list, namely *that email*, is still very much front of mind. *Why did I do it? Why did I open that bloody message?* One word: tequila. Still, what is known cannot be unknown, especially when aforementioned email has been read aloud to the patrons of a Byron Bay beach bar several times over! *FML!* They were all rather invested, has to be said, and after a quick poll we ended up with a 50-50 split between 'Give her another chance' and 'Tell her to go f*** herself, the cheating cow.'

'Well, you know what I think,' Jen says, as we commence a long overdue FaceTime. It's 8 pm there and the London office is pretty much deserted, aside from Jen and Cheryl from Accounts, who has had a perm. Brave choice.

'I mean, I still can't believe she emailed you. The cheek! You'd think she'd get the message after you ignored her text.'

'You'd think! But, hey, you know Scarlet. Persistent.'

'Bullish more like. How about arrogant?'

We sit for a moment.

'It is weird though, hey? That she decided to get in contact now, with all this blog stuff going on. It's like everything is happening all at once,' I garble, 'And did you know she's broken up with Carla?'

'News to me. Look, just don't let her get under your skin, Ave. You've come so far – new career, new carefree you. She can't hurt you!'

'Yeah. You're right, I guess…'

'Err, when am I not?' she winks. 'Don't love anyone who makes you feel ordinary, girl.'

I smile and take a big swig of coffee. 'So, anyway. What did you want to talk to me about, Jennifer? Sounded urgent. Something about *80 Gays?*'

'Oh, yeah. Actually, don't worry about that now. It's just people speculating, you know what it's like…'

'Speculating? About what? Not about the identity of the author?' She doesn't respond.

'Look, we can talk about it when you get to Cape Town. Sooo jel! I've always wanted to go on safari, see all those exotic animals. It's going to be amazing…lions, buffalo, rhino…'

With that, an equally exotic creature comes lunging at the screen.

Shit, Cruella! Stealth attack! Must escape!

'Ava daaarlink! How are the devil are you?'

'Oh, hi Lucrezia! How nice to see you.'

'Ditto. Loving your work. Figures just in. The blog is up 500% week on week. *Fantastico news!* Shareholders v happy. Moi v happy! This is better than snorting Himalayan cave dust!'

'Oh, err, right! Didn't know you could snort Himalayan cave dust.'

'Darlink, you can snort *anything*,' she says exploding with laughter. 'Anyway, back to the blog. Now is the time to amplify, diversify. Ampli-ver-sify! *We need this thing to go big!* Let's lock in a little powwow, discuss some ideas.'

'Oh no! *Crackle, crackle.* I can't hear you, Lucrezia!' I say, fake hissing into my phone. 'I'll call you *hissssss* another time! Byeeee.'

Disconnects and flops back on bed

Pheww! That was close.

I'm not really in the mood for an editorial ambush today, especially not with that face! Not sure if it was the camera but boy, Cruella has overdone the lip fillers this time! You could unblock sinks with those things. #PlungerGob.

I lie for a moment, idly flicking through my phone, looking at the photos from last night. What a collection! Like most evenings out they start off well enough, elegant shots by the bar and dreamy sunset huddles, before quickly descending into lots of silly drunk faces where everyone looks like they've had a stroke.

The last supper with Tom and Dawn was a tear-free occasion, softened by the tequila and fact that we'll be reuniting in the UK in a few weeks. It's been great having them here, a wonderful distraction and now they've gone, I fear Scarlet's email will eat away at me, penetrate my armour. I try to fight it, but I open the email again.

I miss you. I miss us. More than that, I love you and I never stopped. Scarlet xxx

Her words are even more impactful in the cold light of day, with no booze to dampen the blow. They circle round and round in my mind. Words like 'sorry', 'I miss you', 'regret'. And then, the full gamut of human emotion is unleashed. Shock. Anger. Happiness. Resentment. Most terrifying of all, I can feel myself getting drawn in again, like some dim-witted fish nibbling at a shiny lure. *Pathetic Ava! Absolutely pathetic. How can you be bewitched by a few carefully chosen words?* That's all they are – words. But then, what if she really means them? What if she is genuinely remorseful?

What if, what if?

Hannah arrives just in time to avert my emotional nosedive.

'All good?' she asks, still wet from her morning surf. She takes one look at my face and gets her answer. 'Oh, right. Wanna talk about it?' she says, stroking my hair back. I promptly shake my head and lift my face into the sun.

'Nope! I wanna forget about everything and enjoy my last day with you if that's OK?'

'Good answer. So, like I said, I've got a bit of a surprise planned for you later.'

I look at her; half terrified, half intrigued.

'Really? I'm rather partial to surprises and when I say *partial*, I mean I hate them!'

'Oh well. Let's hope this is the exception, the surprise to change it all!' Her eyes grow wide with excitement. 'So…I've booked us…… drum roll…'

'Booked us?'

.

.

The tension grows.

.

.

'A paragliding trip!'

'Sorry, what?' I laugh, 'Could have sworn you just said *paragliding trip*!'

'I did! Well, you did tell me this whole adventure was about facing your fears. So yeah, you're welcome! Just see it as one last hurrah before you head off,' she smiles, tucking a crumpled leaflet into my vest top.

'Umm, it could very well be my last hurrah, period! Shit, Hannah! I'm just not good with heights!'

'All the more reason to do it. Fortune favours the brave, hey? All the info is on the leaflet. I'll meet you there at 2 pm; I've got to inseminate a sow this morning.'

And just like that, any regrets I've been harbouring about not becoming a veterinarian vanish into the air.

Since I have time to kill, I head down to the pool for a quick *pre-shit-yourself-at-2000-feet dip.* I can't quite believe I've agreed to this insanity! Para-bloody-gliding! *Me!* Still, anything to take my mind off the dreaded S-word. I accept a meeting request from Cruella, before googling testimonials about paragliding which range from "best thing ever" to "thought I might die".

I promptly turn off my phone and dive into the pool, leaving it all to fate.

*

The outdoor activity centre is 30 minutes away and I arrive to find Hannah, aka the Sperminator, waiting outside primed and ready for action. Conditions are perfect: clear blue skies and the windsock is blowing at just the right angle, according to the athletic-looking flight instructor who greets us. 'I'm Emelie,' she smiles, lifting her *Top Gun* sunnies. 'Come on in!'

She's a local woman, mid-thirties and we head straight into the air-conditioned office which all feels very professional. Five stars on Tripadvisor – I had D.I. Dawn do some checks. She texted the following intel along with photo of her eating a massive vegan pie in the gorgeous Blue Mountains.

```
Ave. It all checks out ok. Lots of rave reviews. It's
run by a local family, plus an Italian. Doesn't say
how many people have died though. Have fun xx
```

So that's reassuring.

Hannah is super relaxed as usual. I, on the other hand, have taken on the role of her mute companion, making appropriate grunts only when absolutely necessary. This seems to be my M.O. in stressful situations, I've realised. I internalise, hence Scarlet used to run rings around me in arguments.

'Here you go,' Emelie says, handing us a clipboard of insurance papers. I mean, does anyone actually read this stuff? It's like when you download an app and get inundated with pages and pages of terms and conditions that you just tick, willy-nilly, not knowing if you've just given away your firstborn. Emelie must sense my trepidation as she smiles at me very sweetly and says, 'First time, Ava?'

'Oh no, I've been scared lots of times!' I joke, signing away my right to sue should I splatter to my untimely death. Emelie gets on the phone and pretty soon the other instructor arrives. He's not nearly as athletic looking – mid forties, Italian. Little pot belly and no neck.

'Ciao, I'm Marco,' he smiles, munching on a cheese toasty, most of which is stuck in his beard. 'So, let's work out who will fly with who.'

Please let me be with Emelie. Please let me be with Emelie.

'Ava, you'll be with me. And Emelie will take Hannah. Gooda?'

'So gooda,' I lie. 'So gooda.'

And breathe...

My disappointment is soon shrugged off as we settle back for a 30 minute instructional video followed by a final safety drill. That's when it all gets very real. Very fast. First challenge, the harness. A strappy contraption with lots of lines and carabiners, the kind of thing you might find in Carole and Steve's wardrobe. After a couple of 'wrong hole' entries I'm in!

'So Ava, are you defo up for this?' Hannah smiles, 'You can change your mind you know.'

'No, no, I want to,' I enthuse, inspired by a wall of stunning aerial photos and happy faces snapped mid-air. Just before impact.

Stop it Ava! Pull yourself together!

'You girls ready?' Emelie asks, as I give a stoical nod and hobble out to the take-off area. It's a grassy ramp, twenty feet long perhaps, running downhill. Looks easy enough. Two brightly coloured chutes are being laid out by the flight assistants who utter a friendly 'G'day'. Talk about your life in their hands! I watch them fastidiously, looking for signs of intoxication. So far, so good. No whiff of Jack Daniel's. I give an enthusiastic grin, before being instructed to stand in front of Marco while he gets attached to the main chute.

'OK Ava?' he says, connecting himself to me.

Clunk, click. I feel sick!

'They go first, we go after OK?'

'OK.'

We stand in position as Hannah and Emelie start their run; Hannah in front, Emelie behind, blue sky above. They take a few gazelle-like strides down the ramp and then, *whoosh!* The Cape wind scoops them up and they are at once airborne, gliding like a majestic eagle! 'Wohooooo!' Hannah shouts, waving manically from the air. 'This is amaaazing!'

Well, that looked easy. Now it's our turn.

'OK. We run in three, yes?'

'Fuck no!' My inner voice replies.

Of course, I say no such thing, giving a compliant thumbs up as my Norfolk heart thumps out of my chest. *Kaboom. Kaboom. Kaboom.*

'Right. Three, two, one… *Run!*'

I'm like a hare out of a trap as my little jelly legs power down that ramp. One step, two steps, three steps….five. Shit, *it's not happening!* Seven, eight, nine…*Come on wind, take me now!* And then… *WHOOSH! We're up!*

Holy Fuuuuuuuuck!

The upward lift propels my guts into my mouth whilst triggering internal safety mode, in other words, my eyes slam shut and praying bowels do the same. All I can hear is the sound of my own heart, Marco's commentary and the odd 'whoop' from Hannah, as she swoops past, living her best life. Lord, that woman is fearless!

'You OK, si?' Marco shouts and I give a nod as he tugs at the lines, propelling us sideways, before making another tighter turn to the right. I won't lie, I'm not feeling the most relaxed right now. It feels a bit like being on a rollercoaster whilst dangling from a bedsheet on strings. Kind of. As the air rushes over my face and the chute does its thing, it starts to feel better; peaceful even. And next thing I know, I'm half-opening an eye.

Oh wow! I'm flying, I'm actually flying!

A few minutes later, I have the other eye open and I'm gazing through my dangling legs at the turquoise ocean and bright white beaches. It's breathtaking. My confidence grows with every whoosh as I peer left and right, trying to take it all in. What a sight! It's like Legoland down there. Lots of tiny stick people going about their stick people lives. Some walking to the ocean, some playing catch, others lounging on tiny towels beneath equally tiny parasols. Life sure does look different from up here! Everything is so small and well, insignificant. As we soar in the open sky, with no sound but the rushing air, I start to appreciate why Jen had urged me to come away all those months ago. Perspective. It's all about getting perspective. I open my lungs and holler 'Thank you Jen! Thank yoooouuuuu!'

The next ten minutes, well, fly by.

We are lifted upon a massive thermal, soaring high over local beaches and bushland, round past the famous Cape Byron Lighthouse which presides over the rocks below. It's at this point that I realise Marco's on-board commentary has stopped and he doesn't seem to be pulling on the lines much either. Lazy bugger!

'Marco?'

No answer.

'Helloooo Marco? You OK there?'

Complete. Radio. Silence.

.

.

And then it hits me…

He's dead! He's actually bloody dead!

This is not feeling very relaxing anymore and I feel my chest start to tighten. Really tighten. I try giving him a little prod.

'MARCOOOOO!'

Still nothing.

I've witnessed this kind of high altitude headfuckery on the Discovery Channel. Pilots expiring mid-flight, passengers being forced to land planes using only Wikipedia and an iPhone. All very exciting from the comfort of your armchair, but it feels a little different when it's actually you.

I start gesticulating at Hannah. 'HANNAH! HANNAH!' I yell, but she misinterprets my frantic signing as an 'Isn't this wonderful?' wave and bellows back 'Yeah, great isn't it! Wooohoooooo!'

NO, HANNAH! IT'S NOT BLOODY WOHHHOOOOOO!

'MARCO!' I screech, elbowing him hard in the ribs. 'MARCOOOO!'

Heavy breathing. Faint snoring.

Excellent! So, we're losing altitude by the second and the only person who knows how to fly this bloody thing is having a power nap!

FML!

We start to descend, dropping in a big downward spiral. The ground is getting steadily closer and all the little people I was marvelling at earlier no longer look quite as little.

Desperate situations call for desperate measures, so I reach behind me, promptly giving his gnocchi the mamma mia of all squeezes.

'MARCOOOOOO, WAKE THE FUUUUUCK UUUUUUP!'

He suddenly jolts to life, uttering a casual 'Allora,' as if nothing has happened. A few robust yanks on the ropes and we start to slow.

Thank God!

'Here we go…Nice and easy!' he beams, as a last minute sidewind scoops us up and deposits us in the middle of the local market atop a big wooden sign saying 'Organic vegetables'.

'Grazie, Marco!' I smile, legs akimbo on the letter 'V' for Vagina. 'Grazie very much.'

Around the World in 80 Gays
"The perspective from paradise"

Some things in life bring clarity. Travel is one; loss is another; and a third might be dangling from dizzy heights with only a giant handkerchief to stop you plummeting to a bloody death.

Vastly different examples perhaps, but all three have one thread of commonality: they offer us a new perspective. Whether that be a literal one, courtesy of a white-knuckle paragliding adventure above Byron Bay, or by the sheer grace of being able to see things through someone else's eyes.

Truth is, perspective is *everything*.

It can make mountains of molehills and molehills of mountains. It can build empires, start wars and end marriages. A new perspective can alter our understanding of a situation – see us reject things we once held dear or embrace something we once feared.

It's like my aunty always says, 'The real power lies not in how things are, but in how we look at them. We see the world not as it is, but as we are'.

*

'*Narcolepsy!* Who'd have known?' Hannah giggles. 'Quite a rare condition, that one.'

'Not rare enough,' I quip, holding an icepack to my lady regions.

The drive back to our villa takes longer than anticipated and I can't help but feel a little cheated that my last afternoon here has gone so fast. So ridiculously fast that I now find myself in a characteristic rush to get to the airport. *Classic Ava!* Still, maybe it's a blessing, what with my well documented hatred of goodbyes.

Packing happens in a matter of minutes and I throw everything vaguely recognisable in my backpack: T's, bras, knickers, Hannah's sexy bikini (sorry, not sorry). And within 20 minutes, we're out the door and pulling up at Ballina Airport.

'Talk about cutting things fine,' Hannah smiles.

I look over at her. It's odd to think this person was a stranger 10 days ago and now it feels like I've made a friend for life.

'Oh Lord, I hate this bit,' I smile back, dipping my eyes.

'Me too. My grandad had a nice way of looking at it. He always used to say "There are no goodbyes, just see you down the road".'

'Ahh, I like that,' I turn towards her. 'Well Ms Surfing Vet, can't say it wasn't eventful, hey? You saved my life, got me birthing livestock and not to mention a great, big bruise on my lady bits! Shit, it hurts!'

'Ha! See it as a kind of souvenir, a little keepsake from Down Under…'

'A keyring would have been more conventional,' I laugh, as she helps me gather my bits.

'Well, Ava. I can honestly say you're the coolest person I've ever rescued from drowning.'

'Awww. That's nice,' I blush. 'And how many others have you rescued?'

'Just you!'

'Riiiight!'

She gives a little giggle.

'Only kidding! Enjoy South Africa and I can't wait to read all about it in the next instalment. I'm hooked now!'

'I'll do my best. And you enjoy, well, everything! Oh, and hope things work out…with Emma, I mean.'

She looks a little puzzled, 'Why do you say that?'

'Oh, I dunno. Think there might be unfinished business there. Would be a shame to not give it a go, hey? If you think there is a chance?' She gives a coy shrug.

'Maybe. Hey, this is going to sound really weird, but it was your blog that made me rethink things actually. That piece you wrote about not giving up.'

'Really? Wow, that's some pressure! Just promise me one thing – you won't sue me if it all goes tits up?'

'Ha! I promise! Though everyone will think I'm mad if I get back with her.'

'Pah! What was it you said to me, "You can't live for other people". You do you, girl!' I suddenly glance down at my watch, 'Shit! Gotta run. Text you when I get there.'

'Great! I'll see you down the road, Ava Roberts.' She smiles.

I hug her one last time and haul my bag off to the check-in zone.

Late as usual.

CHAPTER TWENTY-THREE -
AIRPORT. TERMINAL

'Bad news is bad news because it drops your
willingness to carry on.'

- Meir Ezra

Sydney International Airport, Transit.

'Shit, Ave! You've cut your hair off,' Jen remarks, mouth agape at the London office. It's 8.25 pm at Sydney International and I'm not looking my best. I jiggle a limp-looking ponytail at her.

'Noooo, it's all there…look,' I assure, attempting to spruce myself up ready for imminent blog summit with Cruella i.e. the woman who wears Stella McCartney to Waitrose.

'Phew! Thought you'd done a Britney on me, what with all the stress. So, how you doing?'

'Bit tired,' I say, having a glorious stretch.

'Can imagine. Another airport, another location. You're such a glam, transglobal super-blogger.'

'Ha! I don't feel like one. Still, only 15 hours of plane smells and I'll be touching down in Cape Town. Guess there are worse things.'

'Like getting a pleading email from your ex, you mean? I'd take the smelly plane any day,' she giggles. 'Did you reply yet or too busy dangling from great heights? I mean, paragliding. Who *are* you even? You *hate* heights!'

'No, I hate *falling*! There's a difference, Jennifer. D'ya know, I actually quite enjoyed it apart from the landing bit. Still a bit bruised.'

'Ouch! Well, I'm just glad you survived,' she says rather tenderly.

'Awww! Were you worried about me, Jennifer Jones?'

'Just a bit,' she blushes, shrugging it off. 'Anyway. How did the farewell go with Hannah? Did you sob uncontrollably?'

'Nah, it all worked out pretty well in the end. In fact, I think she might get back with her ex. You'll laugh, but she said it was partly because of the blog. That piece we wrote in India about the different ways people view love. It made her think about giving it another go.'

'Oh wow! Shit, Ave, this is all getting a bit scary, hey? "With great power comes great responsibility".'

'Is that Churchill?'

'No, Spiderman,' she grins, firing an imaginary web from her palm. 'It is weird though, hey? People seem really into it. Like, I was on the bus and this girl was reading it on her phone. Then yesterday I overheard some people talking about it in the supermarket queue. It's mad! I can't quite believe it's us.'

'Yeah, it is mad alright. And about to get a whole lot madder if Cruella has her way. What's this powwow about anyway?' I say, applying a quick coat of lip gloss.

' "Bigger, better, stronger" I think. Strap on in, girl! Shit, it's half past. Better dial her in.'

'*Urghhh!* Do I *have* to come? Can't you say I'm lost in the Australian bush?'

'Nope! Time to woman up, girl!'

With that, she starts fumbling with her phone and, after a series of beeps and mild expletives, the screen goes black. Perfect! I've evaded the torture after all, but then as if by magic, *poof*, Cruella appears in a cloud of smoke. Like, a literal cloud of smoke.

'Ciao! Just in my sauna releasing some toxins!' she coos. 'The pollution is killing my epidermis! Tell me girls, do you deep cleanse? I mean deep, deep cleanse? You simply *must*, darlinks. Skin and colon. I'll give you some numbers.'

She looks more than a bit ridiculous right now, dressed in a white Prada gown, her hair wrapped up like Norma Desmond ready for her close-up. We quickly lose visuals and have to train our ears to a disembodied voice midst the fog, before she wipes the camera lens with a squeak, and I catch a glimpse what looks like a manservant throwing water on the hot coals.

HISSSSSSSSSS!

'So yah, darlinks! Let's commence meeting, vis a vis *80 Gays*. We've pulled the latest data and it's all looking fabuloso!' she enthuses, flicking to a screen of graphs and pie charts, which like most graphs and pie charts do little for me. 'So, yah, we're now a *top three* Google travel blog, sponsorship fabuloso and we're resonating well with key demo plus millennials from Selsey with a penchant for Lewis Capaldi.'

Hisss! More water splashes upon the coals.

All the marketing spiel starts to make me feel dizzy and I stifle a second yawn before she finishes with the most disturbing image yet, 'In short, we've got the suits upstairs creaming, daaarlinks! *Creaming*!'

'Umm, that's great news,' Jen says, 'Really great. Think we're really tapping into our readership now. You know, content that really speaks to them.'

'Yeah,' I say enthusiastically. 'What she said.'

'Benissimo! Yah! Knew we'd be on the same page. That's why we need to push things further. Give that dial a nudge!' She gazes dramatically into the camera, her face haloed in a mystic haze. 'In short, we need to give them MORE!'

'Oh right, yes! More! Absolutely.'

I nod enthusiastically before plucking up the courage to ask, 'So….. what does *more* mean exactly?'

'Ava, daaaarlink! I'm so glad you asked. It's like this. Imagine yourself as a rocket, an utterly sublime rocket ship, orbiting the earth. Formidable. Dazzling. Unstoppable. And now….'

'Now?' I say, perched on the edge on my plastic airport seat.

'Now, it's time to go…*INTERGALACTIC!* Ava Roberts, let's strap in and ride that rocket ship *harder*!'

'Harder?'

'Yes darlink! More thrust! They want it. They really want it. Yes! Yes! Yes!' She is striking her wooden seat slats like a xylophone. 'They want, they want…'

'What do they want?'

'TO SEE YOUR FACE!'

Water strikes coals with a perfectly timed HISSSSSSS!

The mist eventually clears, revealing Cruella's nose pressed to the screen like a woman possessed.

'Well?'

'My *face*? They don't want to see my face. No, no, no! Use someone else's face. I'm happy being anonymous. It's working well as it is. Just look at all those graphic thingummies.'

Jen leaps in to back me up.

'Yes, I'm with Ava. The whole mystery angle is a good selling point – people love intrigue – I think that's a powerful tool.'

'It *was* a powerful tool, darlink. It *was*.'

'*Was?*' we say in unison.

'Yes. Past tense. Look, I'll cut to the chase; you've been outed!'

'Sorry, what?'

'You've been outed! Revealed. Exposed. Ava Roberts has been named as the mystery writer of *Around the World in 80 Gays: A Journey Through Heartbreak*!'

'*What? But how?*' Jen blurts, 'I knew people were talking, but how did it get out?'

'Cannot confirm, darlink. My guys have got their guys looking into it. Gossip? Data breach? Brought Hillary down in 2016 you know. Loose lips sink ships and all,' she says, pouting her overinflated ones. 'But one thing I do know is that this thing is like a great, big erection; it's not going to go down on its own. Not without some serious fluffing.'

'Err, this is sounding grosser by the minute. Why can't we just deny it like the politicians do. Deny, deny, deny! Or get someone else to front it. There are plenty of people out there who'd love to be famous, some influencer or something.'

'Non possiblo, I'm afraid. BUT, I can tell you what *is* possible, managing it. Using it to our advantage. Darlinks! I've engaged the best PR team in the biz. They will handle things from here: maximum effectiveness, minimum invasion of privacy. In fact, allow me to introduce the guru of PR, the puppet master himself, Mr Andre Untilli OBE!'

With that, a sweaty face emerges from the steamy haze. I assume Mr Untilli OBE has been there all along, as his designer suit is covered with designer sweat patches and he looks ready to combust.

'Enchanted to meet you, Ava and Jen. Enchanted,' he says theatrically. He's a camp, bald guy who looks a bit like Elton John. Without the piano. 'I'm a big fan of your work. HUUUGE fan. So be assured, nay, be confident,' he continues, his Chanel glasses misting up, 'that we are battling for you and we are going to ride this wave.'

'*Rocket!*' Cruella interjects, 'She's a rocket!'

'Oh yes, sorry. Ride this *rocket* and ensure that you don't burn up upon re-entry.' He smiles, clearly chuffed with the analogy.

I feel sick.

This is neither a rocket nor a wave. This is my worst bloody nightmare!

'So yah, darlink. Think we need to prepare for some media interest after the big reveal. Forewarned is forearmed as they say, so we're devising a plan for that, yah?'

Media interest? Not yah, Cruella. Not even in the slightest bit yah!

'Look, I err don't mean to be rude, but I need some time to digest all this,' I say, feeling utterly overwhelmed.

'But Avaaaaa daarlink, we need to...'

'No Lucrezia, we don't!'

With that, I hang up going into full-on protective mode, head in hands.

Everything I was most afraid of has bloody well happened. How is that possible? I feel like that great big cog is turning again and there's nothing I can do about it.

Beep! Beep!

Better not be Cruella again.

She needs to give me some space right now or I'm really going to lose it. I answer the call, rather agitated.

'Look Lucrezia, I really don't want to talk about this anymore, OK?'

Silence.

'Ava Roberts?' a voice says. An Indian voice.

'Indira? Is that you?' Talk about good timing. I can barely contain myself. 'Soo good to hear your voice. How are you?'

'No, dear. This is Indira's sister, Madhvi,' the voice says.

'Oh right….sorry, wow! You sound just like her,' I say, suddenly feeling a little uneasy. 'Is everything OK?'

'Ava, I'm so sorry to have to tell you this by telephone, but I have some sad news. Indira passed away yesterday evening.'

I put my hand over my mouth.

She carries on speaking, but her words just bounce off me like rain off an umbrella.

Words…words… and more words.

All getting jumbled up with the sounds of the airport: tannoys, kids screaming, loud conversations about nothing. Life carrying on as usual.

It's one big, ugly cacophony of sound and I feel sick.

'I know how much she enjoyed meeting you, her *butterfly girl* she called you. She wanted to speak to you herself, but sadly it wasn't to be. She'd been battling cancer for some time and …' Her voice trails off into silence. 'Ava? Are you there, dear?'

CHAPTER TWENTY-FOUR -
THE 'BUTTERFLOWN'

Around the World in 80 Gays
"A butterfly's wings"

It is said that when a butterfly flaps its wings, a typhoon happens on the other side of the world. But what if those beautiful wings didn't bring chaos and angry weather systems; what if they brought positive things – things like grace, accord and understanding? What if their gentle fluttering fanned the embers of hope, the first sparks of love, friendship, goodness and joy? Pure, unadulterated joy.

I think of my friend, of her vitality and grace.

Of that infectious laugh that left cheeks sore and tums aching in its wake, and I remember how brightly she shone. As vibrant as those constellations she would talk so passionately about in the ashram's garden every night.

How sad it is then, when a butterfly no longer flaps its wings.

CHAPTER TWENTY-FIVE – HIDEAWAY

'You may be given a cactus, but you don't have
to sit on it.'

- Joyce Meyers

Cape Town, South Africa

"It never rains but it pours" as they say and this is a cloudburst of epic proportions. A deluge of bad tidings cascading down upon me: Scarlet, the blog and now Indira. It's almost biblical! All that's missing is the damn plague of locusts.

Touchdown at Cape Town International had been a headfuck. An out and out headfuck. I dragged my sorry self through arrivals only to hear my name being called through the crowds, 'Over here Ms Roberts! Over here!' How kind, I thought, they've sent a courtesy bus, thus making the gargantuan error of calling back, 'Yes, I'm Ava Roberts'. Then *WHOOSH,* they were upon me. Photographers. *The locusts! The bloody locusts!*

OK, so there were only *three* of them, but that's still three too many and with every *SNAP,* every enthusiastic holler of 'Miss Roberts' I could feel myself becoming more and more overwhelmed.

It's a surreal feeling to suddenly find yourself the subject of media attention. Albeit minor. People you don't know shouting your name, grinning at you, people wanting to take your photo. Utter insanity.

Close to tears, I put my head down and steamed on through, desperate to get to the hotel. To sanctuary. 30 mins later, I got my wish.

Bath.

Wine.

Zzzzzzzzzzzzzzzzzzzzzzzzzzzz.

CHAPTER TWENTY-SIX - DO NOT DISTURB

Today is cancelled due to lack of interest.

.

.

We apologise for any inconvenience caused.

CHAPTER TWENTY-SEVEN - SHOCKS
AND SHARKS

'There is nothing better than a friend, unless
it's a friend with chocolate.'

- Linda Grayson

It's 9.30pm and I've been holed up in my hotel room for 27 hours now. I'm not feeling or looking my best: big, puffy eyes and hair that you could fry chips in. I know I should be out channelling my inner *Dora the Explorer* and taking in the wonders of Cape Town. However, my current mood has led me down a different path of discovery to the mini-bar, where I have befriended a tub of Ben and Jerry's and a nice bottle of shiraz. Misery loves company.

I can hear Indira's voice now, 'Tut tut, Ava. Tut tut. Such sniffling is most unbecoming.' Perhaps she's right, but fact is her passing at this tumultuous time in my life has knocked me for six. Like being winded by a particularly savage tackle on the footie field. It's as if my whole world is crumbling about me and collapsing into... One. Big. Tragic. Heap.

I didn't know Indira for long, granted, but the lady has left an indelible mark on me, like an inky tattoo. I met her just when I needed to. This big, warm blanket of kindness who wrapped herself about me. A counsellor, a friend, a teacher. She schooled me in the art of meditation and curry-making, showed me the joys of leg-licking cows and the splendour of the silver of first light.

I touch my necklace and raise my glass.

'I hope you're running through a field of butterflies, my friend. Here's to you. And yes, I know binge drinking was top of things *not* to do, but please indulge me this once,' I smile, quaffing my glass in one.

Bang! Bang!

Oh great! So the nympho neighbours are at it again! Just what I need. I curse at them through the paper thin walls. 'Give it a rest will you,' I holler, before pouring myself another wine.

Bang! Bang! Bang!

The distinct lack of panting leads me to conclude that the sound is not actually coming from the happy humpers at all, but from my own door.

A visitor. Really?

I bury my head in my pillow, but the knocking persists. And persists.

'OK, OK,' I snap, dragging my sorry arse to the door and flinging it back. 'What do…'

Jaw.

Drops.

To.

Floor.

'*JEN?* Oh my God….*JEN!*'

I stare at her. This glorious apparition with a bottle of plonk in one hand and packet of dark chocolate Kit Kats in the other.

'Shit here, isn't it?' she winks, pulling me into her arms.

The hug is everything, instantly soothing like a cup of tea. No, better than that, like home. The embrace feels like home. We stand like this for a few minutes before the inevitable happens, the floodgates burst and I start blowing snot bubbles over her nice, new Superdry hoodie.

'Ahh. Come on, Ave, it's OK. It's OK.'

'No, it's not. It's bloody rubbish. Really bloody rub-*snort*-bish. Everything has gone wrong. Everything. Oh, hang on…' My eyebrows suddenly pinch together. 'How can you be here? I was only talking to you yesterday in London.'

'Yep… London Heathrow Business Lounge,' she grins. 'Glad you asked. I managed to get in thanks to that air hostess I used to date. You remember, cute Kel with the killer cheekbones. Oh Ava, you should have seen me. On the massage chairs, at the champagne bar. I got so carried away I nearly missed the flight.'

She eventually comes up for air and plonks herself on the edge of the bed, snapping off a Kit Kat finger. 'Oh, I'm loving the eye makeup by the way.' *Munch munch.* 'Is that what they call the smokey look?'

Bahahahhahhahahahahahahahaha!

God, it feels good to laugh. Big, beautiful belly laughs that turn into snorts and blubs, then seamlessly back into laughter again.

'Ahhh. That's better. So good to see you smile,' she says, touching my hand. 'Seriously though. How *are* you doing?'

'Well, I've had better times.'

'Yeah. It's a lot, hey? I'm so sorry about Indira and then the bloody photographers. Perfect storm. But look, we can stumble through it together now and come up with a plan. Starting with this…' She hands me a plump white pillow from the bed.

'*A pillow?*'

'Not just any pillow, Ava Roberts. This, my friend, is my revolutionary *Stuff-it* therapy pillow, patent pending. *Dragons' Den* is all over it,' she grins. 'You basically imagine it's a problem or a person and then….*bam!* You smash the shit out of it. Here, have a go.'

'Oh no, I haven't got it in me, Jen.'

'Course you do. Smash it,' she says, giving it a good whack. 'Oh yessss! That feels good. Really good. Your turn.'

'Nah, I can't.'

'Avaaaaaa, come on. Have a hit!'

'No, really.'

'Av…'

WHAAAAAAAAAAAAAAAACK!

Punches Stuff-it therapy pillow (patent pending) across the room along with bestie Jen

.

.

'So, yeah, great…you seem to have got the hang of it,' she smiles, smoothing her hair back down. 'Knock yourself out. Cruella will cover any damages.'

'Urgggh! Don't mention that woman's name to me. I'm seriously all out of fucks!'

'I know. I know. It's a mess. A bloody mess. I made my feelings very clear after that summit call. Made some serious demands.'

'You did?'

'Yep. I told her that I was coming to see you and that she needed to sort this clusterfuck out pronto or no more blog!'

'Shit. That's fighting talk,' I say, suddenly inspired to strike the pillow again. One thump for Cruella and a second for life being a bit crap in general.

What release!

The therapy is surprisingly effective and after a few more rounds the session culminates in a drunken pillow fight with feathers bursting forth and raining down upon us like confetti. She looks at me with those big beautiful green eyes.

My lighthouse! My big, strong lighthouse.

'God, I've missed you, Jen. I really have mi…'

Face plants into pillow. Zzzzzzzzzz

*

The African sun streams into the room illuminating the most macabre of crime scenes: the gruesome massacre of a small family of ducks. God rest their souls. White feathers are scattered everywhere, on tabletops, across wardrobes, and I look over at the prime suspect snoring on the bed beside me.

She's here! Jen is really here!

She inhales some of the downy evidence and promptly sneezes herself back to consciousness. *ACHOOOOO!*

'Morning.'

'Oh, morning,' *Yawn yawn.* She takes a quick look around the room. 'Safe to say we got pretty plucked last night then,' she smirks, arching her back like a cat. She catches me looking. '*What?* Bad joke?'

'No worse than usual,' I quip, squeezing one of her gym toned arms. 'I was more looking at you, actually. Bloody hell, Jen! Someone's been working out.'

'What, me? Nah… not really.'

'Err, *yes really!* Look at you. You look greeeeeeat.' I extract another fluffy feather from my armpit. 'Perks of dating a personal trainer, hey?'

'Ha. Well, my endurance levels have certainly improved, which is more than I can say for you. You passed out on me last night. One minute you're Tyson Fury pummelling my head with a pillow and next you're in a coma.'

'*Pummelling?* Ewww.'

She yawns again, giving her tummy a friendly tap.

'Right, I'm starving. Let's grab breakfast, then we can have an explore. Get life back on track. OK?'

'Urrghhh, *no-kay*. I can't face the world yet, Jen. Not today. Not for a few thousand years in fact.'

'Well, you *have* to eat, Ave.'

'Errr, no I don't. Why do you think God invented wine?' I joke, dramatically ramming my head into a pillow. 'I'm just gonna get perma-drunk and hide out here, if that's all the same with you.'

'Alright, alright! You do you, but I, my friend, am off to stuff my face with the "Flavours of Africa",' she says, perusing the hotel menu. 'Mmmmm. Very tasty. And then, we'll sort this nightmare out.'

'How?'

'Absolutely no idea,' she shrugs, grabbing her keys. 'But in tea there is wisdom!'

The door slams behind her and I make the rookie error of checking my phone – 110 new messages. *Urgghhhh!* Not today, thanks. I bury it beneath my clothes and await the return of the hunter gatherer, who reappears 20 minutes later with a mountain of treats piled high upon a big cane tray. She hands me a hash brown.

'Here you go, m'lady.'

I take a non-committal nibble, trying to force it down.

'Come on, Ave. I've seen tortoises eat faster than that,' she says, devouring her body weight in pancakes, French-style omelette with side of Boerewors (curly South African sausage that looks like a child's drawing of a turd).

Two cups of tea later, she's good to go.

I, however, am not.

I just want to fall back into bed and ignore all those messages in my inbox, ignore Scarlet, ignore all the media rubbish. Shut out. The. Whole. Damn. World.

'Sorry Jen, I just can't do today. I really can't.'

She gives me a sympathetic smile and, after a bit more discussion, we agree to make today a day of non-participation. No pressures. No expectations. A day to just 'be'.

The non-agenda runs like this:

1. Netflix marathon featuring depressing Hilary Swank movies, assortment of true crime docos, plus a couple of disaster flicks (mostly nautical themed). Total death count, 183.
2. Indira stories. Tears. Wine.
3. Blog powwow. Nothing resolved. Got angry and ate cheese.
4. Scarlet discussion. More tears, followed by responsible top up of lost fluids.*

*With shiraz.

All in all, a rip-roaring success!

So much so that the 24 hours of non-participation is extended to a full 48. It's like a re-run of the whole Scarlet break up situation, when I camped out on Jen's sofa for weeks on end. Poor girl. Once is bad enough, *but twice!* I can only assume she did something exceedingly wicked in a previous life. She gets me food, filters my messages (mostly positive I'm assured) and she even talks to my mum who is apparently "hugely upbeat" about the whole blog reveal, seeing me as the family celebrity. *Go figure!*

After two days of this Netflix-wine-cry-repeat cycle, even I've had enough. But thankfully, hope arrives in the form of a mysterious package that Jen places on the table.

'What's that?'

'Oh, just something Cruella and Andre DHL'd over. I'll show you later.'

'Jen. What's going on?'

She gives a devilish smile and clumsily pivots to another subject. 'Well, you certainly look brighter this morning, got some colour in your cheeks,' she beams, passing me a delicious smelling samosa. So delicious that I willingly take a bite. Then another. #AppetiteReturned.

'So, I've been thinking. What would Indira make of all this?'

'Which part?'

'The whole blog circus, you rotting away in your PJs like old Miss Havisham.'

'Oh God, she'd give me a right telling off. "Worrying is the stomach's worst poison", she'd say, or something like that. God, she had some good lines.' I feel my eyes start to well up.

'Well, I think that lady knew what she was talking about. She wouldn't want to see you moping about, would she?'

I think for a moment. 'No. Guess not.'

'I'm *sure* not. She'd want to see you out there exploring, not stuck in here stewing in your soup. In fact...' she inclines her nose towards me and gives a sniff, 'You are starting to smell a bit, umm, earthy!'

'What?'

'Yeah, like a turnip. Actually, make that a swede. Defo swede.'

'Stop it,' I laugh, pushing her away. 'Seriously though, how *can* I go out? What about those photographers. They might still be buzzing around.'

'Funny you should mention those pesky paps because I have just the solution,' she says lifting the lid on the mysterious box. '*TADARRRRR!*'

I look inside – a few bits of clothing, sunnies. I'm none the wiser. 'Errr, what is it?'

'It's a media disguise pack!'

'A *what?*' I ask, reading the big red label on the lid. ' "As used by Justin Bieber". Ummm, is this some kind of a joke?'

'Nope. No joke. Bit OTT perhaps, but if it works for Justin...' she winks, having a quick delve inside. 'Just see it as an opportunity to have a little dress-up! Ooooh, look at this!' She starts to wave a curly grey wig in my face.

'No way! That's hideous! Is there not a baseball cap in there, some Ray-Bans?'

'Nope. But there is a note from Cruella.' She clears her throat and starts to read.

Ciao, Ava. Mucho commiserations re photographers. All very normal in these circumstances - they're just after a quick scalp. Shame there were only three of them. Are you sure you didn't miscount with the shock? Anyway, good news! Andre's team is working on a peachy media deal to stop the sharks circling. Benissimo! In the meantime, it's incognito all the way. Can't let a little blip like this slow the blog momentum. Your public is waiting!

'Errr, what the actual fuck? I can't believe the insensitivity of that woman sometimes. And as for *incognito…*' I sneer, dangling the wiggy monstrosity in the air, 'I mean, look at it!'

'It's not *that* bad!'

'Pffft! Says she…who doesn't have to wear the bloody thing. It looks like a dead squirrel! I am NOT doing it…no way Jen. No bloody way.'

.

.

* 30 minutes later *

'Well, I still say you look hot. In an octogenarian kinda way,' Jen winks as we step out into a blaze of sunshine. Needless to say, I'm feeling supremely self-conscious at this moment: curly grey wig, thick-rimmed glasses and detachable prosthetic nose. Don't. Ask.

'I mean, is this *really* necessary?'

'Fuck yes. You looking like Mrs Doubtfire is a small price to pay if it means we get out of that bloody room. The air quality was appalling! I even had Greta Thunberg on the phone earlier,' she giggles. 'Anyway, you won't have to wear it for long, will you? Cruella and Andre are sorting things. You just wait. Now…'

'*Now?* Oh, don't tell me there's more?'

'There's always more, Ava Roberts,' she grins, beckoning me with a snake-like finger. 'Follow me…*MUM!*'

We head out to the car park where I behold the most glorious of sights. A vision to rival the Taj Mahal, nay, the Sistine Chapel, parked in the shade of a Miami-style palm tree.

'So? What you do you think?'

'*OMG! A JEEP?* Really?' I cry, salivating over the sexiest, blackest off-roader with uber butch towbar.

'You like?'

'Err….*I LOVE*. How the hell did you pull this off?'

'Ahh, let's just call it a little treat from Cruella. Otherwise known as a "sorry I ruined your life" gift.'

'Well, I accept,' I smile, running a hand over the hot, silky paintwork.

Jen whips out her phone and starts snapping a few hundred shots of me and sexy jeep in varying poses: casually draped over the bonnet, loading the boot, changing a tyre in my high fashion bifocals.

'You look just like a model.'

'What? For *Hot Flush Weekly*?' I laugh, leaping aboard.

Top down, sunnies on. *Cape Town here we come!*

Whoever said that time spent in nature is the best therapy wasn't wrong. The drive is spectacular, restorative even. Majestic Table Mountain looming above us with its distinctive flat top; the turquoise ocean by our side as we snake along the coast road past countless beaches capped with fluffy, white surf – each one more beautiful than the last.

It's like an instant mood transfusion!

I sink down into my seat, the Cape winds whistling through my synthetic hair as my mind floods with thoughts of Indira. Happy thoughts, and a big wide smile erupts across my face. It's a smile of gratitude: gratitude for having met her, gratitude for this beautiful place and, most of all, for my friend sitting beside me. I look across at her singing her head off to Florence and The Machine, butchering every perfect note, and I realise how lucky I am.

'What?' she asks, suddenly self-conscious.

'Nothing. This is great, Jen. Really great.'

'Well, that's good to hear. And this is just the start. We have a whole day of adventures ahead of us!' she grins, as I'm instructed to cover my eyes in preparation for our first mystery destination.

The anticipation is everything.

'Can I look yet?' I ask impatiently.

'Not yet.'

'Now? Can I look now?'

'Shit, bet you were a nightmare child at Christmas! Go on then,' she smiles as I open my eyes to behold a big wooden sign outside my window.

Welcome to beautiful Boulders Beach – home of the famous Cape Town penguins.

'*Penguins*?' I beam, close to hyperventilating. '*Penguins*?'

It's all too much and we park up and sprint over to a small wooden gate next to the beach. I can barely contain my joy as we come face to face with our first group beside the wooden boardwalk, elegantly turned out in black and white tuxedos.

'It's like Oscars night,' I beam.

'Ha! Actually, that one does look a bit like Keanu, don't you think?' I stand there utterly mesmerised as a dozen of the little barrel chested chaps waddle past us in a perfect conga line. Cuteness on legs! Or flippers. They have such a charm about them. A dignified flippancy that just makes you want to smile. And smile. And smile!

'This is a really good surprise, Jen. Thank you.'

'You're welcome and look, best of all, no photographers! That media disguise kit works a charm, hey?'

'So far so good - though I do look like a twat,' I grin as the False Bay wind wafts some '*perfume de penguin*' up into our faces. *Ewwwww!*

Gag reflex instantly triggered

Jen looks at me and I look at her.

'*PONGUINS!*' we blurt, bolting to the safety of the shoreline. It's stunning, like no beach I've seen before – white sand with little watery inlets pooling between sets of mighty grey boulders. The crystal blue water winks at me seductively. *Twinkle twinkle! Twinkle twinkle!* I can resist no longer. I toss my flip-flops aside and dash in full pelt. And then straight back out again.

'Jesus! It's colder than the North Sea in there. No wonder the bloody penguins like it!'

'Ha! Don't be a wuss,' Jen retorts, ripping off her clothes and diving straight in like some Olympian goddess. She resurfaces with a triumphant whoop, jumping and splashing about with the joy of someone who's never been in the ocean before. I can't help but laugh. 'Come on, Ave! It's lovely... Oh, quick! Look over there!'

I look to my left where a pair of penguins are passionately pecking necks by one of the hulking boulders.

'Ewwww! Get a room!'

'It's mating season,' a voice says. 'Makes the world go round.' I turn to see an elderly man jogging up from the ocean, as the penguin paramours take things to a new level, making the strangest grunts like donkeys at a city farm. I cover my ears.

'Jah, they do make quite the racket, don't they?' he laughs as Jen joins us, blotchy-legged from the sub-zero waters. 'It's quite fresh in there today.'

'Just a bit,' she shivers, attempting to hide her coat peg nipples.

The man runs his hands through his grey cropped hair. 'Are you and your mum here on holiday?'

We both look at him puzzled.

'*Mum?* Or yes, right. Mum! Yes, we are. Mum loves penguins. Don't you, mummy dearest?'

Mum mumbles very bad words

'Well, she's a woman of taste,' he winks. 'They are delightful creatures. You know, this whole colony sprang from just two monogamous pairs. There are hundreds now, hundreds!'

'That's amazing. *Monogamous!* Imagine that. Finding someone who ticks all those boxes for, like, forever!'

'It's not so impossible. You know the secret?' He flashes the proudest grin. 'Knowing when you've found a good one. I've been with my wife since I was 15. A little old-fashioned these days, I know.'

'Awww. I don't think it's old-fashioned,' Jen says, shovelling the sand with her foot. 'I think it's lovely.'

'Not sure my wife would agree with you some days. Anyway, that's marriage!' he smiles, disappearing up the beach and leaving Jen and I ankle deep in ocean and contemplation.

'I tell you what, humans could learn thing or two from penguins. We make such heavy work of this love stuff. I mean, I'm not too sure how advanced homo sapiens really are.'

'Ha! I know what you mean. I fear we might have peaked with the invention of fire,' she laughs.

'You might be onto something there. That whole obsession with fire thing has a lot to answer for, you know. Flames of passion, burning love – maybe that's why we're not very good at the whole mating for life thing. Always chasing a hotter, fiercer flame.'

'I do believe you're writing the next blog entry, Ave!'

'Maybe. It's true though. I mean, look at Scarlet chasing that flame.'

She gazes out to sea for a second. 'Well, Scarlet is an idiot!' she says sternly before turning back to me and erupting with laughter.

'What? It's not funny!'

'Sorry Ave, I'm not laughing at that. It's your makeover – I just can't take you seriously dressed like that.'

I give her a playful nudge. 'It's actually rather liberating in a way. Itchy, but liberating.'

She touches my nylon curls for verification, giving a nod of agreement. 'So, anyway. What about the Scarlet email thing? What are you thinking?'

I roll my eyes.

'Well, for what it's worth, I reckon her behaviour is textbook. Her contacting you like that. It's like they say, "You don't know what you've got until it's gone".'

'Shakespeare?'

'No, Joni Mitchell.'

We stop talking, distracted by another pair of impassioned penguins who are blatantly flaunting their *Happy Feet* bliss in our faces.

'Hey, Jen. Do you believe what that man said. You know, in a *forever* person?'

She gives a shrug. 'Maybe. Guess it's like he said, you just need to find a good one and hang on for dear life.'

'Ha! You make it sound like a rodeo!'

'Well, it is kinda. Oh look!' she says, excitedly pointing at the brightest blue butterfly above our heads. It circles a few times before settling on my hand and extending its wings as if announcing its presence.

'Hi there beautiful!' I smile, gently transferring her to the end of my finger. 'I know someone who would love you!'

I gaze upon her, the most gorgeous iridescent blue creature with black lines radiating out like tiny rivers. And just like that, I'm back in Goa, asking Indira why she loves butterflies so much.

'Because they dare to dazzle!' she answered. 'And that's what we should all aspire to do, my dear! Dazzle! But that's not the best thing about butterflies, you know. The best thing is that these creatures have no idea how beautiful they are. Just like you, Ava.'

*

The thing with cool black Jeeps is that they rapidly become very *hot* black Jeeps in the sizzling Cape Town sun and, after a quick game of toast your tush on the sticky leather seats, we're back on the road and heading to the next stop on our South African magical mystery tour.

'Well, can't see you topping that, Jen!'

'Oooh, is that a challenge?'

.

.

'*SHARKS? GREAT WHITE SHARKS?*' I yell from the blustery deck of *Wild Adventurer III* out of Simon's Town.

There are 11 souls on board today and I pray that all the others are a whole lot juicier than me and Jen.

'It's good to confront your fears,' Jen smiles, attaching her travel sickness bands. 'And you don't get better therapy than climbing into a cage and staring a great white shark in the eye.'

'Umm, I can think of better. Like lying by a pool and *not* facing your fears! Anyway, why's it called *Wild Adventurer III?* What happened to numbers I and II do you think?'

'They sunk!' a low voice responds.

I turn round to see a dashing silver fox of a captain chuckling away at his little joke. 'Welcome aboard,' he says in a heavy Afrikaans accent. 'The swell is particularly big today, so be sure to hold tight, ladies.'

'Oh. Big swell. That's wonderful news! Wonder if the sharks are big today too?'

'The sharks are big *every* day,' he says, completely poker-faced. He educates us a bit more on the local marine life: giant sharks, seals and orcas. This terrifies me all the more, as Jen subtly whispers into my ear, 'I think Captain Jan might fancy a piece of Mumma Doubtfire!'

I promptly give her a little stomp on her toe which seems to shut her up for the moment. She's not wrong though. He *is* being attentive. *Very* attentive. He's an attractive sort; mid-fifties, bright blue eyes, dimple in chin. In short, my Aunty B would eat him alive. We chat some more while motoring further into the wide expanse of sea, nothing but sea, whereupon he informs my 'daughter' and I that we're about to drop anchor.

Daughter?

'I can't believe people are actually buying this get-up. It must be the wig,' I say, trying to reassure my fragile ego.

'Yeah. Either that or you look like you've had a hard paper round!' Jen teases.

The engine stops and we drop a few buoys, as the vessel starts to bob about like a cork in the open water. Up and down, side to side. More upping and downing. I look over the side, the once crystal-clear water is now inky black. Ominously so.

'The sharks will be here soon,' Captain Jan smiles.

We wait. And wait some more, as I witness the faces of my fellow sailors slowly change from perky pink to pale green and finally to a deathly grey. It's the full Dulux colour chart. The lovely Austrian family aboard are looking particularly ill at this point, and within minutes they are standing in height order and hurling over the starboard side.

Look at the horizon, look at the horizon, I tell myself as the bouquet from the spewing Von Trapps wafts back into my face.

Urgghhh! If the sharks don't get me, the fumes bloody will!

Mercifully, my attention is soon diverted by an almighty cheer from a nearby boat.

'Look... look there!' Jen yells, dispensing a sharp nudge to my ribs. I reposition my eyes just in time to witness a gigantic grey torpedo dramatically breaking surface a few metres away.

'OMG! Did you see that? Did you see that?'

The shark soars two metres into the air before slapping down on the surface and disappearing into the depths.

'Errr, *did I see it*? You could see that bloody thing from space!'

'She's a beauty, isn't she?' Captain Jan interjects. 'Five-metre female. We call her Fin, because of the notch in her dorsal – see!' He hands me his binoculars and I focus on the distinctive fin appearing in the waves again.

'Oh, yes, yes! I see her!'

It's quite a notch, like a giant Dorito that someone's taken a good bite out of.

'She comes here every year. I think she must like the tourists!' he laughs.

My face must say it all as I gracefully return his binoculars and start gripping onto the handrail with such vigour that my knuckles turn white.

'You're perfectly safe with us,' he reassures. 'Nothing to be afraid of!' He then nods to a bearded man who gives the order for us all to don wetsuits, ready to take to the cage.

OMG!

This is all starting to feel dangerously real, dangerously fast and frankly it's a reality I could do well without. Jen is much calmer and slips into her suit before zipping me into mine, a tight pink number clearly intended for the tiny body of a tween.

'And I thought I was here to see the sharks!' she winks, gesturing to my vacuum-packed front bottom.

'What?'

'Err, camel toe alert!'

'Oi!' I laugh, stretching the rubber to make some much needed space downstairs. I take a deep breath and mince my way to the side of the boat, ready for launch. *Squeak squeak. Chafe chafe.*

The tension is palpable as two burly crewmen unfasten a series of thick ropes and pulleys, gently lowering the cage into the water. I find myself staring at it. It's much smaller than I imagined, around 1m by 2m I'd guess, not a bit like the cages they use on *Discovery Shark Week*. Those things look big and solid, thick galvanised steel that nothing or nobody can get through. The bars on this one, however, look markedly thinner, and I get the sense that I'm about to step into a Tesco's shopping trolley and head straight down the big fish aisle!

'I'll let you go first,' Captain Jan says with a playful wink.

OK, so now he really *is* flirting with me! *FML! Sharks above and beneath!* I'm so terrified at this point, I can barely speak.

'Are you OK?' he asks. 'You look a little pale.'

'Oh yes!' Jen interjects, tossing an arm round my shoulder. 'Don't worry about mum, she's got a 20 year old lover back home. I'm sure she can handle a big old fish! Hey mum?'

I shoot her a look.

If I wasn't so bloody nervous, I'd shove that plastic snorkel right down her throat! Instead, I do the next best thing and shunt her towards the cage with a gleeful, 'In you pop, my dear. Don't get eaten now!'

The crew hold the cage steady as she lowers herself inside. Nice and easy. Gently does it. She's in! Now it's my turn. The ocean swell raises the cage and drops it again as the crew give me a look that says, 'It's now or never' to which my inner voice retorts, *'It's never! Definitely a never!'* Seeing opportunity in my hesitation, the youngest son from the Austrian family strides on up and climbs inside, no fuss, leaving just one more spot.

'Come on Ava! It'll be amazing!' Jen warbles through her snorkel.

Will it? Will it really?

I stand there, teetering on the edge of a massive decision.

This is one of those pivotal moments in life and the 60 year old woman I now am feels the full weight of the baby boomer generation on her quaking shoulders. I channel my inner Meryl, looking at the dark water, then at the cage, back at the water and next thing I know...

SPLOOOOOSH!

The lid slams behind me. No turning back.

'Yayyyy!' Jen sings as I attach mask and settle into my spot in the tiny cage: Jen to one side, boy to the other and me as the filling in this charming sharky sandwich. The boy is not looking too chipper must be said; he's almost translucent at this point. I nod at him by way of support, but he just stares through me, like when you've had one too many and are trying not to hurl in the Uber home.

Not much happens for the next few minutes.

We bob about in the murkiness, three human McNuggets in our tiny metal basket, as the crew toss out a seal decoy on a fishing line and tow it around the cage to attract any passing maneaters. Basically, the equivalent of ringing the dinner bell. *Ding ding!*

We wait. And wait.

Images of every shark movie I've ever screamed through flash into my mind: *Jaws, Open Water* and then Blake Lively in her very nice bikini in *The Shallows. Not now, Ava, not now!* My heart starts to pound and I'm suddenly aware of some wildly erratic breathing happening through a snorkel, which I quickly realise is my own.

Kaboom. Kaboom!

Wait. Some. More.

And then, finally…

Out of the blackness, a long, shadowy shape catches my eye.

I see it! I see it!

I instinctively hold my breath, utterly transfixed as the torpedo-like form becomes more solid, more fish-like, more…

'FARK IT'S A SHARRRRRKK! IT'S A SHARRRRRKK!'

I latch onto Jen's arm as it glides up slowly at first, almost warily. Its snout becomes brilliantly clear, triangular and pointy, and it pushes it up to the cage giving the bars an exploratory nibble. Oh. My. God. Those teeth! My grip on Jen's arm tightens. It's so close now that I can make out the deep pores on the tip of its nose. Pores designed to detect tiny electrical impulses – impulses from a terrified human heart thumping out of its chest in a shark cage for instance.

Kaboom. Kaboom. Kaboom!

Calm, Ava. Calm.

It's the strangest of feelings to come face to face with an apex predator. Exhilarating. Horrifying! The ultimate primal fear. Like staring your own mortality in the face, knowing all too well that this creature could take you in its big, toothy mouth and chomp you up as easily as me munching a french fry. Aside from all the teeth, it's the size of the thing that strikes me most. Not just the length, but its mighty girth as broad as a family sedan.

The Austrian boy clearly echoes the sentiment.

He is now all eyes and terror, and suddenly, his body starts to jerk, convulse even. *Oh God, he's having a bloody fit! He's actually having a fit!* I go to steady him but soon realise that he's not having a fit at all, but chundering as chunks of carrot start spurting from his snorkel like he's struck oil. Bright. Orange. Oil!

FML! Not again!

I'm soon dry retching into my mouthpiece as bits of perfectly diced carrot float by, attaching themselves to my wig. *Ewwww.* It's like a magnet to the stuff! I give it a rub, dislodging bits of vomit as well as the odd clump of hair as Mrs Jaws stares at me with those big black eyes, clearly unimpressed. She gives the cage a final nibble before disappearing into the inky blackness, never to return.

Way to kill a vibe, Johann!

Abandoning hope of any further sharky encounters, we head back on deck only to discover an altogether bigger commotion happening. I remove my mask and look over to the side rails where the Austrian mother is pointing into the water and yelling,

'Oh my Gods! Looks! Zere is a persons in ze waters! There is a persons in ze waters!'

'What? Who?'

The news sends shockwaves around *Wild Explorer III* as everyone rushes to the starboard side, ogling what looks like a head rising and falling in the swell.

'OMG! Who is that?'

Jen grabs my hand, I grab hers as Captain Jan calmly orders the crew to up anchor and motor closer to the poor floating wretch.

'Nobody panic, please!' he says sternly. 'Nobody panic.'

Everything is happening so fast, so frantically and I squint down into the water, catching sight of the mass of hair on the surface.

'I can see them! I can see them!' I yell, as all eyes fix upon the head, hoping for some sign of life. Any sign. I stare and stare, looking closer at the curls. Tight. Grey. Curls. Curls that look oddly familiar, and then..... *Oh dear.*

Subtly nudges Jen

'Not now Ave! This is serious.'

'Yeahhh, so is this,' I implore, pointing at my head and then at the hairy mass floating in the water. She stares at me, not quite connecting the dots.

'What is it?'

'Umm, err….that's my wig, Jen!'

Her face drops as she reaches out her hand to touch my wet, blond head. A head now devoid of nylon wig as worn by Justin Bieber.

'Fuck, Ava! Oh. Fuck!'

At that moment, there's a collective gasp from the group as we turn to see a huge mouth breaking the surface to engulf the mass of hair in… One. Merciless. Bite.

MUNNNNNNNNNCH!

'Oh my Gods!' Poor Mrs Von Trapp shrieks before promptly fainting into the on board buffet as Jen and I stand there completely motionless.

.

.

'Errr…. are you going to tell them or am I?'

The trip back to Simon's Town is a subdued affair and I get the impression everyone is a little peeved with us causing a minor maritime incident. #ThrowThemToTheSharks. We try to make amends, but the Austrian family just give us the side eye, while Captain Jan opts for a highly effective 'you're dead to me' approach.

'Maybe he thinks you catfished him?'

'What?'

'You know, him thinking you were more of a *mature* lady,' Jen shrugs.

I don't respond.

CHAPTER TWENTY-EIGHT – UNEXPECTED ITEM IN BAGGING AREA

`'Happiness is the china shop. Love is`

`the bull.'`

`- H.L Mencken`

'Lucrezia! Are you OK?' Jen asks.

It's blog summit part 2: big media plan reveal.

Expectations are high, although not as high as Cruella who is currently dangling upside down on my screen.

'Just doing some inverted yoga, darlinks!' she coos. 'Nicole Kidman swears by it you know, hangs like a bat for days! And I mean, have you *seen* that woman's face? Skin of an embryo! Course, I suspect she's on the placenta smoothies too.'

'Aren't we all, Lucrezia?' I tease, sucking in my cheeks.

'Oh Ava, you *are* funny! Funny, funny, funny! So, yah. Tell me, how are my superstar bloggers? Busy on the next thrilling instalment, I hope. We are number 2 in the charts, girls. *Number 2!*'

'Wow, really?'

'Yah. Just inches from the summit. Teetering on the precipice of greatness, like Tenzing Norgay and Hillary on the crest of Everest, Rosa Parks on that bus! We can't let a little media intrusion stand in the way of number 1 glory! One extra push. *More, more, more,* remember!'

'Are maneating sharks *more, more, more* enough?' I say, half-sarcastically. 'Jen almost fed me to one earlier.'

'Ooooh, sharks! Sexy *and* dangerous! *So* on brand,' she beams, her cheeks flushing even redder. 'Tell me, did anyone lose a limb?'

'Sorry, what?'

'With the maneating sharks? Any severed arms? Cheeky finger perhaps?' She wiggles her pinky to camera with an excited squeal.

We maintain a dignified silence.

'Pity. We champion diversity here at *Marshall Media*. Anyway, can't be helped. Right, let's get down to business.'

She instantly switches to full-on pitch mode, like she's about to sell us something. Something we doubtless do not want. I brace myself. 'So yah, I know the last few days have been *un peu* challenging, but girls, as promised, Andre has worked his tush off to sort this media debacle and we have spectacular news!' She snaps her fingers, 'ANDRE?' and he magically appears like a bespectacled genie.

'Grazie Lucrezia. Hello girls. So, yes, I'm pleased to report that as of today - *dramatic pause* – ding dong, the witch is dead!' He thrusts his arms skyward like a portly Judy Garland.

'Riiiiiight! Greaaaaat!'

'Isn't it just? Wohooooo!'

'So, errr, what does that mean exactly?' I ask.

'It means the press agencies have called off the hounds, dear. No more paps!'

'They have? Really! Wow! Well, that is great news, amazing news in fact! Thanks so much Andre.'

'Oh please, anything for my top bloggers!' he beams, before pausing to take a deep breath. 'There is of course one teeny, weeny catch...'

I knew it! There is always a catch.

'Err. What kind of catch, Andre?'

'Nothing big, dears. They just want an exclusive interview with our superstar blogger, plus a few photos. Quid pro quo, darlinks! Quid pro quo!'

Interview? With me? Errr...how about QUID PRO NOOOOOOOOOO!

I can feel myself getting all discombobulated.

'Don't worry Ava. Nothing too probing,' he reassures. 'Just the usual stuff – you know, life as a top travel blogger, thoughts on global warming, fave sexual position. Do you have one?'

'A favourite sexual position?'

'Actually, don't have to tell me now. Just a good idea to not say anal. Sounds slutty.'

'Noted,' Jen says, shaking her head. 'Seriously though, if Ava agrees to this, that will be the end of the whole nonsense, yes? Cos it's been really stressful for her. It's not what we signed up for, it's…'

'Jennifer, Jennifer!' he interjects, removing his orange spectacles. 'Consider it handled. Fixed. Sorted. I swear on my Princey's life.'

With that, a bulgy-eyed pooch leaps up and starts to slather all over daddy's face like it's a juicy pork chop.

Slurp slurp.

'Who's the goodest boy then? Come on Princey, say woof to the famous bloggers!'

Princey shoves bum into camera

'Bad boy!' he scolds. 'I'm so sorry girls – he's not very keen on women. I fear I've raised a misogynist!'

Lick lick!

I attempt to ignore the canine tonguing and accompanying slurps, determined to reach some kind of satisfactory resolution.

'So, *if* I do agree and I'm only saying *if,* where is this interview happening?'

'On location,' he says sheepishly.

'On location where?'

Cruella instantly leaps in, 'At your cousin Maria's wedding, darlink!'

'*What?'*

'I know! Genius, isn't it? It's all arranged. Such a lovely couple and the venue, the Aquila Game Reserve! Perfect backdrop for the photo shoot. Raw, wild, untamed…'

'But…what…how?'

'Ava, look at me, look at me…' she says, the veins bulging in her upside down head. 'Action needed to be taken. A crisis had to be averted. Fear not, the happy couple will be handsomely compensated. In fact we're paying for the whole affair: catering, accommodation and the venue. The whole glorious event will be sponsored by *Around the World in 80 Gays*! Isn't it just wonderful?'

'And Marcus and Maria have actually agreed to this madness?'

'*Agreed?* Darlink, they are EUPHORIC! The groom is particularly happy – I threw in a cheeky Porsche hire. I mean, who can resist a Boxster?'

Before I can tell her where to shove her Boxster, inverted Cruella breaks into a coughing fit. I fear she has swallowed her own tongue.

'Just try to see it as a *cough cough* wonderful gift as they set out on their journey to happily ever after.' *Cough cough.*

'But…'

'Benissimo! All settled then! See you in a couple of days!'

'Wait, *you're* coming too? To the wedding?'

'Wouldn't miss it for the world!' she grins. 'I have my safari suit fitting this afternoon. Donatella, darlink! Donatella! Honestly, the things that woman can do with a khaki breastplate is a revelation! Hakuna matata, darlinks. Hakuna matata!'

*

The blog summit is commemorated with a celebratory tipple at one of Camps Bay's trendy beachside establishments.

'Here's to the Crunts! They came through in the end.'

'*The Crunts?*'

'Yeah, Cruella and Andre Untilli, I've rebranded them the *Crunts*! Kinda suits, don't you think?' Jen laughs, slurping another lychee martini. I must admit that, although not yielding a *perfect* outcome, blog summit 2.0 has brought some relief, eliciting one of those delicious *phew* moments, like when you make it to the loo just as your bladder is about to burst. Andre's deal will spell an end to my press woes and more importantly the need to dress up as Mrs Doubtfire. Just as well, since my hairpiece is now in the digestive tract of a five-metre great white.

#HairyScary.

'You know what,' I slur, 'I don't know what's more terrifying, the thought of Cruella rocking up or that bloody interview!'

'Ha! The stuff of nightmares, hey?'

Slurp slurp!

'Now, about that interview. I know it's not ideal, but it's just a few silly questions and then it's over. You've faced a lot worse.'

'True that,' I smile, coming over all philosophical. 'Hey Jen, maybe all my wild adventuring has been training for this very situation?'

We stare at one another for a moment before blurting a unified 'Nah!' and furiously necking our drinks. 'Fancy another?'

Jen swaggers back to the bar leaving me alone with my thoughts. Dangerous. I do feel less anxious, I have to say. Heart palpitations have ceased, head no longer feels like it's stuck in a vice. Maybe things really are on the up. *Just have to believe.* I give a contented sigh, settling back to survey the bar clientele. Rich pickings here tonight. Not surprising as it's one of those super chic joints just on the oceanfront. A magnet for the *glamarati*, stick thin models with angular faces, who look like they haven't seen a chip in years. As I watch them pout and pose, I'm reminded of my own modelling days – 2005, local garden centre brochure. (Girl on left, pushing yellow wheelbarrow.) Glory days that resulted in me keeping the wheelbarrow. My dad was overjoyed.

Sadly, not everyone is as appreciative of the Cape Town buzz, namely an older couple sitting out on the balcony. I watch them starring out at the most glorious view of the ocean and palm trees, not exchanging a single word. My heart sinks.

'Don't let me end up like that,' I slur as Jen returns with two more lychee delights.

'Like what?'

I gesture over to the balcony, 'Stuck with someone I can't even speak to!'

'Never,' she smiles. 'Not on my watch!'

We sit a moment observing them further, wildly theorising on their relationship. Is it him who's lost interest, is it her? We can't quite agree.

'So, when does it happen do you think? When do you stop having anything to say to someone?'

'Dunno,' Jen sighs, having another slurp. 'It's funny. Everyone thinks ending up alone is the worst thing, but I think that ending up with someone that makes you *feel* alone is a million times worse.'

'Very profound.'

'Still, on the plus side at least that won't happen to Maria and Marcus. The pair of them never bloody shut up!'

'Ha! Actually, Maria just texted,' I say, looking down at my phone. 'She's LOVING the idea of an *80 Gays* sponsored wedding or how did she put it?

Oh yes, *this is the bestest news ever*, quote unquote. God knows what Cruella promised them?'

'Untold riches, eternal youth?'

'*Porsche Boxster!'* we blurt simultaneously.

Bahahahahahha.

'You know what? I wasn't looking forward to this wedding, but now you're my plus one, I reckon it will be fun! Plus we get to go on safari! See the Big Five!'

'Yaaaassss! The Big Five! Sounds like an overweight boy band,' she giggles, prodding the lychee like a cat pawing at a goldfish.

More slurring.

All the talk of relationships gets me thinking of that other great matter… my betrayal.

'So, who was the snake who did it, d'ya think? The dirty rat that outed me?'

'Ooh, the blog Judas? Now that's a question!'

We reel off a few possible suspects (however unlikely) and end up with a shortlist of ten: Tom, Dawn, Hannah, Sara, the rest of the ashram gang, mum and outside shot, Nandi the cow. All parties are eliminated from our enquiries as no motive can be established, plus one of them can neither speak nor type due to having cloven hooves.

'It's a biological certainty!'

'Hmm, maybe. But I still reckon it might be Nandi!' Jen teases, letting out a big snort.

'Ewwww! Sexy.'

'Whaaaat? You can talk. You make the weirdest sounds.'

'Whaaaa? When?'

'When you sleep. You kind of growl like an asthmatic tiger mixed with a snuffling pig. *Tiger pig!*' she blurts, doing a rather loud impression which, although excruciating, gives the mute couple on the balcony something to talk about. We look over as they break into laughter and then, miracle of miracles, they lean in to share a kiss.

'I think our work here is done, Jennifer.'

HIC!

The stagger back to the hotel takes us along Camps Bay's gorgeous beach front. The place is buzzing! Drinkers, street sellers, local kids singing their hearts out way past their bedtimes and by the time we settle into the hotel bar, I'm feeling the lightest I have in a while.

'What are you grinning about?'

'Oh, I dunno. Life. The blog. It's been quite a ride, hey? I mean, who'd have thought it would go off like this,' I marvel.

'I know. It's mad. Like, one minute we're writing stories about Goan sunsets and next you're getting pursued by all those bloody photographers!'

'*All* those photographers? Jen, there were three.'

'Err, never let facts get in the way of a good story! Have I taught you nothing?'

I look at her, feeling a little drunk and emosh.

'Seriously though, it *is* pretty amazing. Well, to be accurate, *you're* pretty amazing.'

'Oh hello, someone's drunk!'

'No, noooo. Well, yessss, I am a bit. Well, a lot. But lizzen, I'm trying to be serious here.'

'Sorry. Go ahead.'

'Well, I just want to say that it's all down to you really. You make all my stories come alive and honestly you really are the best. Truly.'

'No, *we* are the best, Ave! It's a team effort. I'd have nothing to write about without your crazy antics.'

'Awww. Yeah but, no …beyond the blog. I mean, you came over here, got me out of that room and I just want to say that I appreciate it.' I look down into my lap. 'It's just with Indira passing and everything, it makes you appreciate, well, people and you're, you're… my…. lighthouse!'

'Your what?' she chuckles.

'My lighthouse. Oh I dunno. Just something Dawn said. Too drunk to explain. Anyway, I'm going on…'

I feel a lump forming in my throat as she reaches for my hand. 'Well, I'm proud of you too. And I know Scarlet getting in touch has wobbled you a bit but look, the worst is over, Ave. And the best is yet to come. I just know it.'

'Well, I'll drink to that,' I declare as our drinks arrive right on cue. 'To adventures.'

'And amazing women! God bless them all!'

Big slurp.

'You're right though. We do make a good team, hey? Ever since that first day at Uni. OMG Jen, I remember seeing you at freshers' week. In your cool dungarees.'

'Oh, stop! What was I thinking?' she laughs, throwing her head in her hands.

'What? You looked hot.'

I paw at my drink for a while, lost in the moment.

'Hey, do you ever wonder what might have happened that night, the night we met, you know…'

'Oh, if you hadn't snogged the face of sexy Salma Jessop?'

'Nooooo! She pounced on *me*! I was terrified. Anyway, you seemed pretty taken with that girl with the teeth. What was her name?'

'Bugsy Belinda! Ha! I'd forgotten about her! God, she did have big teeth, hey? I was never interested in her. I was just saving face you know,' she smiles, all heavy-eyed with drink.

'How do you mean?'

She goes to speak but is suddenly distracted by a giant plate of oysters at the next table.

'Oooh! Oysters. The mystery of the ocean in a single mouthful.'

'Such a poet!' I laugh. 'So, what were you saying?'

'When?'

'Just then…'

'Huh? Oh, doesn't matter. Hey, let's order some oysters! I looove oysters!' she grins, summoning the waiter with an enthusiastic wave.

I gaze over at the next table, at those big, plump oysters shimmering on a bed of ice. And just like that I'm back in Whitstable, Kent, my feet crunching along the pebbled beach, the salty wind in my hair. That town has a special place in my heart, not only because of childhood holidays, but because it's the setting for one of my favourite novels, *Tipping the Velvet*.

What a read!

That story meant everything to me as a fledgling lady-lover. I remember obsessing over the DVD, enjoying the kissing scenes a bit too much, rewinding them over and over just to get that funny feeling in my tummy again. I lived every step of that journey with heroine Nan Anstey – falling in love, falling apart and now years on I can relate more than ever.

I'm suddenly possessed by the spirit of Nan and I blurt in my deepest voice.

'I love you Kitty!'

Bahhahahahaha!

Jen lets out a laugh of recognition before coming back at me with a "Ooh Nan, your hands smell like mermaids!" quip and after that, we're gone! It's a *Tipping the Velvet* free-for-all. Kitty this, Nan that. "Exquisite little tarts" everywhere! We barely come up for air.

'Ahh. God it was good! And Keeley Hawes…'

'Keeley *Phwoarrrs* more like! Now she was *hoooottttt!*'

'Hot, but dangerous,' I say pointedly.

'Aren't they always?'

We sit for a moment, set adrift on memory bliss. Analysing the plot, the costumes, the wonderful characters.

'So, Ave. D'ya think Nan made the right choice zhen? You know, between Kitty and Florence?'

'Hmmmm, that's a tough one,' I say, taking it all rather seriously. 'The choice between the repentant cheating first love or the new belle, who has never let you down?'

'The one who broke your heart…'

'Or the one who stuck it together again?'

'The one who makes you feel alive…'

'But burns you!'

We sit in a prosecco-induced haze, contemplating the question that's divided lezzakind for decades.

'Shit, girl! I can't believe we're agonising over thish as if this is an actual thing!'

'You know what Ava Roberts, I zink it izzz!' Jen says, now slurring for England.

She leans in, dipping her chin like she does when she's about to say something profound.

'I reckon when a girl decides whether she wants a Kitty or a Florence, life gets a whole lot easier. It's like the whole Darcy or Daniel Cleaver thing.'

'Yesssshhhh,' I say giddily. 'Darcy or Cleaver? Florence or Kitty?'

'So come on then. Who's it to be, Ave? Kitty or Florence?'

I stare over at her, entangled in the moment.

Kitty, Florence, oysters, prosecco, my beautiful best friend Jen. Those big green eyes, that bright smile and I lean forward, intoxicated in the moment.

'I'd pick...'

'Yes?' she says, leaning towards me. 'I'd pick...'

.

.

Suddenly her face drops. I have that horrible feeling that I've done something wrong. Overstepped a line.

'What's wrong?'

She just sits there, staring into the space behind me. Not saying a word. Not moving.

'Ummm, Ava....I think your Kitty might have arrived!'

'What?'

I turn to look over my shoulder and my heart stops.

.

.

'Hello Ava.'

.

.

'Scarlet?' I stammer. 'What are you doing here?'

CHAPTER TWENTY-NINE – SHOWDOWN.
AN ELEPHANT NEVER FORGETS

'The ghosts of the past speak to all those
who listen.'

- Naya Ventura Gv

Cape Town, South Africa

One of the many changes that comes with age, aside from awful hangovers and disproportionately large ears, is a person's ability to deal with surprises. As children, we love them – surprise parties, surprise gifts, we can't get enough! However, with the advancing years comes the realisation that surprises can actually be pretty shit and in some cases lead to death. Case in point, my friend's great aunt Dot who keeled over in the victoria sponge just as everyone yelled 'Surpriiiiiiiiise! Happy 100th!'

Similarly, last night's blast from the past completely floored me. Scarlet's sudden arrival was the romantic equivalent of an 'unexpected item in the bagging area' and, aside from the initial trauma, there was also a strange sense of annoyance. *How could she turn up now? Out of the blue?* It's like when you've spent all day cleaning your car, only for some seagull to take a giant dump on the windscreen. Scarlet is the seagull. I am the windscreen.

Clearly disturbed, I ended up having the most horrific nightmare in which I was besieged by a trio of evils: Scarlet, sharks and snakes. The unholy trinity of S's! I was back in that shark cage, back in the inky black water with the giant predator ramming its nose against the bars. Only this time it had the face of Scarlet: big red lips, blond hair and killer cheekbones (no pun intended). Every time I tried to escape, the angry snake would wrap itself around the bars, opening its mouth with an evil *'Hissssssssssssssss!'*

Hissssss.
Hissssssssss.

The hissssssssssss seamlessly mutates into the sound of a boiling kettle, thus bringing me back to reality in our hotel room with Jen making her morning brew. She looks pensive, dunking the tea bag into the steaming water with all the glee of a medieval torturer.

'Shit, Ave! Is it just me or was Scarlet turning up *the* headfuck of the century?'

So, it did really happen then? Scarlet is actually here!

Burrows head into duvet like ostrich in sand

'That girl must have bloodhound DNA, that's all I can say,' she continues, having a big slurp of tea. 'I mean, how did she know you were here? Oh, hang on.' Her eyes widen.

'What?'

'The blog betrayer strikes again?'

'Nooooo. D'ya think?' I say, feeling utterly sick.

'Either that or she's been getting intel from your mum.'

'Yes, it must be mum. She's been so carried away with that bloody book club and Virginia Woolf that she's making it her mission to get us back together. Odd really, she never seemed that keen on Scarlet before.'

Jen stays silent for a moment, before the wisdom of the Tetley tea starts to diffuse.

'Of course, you do have a choice in all this. I mean, you don't *have* to see her you know.'

I pause for a moment, contemplating this boldest of concepts. I don't *have* to see her. **I don't *have* to see her.**

'You're right. *I didn't invite her here.* I don't owe her anything, do I?'

'Not a thing.'

It's the starch my spine needed, the reclaiming of power and my shoulders instantly draw back, giving me a whole new courageous stance.

'Yes. It's my choice and I choose *not* to see her,' I declare.

'Great.'

Slurp.

'Yeah, great. Mind made up. Move on.'

'Cool.' Another big slurp. 'If that's what you want…'

'That's *exactly* what I want, Jennifer Jones. Thanks for double checking.'

Deafening pause leading to moment of overthinking and self- doubt

'Ummm, what do you mean "if that's what I want?" '

'Oh, ignore me. I'm no expert. I mean, a mayfly has longer relationships than I do.'

'No, tell me what you think please.'

'Well, I'm not her biggest fan as you know. But, I dunno, you've got so many unanswered questions, maybe it would be good to see her and put the ghosts to rest. You know, closure.'

I tug at the bed sheets.

Closure. The second best C word. The holy grail of the broken hearted.

Closure can bring an end to all those unanswered questions.

A final curtain falling on those nagging doubts. A line drawn in the sand.

The decision is all too much.

'Urrghhhh! I don't know what to do. I mean, do I *really* want to share a latte with the woman who ripped my heart out and blitzed it in a Nutribullet?'

'Ha! Well, to be honest, all this is a little academic actually. I just remembered something...' Jen sighs.

'Yes?'

'I think drunk Ava might have already agreed to meet her.'

'Sorry, what?'

At that very moment, my phone offers a little beep of confirmation, as if to say 'Yep, you so did!' and I look down at the screen.

```
See you at breakfast as planned. Can't wait! S. Xxx
```

Well, isn't this poetic?

Like all tragic heroines, I am to be the orchestrator of my own downfall, the architect of my own fate. Or as Aunty B would say, 'You've well and truly cooked your goose!'

I steady myself.

Come on, girl! Is there really so much to be afraid of?

I've come a long way since that snivelling girl on Jen's sofa. I'm a global traveller for heaven's sake! A badass adventurer, a birther of cows, alleyway lover, not to mention top blogger. If I can do all that, I can face *her!*

'Boats don't sink because of the water around them, they sink because of the water that gets into them!' I declare, suddenly leaping up. 'Right, Jen. I've decided. I'm going to meet her. Face my demons. I'll hear her out and then we can head to the wedding and get completely wasted. Deal?'

'Deal. Now please can I go back to sleep? My head hurts.'

Meeting an ex is not an enterprise to be taken lightly. Protective strategies need to be put in place; plans need to be hatched. In fact, the whole thing is akin to a military operation and it all begins with the armour, aka the outfit.

According to *A Modern Guide to Heartbreak, Volume 3,* "the outfit must strike a keen balance between looking fabulous but not so fabulous as to imply you give a damn." Excellent advice! Thoroughly concur. I begin by selecting the most important item, *knickers!* Yes, funny as it might seem, knickers, briefs, trollies, panties, whatever you care to name them, are never to be underestimated. They are the foundation of any outfit, the bedrock on which everything else sits. As such, knickers need to be sound. No baggy elastic, no gaping gusset. I opt for sexy black briefs with Wonder Woman logo. *Nothing says boss like a badge on your vag!*

Now for the outer layers, cool but understated. I go for black denim shorts and cut-off white Tee to show a bit of that newly toned midriff. Next comes the war paint, another powerful weapon in the spurned lover's arsenal. Lipstick, mascara, eyeliner. Not too subtle. Not overdone. Girl-next-door vibe. I round it all off with the ultimate 'power' accessories: butterfly necklace and lucky pink Havaianas.

Operation complete, I leave the bedroom 30 minutes later.

'Well?'

Jen looks me up and down. 'Gorgeous, Ave! Just gorge!' she smiles, giving me the kind of embrace usually reserved for soldiers heading off to war and likely never to return. 'You've got this, my friend.'

Yep, I've got this. I've got this…. horrible feeling in my stomach. What was it Indira said about trusting your gut?

The walk to the beach café is faster than anticipated on account of my nervous jog and I arrive ten minutes early. Not ideal. Do not wish to appear overeager. *Must not give my power away!* On the plus side, it gives me the perfect opportunity to survey the field of engagement: small café, ten tables or so, counter at front. I make for the small table in the corner and sit down, back to the wall, thereby eliminating stealth attack from the rear. #ThingsIlearntFromJamesBond.

My heart is going like a jackhammer and I order a large flat white with complimentary biscotti.

Tick tock. Tick tock.

There aren't many things in life as anxiety-inducing as waiting for an ex. Waiting for that agonising moment when two worlds collide, the romantic past and the estranged present, terrified you'll be horribly crushed between the two.

Five minutes pass, then ten, as I scroll nervously through my phone. Two notifications: a text from Dawn about an unsightly pimple, and a Facebook memory, me and Scarlet in Paris two years ago today. *Merci beaucoup FB!* I flick her face from my screen only to magically swipe her to life…Right. Before. My. Very. Eyes.

'Hello Ava,' she smiles. 'How are you?'

My heart stops.

It's her. Scarlet in the flesh. For real.

She stares at me. I stare back at her.

I hadn't factored in the full impact of seeing her again, facing those intoxicating eyes, those piercing blue eyes that bewitched me from the first.

'I'm so glad you came,' she says, flicking her hair back. 'May I?'

She pulls out a seat and sits down.

She looks the same, her hair a bit shorter perhaps, but other than that, the same. She extends a hand over the table and I stare down at it. It feels odd to shake the hand of someone you've been so intimate with. The hand that knows every inch of your body, the hand that has given so much pleasure and such devastating pain.

My hand touches hers. Skin meets skin and I pull away.

'So, it's a bit different to our coffee shop in Shoreditch, hey? What was that little place we used to go to?'

I detect a nervous tremor in her voice.

'Smiths,' I answer.

'Oh yes, Smiths! I used to love it there.'

Pause.

Biiiiiiiiiiiiiig. Pregnant. Pause.

.

.

'Well...you look amazing. Travel clearly suits you, Ave!'

I feel myself blush, but, unlike the old me, I accept the compliment with a casual 'thanks' as if it's no biggie. As if her presence is not affecting me. Not making me feel weaker by the second.

'Do you want another coffee?' she says, gesturing to my half-empty cup.

'No, thanks. Sorry, I went ahead and ordered without you.'

She responds with a knowing giggle.

'All good, I know how you can't function without your coffee. Some things never change, hey?'

She orders a latte. Double shot. Oat. Not too hot. Not too cold. Complicated. Just like her.

'Congratulations on the blog by the way. Everyone's reading it back home.'

'Oh really?'

'Yes. It's a really big deal, Ave. I didn't even know you were a writer. You must be so proud.'

'It's Jen really, she's the talent. I just do all the ridiculous things and well...'

'Well, however it's working, it's great.' She starts to look down at this point. 'Can't say it was the easiest of reads in parts though – you know, hearing how much I'd hurt you.'

Her remark strikes a nerve.

'What makes you think it's about you, Scarlet? Lots of it is fictional,' I snap.

'Oh, I just thought...'

She stares at the table and I instantly feel guilty.

'Anyway, I'm feeling a lot better now. Like you said, travelling has been good for me. Really good.'

My palms are sweaty. My mouth dry.

How is it that after all these months she can still make me feel so nervous? All those months of rebuilding, sticking my broken self back together and now after just five minutes I feel like the glue is starting to dissolve.

I take a deep breath and return to the small talk.

'And how about you, Scarlet? How's London?'

'Oh you know, grey. A lot grey,' she shrugs, 'Especially since you left.'

BOOOOOM!

And there is! First bomb delivered. Target hit. Shaken, but no major damage. She looks into my eyes again, desperately trying to connect.

'Anyway...'

It's funny, I've imagined this scene so many times, pictured us sitting down together talking, visualising what I'd say. What she'd say. I'd rehearsed it to the line, the word even, but now the moment is here, all that has gone out the window and it's like it's happening to someone else.

She starts thumbing her hair between her thumb and fingers, the way she does when she's nervous. The way she did that night when I walked in on her and Carla.

'So, Jen is here I see. Your faithful sidekick.'

'*Sidekick?* She's my best friend!'

'Yeah, course. Partners in crime. She's looking great. She looks different, what's she been doing?'

'Oh, dating a personal trainer,' I respond with a wry smile, accidentally letting my guard down.

Be strong, Ava! Strong!

She smiles again and takes another sip of her coffee, which leaves a little foam moustache around her gorgeous red lips. Instinctively I go to wipe it away but stop myself. Crazy how easily you slip back into old rhythms, like a train gliding on rails. Seamless. I guess there's a comfort in old intimacies: a familiar voice, a smile, a little look that to anyone else would go unnoticed, but to you, says so much. All these little things conspire to lure us in, to weaken our resolve.

I touch my necklace and address the elephant in the room.

'So, what is it you want, Scarlet?'

My tone is much stronger than intended and I see her physically flinch.

'Wow. That's pretty direct.'

'Well, you have just appeared out of the blue uninvited. It's not such an unreasonable question, is it?'

'No, no, it's not.' She starts to play with the folds in the tablecloth, as if calculating her next move. 'I guess I just wanted to talk,' she says, leaning in. 'Did you get my texts?'

'Yes.'

'And my email?'

'Yes.'

'But you didn't reply?'

'No, I didn't. I've been umm…'

'Yes?'

'Busy.'

I must have hit a nerve as her eyes flash at me, full of hurt.

'*Busy?*' she repeats. I stare over at her.

Yes, busy.

Busy dreaming of the day when you're not the first thing I think about when I wake up and the last thing I think of when I close my eyes. Busy dreaming of the day when you don't occupy every waking thought or dream. Busy wishing every song didn't remind me of you. Every smell. Busy trying to forget how the sight of you makes me melt into a big, wet puddle.

Yeah, I was busy all right. Busy getting over you.

I share none of that of course, retreating to the safety of my coffee.

She doesn't let up.

'But… you *did* read them?' she says, desperate for some tiny reassurance. I stare over at her, at those beautiful eyes, at those lips I've missed so much and then I speak.

'Yes, I read them, Scarlet. Not that I wanted to.'

My voice suddenly cracks, so I break off.

I can feel a ball of emotion forming in my throat, a ball of anger at having to justify myself, at having to explain *my* actions. Jen's right, I don't owe her a thing. Least of all an explanation as to why I didn't answer her bloody messages!

She pushes her hand out across the table.

'OK. Look, let's forget about all that. I'm just happy you came, Ave. It's so good to be able to talk, to try and make you, well ... understand.'

I instantly recoil, pulling my hand away.

'*Understand?*' I snap, 'Understand what exactly? Why you were shagging your workmate you mean, or why you proposed to me in the first place? Because, to be honest, I've had a hard job comprehending either!'

Her mouth goes to open, but for once the floor is mine. I am a she-wolf. Fierce, unyielding, savage.

'I mean, why in God's name did you push for that big party, Scarlet? So you could humiliate me in front of our family and friends? So you could make me feel the worst I've ever felt in my whole fucking life?'

I'm unstoppable.

All the months, weeks, days of hurt come spewing out of me like steam from a pressure cooker. *Speaking my truth at last!* The honeymooners at the next table are far less appreciative of my candour and I feel the weight of the new bride's gaze upon me. Her disappointment. It's as if she's getting a tiny glimpse into love gone sour. The shape of things to come, perhaps. I feel bad for her. I have no desire to subject anyone to our happy *never* after, so we head off towards the beach.

It's roasting outside.

Oppressive. The sun every bit as intense as the conversation. Scarlet clears her throat.

'Believe me, Ava, I know what I did was beyond awful. It's the worst thing I have ever done and if I could undo it I would. If ...' Her eyes well up. 'Look, I just want to tell you how sorry I am about hurting you, about it all. The lying, the cheating...everything!'

It's a lot to take in.

Every word I've dreamt of hearing her say is now pouring from her lips unprompted, unsolicited. Remorse, guilt, regret. But now that I'm finally hearing those words, I just feel numb. Numb and profoundly sad.

We sit for a moment, staring into space, not knowing where to go from here. The sun beats down, the wind breathing hot air upon us, adding to the discomfort. She grabs my hand.

'I didn't come here to fight, honestly. I know I have been stupid, so fucking stupid. I have missed you *so* much.' She stops for a moment, looking me full in the eyes 'Have you missed me?'

I stare at her half-blinded by the glare, half-blinded by my own rage.

'Fucking hell, Scarlet! What do you want me to say?' I spit. '*You* did this. You did all of this! You killed me that night. I swear to God, you fucking killed me. And now you've come over here in what, some kind of grand gesture, and I just don't know what you expect from me. Forgiveness? Redemption?' I feel my temples thumping, the sun more intense by the second. 'I mean, where's Carla in all this? Did she dump you or something? Did her boobs explode at 35,000 feet on the way over?'

'No, Ava! It's over with her. I don't want to be with her. I never did. It all got out of hand and I couldn't get out of it. It's you I love. It's only ever been you.'

With that, the dam bursts and the tears cascade down her cheeks, but rather than deriving any satisfaction from it, I feel sad for her. Sad to see her in all that pain. That searing pain that used to be mine. I look into her eyes and, in that moment, I believe her. I pull her into me, holding her trembling body against mine while the seagulls scream, and the kids play about us. It is like the first rain after some godawful drought, all the anguish of the past spewing out of us and leaving little wet patches on the Camps Bay sand.

Around the World in 80 Gays
"The other *C word*"

The most potent C word is not the one most might imagine.

It's not that four-letter stinger that divides a room – leaving some in hysterics, while mortally offending others. No. The *truly* powerful C word is much less controversial. Boring even.

I'm talking about *'Conversation'*.

Doesn't sound very powerful, does it?

Not quite packing the punch of its cruder cousin, and yet it contains all the clout, and more: *the power to heal.*

As I walk away from my ex, feeling utterly exhausted, I also have a strange sense of lightness, as if unburdened of an emotional load. One packed with questions, confusion, anger, resentment – feelings that eat away at us, emotions that we carry into other relationships.

And on and on.

The damage being passed along.

The truth is, some conversations simply need to be had, however uncomfortable they might feel. How many family rifts would be sorted with an honest conversation? How many fragmented friendships would be repaired and laughed about after a good, candid chat?

In short, however painful airing a grievance might be, it's far better than the alternative: allowing things to fester.

This is doubly true with romantic love.

Passion gone bad leaves a terrible smell, or as Shakespeare more elegantly put it, "Lilies that fester, smell far worse than weeds."

CHAPTER THIRTY - SAFARI TIME!

The drive to Aquila Game Reserve, location of highly anticipated wedding and dreaded blog shoot, is gloriously uneventful, aside from squishing a few hundred dung beetles en route. *C-ruuunch!* I can only hope it's not an omen for things to come.

The little critters are everywhere.

Armies of them lining the red dust road up to the safari lodge, all diligently rolling turd into little round balls to take home for dinner. *'Poober Eats'* delivery as Jen coins it.

'Hey, must suck being a dung beetle,' I laugh, as we steamroll corpse 68. 'They quite literally eat shit and die!'

'Ha! That'll be you at this wedding,' Jen teases. 'I mean…WTF!'

'Oh dooooon't. It's not my fault.'

'What? Not your fault that your ex is coming to your cousin's wedding you mean? No shit, Sherlock! In fact, please explain to me one more time how Scarlet got herself invited, 'cos frankly it's a complete headfuck.'

'I know, I know. Urgghhh!' I say, my anger reignited. 'I told you what happened – it was Marcus – the gruesome groom! Scarlet and I had our chat and big cry sesh on the beach and then…'

'You instantly forgave her and fell tongue first onto her gorgeous, plump lips?'

'Noooooo! Course not. We bumped into Maria and Marcus, and they insisted we went for a drink and, well, that's when Marcus bloody invited her! I swear he did it on purpose, the little weasel.'

'Yep. Doesn't sound any better the second time I hear it. I mean, talk about complicated. You now have Cruella, all the media stuff AND Scarlet to contend with.'

C-RUUUNCH!

The girl's got a point.

The shock of Scarlet turning up has left me feeling a whole heap of confused. Lighter but confused. Seeing her so upset, listening to her poignant *mea culpa* confessional, hearing that she still loves me; it's a lot! I feel all shaken up like a can of coke that's rolled down a few flights of stairs. And then some. Frankly, I'm doing all I can not to explode in a big frothy mess right now.

Aquila Game Reserve, Touws River, The Karoo

The entrance to Mandela Lodge is suitably impressive and we stop before a pair of wooden gates, not dissimilar to *Jurassic Park*, only smaller. I watch incredulously as my water bottle trembles on the dashboard and an almighty trumpeting sound blasts from behind the gates.

'Oh Lord, is that what I think it is?' I stammer.

'It's just the elephants, Miss. No T-Rex!' the lodge guard laughs, handing me a neatly folded map. 'A big bull whispering sweet nothings to his wife.'

'Oh right! Just the elephants!' I smile. 'Oh, hang on, what am I saying – *just the elephants!* WE'RE ABOUT TO SEE ELEPHANTS! ELE-BLOODY-PHANTS, JENNIFER! You know what? This wedding might just be fun after all!'

We set off again, our tyres kicking up a cloud of dust as we negotiate a few more tricky bends along the track. We come to the last, a particularly tight hairpin which uncoils to reveal our first glimpse of the five star safari lodge. It. Is. Stunning! A dozen or so wooden buildings with triangular thatched roofs, nestled amongst the brightest flowers and bushes. Apparently, Kate and William stayed here Maria told me, although she didn't specify *which* Kate and William, so I'll refrain from any further bragging.

'It's mad to think we're only a few hours from Cape Town,' Jen remarks, gazing across the plains. 'Look at that landscape!'

I remove my sunnies and look about me.

Gone are the white, sandy beaches and turquoise ocean, replaced by wild, untamed Africa with its dry, bushy plains stretching as far as the eye can see. There is the most gorgeous sense of peace here. Calm. A feeling of complete and utter tranquili...

'AVAAAA! You're heeeere!' a voice sings, thereby shattering the peace and tranquility bit. I leap out of the car.

'Maria! Awww! Look at you - you look amaaaazing!'

'Oh, d'you like it?' she beams, adjusting her spotty leopard print scarf. 'I got it online. *RealAfrica.com*. Thought I'd go all out, you know, when in Rome or *Africa* I should say.'

Snort snort.

She's very on theme, I have to say. Khaki onesie, animal print head scarf, zebra striped nails. What is it with people dressing like safari animals when they visit Africa? At best it's a fashion faux pas, at worst, they run the risk being of being taken out by a poacher and their heads unceremoniously mounted on the sitting room wall.

'Oh Ave, you should see my Marcus. He looks just gorge. MARCUS!' she yells, 'MARCUUUSSSS!' and right on cue, the little Napoleon comes marching out in cut-off safari trousers and matching khaki hat. *Cringe!* We struggle to stifle giggles as he removes his hat giving a long, low bow.

'Greetings, ladies. Looking lovely, looking lovely.' He instantly peers over my shoulder, 'Oh, is Scarlet not with you?'

'No. She's not. But it was thoughtful of you to invite her, Marcus,' Jen smiles with more than a hint of sarcasm.

'Just trying to help out,' he winks, adjusting his crown jewels. 'She's quite a girl, that one! Quite a girl!'

We give him the side eye, knowing that 'quite a girl' is Marcus code for hot.

'Well, we're just *so* happy you two are here,' Maria grins, quelling any awkwardness. 'Look at you...my cousin Ava, a famous blogger and all. Who'd have thunk it? And hasn't it all worked out a treat? Lucrezia and Andre have been amazing with the wedding arrangements, you know. Nothing too much trouble, they've done it all.'

'Oh right, are they here already?' Jen asks, the colour draining from her crimson cheeks.

'Not yet. Detained in Customs apparently – some mix-up with a bag of talc or something. Anyway, the vans and decorations have all arrived. You should see them. This wedding is going to be bigger than *Ben-Hur*. And it's all thanks to you, Ava!' she gushes, showering me in sticky champagne kisses. 'Thank you! Thank you!'

'Well, I'm just glad you're happy, Maria. I...'

'Happy? She's over the friggin' moon,' Napoleon interrupts. 'You know what you girls are like. Love all that glitz and glamour, don't you? Still, can't believe all this fuss over a silly blog. I mean, it's hardly Doffdoy, Doffdoyosly...'

'Dostoyevsky?'

'Yeah, that's it.'

The man is an ungracious little twat, but for once we are in agreement.

It *is* a lot of fuss over a silly blog.

The world has gone mad and it would seem that a good few of the genuinely mad ones are here at this wedding. Case in point, inappropriate Uncle George, who starts to bellow at me from the main terrace.

'Ava Roberts! Is that you? Last time I saw you, you were stuffing your bra with tissue! Hahahahaha!'

Not strictly true since I saw him at my engagement party a few months back. Not a hint of stuffing. Not that he'll remember. #LikesASherry.

'Uncle George,' I smile. 'How very nice to see you.'

Awkward hug.

George is not my blood uncle I should add, though I do often fantasize about him lying in a pool of the stuff. Jokes. He met my Aunt Mary following a stressful divorce, after her hair fell out. He has a thing for bald women, *acomophilia* I think they call it, and they married soon after, much to my mum's horror.

The chat quickly switches to my love life. Or lack thereof. I fear it's going to be like this for the next day or so – me explaining to relatives why I'm not married, or worse still, why I'm not married to Scarlet.

Urrghhhh!

I'm on the cusp of becoming a little agitated when I'm rescued by an enthusiastic 'Yooo-hoooo!' from the bar. I spin round to see her, my knightess in shining Armani, wielding a pina colada as big as her smile.

'Aunty B! You're here!'

I leap up the steps and embrace her with a vigour that's close to asphyxiation.

'I'm soooo happy to see you,' I enthuse. 'So happy!'

'Of course you are, dear – you're only human. Now let me get you girls a drink!'

Aunty B is everything. My mum's youngest sister who caused quite the scandal when she eloped with a Dutch sailor aged 16, before dumping him for a novice priest. 'She had a bit of how's your father with a Father!' as dad likes to joke at family gatherings.

'So, how are you, my dear?' she smiles. 'And hello Jennifer. My, you're looking lovely! What beautiful eyes you have. Beautiful!'

'Thanks,' Jen blushes.

'Such a shame your parents couldn't make it to the wedding, Ava. Still, knee replacements are never fun and good of your brother to stay behind and look after your mum. I've had two new knees myself you know. Can't possibly imagine how I'm wearing them out so fast,' she laughs, winking at one of the hot, young barmen.

'Aunty B! You're wicked!'

'I do try!' she grins. 'So, will you lovely girls be coming on the game drive later?'

'We sure will. You?'

'Wouldn't miss it for the world, dear. Besides…' she says in a whisper, 'With any luck, a lion might eat the bridegroom!'

Bahhaahahahaha!

*

The aunty/niece catch up lasts longer than anticipated and two and a half pina coladas later I sway my way to our room for a quick change before the inaugural game drive. We're in the Royal Zebra Suite, overlooking the pool. Cruella upgrade. It's utterly gorgeous: marble bathroom, outside shower, luxury recliners, all housed beneath a high timber roof that would happily accommodate a giraffe.

'Right!' Jen grins, spraying mosquito repellant like it's Chanel No5. 'Simba, here we come!'

'Shit girl. Go easy with that stuff.' *Splutter splutter.* 'Hey, don't suppose it repels ex-girlfriends and annoying relatives, does it?'

She has a quick scan of the label.

'Nope. Just mozzies and midges.'

'Ha! Shame!'

'Have to say, Ave, your family is a bit...interesting. I mean, Uncle George! I swear he's gets worse every time I see him! And are they *all* in love with Scarlet?'

'All except Aunty B. Think she's more taken with you. She kept saying, "Jen has eyes like emeralds!" ' I laugh, stifling another Deet-induced splutter.

'Well, I'll take that. She's cool your Aunty B, a lady who knows what she wants.'

'Yeah and tonight it's that cute bartender with the tight buns!'

There are few things as thrilling as an African safari. Not surprising that they feature on 98.99 percent of bucket lists, right up there with travelling the world, parachuting and the Egyptian pyramids. Visiting them I assume, not building. Tonight, we're all about the 'Big Five' or medium four even. In fact, anything badger-sized and above will do. We're just happy to be here in beautiful Africa. There's something truly magical about this place. Even the air smells different, thick with the musk of rutting beasts and sun-dried vegetation. And as for the noises! My ears delight to a symphony of animal grunts, insect clicks, cackles, and some weird bird that sounds like a ring tone and has everyone checking their phones every few seconds.

We make it to reception just in time to board the awaiting chariots, four dusty Land Rovers each modified with an elevated platform behind the driver's seat: six rows of bench seats, open sides and beige canvas roof. In short, it's like a charcuterie board on wheels, easy game for any passing lion!

The last car looks like a good option – half empty thus eliminating the need for small talk whilst awaiting the arrival of Mr Rhino and chums. We go to slip in unnoticed, when an excited Maria bellows,

'Ava, Jen! Over here! I've saved you a seat in VIP!'

Dutifully disembarks, rolling eyes beneath sunnies.

The bridal jeep is a sight to behold, decorated with hundreds of fabulous native flowers and a tasteful orange banner advertising *Bovine Weekly (South African edition)*. #SafariSellOut. We clamber aboard with a joyful 'Wohooo!' acknowledging the bride and groom who are sitting up front with Maria's sister Jane, fiancé Mark and their two children, Oli and Tabitha, who keep demanding to watch TikTok videos on daddy's phone.

'Remind me not to have kids,' Jen whispers, as Ollie proceeds to smash screen number five, thus causing an uncontrollable tantrum. Daddy's, not Ollie's.

We leave them to it, clocking Uncle George and Aunt Mary in the row behind.

'Oh, hello girls,' Aunt Mary smiles, spraying us with a hearty welcome sneeze. *ACHOOOO!* Classic Aunt Mary! The poor woman's allergic to everything – nuts, hair, horses, magazines (the ink), dust, daffodils, lightbulbs and most recently smoked ham. She consequently spends most of her time asleep due to overuse of antihistamines. We exchange pleasantries and plonk ourselves firmly at the back, across from Aunty B and mysterious beau, who I soon recognise as said bartender with tight buns. *Fast work indeed!*

Safety belts affixed, we're ready to go.

'Hello ladies and gentlemen,' our driver says, rising up from his seat. He's a remarkably tall man with long, long limbs that must be concertinaed into that tiny seat. 'A warm welcome to Aquila Game Reserve. My name is Thuto. I will be your guide this evening. It is wonderful to have the bride and groom with us today. What a blessing love is. Just a few rules for the drive this evening. Firstly, have fun and secondly, please keep your hands inside the vehicle. Everything in Africa bites! But…' he pauses, flashing the toothiest grin, 'Nothing bites harder than the safari bug, so prepare to fall head over hooves in love with the beautiful animals of Africa! Thank you!'

With that rousing introduction, the engine rumbles to life and our African odyssey begins.

'I'm sooo excited!' I beam, as we start to chug away.

'Same! This is the best, Ave! The best!'

The euphoria lasts all of two metres, before we are cruelly halted by an excited yell from reception.

'OH, HELLOOOOO! WAIT FOR ME! WAIT FOR MEEEE!'

The brakes squeal and all eyes divert to the side of the vehicle as a tall, blonde figure clambers into the van. 'Room for one more?' she smiles.

Scarlet. Just perfect!

Uncle George is beside himself with the arrival of the latecomer.

'Squeeze on in, my dear! Plenty of room!' he smiles, his tongue rolling out like the Oscars' red carpet. 'Any more in here and we'll need lubricant, hey?'

Snort snort.

'Did someone say lubricant? We've got bags of the stuff!' Marcus grins, tossing a handful of fruity lube sachets our way. 'They're one of the sponsors of the wedding!'

'Ewww! You are kidding?' Jen grimaces, 'Lucrezia really sent you strawberry lube?'

'Not just strawberry! Peach, lemon, papaya - even watermelon! Though it tastes more like grape,' he grins, revealing a big stash in his day bag. 'I'm selling them on eBay. Making a killing! Maria tried some earlier, didn't you my angel? Spread it on her ciabatta, *thought it was jam,*' he laughs. 'JAM! Not the brightest spark...'.

I'm just about to tear a strip off him when I realise I have bigger problems right now, as Scarlet plonks herself down in the only free seat available. Right. Next. To. Me.

FML!

I don't know what's more dangerous at this point, the creatures outside the jeep or the tall, hot blond ones within! I glance at her in her safari shorts with those long, long legs; the eighth wonder of the world as we used to joke. She's even wearing that perfume I love. I can't help but inhale a lungful as she pushes her body against mine.

'Hi there, Ave. This is cosy!' she says before leaning forward to greet Jen. 'Hello Ms Jones. It's been *ages*!'

'Yes, it has been a while. How are you, Scarlet?'

'Much better….now,' she says looking directly at me.

I get the impression Jen is a not best pleased with the cuckoo in the nest and she turns to look out of the vehicle as Thutu calls, 'Hold tight everyone!'

Thud, thud, bounce, bounce!

It's not the smoothest of rides I have to say, but we skillfully negotiate the craters, potholes and dung beetles, *cccc-rrunch,* while people periodically strike their heads on safety bars and handrails. On the plus side, it does wonders to relieve tensions within, and pretty soon everyone is laughing and joking as we bounce our way across the magnificent Karoo.

BOING! BOING!

'Mummy! Mummy! Look at Aunty Beryl's boobies!' Oliver sniggers.

'Hahaha! Oh yes, look out B. You'll end up with two black eyes at this rate!'

'I won't George, but carry on like that and you sure as hell will!' she retorts, shoving oversized puppies back into their lacy black kennel. Aunty B's breasts aren't the only bruised items aboard today. I myself am being unceremoniously jostled between Jen and Scarlet, flying back and forth like a pinball.

Jen to Scarlet. Scarlet to Jen. Back to Scarlet.

Ding ding ding!

Mercifully, the pinballing ends when we pull up at a watering hole where we are informed we will likely see our first animals. The excitement is palpable. Everyone sits quietly, all eyes trained on the vast plains. Watching. Waiting. Every rustle of the bush, every swish of a tree provokes a new wave of excitement. I wrinkle my nose to inhale the musky air, imagining I am some kind of animal scout, like in the movies and then…

'*Kudu! Kudu!*' Thuto announces, 'Over there!'

Hearts leap from chests as we spy a small group of antelope-looking creatures to the left; one male with the most spectacular spiral antlers and four females. Absolutely gorgeous. There's a mad scramble for cameras and phones as everyone dashes to our side of the jeep to snap the first spot of the day. Elbows in eyes, noses in armpits, and Jen and Scarlet in hysterics as I grapple with a face full of Uncle George's groin. The stuff of nightmares. There's a second flurry of camera action and next thing I now, everyone is scampering back to their side of the jeep, shouting 'GIRAFFE! GIRAFFE!' at a ridiculous volume.

'Giraffe? Where?' I squeal, as I look to a cluster of pointy trees to my right. I see it! The tallest, leggiest creature I've ever laid eyes on. A young male, we're told, and I watch him feed on a nearby tree with a neck 'as long as an Indian summer', as Aunty B eloquently puts it.

'The giraffe is the tallest creature on earth. Adults grow to around five metres, which makes birthing very interesting,' Thuto explains. 'You see, the giraffe gives birth standing up and the baby falls two metres to the floor.'

'That's why they've got those lumps on their noggins, hey Thuto!' Marcus quips, thrusting his four inch telescopic lens in our faces again.

Click click.

'Jeez! What is it about little men and big lenses?' Scarlet whispers as Uncle George whips out an even bigger one, and the two of them engage in a homoerotic lens-off, wielding their weighty appendages like light sabres. Mr Giraffe is equally unimpressed, promptly retiring to the bush just as a second wave of beasts arrive for happy hour. Springboks, oryx and then to my delight, the cutest family of warthogs, who merrily trot out in single file to join the pool party.

'It's like waiting for a bus, isn't it? You wait and wait, and then eight come at once,' Maria giggles, as the most beautiful ostrich dashes out and flutters her glorious eyelashes my way.

'Awwww! She likes you, Ava!' Scarlet smiles, 'She clearly has taste.' She touches my leg in a not unflirtatious way and I try not to react, as Madame Ostrich treats us to an impromptu dance, fanning her wings and crossing them back and forth across her face like a burlesque dancer.

'Reminds me of our trip to Paris and all those feathers at the Moulin Rouge! Do you remember?' Scarlet smiles. 'What a city. Not that we left our hotel room much.'

I give a nervous little cough.

Paris! How could I forget Paris!

The city of romance, the city of food and wine, the city of not-being-able-to-keep-our-hands-off-each-other!

My mind starts working overtime, recalling all the things we did there together – nighttime walks along the Seine, jazz clubs – before Marcus jolts me back to the moment.

'Hey, Thuto mate. Where's the big stuff? We wanna see the *proper* animals; rhinos, hippos and the ones with the big teeth!'

'I will see what I can do, sir!' as right on cue a two-ton rhino trundles up for a quick sundowner. *It is HUGE!* An incredible looking creature, almost prehistoric in appearance and its tank-like body is covered in a thick layer of dust, like a hessian sack.

Cue next mad wave of camera activity

'Now, that's what I'm talking about! Christ! Look at the size of that horn!' the groom smirks. 'Course you know what they say about rhinos?' He doesn't wait for a response, 'They're unicorns that have let themselves go! Hahaahahah! Good, hey?' He turns to his bride-to-be. 'You better not do that when we're married, Maria – let yourself go!'

Prays to heaven for lion to savage groom quick smart.

The banter subsides and for once all is quiet both inside and outside. The humans watch the animals, the animals occasionally watch the humans, and I surrender to the magic of the moment. #GratitudeGratitude.

Even Scarlet's body pressed so close to mine in those cut-off safari shorts and tight white vest seems less dangerous.

'What's that?' she blurts, grabbing my hand.

Gentle movement in the trees just 20 metres away!

All heads turn to two o'clock where there's a further swooshing of leaves, then suddenly the branches dramatically part and a colossal grey shape emerges.

'*HELAPHANT,*' little Oliver blurts. '*HELAPHANT!*'

'Hella-HUUUUGE more like!' Marcus grins, frothing at the muzzle.

What a sight! Encountering a wild elephant up close is near indescribable. Words like amazing, awesome, spectacular, simply don't cut it. In fact, it's probably best explained as a rush, an excited high like downing a glass of champagne too quickly, and I can't help but pop!

'This really is the best day *ever!*' I beam.

'Isn't it?' Scarlet smiles, 'I'm so glad I'm here with you, Ava!'

She presses her leg against mine as we watch the creature artfully strip leaves from the trees with her massive trunk, wielding it like a giant arm. I'm mesmerised by the size of the beast! It must be over three metres tall with its gargantuan body and feet, not to mention its head! Gi.Nor.Mous! And yet, despite its size, there is such an elegance about it, a gentle majesty as if it's walking in slow motion.

'OI, BIG EARS! OVER HERE!' Marcus bellows, thereby shattering the poetry of the moment.

Click click!

The elephant stops in her tracks. I fear she doesn't much appreciate the big ears heckle or the ferocious clicking for that matter. She starts to kick the earth, swinging her trunk back and forth with a few irritated grunts.

'No shouting sir and kindly sit down!' Thutu says sternly. 'We do not wish to startle her.'

For once Marcus complies and we sit there, torn between terror and awe watching her defensive displays. She's so close now that I see all the folds in her thick, grey skin. It's rather like the texture of tree bark.

'If only humans were as proud of their wrinkles,' Aunty B quips. 'I'd save a fortune on Botox!'

Bahhhahahha!

The giggles morph into a collective 'Awww!' as all of a sudden a baby elephant trundles out of the bush! He's almost drunk-looking, waving his little trunk high in the air, as if he hasn't quite got the hang of it yet. I watch the pair interacting, mummy nuzzling baby with a tenderness that makes all the hairs on the back of my neck stand up.

The private audience doesn't last long and we are soon joined by two other jeeps that draw up on the other side of mummy and baby. The competition is too much for Marcus who rises up almost in protest and starts clicking more frantically than ever.

'Come on Nelly! Look at us, not at that lot!' he snarls, getting ever more frustrated. Nelly doesn't comply, so he jeers at her again even louder. 'Big Ears, oi!'

It's one step too far and this time she takes real offence, nodding and shaking her giant skull with more and more vigour.

'Please be calm everyone. She is signalling her annoyance,' Thutu warns.

'Annoyance? Errrr, not sure I want to be near when this lady gets annoyed,' Jen whispers as everyone starts to get a bit jittery or, in Aunt Mary's case, starts snoring louder than the resident buffalos. #IBlameTheAntihistamines.

The head bowing carries on for a big longer before…

BAHHRROUUUUUUUUU! BAHHRROUUUUUUUUUUUUUUUU!

Nelly trumpets the mother of all warnings, angrily swinging one leg back and forth above the cracked earth.

'Umm, is it me or is she walking this way?' Scarlet says.

'Err, I'd go with trotting!' Jen stammers. 'Defo a trot!'

STOMP STOMP STOMP!

The vehicle instantly cranks into reverse as Nelly and baby upgrade their trot to more of a leisurely gallop.

'She's gonna charge, people! *SHE'S GONNA BLOODY CHARGE*!' Marcus spits as everyone starts grabbing their loved ones, others burying their heads in their backpacks.

'Please remain still!' Thutu warns. 'Very still!'

STOMP STOMP STOMP!

There must be a word for the feeling you get when you see a two-ton African elephant jogging your way, but in want of that I'll just utter an unimaginative 'FUUUUUUUUUCK!' and grip onto my seat buddies. Marcus' fear response is radically different. He starts getting aggressive, yelling 'Screw this!' at the top of his lungs, whilst propelling himself over to our side of the jeep, thereby creating a mini stampede! Everyone scrambles to follow suit, as the jeep starts to pitch.

'Please remain seated!' Thuto implores. 'Please remain seated!' The gears grind, the elephants trumpet and the jeep leans.

Grind

Trumpet

Leeeeeaaaaaaaaaaan!

'We're tipping! We're tipping!' Marcus wails, as the Jeep starts to seriously lilt to the left like a drunk at a bus stop.

'I can't die! Not before, not before…'

'Not before we marry, darling?'

'No, not before I've driven that Porsche!' Marcus yells, grabbing a fistful of lube sachets, which he promptly starts to lob at poor Nelly and child.

'For fuck's sake Marcus!' Jen shouts, grabbing the sachets from his sweaty palms. 'Stooooop!'

Too late! One sachet strikes baby square on the head, as Nelly quickens her pace.

STOMP STOMP STOMP!

'We're going to die! We're going to die!' Uncle George blubs, as we assume brace position. 'Farewell cruel world! Farewell!'

And then suddenly, BEEEP BEEEEEEEEP!

Out of nowhere, the sound of a car horn!

The honking is enough to stop Nelly in her tracks, as we direct our attention towards a giant dust cloud hurtling along the track ahead.

'What the fuck is that?' someone shouts, as we watch the unidentified dusty mass moving closer. Then, from amidst the cloud, a revving beeping Jeep dramatically bursts forth! *It's neon pink with animal print rollbars!* We watch in disbelief as it leaps over the brow of the hill, like something out of *Mad Max*!

WTF!

Nelly's ears pin back, our ears pin back, as we strain to hear the sound of music blasting from its pinkness!

That drum beat, those unmistakable opening notes.

.

.

'Err, is it me or can you hear Toto's "Africa"?'

"It would take a lot to get me away from yooooou….."

Nods all round as the neon Jeep thunders over to us, with a wild-haired warrior woman standing atop! I stare at her in disbelief.

OMG! It can't be. It can't be....can it?

'Holy crap! IT'S CRUELLA!' Jen gasps, as the Jeep screeches to a halt and then, out she leaps,

'HAKUNA MATATA, BITCHES!'

Jaws drop, hearts pound as Nelly stares at her, utterly bewildered by this strangest of sights in head-to-toe animal print.

Cruella starts to stride towards her, throwing her arms into the air like the ancient warrior Boadicea.

'Be gone mighty elephantus!' she commands. '*Ungawa!*'

It's utterly trouser-pooping!

Two mighty opposites in a spectacular safari stand-off!

Nelly's great ears beat back and forth.

Cruella's kaftan flaps out behind her like a pair of majestic wings.

I can't look at this point, foreseeing the bloody confrontation that is about to ensue, whereby Cruella will be rendered a mangled pulp of designerwear in the Karoo dust.

Jen grips my right hand, Scarlet, my left. Nobody. Uttering. A. Sound.

And then….. the unthinkable happens.

Nothing!

Absolutely. Nothing!

I peel back an eyelid to witness the mighty Nelly shaking her great head one final time before trumpeting the loudest retreat and disappearing into the bush whence she came.

Sighs of relief all round. And then, a solitary snort, as Aunt Mary awakens from her antihistamine coma.

'Oh my! Did I miss the elephants, George?'

*

Nobody mentions the unpleasant aroma in the Jeep or the fact that Marcus has changed his trousers; instead, we head to the lodge terrace to raise a glass to the hero of the hour.

'To Lucrezia! Hip hip…!'

'HOOOOORAY!'

'Darlinks, pleasssse! It was nothing!' she coos in such a way as to garner even more praise. 'I've always had an affinity with the African beasts you know – it's in my blood. I'm part African,' she smiles, fanning herself with a huge ostrich feather.

'*African?* I didn't know you had African heritage?' Jen says incredulously.

'Yes, darlink, I did one of those ancestry tests. It was conclusive. I'm a resounding 0.000000000001 percent Namibian.'

'Well, we're just grateful you were there today, Lucrezia!' Uncle George roars. 'What a woman, taking on the might of an elephant!' he gushes, attempting to hug her for the sixth time. And missing.

'TO LUCREZIA!'

Tonight is the official start of Marcus and Maria's nuptial celebrations: the pre-wedding braai. A South African brai is a more sophisticated version of our English BBQ, in other words, not an uncooked pork sausage in sight. Imagine if you will, steaks as tender as butter, prawns the size of a baby's forearm and an array of rainbow-coloured salads made from the finest local produce.

'The chef is Michelin-starred!' Cruella coos. 'We had him flown in.'

'Oh, how lovely,' Maria enthuses.

'Yah, yah. He's exquisite, a raging alcoholic of course! But all the greatest artists are – misery maketh a good roux, n'est-ce pas?' she grins, picking at the plumpest lobster tail.

'Well, all I can say is it's delicious, Lucrezia. In fact, I just can't stop eating,' Maria giggles, poised to eat another juicy pink prawn.

'Well try to my love,' Marcus snipes, snatching the food from her hand. 'Remember what I said about rhinos and unicorns!'

Heckles instantly go up

'Ignore him, Maria. Eat what you want, it's *your* wedding,' I protest, returning said prawn to her plate, which Marcus immediately snatches back, thereby making it the most manhandled crustacean in Christendom. He shoots me a look as Jen swoops in for backup.

'Hear hear! You go for it, girl! I intend to eat my entire body weight over the next two days!' she winks, patting her tummy. 'No shame, all gain!'

Everyone nods in hearty agreement as Cruella (self-appointed M.C.) raises her glass skyward and declares, 'To the bride and groom!'

'To Marcus and Maria!'

'WAHOOOOO!'

I can't help but watch her. Cruella is a woman in her element tonight. Laughing uproariously, charming my family and friends. It's a bizarre scene! The union of two different worlds. Ying and yang. Chalk and brie! I look around the terrace at all the guests drinking and laughing, and I can't help but feel I'm in some weird French farce. The cast are assembled – irresistible ex, arsehole groom, inappropriate uncle and oversexed aunt. It has all the makings of a blockbuster and I can only pray that whoever is directing this crazy life of mine will come up with a half-decent ending.

'Here Ave, I got you a top-up.'

I spin around to see Scarlet standing there with champagne flute number five. I'm not entirely sure of her motives to be honest. Perhaps she's being kind. Perhaps she is trying to ply me with drink and weaken my defences. The cynical me thinks the latter. Whatever her intentions, she is being supremely attentive. Everywhere I go I feel her eyes upon me, watching, waiting to catch my glance, to beguile me with those eyes.

'So, today was terrifyingly great,' she smiles. 'Can't say I've been chased by an elephant before!'

'Ha! Me neither!'

'But we have been chased by a cow, a whole herd of them, in Cornwall. D'you remember?' she laughs, brushing my hand. 'It was after that awful surfing lesson!'

'Oh God, yeah! They pinned us against the fence!' I giggle, giddy on bubbles and nostalgia. 'I'm much better with cows these days, a big hit in fact.'

'Oh yes! Andi the cow in your blog?'

'Nandi. It's Nandi,' Jen says, wandering over to join us.

'Handi, Nandi, whatever!' Scarlet retorts, instantly cutting her down. 'Well, I just can't believe how brave you were today, Ave. Everyone was panicking, but you were so calm. A whole new you!' she smiles, holding my gaze.

'Well, I'm not sure about that,' I blush and sensing an in, she strikes.

'Hey, I was thinking. Maybe we could we go for a little walk later? Just the two of us. I'd love to show you…'

Before I can reply, Cruella glides up as excited as a kid at Christmas. 'I don't believe we've been introduced?' she coos, extending a manicured hand to Scarlet. 'I'm Lucrezia De Silva – CMO, CCO at *Marshall Media*. We produce Ava's tremendously successful blog.'

'Nice to meet you. I'm Scarlet, Ava's…'

'No introduction necessary, daaarlink!' she beams, giving her an air kiss. 'I know *exactly* who you are!' She stops for a moment to examine her. 'Aren't you exquisite? Just exquisite!'

'Oh, thank you!' Scarlet smiles.

FML!

Cruella's been gagging to meet my infamous ex ever since she arrived, desperate to unwrap this very special gift, and she wastes no time in diving on in and ripping off the ribbons.

'So, tell me, Scarlet. Do you read *Around the World in 80 Gays*?'

'Yes, I do. I'm a big fan.'

'Yah, yah. It's simply enchanting, darlink!' she says, leaning over her like a praying mantis. 'It has everything! Adventure, pathos…. *passion!* And I suppose we have *you* to thank in some part. *Indirectly* at least!'

'Oh, well err…'

'In fact, I'd *love* to buy you a drink, darlink!' she coos, sweeping her off for a cosy bar side tete a tete.

I stand there in disbelief.

'Well, that must be a record, even for Scarlet! I mean, her charm normally takes a bit longer than that to work,' I throw back my drink.

'Seven seconds, they say.'

'Hey?'

'It takes seven seconds to form an opinion of someone,' Jen slurs. 'More to the point, what a bloody cheek! Cruella giving Scarlet credit for all our hard work!' She breaks into a full-on Cruella impression, *'Oooh, can I buy you a drink, daaaaaaaaaaaarlink? Can I lick your bloody gold plated rectum?* Pffft!'

Our giggling soon catches the attention of Aunty B, who wanders over with cocktail in hand and naughty grin on face.

'So, what are my two favourite girls conspiring?'

'Oh, not much. We were just talking about Cruella, I mean Lucrezia, and Scarlet suddenly becoming BFFs! Sickening!'

'*Lucrezia?* Oh, is that the painful woman in the kaftan? I know she's your boss girls, but I've got diamonds that are more genuine!'

Bahahahahahhaa!

'Seriously though, I've known plenty of her sort, rarely what they seem. Mind you, this is the first one I've met who travels with a new age fire guru!' she grins, stumbling over the words. 'What is that by the way?'

'Not sure to be honest! Is he here yet?' I ask, looking about the terrace.

'Oh yes, he's here alright! Wafting his burning bush in the reception area. The smoke alarm has gone off twice already!'

'Oh God, nooooo!'

'Apparently, he's *cleansing* the area. Exorcising the spirit of an angry beast! Mind you, I could do with an angry beast myself right now!' she winks. 'Now where did that delicious barman go?'

The night goes off rather well, aside from the best man choking on a dill pickle and Uncle George getting so drunk that he has to be put to bed. 'It's the heat!' he slurred as they carried him to his room, clutching an empty bottle of Baileys.

By midnight, I'm out and out beat. I give a little yawn and commence farewells, only to be ambushed near the cheese board.

'Ave, you're not going to bed, are you?' Scarlet says, her eyes heavy with disappointment.

'Yes! I have to. I'm soooo shattered.'

'But it's still early. Thought we could have that drink – you know, just us two. Like we said.'

Like you said, Scarlet. Like you said, I mutter beneath my breath, trying to remain strong.

I throw in another little yawn, but she just shoots me one of those hurt puppy dog looks which makes me feel mean. I promptly remind myself that

I had promised her nothing. Raised no expectations. In short, nothing to feel guilty about.

'Right then,' I smile, putting my empty glass down, 'See you tomorrow for the big day.'

I'm two seconds away from a good decision when a rather merry Cruella inserts herself slap bang into our conversation.

'Bed so soon? But you're in Africa, daaaarlink!' she implores. 'I mean, how often does one stand beneath a canopy of twinkling stars, listening to the calls of the impala, bewitched by the song of the *Loxodonta Africana*?'

I pause.

My head is drenched in champagne and Scarlet is working her magic, conspiring with a sky full of the brightest African stars I've ever seen.

Must resist. Must resist.

'Well?' she says.

I turn towards her, 'Oh, go on then, just the one!'

CHAPTER THIRTY-ONE - WEDDING BELLS AND ONE HELLUVA DING DONG

'Marriage: sometimes soulmates, sometimes cellmates.'

- Rory Elder

You are cordially invited to the Wedding of:
Marcus Von Strondleberg and Maria Jane Roberts

~

Sponsored by Around the World in 80 Gays in
association with Bovine Weekly &
Nandi Shakes. 'Shake it 'til you make it!'

It's a glorious day for a wedding. Especially one proudly sponsored by *Around the World in 80 Gays* plus highly reputable brands. *Cough. Cough.* I throw back the curtains like a regular Snow White, 'Morning Mr Rhino! Morning Mrs Bird!' I sing as the beasts respond with equal fervour: elephants trumpeting, buffalo snorting, while the baboons take it one step further presenting bottoms as I nibble on my breakfast bap.

'It's a sign of affection,' I smile as one gives said derriere an enthusiastic scratch.

'*In-fection* more like,' Jen yawns. 'Ewwww! Look at that! Doesn't look very healthy, does it?'

'Bet you've seen worse on a Friday night!'

'Ha! Maybe. You have to watch those baboons you know, they're right cheeky buggers. One ran off with someone's phone yesterday.'

'Really?' I giggle, as I imagine a baboon playing *Angry Birds* on a Samsung Galaxy. 'Didn't one steal a baby once? Saw a film about it with Meryl Streep.'

'Errr, I think that was a dingo.'

'Nah, it was definitely Meryl!'

The baboon debate is a welcome diversion from the underlying tensions of the day. Weddings are emotional affairs at the best of times; lovers gazing into one another's eyes, pledging their forevers. Add to that a hopelessly romantic setting, copious amounts of alcohol and an ex on the charm offensive, and we're talking potential disaster of Titanic proportions.

I will not meet my iceberg today! I will not meet my iceberg today!

Jen can read me like a book.

'So, how did your nightcap with Scarlet go?'

'Urgggh! I can't believe I weakened. I was doing so well and then I had all that champagne, and she was so persuasive and nice, and....'

Her face drops, 'Oh, right. So, you two...'

'Nooo! We just chatted – mostly about London things. I steered well clear of any dangerous talk. I mean, she tried to go there but, hey, I handled it, girl! Just gotta do the same today, hey?' I say confidently, reaching for my towel. 'Right. Prenuptial dip?'

The infinity pool at Mandela Lodge is Insta-perfect to quote editor-in-chief Lucrezia Da Silva. A turquoise water oasis, enclosed within a natural stone wall and as such has been earmarked as one of the locations for tomorrow's blog photoshoot #KillMeNow.

It *is* beautiful here; Maria has certainly aced the location, if not the groom! Mr Marcus Von Strondleberg! I can only imagine she sees something in him I don't, that he's truly wonderful deep down – the kind of deep down that requires heavy duty excavation equipment.

The pool is packed.

Wedding guests bubbling away in the shallows like lobsters in a pot, others loafing on giant bean bags. All. Semi. Naked.

Quickly averts eyes

Seeing a family's member (sorry, family member) in their swimwear is akin to using a hairdryer in the bath – shocking. Particularly when said relative is sporting tight orange speedos with half a testicle peeping out the side.

'Hi Uncle George,' I smile, framing out the offending hairy peeper before I clock Scarlet waving from a secluded corner.

'Ava! Ava!' she calls, drumming the lounger beside her like a snare. 'I saved you one!'

It's a rock and hard place situation: Uncle George and stubbly scrotum versus Scarlet and vacant lounger. Scarlet wins and I drag another bed over for Jen, thus forming a cosy throuple right beside the African violets.

'Beautiful day,' Scarlet smiles. 'Soo nice to get some sun in.'

She runs her hands through her hair and arches her back, instantly drawing my eyes to her body: those curves, those shoulders and that tiny little mole just above her belly button.

Dear Lord above!

It's like Aunty B said last night, 'Exes are just like cream cakes'. They sit there oozing their deliciousness and crying *'Eat me, eat me!'* And no matter how much we tell ourselves we should resist, it's almost impossible. 'A moment on the lips, a lifetime on the hips' as they say. Only in this case, there's a lot more at stake than gaining a few pounds. Like losing your heart and sanity all over again.

I take a massive glug of water to quell the fire within.

'Someone's thirsty. Must be all that champagne we had last night.'

'Ha! Don't know what you mean, Ms Tennison!'

'Well, hangover or not, I intend to make the most of the sun today girls,' Jen grins. 'It's pissing down back home.'

'Aww! Don't talk about London! Can't believe you have to head back tomorrow. Please staaaaay! It's been so great having you here.'

I feel the full weight of Scarlet's eyes upon me.

'I know! It's been the best, hey? Still, at least I have my birthday party to look forward to. *Thirty-one!* Shit! How did that happen?' Jen removes her sunnies. 'And how about you Scarlet, how long are you here for?'

'That depends…'

She glances over at me.

.

.

'Lord, it's hot!' I blurt. 'Hot hot hot!'

My evasiveness is transparent, but thankfully any awkwardness is soon dispelled by the arrival of Aunty B, who gives a chirpy 'You-hooo!' from the other side of the pool, before gliding over in a silver one-piece and matching kitten heel sandals.

'Hello girls! Room for a little one?' she sings, pulling up a seat.

'Of course! How are you, B?'

'Oh peachy. Just peachy.' She gives us all a quick inspection. 'And just look at you three lying there all gorgeous in your bikinis! I do love that about young women these days. Oozing power... oozing what do they call it...F.B.C?'

'*F.B.C*?'

'Front bum confidence! I read about it in *Cosmo*. It's like big dick energy, but much more potent.'

Bahahahahaahaha!

'Aunty B – you are incorrigible!'

She gives a cheeky grin and offers us a slice of pineapple, the secret to her youthful looks. That and sex. Lots of it in multiple positions, or so she told us last night. #AuntyLovesReverseCowgirl. 'Do you know, I had the best sleep last night! The best!'

'Wish I could say I did,' Scarlet scoffs. 'I hardly slept at all; the animals were so bloody noisy! I swear there was something pacing outside my room.'

'Big-bummed baboon.'

'Sorry Jen?'

'Probably a baboon making all the noise, I mean. Still, guess that's what you expect at a game reserve. Right, swim time. I am melting!'

She scoops her hair into a ponytail and dives in with an elegant SPOOOOSSSSHHH!

I love that sound!

The sound of summer! Like cicadas and croaking frogs, sizzling BBQs and late night laughter from garden parties. *Bliss!* I watch her glide up and down the pool while Scarlet leers at her, eyeing her every move from beneath her sunglasses.

'You can tell Jen's been dating a personal trainer. Must be rubbing off, hey?'

I don't respond, far too preoccupied with some rubbing of my own, namely my Ambre Solaire factor 30, which I'm making a right bloody mess of! I squeeze the tube a little too zealously, thus torpedoing a big white dollop onto the top of my leg. Scarlet gallantly comes to the rescue. 'Here, let me help.'

Before I can object, she's scooping up the cream from my thigh and massaging it over my shoulders in a sensual figure of eight motion.

Bites lip. Grips lounger!

Oh Lord, Oh Lord. Hold it together.

What is wrong with me? How can I still be attracted to her after all that's happened? And yet, attracted I am. It's like, despite all the warnings from that sensible part of your brain, your body has other ideas. Other wants and needs. Desires. My skin tingles in recognition of her touch and I'm instantly transported back to our intimate moments together, the feel of her body on mine, her mouth on mine. Her soft, beautiful…

SPLAAAAAAAAAASSSHHHHHH!

The erotic flashback is shattered by Marcus who bellyflops into the pool, taking out two children and soaking everyone in the vicinity. Zero. Fucks. Given.

'Wow, thanks Marcus!' I say, dabbing my face. 'Maria sure is one lucky lady.'

'Haha! You know it, Aves! You know it!' He starts to spurt water into the air like a medieval gargoyle, looking at Scarlet and then back at me. 'Talking of getting lucky, are you two girls back on again? If so, I want a commission.'

What a cheek!

The guy should concentrate on his own love life. He is after all the man who thought clitoris was a Greek island! He rests his chin on the pool edge, thereby prolonging the torture.

'So, I guess this is the kind of luxury you're accustomed to – now you're a fancy blogger?'

'Err, hardly! I don't usually stay in five star game lodges – *Travelodges* more like!'

'For real? Well, your boss was certainly generous with the wedding donation,' he grins, rubbing his fingers together like Fagin. '*Kerching*!'

'Oh right, that's good then. Glad it helped.'

'Yeah, saved us a packet. So come on then, how much do you make, Ave?'

'What?'

'Ballpark figure. What are you netting for the blog? 50K? 100K?'

Thankfully, Jen exits the pool just in time to spare any potential financial blushes.

'Why so interested Marcus? Are you inspired to write a blog of your own? If so, I'm sure Ava would be happy to share some tips.'

'Nah. I'm more of a figures man,' he says, staring right at her cleavage. 'Though I reckon I'd do a decent job. I mean, how hard can it be? Can't say I've read much of yours, but Maria's well into it. She was convinced you were the mystery writer all along - even before it came out. She kept saying "I bet it's Ava, bet it's Ava!" '

'Family intuition I guess.' I try to quickly derail the subject. 'Anyway, how about you, Marcus? I hear you guys are buying a fancy new house. Business must be good.'

'Yeah…blinding!' he says, half-submerging his face in the water.

'So where is it?'

'Where's what?'

'The new house?'

'Er yeah, Surrey. Near Guildford.'

'Very ni…'

My sentence is interrupted as a frenzied Marcus suddenly starts splashing about, yelling, 'Fuuuuuck! What time is it? Maria will castrate me if I'm late!'

And just like that, he's doggy paddling off and we're rushing back to our room to get changed.

*

The Wedding Ceremony.

1.45 pm. The Zebra Suite is alive with the whoosh of showers and the hisssss of perfume, and 43 minutes later transformation from drowned rats to wedding sophisticates is complete.

'Shit! Ave! Come on, the ceremony's about to start!'

'Cooomiiiing!' I yell, squashing size 12 thighs into size 10 dress #TooManyCocktails. I take a deep breath and zip myself in, only to have my breath taken away again. Absolute. Vision. In. The. Doorway.

'*WOW!* You look just wow, Jen!' I effuse, causing her to glow a bright pink, thus clashing horribly with her elegantly tailored electric blue suit.

'Oh, this ole thing?' she mocks, flicking up the collars. 'Well, you're not looking too shabby yourself. Come on! Selfie time!'

Click Click!

The congregation is already assembled when we squeeze our sweaty bodies into the third row bride's side, right next to Aunty B. It's hot – that hairdryer kind of hot, where the breeze just blasts more heat upon your near-combusting flesh.

Our timing is immaculate and as soon as we plonk ourselves down, the celebrant rises to her feet to address the congregation.

'Welcome everyone,' she smiles, her whole face lighting up. 'Or as we say in South Africa, *Sawubona!*'

'Sawubona!'

Now that's a nice word.

Doubly so when spoken in that soft South African accent. *Swoon!* She introduces herself as Lesidi, extending her toned arms long and wide as if to embrace us all.

'What a delight it is to be here!' she beams, inviting us to be seated. She has a commanding presence; six feet tall in a patterned yellow dress, her skin flawless. She gives a subtle nod to the string quartet who instantly take up their bows and, just like that, I'm swept away, lost in the most gorgeous orchestral rendition of…..oh no…..Celine Dion's "My Heart will go on"!

Cue terrifying flashback of flying dildos and fluffy cuffs

FML!

I shudder, pushing those memories from my mind; today is not a day to be sullied with such matters. Today is a day to get deliriously lost in the romance of the occasion…wild Africa about us, sunshine above and hundreds upon hundreds of smiling daisies lining the aisle all the way up to a huge, carved wooden elephant at the top. Perfection! Until I notice a vivid orange banner draped across its back, an advert for Nandi Milk Shakes. '*Shake it 'til you make it.*' Gulp! I can only imagine the ads will be centre stage at tomorrow's photo shoot too. #SoldOurSoulsToTheDevil.

I feel a little nudge in my ribs.

'Someone's got ants in his pants!' Aunty B whispers, giving a nod in Marcus' direction. He's very agitated, pacing up and down like a nervous hyena. In fact, it's no exaggeration to say the man looks positively petrified and I find myself softening towards him. Maybe he does have a heart, maybe he's nicer than I thought, maybe he's…. Winking. At. The. Celebrant.

Yeah, nah. Please see earlier notes.

The groom's manic pacing soon turns into an on-the-spot jig, thus making everybody else that bit more anxious, including the string quartet who quicken their tempo to keep up with him, playing faster and faster until their elbows are pumping like pistons on a steam engine. *Back, forth, back, forth!* I can't watch, it's so comical.

I avert my gaze to the assembled crowd, aunts and uncles in their wedding finery, toddlers exasperating their parents, and then *I sense her!* Like the antelope senses a predator…. *I sense Scarlet*!

I shrewdly scan the rows peering over the fancy feathered hats and over-lacquered hair, and within seconds I locate her just across the aisle beside Uncle George. She looks beautiful. Sizzling hot in her signature red dress and staring right back at me like she's been waiting for me to notice her. And getting her wish, she breaks out into the most glorious smile.

'You look beaut-i-ful!' she mouths. 'Beautiful!'

I pretend not to comprehend as my attention is snatched away by the bizarre sound of chanting and a strong burning smell, the kind of smell that gets right into the back of your throat. I peer down the aisle to see a woman in a full ostrich feather bodysuit striking a tiny xylophone. *Bing! Bong! Bing! Bong!* As she nears, her features become clearer; that shiny botoxed face, lips that only a fish could love. *Cruella! Of course, it is!* She is dutifully flanked by her fire guru, who is wafting his burning bush in everyone's face again.

Cough cough, splutter splutter!

'Just getting rid of any bad energy darlinks,' she whispers.

Now, I don't usually object to a bush in the face, but the fact is the accompanying smoke has now merged into a thick ball of fog, so you can barely see your hand in front of your face. Not ideal for the bride's arrival. A few splutters later, plus some frantic wafting by the ever attentive Mandela Lodge staff, and the smoke lifts. Hoorah!

The congregation falls into a reverential hush as the string quartet start to play the most recognizable opening bars on the planet, "Here Comes The Bride"!

She's here! Maria is here.....in a big puffy meringue dress on the arm of my dear uncle Tom.

We rise to our feet.

'Add a dollop of cream and she wouldn't look out of place in a bakery!' Uncle George says a little too loudly and just like that my eyes are springing a leak as Aunty B clutches me to her bosom and rocks me like a newborn.

'There there! There there!' she coos, as the bride takes her place next to the teary groom and the celebrant opens her arms in a gesture of welcome.

'Family, friends, please be seated.' She pauses for a moment to let us settle. 'We have a proverb in South Africa. It says "Love, like rain, does not chose the grass on which it falls". And today, we celebrate the beautiful rain that has fallen on Marcus and Maria; two young people pledging their lives to one another.'

It's a touching start and the more she speaks, the more I am swept away by the beauty of every well chosen word. Poetic, with not a hint of pretentiousness. It's glorious! Next, my cousin Anna rises from her seat to deliver the first reading. She looks nervous, the paper shaking in her hands as she looks into the crowd and begins.

' "Love is not rude, is not selfish, and does not get upset with others. Love does not count up wrongs that have been done." '

Instant lump in throat

Corinthians.

The verse that Scarlet and I had selected for *our* wedding day.

I sense her gaze upon me, willing me to look over as the words whirl round and round inside my head.

' "Love does not count up wrongs.

Love does not count up wrongs.

Love does not count up wrongs." '

.

.

Don't look at her Ava, don't look!

.

.

And then…I look. *Of course I do!*

I look long and hard at the tears tumbling down her flushed cheeks while she just stares over at me. I'm momentarily sucked in, breaking away to return my attention to the bride and groom, and to something equally magical happening on the plains behind them. Two amorous elephants caressing one another with their trunks, having their own special moment! There's a collective 'Awww!' as Maria's mum dabs her eyes and Aunty B smothers me deeper into her doughy cleavage.

'I, Marcus Oliver Von Strondleberg, do take you, Maria Jane Roberts, to be my lawfully wedded wife.'

'And I, Maria Jane Roberts, do take you, Marcus Oliver Von Strondleberg, to be my…'

BAHRUUUUUUUUHHHAAAAAAAAAAAAAAA! BAHROOOAAAAAAAAAA!

The moment is interrupted by an almighty trumpeting from the elephant paramours as the excited bull, with a formidable fifth leg, proceeds to mount the cow right in the middle of the 'I do's.'

'Awwwwws' quickly turn into 'ewwwws' and frankly, nobody knows where to look. A few grunts later and some wag yells out, 'Your turn next, Marcus!' alleviating the tension of the moment as the celebrant battles on, straining against the visceral groans of the mid-coitus elephants.

'Marcus and Maria, your love for one another is huge.'

BAHRUUUUUUUUHHHAAAAAAAAAAAAAAA!

'And you know, the more love you put in…'

GRUNT GRUNT.

'… the more love you will get out.'

GRUNT GRUNT. GROAAAAAN!

Her elegant words are instantly gifted a whole new meaning as the elephants echo… Every. Poetic. Sentiment.

'And rest assured, Marcus and Maria, as hard as things might get…'

HUUUUGE GRUNT.

'This love will nourish you… for… whatever… might … Come.'

***Final orgasmic trumpeting. Congregation lights up imaginary fag. ***

*

The African-themed marquee is refreshingly cool, courtesy of a light breeze sweeping in off the plains. It's the perfect place for the reception, 360 degree views of the Karoo and very roomy. Just as well, since there are so many carved animals inside that you might think you've stepped onto Noah's ark.

'Let's hope the wooden ones are better behaved than the real ones,' Jen giggles as the happy couple arrive, all blushes and smiles.

'Welcome, Mr and Mrs Von Strondleberg!' the best man announces.

'Wooohooooo!'

They both look so happy, I must say, as they commence the customary marathon meet-and-greet sesh with the awaiting guests. They are adopting a 'divide and conquer' approach commonly used by the Royals, with the bride focusing on the older demo and the groom on hot women under 35. Very noble. I watch his beady eyes light up as Scarlet gives him a reluctant peck on the cheek before bidding a hasty retreat over to us.

'Well, that was a memorable ceremony,' she grins, leaning in for a kiss.

I instinctively give her my cheek as the conversation turns to the usual post-ceremony debrief – bride's dress, groom's nervousness, plus your standard elephant fornication with special reference to ridiculously large appendage.

'Big! It was bloody maaaaassive!' I giggle, not able to extend my arms nearly wide enough to do it justice.

'Wasn't it just?' Aunty B winks. 'Lucky Mrs Elephant!'

Bahahahaahahaa!

Cruella's burning bush antics are another hot talking point, smoking hot, and we learn that somebody had to be escorted out with a full-on asthma attack. Poor Aunty Mary, God bless her.

'Your boss is certainly very *involved*, isn't she?' Scarlet remarks, as we watch Cruella commanding a terrified army of assistants by the stage area. 'What's going on there?'

'Oh, she's organising some big surprise for later apparently,' Jen shrugs.

'Well, as long as she leaves me alone, I'll be well hap…'

'Ava, daaaarlink! I've been looking for you!'

WTF!

I look to my left to see Cruella standing there. This woman has supernatural powers!

'Oh, right, well I'm here, Lucrezia!'

'Aren't you just, darlink! Illuminating the room. So, yah. We need to arrange a little briefing for tomorrow's photo shoot.'

I dutifully nod, 'That sounds lovely. Just lovely!'

'Yah! Yah. And a little update on that interview, darlink! We'll be supplying your answers via email, safer that way. Don't want you saying anything, well, off-brand, do we?'

'God forbid!' I grin.

Scripted answers, yessss! That's one small mercy at least!

Cruella gets distracted by a very important call from New York, so I make my escape only to wander into the path of an even greater evil. Great. Aunt. Agatha. Nothing great about her really. The woman is a notorious gossip and horrendous snob.

'Ava Rrrrroberts! There you are!' she says, rolling her r's like a deranged feline.

'Oh, hi! Lovely to see you, Aunt Agatha!'

Air kiss, air kiss

'Oh, don't call me that dear, makes me sound so decrepit. It's Aggy! Call me Aggy!'

That sounds about right. Aggy for Aggy-nising!

'So, tell me, Ava. Which one of those lovely ladies is your fiancée?' She proceeds to peer over her Gucci frames at Jen and Scarlet like they are exotic insects.

'Err, neither actually…'

'Oh yes of course, your mother did tell me. Frightful business, the whole engagement party debacle. And that *washing machine*! Shocking! Which brand was it?'

'Sorry?'

'The washing machine, dear. Which brand? Some of them can be so unreliable. I always say one should take as much time picking one's household appliances as one's spouse! But I don't need to tell you that, do I? Anyway, I imagine you're fighting them off now?'

'Fighting who off?'

'Why the *lesssbians,* of course! I hear you're doing rather well for yourself writing a column of some sort?'

'It's a blog.'

'Oh, how charming! No greater aphrodisiac than fame,' she says blowing her Tanqueray breath in my face. 'Though now you'll have to be *doubly* careful of course. Word of warning…' She shoves her pointy nose deep into my ear. 'They might just be after the fame, dear!'

The advice is punctuated with a satisfied nod, indicating that she is happy with her good deed. I, however, am less so.

Get me the hell out of here!

Fortunately, Jen recognises the code red situation and courageously enters the fray.

'Aren't you going to introduce us, Ave? I'm Jen!'

'Oh, how lovely to meet you! I'm Ava's Aunt Aggy!'

Scarlet soon appears at my other side, thus forming a kind of Ava sandwich which sets Aunt Agatha's mind working overtime. Her eyes dart from Jen to Scarlet, Scarlet to Jen and then finally back to me.

'Ooooh! I seeeee! There are *three* of you now!'

'Sorry?'

'You're in a throuple! How very modern!'

'No-no-no! We're just…'

'Oh, I'm not shocked dear! *Au contraire*! I hear it's quite *de rigueur* these days! Though I imagine it must be rather crowded – what with all the cats!' she snipes, revealing a thick smear of lipstick across her dentures.

'Um, I don't actually own a cat!'

She pats my hand condescendingly, 'You will, dear. You will!'

And just like that, she's off to terrorise her next victim. I stand for a moment, utterly traumatised.

'Jeez! I feel like I've been shafted by that bloody elephant!' I wince, downing champagne flute number three. 'I mean, can you believe that woman?'

'Don't worry, Ave. *Haters gonna hate!*' Jen teases. 'Don't pay any attention! Oh look... the speeches are about to start! Come on.'

I turn to see Uncle Tom, father of the bride and all-round good egg, stepping onto the stage to rapturous applause. Gotta love a good wedding speech or a bad one for that matter. Either is good, so long as you're not the poor bugger delivering it! #GladItsNotMe. Lord it's nerve-racking! I've seen the most eloquent of orators plummet to their untimely stage deaths, reduced to a sobbing wreck by some mistimed jokes. Hopefully not this one.

After a few teething problems with a squealing microphone and lost script (discovered in gent's bathroom), Uncle Tom is off!

'Good evening everybody!' he grins, instantly enchanting the room with his jovial demeanour. 'How are we all enjoying Africa? *Safari, so goodie*, hey?'

Cue enthusiastic applause

Solid start. Strong enough to allay any nerves. He continues. 'I'm just so proud of my lovely daughter Maria who, I'm sure you'll agree, is looking beautiful today. And as for the groom, Marcus, well I cannot think of a better man for her to marry...'

Yeah, nah. That's where we differ Uncle T!

I can think of several: Attila The Hun, Jeffrey Dahmer, even Donald Trump and he's got a combover and tiny orange hands. But hey, it's not my gig, so I stand back and watch the magic unfold. The speech progresses beautifully, a perfect blend of humour, heart and impropriety and, by the end, I'm blubbing into my hanky with the rest of them.

'Bravo Tom. Bloody great!' the crowd yells as Uncle Tom takes a well-earned bow and welcomes a teary bride to the stage. *How refreshing!* Maria's going to say something! They share a heartfelt hug as she takes the mic and clears her throat.

'Thanks so much for your touching words, dad. I love you very much! Now, as you all know, I'm not one for public speaking. I was leaving that honour to my best friend Mary-Ann Hargreaves. However, poor Mary-Ann injured her coccyx earlier...'

Cue smutty comment from best man.

'Soooo, in her absence, I can think of only one person who can fill her stilettos! It's short notice, well zero notice really, since she doesn't know anything about it! Dear wedding guests, please welcome to the stage the famous one in the family, our travel blogger extraordinaire... my cousin, Ava!'

Spurts mouthful of Pinot gris down front of dress

'Sorry, what?'

All eyes fall upon me as I stand like famous rabbit in the headlights, desperately hoping that this is some elaborate prank that I will doubtless laugh about later. Confirmation not forthcoming. This is not good. Not good at all. The crowd stomp their feet while Maria claps like a demented seal – a demented seal that's looking more annoyed by the second.

'Come on Ava! Come on up and say a few words!'

She starts cracking the microphone wire like an angry cat flicking its tail. I look to Jen, then to Scarlet, as the crowd chant, 'Ava, Ava!' and I realise that resistance is futile. I take a deep breath and go unto my fate, like Marie Antoinette to the guillotine minus big hair and brioche.

There are just three steps up to the stage, but there might as well be three hundred as my jelly legs struggle to propel me to the top. Everything looks so different from up here, like the whole room has suddenly expanded! Row upon row of faces staring back at me. Waiting for me to speak. I grab the mic and commence.

'Errr.... hello everyone....' *SQUEAL! SQUEAL!*

'Sort the mic out, Ava!'

Hahahahahaaha!

'Oops, sorry!' *SQUEAL!* 'Well, this is a surprise! Me doing a speech that is, not the wedding! I mean Maria's not pregnant or anything, although you never can tell with those big puffy dresses. Ha!'

Three encouraging whoops from party faithful down the front

'No, um, it really is wonderful to be here in beautiful Africa! It's everything I imagined. The spectacular Karoo, the incredible wildlife and I have to say seeing that elephant earlier brought me great joy...'

'NOT AS MUCH JOY AS MRS ELEPHANT!' the best man heckles.

Massive roar of laughter

'Indeed! Ummm...'

This is not my finest moment I have to say.

It's right up there with that time I set fire to myself during school assembly, aged seven. I take another deep breath and resume my enthralling rhetoric, ad-libbing a few anecdotes about married life, his and her pjs, before ending with the latest stats on soaring divorce rates. 'Up 60 %, who'd have thought it! So yeah, that's ummm...'

Tumbleweed

In short, I'm going down like a cold cup of sick.

The crowd are shuffling, some are checking their phones while the old folk pretend to adjust their hearing aids, even those who aren't wearing one.

Kill me now!

'Soooooo yes, let me say the bride is looking simply...errr.'

.

.

' "SIMPLY THE BEST!" ' a lone voice bellows from the crowd.

'Right! Yes, thank you. She does indeed look... err...'

' "BETTER THAN ALL THE REST!" '

And again! FFS! So now I'm being heckled by a bloody Tina Turner fanatic! #BestDayEver. I battle on, 'Maria is indeed the best, she is err....'

' "BETTER THAN ANYONE!" '

Another prompt. Louder this time, as a wave of laughter starts to ripple through the crowd.

Hang on a minute! I know that voice!

I gaze out into the sea of guests trying to locate the mysterious heckler. Face upon face upon face as suddenly the crowds part and I see her! *JEN! IT'S BLOODY JEN!*

'Sing, Ave! *Bloody sing!*' she mouths.

'Huh?'

'*SIIIIIIIIIIIING!*'

She has a weird constipated look on her face like she's about to burst. As she starts to warble, I'm taken back to our drunken karaoke nights doing dodgy Tina Turner impressions in equally dodgy venues and the penny drops! *I know what I have to do!*

I bring the mic closer to my mouth and let rip!

' "Better than everyone, anyone I've ever met!" '

Wohoooooooo!

Admittedly, it's not the finest rendition of this 80's classic, but at least it's something. I grip that mic and sing my little Norfolk heart out massacring line after line, note after note, which miraculously the crowd don't seem to mind. In fact, their whooping continues and next thing I know, Jen is wandering on stage to join me! It's just like the Robbie/Take That reunion! She gives a casual nod to the string quartet who reach for their bows and start to play along. It's just a few notes at first, a subtle plucking of strings, but it soon builds into an arrangement worthy of the Royal Philharmonic!

' "I'm stuck on your heart, I hang on every word you say,
Tear us apart, or I'd rather be dead!" '

Things reach an altogether higher level of WTF'ery when Aunty B joins in with the soprano section, followed by Uncle George (chesty baritone) and finally Uncle Tom, who surprises everyone with a not unimpressive falsetto! *Inspired!* Champagne glasses might be shattering throughout the land, but by verse two the whole bloody room is with us! Young, old, drunk, really drunk, all singing their little hearts out and wielding their smartphones skyward like at a Coldplay gig.

What a turnaround!

I look into the crowd to see Maria clapping and Marcus crooning as we pull them up on stage for the emotional finale.

'Everybody…let's hear it for the happy couple, Marcus and Maria!' I yell, working the crowd like a pro. 'They're…*c'mon everyone…*'

' "*SIMPLY THE BEST!*" '

Mic drop. Exits stage left.

There aren't many times in my life I've felt this high (legally) and I leave the stage like a regular Beyonce. Admiring looks, pats on backs. Even Aunt Agatha manages to muster a compliment.

'Bravo, Ava! Where would we be without friends, hey?'

'Errr, sad and lonely like you!' I mutter under my breath, before running face-first into Scarlet, who plants an opportunistic kiss full on my lips.

'That was brilliant, Ave! Just brilliant!' she grins, hugging the life out of me.

'Ha! It was Jen really or should I say Tina! Where is she?'

I spin round to see the hero of the hour dancing towards me, all red-faced and fabulous. I make a lunge for her, giving her a full-on champion's hug.

'Thank you, bestie! I can't believe you thought of that!'

'Well, it was either that or fake a coronary! I mean, you were *bombing* up there, girl!'

'Err, I wouldn't say *bombing!*'

She pulls a face that says otherwise.

'Ok, I was bombing! I was definitely bombing!'

Bahahahhhaha!

Scarlet stands there looking more than a little put out.

'Yes, well, I was just about to join you up there, but I knew you'd be OK, Ave. I had faith in you! I *always* have faith!'

Rather than reacting, I turn my head towards the DJ booth.

' "FAITH". *Listen*, he's playing "Faith"! It's a sign, girls! It's a sign,' I quip, charging onto the dancefloor like a woman possessed.

The euphoria is real and I leap about with the joy of someone who's just escaped a near 'stage' death experience! I throw my arms in the air and bust out some of my best wedding moves, spinning children by their ankles, high-kicking with great aunts. It's utterly liberating! This is one of the best things about weddings – families coming together on the dancefloor, all their petty differences evaporating over a quick chorus of "Chumbawamba". It's miraculous! Even those barely able to walk toss their zimmer frames aside, reborn to the sound of "Uptown Funk"!

'Oh, what a night, Ava! What a night!' Maria grins as I spin her around by her ponytail.

'Best. Wedding. Ever. Mrs Von Strondleberg!'

'And the best is yet to come, Ave! Lord, I *love* being married!' she giggles before being unceremoniously thrown over hubby's shoulder and bundled off to the stage. I wave her off, taking a well-earned breather by the buffet table. *Munch munch!* I'm a few bites into my butternut quiche, when I spot Jen and Scarlet deep in conversation at the bar. I head on over.

'Hey, you two! I think the big surprise is about to happen. We need to get to the front.'

Their faces instantly change and, drunk as I am, I pick up a weirdness. 'Oh, hello. What's going on here?'

They both stand there, smiling awkwardly.

'Jennifer?'

'Oh, nothing! Just chatting.'

'Hmm, looks very conspiri...conspire...looks like you two are up to something!'

'Nope. Like Jen said, just chatting.' Scarlet explains. 'Actually, she was just saying she might have to go back to the UK earlier than planned, weren't you Jen?'

'*What?* Back to London? How come?'

Jen gives me a sheepish look. 'Oh, something's come up. Nothing to worry about! I'll explain later. Anyway...' she grabs my arm. 'We don't wanna miss the surprise, do we? Come on!'

I find myself being dragged off to the stage where Cruella, self-appointed MC and Queen of wedding proceedings, is about to address the crowd. Again. Her outfit change has not gone unnoticed; she is now rocking a heavily beaded onesie, plus matching headscarf. Very fetching! 'Must be that Donatella number she was talking about,' I whisper as we take prime spot right in front of the newlyweds, who are regally posed above us on two bejewelled thrones. It's all a bit Posh and Becks 1999 to be honest and Marcus is loving every second.

'H.R.H. His Royal H'arsehole!' Aunty B quips, as Cruella cracks the microphone chord like a dominatrix.

'Sawubona! Daaaarlinks! Sawubona!'

'SAWANABBAWAWWWBONAAARRR.'

'I don't know about you, but today has left me feeling utterly intoxicated!' she beams, '*HIGH, HIGH, HIIIIIGH*! Which is exactly what our newly-weds are going to be soon! Yes, Marcus and Maria, you might be *flying* on the wings of love right now, but tonight....

Dramatic pause

.

.

Milking it

.

.

Churning it to butter.

.

.

'Tonight, we want you to fly...*IN THIS!*'

She throws her bangled arms into the air, as all eyes divert to a bizarrely shaped hot air balloon coming in to land just fifty metres away. It's all a bit blurry. #TooMuchChampers. But everyone else seems hugely excited and there's a lot of whooping and 'Ahhh's!' before Jen blurts...

'HOLY COW, AVE!'

'*Holy cow?* Who even says that?'

'No, Ave. *LOOK UP!*'

She grabs my chin and inclines my face towards the giant inflatable creation floating above us, which upon closer inspection does indeed look, well, *cow-like*. Four legs.....black and white colouring... massive set of inflatable teats!

'Yep, defo an inflatable cow!'

She nods in agreement, pointing out a bright banner plastered across the thing. I squint up trying to read the yellow block lettering across teats four, five, six and half of seven.

'OMG! *Nandi Shakes*! It says *Nandi Shakes*.' I cringe, as airborne Nandi's basket touches down dramatically evacuating her unexpected cargo, Andre Untilli OBE plus some exquisitely dressed dancers.

WTF!

'AVA! JENNIFER!' he hollers, running toward us. 'What do you think of my creation? Beautiful, isn't she?'

'Well, errr…'

'I know, I know, words are inadequate!' He stares up adoringly. 'It's for the shoot tomorrow. But no harm in sharing with the happy couple first. I mean, can you imagine a sunset safari aboard this beauty?'

Errr, no Andre, I cannot! And to be clear, I will not be jumping aboard a flying cow for a photo shoot tomorrow or any day for that matter. So. Help. Me. God!

Evidently Marcus and Maria share none of my misgivings and are ecstatic about the prospect of a sunset safari aboard a flying ruminate, but before that can happen, there's just 'one final surprise'.

'Ladies and gentlemen, I am beyond proud to present the ultimate wedding gift!' Cruella pauses to take a breath. 'Here to join our happy couple in their first dance is a supremely talented group of performers. Please welcome, the award-winning cast of… *THE LION KING*!'

Cue African drumming, harmonious chanting and rapturous applause

The rest of the dance troupe come galloping out in the most incredible animal costumes! Some on giant stilts, some on wheels. Zebras, antelopes, giraffes and then a magnificent lion with the brightest, yellow mane!

'Jeez! She's outdone herself this time!' I gasp, as the beasts start to encircle the newlyweds for a rendition of *The Lion King* classic, "Can You Feel The Love Tonight?"

Goosebumps. Instant goosebumps!

The harmonies are perfection! The choreography sublime, as they leap and spin six feet in the air. I feel Scarlet's arm slide around my waist as she whispers, 'Remember that show we saw in Italy, Ave?'

Italy! *That* weekend. The weekend she proposed.

Of course, I remember, my drunk head screams. I remember everything!

I resist being pulled back there, back to romantic Italy, to us, the happy us before Carla. I switch my attention back to the performance, to those divine voices and the delicious champagne, both of which are conspiring to heighten my emotions further. *Urggh.* She leans in closer and I feel her breath on my neck, her hands on my waist, as "Can You Feel The Love Tonight?" takes an altogether unexpected twist.

'Wedding guests, friends and family...'

DJ appears on decks

BOOM BOOM! BOOM BOOM!

'Check this out!'

There's a distinct change of vibe as Marcus bolts off stage, only to return as what I can only describe as 'Marcus O.G.' in thick, gold chain, Gucci shades and jungle shell-suit.

OMG!

It's a lot to behold as the groom and his bro crew break out into a full-on choreographed street dance, which mostly involves them bouncing about a bit, whilst saying 'Yo'. There's hip thrusting, the grabbing of crotches (lots of) and just when I think it can't get any worse.....Marcus starts to rap!

> *'Yo, yo, can you feel the love tonight?*
> *Me and my Maria, passion burning bright.*
> *Africa massif, jungle beats galore,*
> *Spitting my bars, yo, Marcus know da score. Word!'*
> ***Crotch grab***

It's like a Vanilla Ice/Bob the Builder mash up and pretty soon, other male family members are joining the posse. Uncle George, Uncle Tom and then Cruella's fire guru, who accidentally gets pulled in along with his burning bush.

> *Marcus O.G, 'Yo yo! Can you feel the love?'*
> *Bro B.Vs, 'Yeah, yeah, feel it from above!'*

Marcus is completely lost in the moment, not to mention drunk, as he unceremoniously snatches the burning bush from the guru's hand and starts waving it around, dangerously close to the white flowing voiles. *Whoosh whoosh! Inflammable inflammable!* I can hardly look as we're treated to more crotch grabbing followed by a woeful attempt at a head spin, which doesn't go to plan. They turn to the audience:

'Yo yo, can you feel the love?
'Yo yo, can you feel it from above?'

'Err, *feel* the love? I think I can smell it!' Aunty B says, wrinkling her nose. 'Is it just me dear or is something burning?'

It's not just her, and before long everyone is getting a whiff!

'Whatever is that smell?'

.

.

'OH MY LORD! THE ELEPHANT! *THE ELEPHANT IS ON FIRE!*'

I look over to see the ornately carved sculpture engulfed in a cloud of grey smoke and the poor staff frantically wetting it down with buckets of water and a couple of floppy garden hoses.

'NOBODY PANIC! NOBODY PANIC!' the manager shouts, which of course has never stopped anybody panicking in the history of time and we all file out drinks in hand, PANICKING!

PANIC, PANIC, PANIC!

It's utter pandemonium!

Aunt Agatha is saying a few 'Hail Marys' and Cruella's poor fire guru is having a meltdown chant as the unrest spreads to the resident baboon population, who start barking and grunting around the balloon basket. This does not look good! Pretty soon they're yanking and biting on the guide ropes, biting some more and then, *PING,* a rope comes loose! A few nibbles later another one pings off and next thing I know, WHOOOOOOSH!

Nandi, we have lift-off!

Jaws drop. Cameras snap as the basket rises up into the smoke-filled air.

'My creation! My beautiful creation!' Andre wails, as Nandi slowly disappears from view, happily on her way to Mozambique.

.

.

The commotion feels less intense from the pool area, the peaceful idyll that Scarlet has dragged me away to, 'Just to be safe'.

We sit side by side, our feet dangling in the warm water.

'Well, can't say your family do boring weddings,' she laughs. 'Balloons. Baboons. *Fire!*'

'Oh don't! I hope it's alright! Maybe we should go back and help?'

'Nah, it's fine. They have it under control. Look!'

I glance back at the once white marquee, which looks much less smoke-filled now and, more importantly, the screaming seems to have subsided. She sees I'm not convinced.

'It's definitely fine, I promise. Hey, I was going to say you look smoking tonight, but feels a bit wrong now!'

Drunk Ava laughs. Drunk Ava laughs a lot.

Perhaps it's the champagne or the smoke inhalation, or PTSD from that godawful rapping! Whatever it is, it's fast breaking down my carefully constructed barriers and before long we're laughing and chatting like it's 2018 B.C. *Before Carla.*

'I've missed this. Nobody makes me laugh like you do.' She magically produces a bottle of wine.

'Errr, where did you get that?'

'I'm resourceful.'

She's that alright. Resourceful, dangerous and now she is leaning up against me, against the very drunk me, under the light of the full moon.

'Well, I can't promise you any rapping, but we have got these lovely stars to keep us entertained,' she says, gazing up at the sky full of twinkling diamonds. 'Beautiful, isn't it? All those little worlds up there make you realise how small we are.'

I don't respond, not wanting to be drawn into anything.

'Hey Ave, do you believe in the stars?'

'How do you mean?'

'You know, in destiny? That some people are meant to be together I mean?'

'What, like Romeo and Juliet? "Star-crossed lovers?" ' I scoff. 'Not sure what I believe any more Scarlet. I did once maybe.'

She touches my hand.

'And you can again, Ave. You know how sorry I am. That's why I flew all the way over here. I messed up. People do mess up, you know. They make mistakes, terrible ones and...'

'I know they do, Scarlet! But...'

'But what? Don't you believe in second chances? New beginnings?'

I can't help but snap.

'Ha! Said the person that didn't get the stuffing knocked out of her! It's not that easy, is it? There are things like trust, there's, there's...'

I can hardly get my words out. All the resentment rising within me again, the months of anger bubbling to the surface.

'I mean, bloody hell, Scarlet! You asked me to marry you for God's sake. I'm not sure how you come back from that!'

I feel her breath on my cheek and I turn away. 'Anyway, where's Jen?' I snap, looking for an out.

'Don't worry about her. She's with the others.' She pulls me into her again. 'Look, Ave. There's still something between us, it's obvious. Just look at us!'

I keep staring out into the blackness refusing to meet her gaze, refusing to weaken and then I do it. Giddy from the drink, with the stars glimmering above, I look into her eyes.

'We *can* come back from this. I know we can. I love you Ava and I'm not ever going to stop. That's *my* fate. I love you.'

I stare back at her.

It's like all my resolutions, all my good intentions are about to go up in smoke just like that ornately carved wooden elephant.

CHAPTER THIRTY-TWO – SCARLET FEVER:
A REINFECTION

'Life's too short to drink a margarita slowly.'

- Aunty B

Q. What do you get when you cross two drunk exes, romantic Africa and a minor hotel blaze?

A. Extreme nakedness and a whole heap of self-loathing.

In a word, shit, tits and FUCKETY FUUUUUUCK!

OK, so that's four! Entirely justified given current *shituation.*

In short, I seem to have woken up in bed with my ex, plus bonus hangover. *Ultimate threesome!* All the work of the past few months has been spectacularly undone along with my bra, which is lying cup-side down on the bedroom floor.

To my earlier point, *WHAT THE ACTUAL FUUUUUUUUU-UUUUCKKKKKKK!*

Scarlet is beginning to stir.

I play dead, secretly plotting my escape. I just need to get the hell out of here and have Jen cast some light on last night's Herculean relapse. The escape part of the plan instantly stalls, since I am pinned down by Scarlet's arm which is casually draped across me like in the movies, post hot sex scene.

I attempt to extricate myself, wriggling down the bed like a giant worm but alas, the lioness awakens.

'Argggghhhhhhh! Morning gorgeous,' she yawns, having the most luxuriant stretch across my side of the bed. The sheets fall away…

***HOT NAKED BODY ALERT! ***

I bury my head beneath the covers, uttering a muffled 'Morning!' as she lays a long, slender leg across mine.

'So, last night was fun,' she says in that *we've got a sexy secret* way. Though, in this case, I'm not 100 percent clear on details of said sexy secret. #DrunkestGirlAtTheParty

'Oh right. So, umm, did we err…?'

'What? Have wild makeup sex in multiple positions?'

My head shoots back over the covers like a periscope. I stare at her, not blinking, not breathing, awaiting the answer. It's a poker face to rival Dawn's, but eventually she cracks.

'Way to make a girl feel special! Now I just feel used…….and I like it!'

So that's a yes. A big, fat, sexy, yes. Nice work Ava!

I feel utterly sick as I'm drip-fed details of the night before: the bad rapping, giant cow balloon, the fire, plus another four-letter F-word, which sounds every bit as hot as the blaze. She leans over to me.

'I don't need to ask if you slept well, you were purring for Africa this morning.'

Purring! Nice play, lady!

That used to be her pet name for my snoring. Very cute snoring, I might add. *Jeez, this girl knows how to get under my skin!* That's the danger with exes, they have insider knowledge of all your vulnerable spots, and boy, do they work them! They scatter little love grenades; dropping a cutesy nickname, that special song you shared and, just like that, *kaboom!* They've blasted a hole right through your armour.

'So, what do you want to do today? Pool day, little walk round the…'

'Shit, shit, shit!' I blurt, leaping to my feet. *'B-DAY! IT'S B-DAY!'*

'Whose birthday?'

'Noooo – *Blog Day*! I have to meet Andre and Jen for that stupid photoshoot. Shit, what time is it?'

'Calm down, Ave,' she says looking at her watch, 'It's just after 7. Do you want me to come with you for moral support?'

'Nah – it's okay, Jen will be there. Thanks though,' I smile, hunting for my second shoe. *Now where did I put it?*

'Jen? Jen left last night. Got called away or something. Probably that new girlfriend of hers! You know what it's like…'

'Don't wind me up, Scarlet!'

I feel sick again. Sick and angry.

'I'm not. She went back to Cape Town with Maria's friend, the one with the sore coccyx. You had a big drunken goodbye, don't you remember?'

Maria's friend. Coccyx. Drunken goodbye.

The more she explains, the more I do recall some kind of conversation and Jen getting into a car.

I can't do this without her! I just can't!

Scarlet senses my panic.

'It's ok, Ave! I'm here. How about you go get showered and meet me by the pool. I'd like to be there for you…really.'

I don't have the brain cells to argue, so I nod and her whole face lights up like she's won the lottery. She takes my hand in hers.

'Look…I know last night was just a first step, but it could be the start of a whole new chapter for us. *You and me.* Better than ever. We can make this work, Ave. I just know it.' She kisses my forehead, then my neck, and then that special place just behind my ear and, *ding-a-ling-a-ling,* I'm inches away from falling fanny-first into more trouble.

'No, no, nooooo!'

I grab my phone, slamming the door behind me.

The walk of shame is mercifully short. Short and torturous. As if sleeping with my ex wasn't bad enough, now I have this whole blog circus to contend with *without Jen!* I call her, but it goes straight to voicemail. There's no way she'd have left without a good reason, just wish I could remember it! Note to self: must not drink oneself into a coma at weddings.

I get one hand on the door, when….

'Lovely day for it, Ava!'

It's Uncle George, binoculars round neck, en route to some ornithological jaunt. Well, he's certainly spotted himself a fine specimen this morning! *Sluttus maximus!* Dressed in yesterday's clothes, creeping home after a night of ferocious rutting. He can see I'm squirming.

'So, quite the wedding, wasn't it? All got rather overheated at the end, pardon the pun! Still, the staff were on top of that fire quicksmart.'

'Yes, they were, thank God….Sorry, Uncle George, I gotta run.'

'Oh yes, yes. I quite understand my dear.' He gives his nose a conspiratorial tap. 'Escaping, are we?'

'Sorry?'

'It's the chemistry you know! Unmistakable. Me and your aunt had it in bucket loads. Mind you, she was bald as a coot back then,' he sighs. 'Happy days!'

Slams door

The shower is heaven. A purifying oasis and I give myself a good cleanse and thorough talking to. As the water drums upon my head, I'm bombarded with images of the night before. Scarlet's naked body, her lips on mine, the arching of backs.... I twist the temperature dial round to cold. *BRRRRRRRR!* Instant reset. If only feelings could be washed away as easily: no more brokenhearted wretches blubbing into their beers at closing time, no more Mariah ballads at Xmas and no more of those (un)inspirational quotes on Insta that make you feel a million times worse.

I emerge a few minutes later, resolving to get my head straight for the day ahead.

It's just a day. One single day to get through. I can do this!

I grab my phone. Nothing from Jen still, but then I catch sight of a little note on the bedside table.

Good luck today, Ave. I know you will be <u>amaaaazing</u>. Sorry I had to leave. Love you, Jen xx

I trace my fingers over her writing.

Gutted doesn't come close! Her not being here is an out and out disaster, and I can't help thinking that last night's relapse wouldn't have happened either, if she hadn't left.

Urggh! Jen, Jen, Jen! Why hast thou forsaken me?

I'm not sure how I'm feeling right now other than a whole heap of confused.

*

Mandela Lodge infinity pool, first location of today's photoshoot, is a hive of activity. It's barely 8 am and Andre is already buzzing about like a hyperactive bee, styling everything in sight: plants, cushions, loungers, the odd fruit fly.

His attention to detail is astounding, right down to the angling of cocktail straws. I look about me at the giant studio lamps, big white reflectors and fancy camera on tripod, and can't help but think I've walked onto a Hollywood film set. There's even a crew – half a dozen assistants with asymmetric hair, plus 'the model twins' as they are dubbed, stick-thin creatures exclusively dedicated to Cruella's every whim.

I see her reclining beneath an elegant cream pagoda and start to wander over when Andre bounds at me like an excited puppy.

'Oh, fantastico! My star is here! Ava Roberts, today is going to be lit! LIT, LIT, LIT!'

Unfortunate choice of words considering last night's incendiary incident. A quick scan of the area confirms no major damage to premises or persons. Hallelujah! Only casualties appear to be the big wooden elephant, that's now a small, charred elephant, plus a semi-flaccid cow balloon, currently being resuscitated by burly types in Crew T-shirts.

Andre catches me looking.

'Oh, I know! Tragic, isn't it? My creation got punctured last night. Pricked in her prime. Can you conceive of it? Still, nothing that can't be fixed,' he smiles, assuring me Nandi blimp will soon be 'patched and pumped' ready for this afternoon's stunning aerial shot. 'They'll be nothing flat about today, Ava. *Nothing!*'

He flits off again and I wave to Cruella who is immersed in an intense tête-à-tête with Scarlet. I give a follow-up 'you-hoo!' and she looks up.

'Ava darlink! I was just talking about you! Come on over!'

She looks every inch the part in a white linen suit and Hepburn sunnies. Sidekick fire guru is notably absent this morning, left under a bit of a dark cloud she tells me and is suing for damages to reputation and bush.

'Ha! Sounds like a lawsuit for a porn star!' I quip, but she doesn't laugh, far too distracted by my face it would seem.

'Ava, darlink, we all love designer bags, but not under our eyes,' she tuts. 'Right, we have to get you straight to makeup.' She quickly turns away, bellowing '*J.C! Armanitti!* We'll need *two* makeup artists today. Maybe three. Oh and Touche Éclat, industrial strength!'

I instinctively feel the need to apologise.

'Sorry, Lucrezia. I didn't get much sleep last night.'

'Entirely my fault,' Scarlet winks. 'And I look forward to depriving you of more of it tonight!'

Big grin.

The next hour sees me professionally preened, poked, plucked, painted, blow-dried, freeze-dried, washed, waxed, teased and tonged, and by 10 am I'm unrecognisable to my own mother! I'm led onto the set and carefully positioned for shot 1, 'Ava casually seated by pool drinking a pina colada', the sight of which makes me want to heave. Scarlet waves over. 'You look gorgeous', she mouths which makes me feel a bit better and just like that it starts! Andre removes his lens cap and fires off a few preliminary shots while I sit there like a lemon.

'Yes, yes, give it to me Ava. Don't hold back!'

Click click click.

'I didn't know you were a photographer Andre,' I remark. To which Cruella retorts, 'Oh yes, darlink! Andre has shot all the greats: Kylie, Kate, Kim. He used to work for *Dogue*, you know.'

'Don't you mean *Vogue?*'

'No, *Dogue*. Fashion for pooches. Same principle, higher IQ. Oh hold on! *CUT! CUT! CUT!*' she barks, instantly leaping up. 'Ava, darlink! That necklace needs to go!'

'Sorry?'

'The necklace, it's just not working. Not working at all. We need something less …'

'*Less?*'

'Less….*butterfly-ey!*' she sneers. 'We need a statement piece!' She takes a short breath before hollering '*WARDROBE!*' at the top of her lungs, whereupon a terrified assistant scurries out with a box of high fashion jewellery and starts placing them against my neck.

'I'd rather wear this one,' I repeat as she tries piece after piece to check they 'work with my skin tone'. There must be a dozen options, each one rejected with a 'No', 'Hideous!', 'Ewww!', 'Too shiny!', 'Too dull!', 'Too vulgar!', 'Too tame!', 'Too short', 'Too long' or a 'Too ….*necklacey*'. And then at last, 'That's it!' Cruella declares, like Goldilocks sampling the perfect porridge. '*This* is the one!'

It's a chunky silver piece, rather heavy for the pool. In fact I suspect you'd drown if you attempted to swim in the thing.

'I love it, daaarlink, *love it*,' she beams. 'It says it all. Strong yet vulnerable, happy yet sad, pure yet sluttish.'

'Really? It says expensive yet ugly to me. Can't we just go for something that says, I dunno, *I like butterflies*?'

She glares at me like I've just eaten her newborn, before Scarlet wades in.

'You know what, Ave? I think Lucrezia's right. That one looks much better! The butterfly is cute I guess but...'

'But what?'

'Well, since when did you like butterflies?' she laughs, stepping forward to take it from me.

And since when did you tell me what to wear, Scarlet Saint bloody Laurent?

Then I remember she did often 'advise' me on my wardrobe choices.

My food choices.

Movie choices.

Music.

Hair.

Socks.

Tampons.

Come to think of it, *did I even have a mind of my own?*

I feel the venom rising again. I think of Indira and everything that necklace means to me, and with a demeanour that is calm yet firm, I find my voice.

'I appreciate your help everyone, but the butterfly necklace stays. Thank you.'

I can only imagine the quiet defiance gives me a whole new allure, as Andre leaps back into action while Cruella looks at me like I'm the second coming!

'Oh yes! Yes! I see the fire in your eyes, Ava. *FIRE!* We need to capture that! That rebelliousness. Sexiness. Fuck off-iness... *I'm a survivor!*'

Presses play on Destiny's Child remix

CLICK CLICK CLICK!

1 pm comes and goes, and after a quick bite for lunch, stick of celery and half a radish, we move on to the third and final location of the day, 'Beachside paradise shot'. Huge relief, as frankly I'm exhausted and busting for the loo.

'I don't know how models do it,' I gripe as I'm told to lay back and channel my inner mermaid. Rather challenging when you're in a fake sand pit hundreds of miles from the ocean.

'You're doing great, Ave! Really great,' Scarlet assures, adjusting the tilt on my hat.

I have to say that she is being supremely supportive today aside from the butterfly remark, which makes me feel guilty about all my 'I wish Jen were here' comments. I resolve to zip it and carry on splashing about in the imaginary ocean with my imaginary modelling talent.

Cruella calls over to me, 'Tell me Ava, have you modelled before?'

'Err, just with lawn mowers!'

'*Lorne Mowers?* Isn't he with Tommy Hilfiger?' she enquires, before subjecting me to costume change number 412. FML!

I'm just about ready to quit when her eyebrows suddenly shoot up to the heavens like she's having some kind of creative epiphany, and we are all summoned in for a big powwow.

'So, yah, for this final shot, I'm seeing something different, something special, something *…more more more!'*

Oh, shit shit shit! Heard this one before!

I look about me expecting a herd of zebras to gallop up or a chariot drawn by a dozen golden-maned lions, but nothing appears. We stand there, waiting for the creative guru to speak.

'Darlink, I'm seeing…'

All lean in

'Yes?'

'SCARLET! I'm seeing Scarlet in the next shot!'

She steps back, throwing her arms into the air like she's just solved the global climate crisis, while I stand there utterly blindsided.

'*Scarlet? In the shot?* But, why?' I blurt as a makeup artist dashes out, brush in hand and starts painting my new co-star's near perfect face.

'Because Ava, this is the fairytale! *The reunion* in untamed Africa! I can see the headlines now, "Untamed love. Untamed passion". *It's poetry*! Poetry!'

'But...'

'Yes?'

'Well, it's not true, is it?'

Scarlet's face drops. She lifts her sunglasses.

'But we're hoping that it will be, aren't we? Well, at least *I* am.' I go to respond, but Cruella takes the floor again.

'Oh Ava, darlink, you're far too hung up on facts! Facts are the worst kind of F-word. At *Marshall Media*, we are in the business of selling dreams! And our readers deserve a happy ending! Surely you can appreciate that?'

Any further objections fall on deaf ears, literally, as she inserts ear pods and takes a call from a potential sponsor, thus leaving Andre with the hefty task of convincing me. He takes me to one side, assuring me that the 'lovers reunited' photos will only be published with my agreement.

'Really?'

'Pinky promise.'

I think for a moment, but before I can answer Scarlet does.

'No harm then, I guess? You get full approval. What do you reckon, Ave? Go for it?'

Next thing I know she is slipping into something sexy and cuddling up to me, while Andre jumps behind the camera and starts making a series of contented grunts. Every click sees us in a new pose, gazing into one another's eyes, casually throwing a beach ball (possible tampon/deodorant ad) and frankly, it all starts to make me feel a little bit sick.

'Oh, yes! Yes! *This* is the dream!' Cruella coos. 'The dream that will blast us all the way to the number one spot! Look at you both! Gorgeous! Now, for God's sake give her a snog!'

THUD!

Odd to say, but the next thing I know I'm flat on my back with Scarlet, Cruella and Andre staring down at me. I go to move, but I feel a sharp pain across the bridge of my nose and something warm dribbling from my nostril.

'OMG! Blood! I can't look!' Cruella winces, before dramatically fainting into the sand pit. I look about me bewildered.

'Wha-what happened?'

'You got hit in the face with the volleyball!' Scarlet smiles, handing me an iced towel. 'We were doing the *lovers fit and fun* shots.'

'*Fit and fun?* I don't feel much like either of those right now,' I laugh.

'Haha! Witty even with concussion. That's our blog superstar!' Andre gushes, giving me a playful nudge. He looks rather odd from this angle, all jowly, like a Saint Bernard. 'Fear not, Ava! Your injury has not been in vain. I got some *fantastico* content and, most importantly, an amazing aerial shot from all the…Way. Up. THERE!' He points up at the reinflated Nandi balloon floating above us. 'I can see the copy line now, "Living the High Life"! Genius! D'you know, I think this might be my best work since Kim?'

'*Kardashian?*'

'No, Kim Jong-Un. We met on my gap year. Lovely chap.'

WTF! Anyone would think that he's the one that's been hit on the head with a bloody volleyball!

I smile and nod though I can't say I remember much of what he's describing – the 'fit and fun' shots, Nandi's triumphant return to life, let alone him climbing aboard her for the stunning vista shot.

Scarlet stares down at me, lovingly brushing the hair from my eyes. 'You had me worried for a minute, Ave.'

'Don't be silly! I'm fine.'

'Yes, but…'

Her eyes start to fill up. I gently wipe her tears away.

*

The last few months have been a catalogue of firsts, paragliding, cow birthing and yoga, and I can now add *fashion model (beginner level)* to my ever-expanding repertoire. Andre declares it a wrap and, after quick nose clean-up and awkward group hug, we reconvene at the infinity pool for a well deserved post-shoot prosecco.

Lord, it feels good!

B-day is over! And not half as hideous as anticipated.

'Things are rarely as bad as we imagine Ava,' Aunty B pontificates. 'Rather like childbirth.'

'But you haven't had any children, Aunty B.'

'I know dear, but I have dated some *very* big men!' she winks, siphoning a strawberry from her second glass of fizz.

The newlyweds soon rock up and everyone remarks upon how decidedly perky they look today. Can only imagine last night's blaze led to some heat in their bedroom and Marcus made it to the Island of Clitoris at long last! Maria as good as confirms the news via a little blush.

'Soooo...how did the photoshoot go? Must have been sooo exciting,' she gushes before clocking the plaster on my snout. 'Oh, apart from your nose.'

'It went as well as the wedding – *apart from the fire*,' I tease, which makes her snort bubbly up her nose. Never nice.

Cruella is now fully recovered from her fainting spell and leaps in to deliver a toast.

'Well, darlinks, I think Africa has been a staggering success! Staggering! The wedding, the shoot! Do you know, I feel we really captured the essence of *80 Gays* today: the pathos, the pain, the rebirth!' She bites her bottom lip as if on the point of orgasm. 'And as for those reunion shots...'

'*Reunion shots*? So, you guys are back on?' Marcus interjects, 'Worked out well for everyone then.'

I peer at him suspiciously, 'For *everyone*?'

'Well, no, yeah. For you and Scarlet, I mean...worked out well for you two!' He starts to tug at his snub nose, deflecting my interest with a quick Cruella admiration session. 'Lucrezia's spot on, isn't she? It *has* been a great wedding! Class, Lucrez. Absolute class!'

Lucrez? Urrgh!

Could the little dweeb crawl any further up that woman's bottom? Maria leans in, giving him a little peck on the cheek.

'Well said, hubby. It's been magical: the dancers, the hot air balloon, the rapping! And we can't forget Ava's performance. Oh Ava, it was *the* best surprise! Or should I say, *simply the best* surprise!'

Snort. Snort.

'Errr, for me too, Maria! Bloody hell! Talk about putting a girl on the spot!'

'Ahaaaa! But you know what they say, Ava – pressure makes diamonds,' Aunty B grins, giving my hand a squeeze. 'And look how well it all turned out! Teamwork makes the dreamwork!'

'I know. Jen was great, wasn't she? *She's* the real diamond in this.'

Scarlet's face drops.

'I actually thought it was less diamond more *corn,* her rescuing you like that. It was all very, well, *rom-com!'*

'*What?* It was a lovely thing to do. And I happen to *love* rom-coms.'

'Me too.' Maria smiles. 'Especially that bathroom scene in *Bridesmaids*! Classic! I think Jen did a stellar job. I mean, you were dying up there. Dying.'

'Thanks for that!'

Marcus is now hovering around me like an annoying fly, an annoying fly waving an iPhone X in my face and demanding we take a nice group photo.

'Come on. One more for the album,' he grins. 'The light is perfect now.'

We dutifully comply; what's one more photo when you've just taken 4,000? We get into a little line donning our best smiles, which is a major effort since I've been doing smiley-smiley all day and have serious face fatigue. I think it's over when Marcus 'Testino' herds Scarlet and I off for a couple more couple shots, which feels a little uncomfortable. Especially when he requests a kissing pose.

'Right, that's it for the photos, Marcus!' I say, returning to the safety of the group where Cruella is mid-toast. Again.

'Everybody, please join me in a toast to the master, the artist, the photographic legend that is Andre Untilli! The man is touched by God!'

'No, no, no! I was merely inspired by my subject! My muse! Ava Roberts!' He gives me an affectionate little nod before Cruella jumps in again.

'*Subjects*, Andre! *Subjects!* Those last shots with Scarlet were sublime! I mean, look at those cheekbones!' She turns to Scarlet in a whisper, 'Well done darlink. I knew you'd come through for me!' *Little wink.*

Now call me paranoid, but I sense something in that little wink, something conspiratorial, and despite the chat moving on to Aunty B's tenure as head physio at Woking F.C., I can't let it slide.

'*Come through,* Lucrezia? What do you mean by that?'

'Just a figure of speech, darlink!' she says dismissively. 'Anyway! *What a day*! *What an enchanting day*!'

I'm not entirely convinced. I've worked with the woman long enough to know when she's lying; her lips move. I go to push her on it when Scarlet swoops in to top up my drink.

'There you go Ava! Our supermodel extraordinaire!'

I put a defiant hand over my glass.

'No more thanks,' I object, looking straight into her eyes. 'Have you two been planning this reunion thing all along?'

'*Planning?* Oh darlink! I think that volleyball might have damaged your frontal lobe!' Cruella interrupts. 'Perhaps we should get you checked out!'

Scarlet looks down into her glass.

'Come on – I can tell something's going on. I'm not stupid.'

'You make it sound so dramatic, Ava! Nothing has been *going on* as you put it! I might have merely *encouraged* Scarlet to be bolder with her feelings, nothing more! "A faint heart never won fair maiden." '

'Be bold? How?'

'To fly over and tell you how she felt. I got the sense that you might be ready to, well, forgive. I noticed a change in tone in the blog. A softening. I was right, wasn't I? I can see it in your eyes, darlink! Lucrezia was right, wasn't she?'

Lucrezia was right out of order, more like!

My stomach starts to churn.

Those gut feelings Indira talked about - I have one of them now. I turn to Scarlet.

'Shit, Scarlet! Lucrezia *told* you to come here? For real?'

'Noooo! I was already coming, Ave. I swear! I've been texting you for months, you know that! Not that you replied!' she says sarcastically.

'Really? That now?'

Everyone starts to look into their drinks, but I dig my heels in deeper. 'Do you know what, Scarlet? It makes me wonder what else you've been doing behind my back?' My head starts to work overtime. The heat, the champagne. 'Oh God, tell me you didn't?'

'Didn't what?'

'You didn't out me about the blog – give my name to the press?'

'What?'

'Did you, Scarlet? Did you?'

Her face changes. It is now a face of thunder. Of dark clouds and anger.

'Fuck, no! Are you being serious right now? I would never do that. I would never betr…'

'What, *betray* me? Pah! It's not as if you don't have form in that department, is it?'

Low blow. Sorry, not sorry.

I scull my drink while Scarlet stares at me like a wounded animal.

'I think we both need to calm down. This is ridiculous, Ave.'

'Is it?' I spit.

'Yes, it is. I didn't *out you!* On my life I didn't,' She starts to gather her things. 'Look, I'll see you back at the room when you've come to your senses.' And with that she is gone.

I plonk myself down on a lounger confused and annoyed. At Cruella, at Scarlet, at Jen for leaving, but mostly at myself.

You're a bloody fool Ava Roberts! A stupid, bloody fool!

This is exactly what happens when you let people back in. When you trust people who have hurt you. Aunty B gives me one of her 'it will be alright' smiles and I close my eyes trying to channel 'Goan Ava', the chilled version of myself that I discovered back in India. *Deep breath. In and out. Nice and slow.* I think of all those long walks with Indira, our talks, the leg licks from Nandi, and I open my eyes to behold something truly spectacular.

A giant inflatable udder floating right above me!

'*Nandi!* You haven't deserted me!' I gush, as the big goofy face with lop-sided mouth hovers over me, gurning like a lunatic.

She lingers for a moment, as if to offer comfort in my moment of need, before the gas burner breathes fire into her undercarriage and she drifts off again with some lucky prize winners on their *80 Gays* safari extravaganza.

I interpret the visitation as a sign; a sign to dry my eyes and take back control.

CLICK CLICK!

FML! Not more bloody photos for God's sake!

It's Marcus snapping away at me again, the insensitive little worm.

'Sorry, Ave. Just taking some shots of the...err balloon. It's cool, hey? A flying cow! Ha! Brilliant!'

'No, you weren't. You were taking them of me!'

'*What?* Are you mad? You need to cool it with the accusations. You've already sent Scarlet packing! Holy fuck, woman!'

I stand firm, 'Don't be a jerk, Marcus. I saw you! You were pointing your phone right at me! Let me see!'

Maria looks up from her *Hello!* magazine and gives him a look. 'Marcus?'

He completely ignores her and, next thing I know, she's grabbing the phone from his greasy little hand and scrolling through the photos.

Her face grows paler with every swipe.

'What the hell, Marcus? Why have you got all these photos of Ava?' *SWIPE SWIPE.* 'And Scarlet too? Oh my God! Have you, have you been... tugging off to these?'

It's a comment worthy of a snigger but frankly, I'm so bloody furious I can't manage it. I watch Maria's face as she examines his phone further, while Marcus squirms like a fly at the end of summer.

'Maria, babe! It's not what it seems. I'm not perving, I'm ...'

'What? *Sick?* That's what you are! Oh Lord, what have I married?'

Marcus looks more red-faced by the second.

'Babe, they're not for me. I swear on my life, they're not mine! I've been sending them to ...'

'Who? Perverts.com?' I interject, 'Jesus Marcus! You're such a pig!'

'But, but...'

He has the look of a cornered animal.

Everyone is glaring at him: Aunty B, Cruella, Andre, random couple by the African violets. He starts to tug at his thinning hair and then finally he breaks.

'OK, OK! I was sending them to a journalist, alright!'

'A journalist? But why would you send them to a............... ohhhhhhhh!'

.

.

Penny. Drops.

'Shit! *It was you!* You're the blog Judas!'

'The *what?*'

'You're the one who outed me, aren't you? *YOU COMPLETE AND UTTER CREEP!*'

Poor Maria looks absolutely horrified, desperate for it not to be true.

'What? Nooooo, surely not? Marcus! Say something for God's sake!'

It's all too much for the little toad and he finally jumps to his feet, as it all comes spewing out like a burst water main.

'Oh, for fucks's sake! Yes, yes – it was me! I told them! I don't see the big deal though. I mean, it all worked out, didn't it? Ava's living the dream!' He stops to look at me. 'Plus, you got your girl back! In fact, you should be thanking me, Aves!'

'*Thanking you?* How about I bloody drown you?' I launch myself at him with such velocity that he is propelled fully clothed into the deep end.

SPLOOOOOOOOOOOOOOOSH!

'You know what, Marcus? I always thought you were a twat and now I have confirmation! Have a nice swim!'

He resurfaces, splashing around in circles like a squinty otter, calling out for Maria.

'Babe, babe! Don't be mad!' *Splutter splutter.* 'I did it for us! Houses aren't cheap you know!'

'Oh! You're so right,' she says. 'How ungrateful of me, Marcus!'

'Ahh, that's my girl. I knew you'd understand!'

'Oh, yeah, I understand alright. Here, let me get your towel, my love.'

She picks it up and hurls it straight at him, along with his designer sunnies, wallet and best of all brand new iPhone!

SPLOOSH! SPLOOSH! SPLOOOOOOOOOOOOOOSH!

'Screw you, Marcus! I'm done!' she yells, storming off to the bar, as the phone sinks to the bottom along with Marcus' hopes of ever having sex again.

I don't remember leaving the pool or walking to Scarlet's room, but next thing I know I'm knocking at her door with my heart thumping out of my chest. I feel like I've been on a rollercoaster with all the twists of the last 30 minutes! And worst of all, *I* am now the villain in this story since I wrongly accused Scarlet.

What a mess!

I try to gather myself, as she opens the door in an angry red sarong.

'Oh hello. Come in.'

She seems a little subdued and perches on the edge of the bed leaving a space for me, but I opt for the wicker chair opposite. Safer ground.

'So, have you come to your senses? Or do you still think it was me?'

I immediately look down, embarrassed.

'No. I know it wasn't you Scarlet and I feel just terrible,' I lament, tugging at my necklace. 'I'm so, so sorry.'

She instantly looks relieved, relieved but still a little mad.

'Well, I did tell you. I mean, fuck, Ave! Is that really what you think of me?'

'I know. I know. I don't know what I was thinking.'

She twitches her foot.

'So, who was it? Do you know?'

'Marcus.'

'*Marcus?* You're kidding me! The little dick stood there while you accused *me*? Shit! I'm going to rip him a new one.' She starts to walk towards the door.

'No, no. Leave it.'

'Seriously? After all the shit he's caused you – *us!* He could have ruined everything!'

'I know and I'm sorry. Honestly.'

We sit for a moment in silence; her on the bed, me on the chair.

How quickly things change. Now it's me who's in the wrong, the one asking for forgiveness! She leans over to take my hand.

'Look, it's OK. I can't blame you for thinking the worst. I haven't exactly been my best self of late, have I? And at least you know the truth now, so we can try and get past this. Because that's what I want. More than anything.'

'I know you do, Scarlet.'

'And you? That's what you want too, isn't it?'

She doesn't wait for an answer, afraid of hearing a 'No' perhaps.

'Sorry. That's unfair of me. I know you're still working through things. It will take time. I know that.' She pulls me over to her. 'I want you so much. I love you, Ava Roberts! I really do.'

Her lips touch mine. I don't push her away.

*

Makeup sex is the best. Officially. In fact, there are extensive scientific studies on the very subject and they regularly appear on women's sites, right next to articles on "Eat Yourself Thin" and "My Sister: The Zombie Health Worker".

It has something to do with endorphins, apparently.

Whatever it is, I wake up an hour later feeling a lot less stressed.

Scarlet is asleep at my side with the cutest little smile on her face. Angelic even. I don't wake her but throw on some clothes and head off in search of an ice-cold Coke. Lord, I'm dehydrated! I feel like one of those mummified corpses that they periodically dig up in peat bogs.

It's still sunny out, a few people lounging by the pool and a good few more in the bar. I wander inside, immediately clocking Aunty B in her favourite spot between giant wooden giraffes and portrait of Nelson Mandela. Perfect view of hot bartenders.

She beckons me over.

'So, is my favourite niece feeling any better?'

'Yeah, I think so! God, what a mess! And Marcus! I mean, he's lucky I didn't kill him!'

'Oh, don't worry about that my dear, Maria will do that for you,' she grins, impaling the olive in her martini glass.

'Ha! Roger that. And where is he now?'

'Divorced, I'd say.'

Bahahahaha!

'Anyway, let's not worry about that waste of space.' She pushes the hair back off my face. 'What about you? You're looking a little flushed. I take it the makeup with Scarlet went well?'

'*Aunty B!*'

'What? Sex is an important part of any relationship, Ava. Not *the* most important thing, but it's up there!'

'Well, let's just say I apologised and she was very nice about it. So it's not a complete disaster.'

'Well, that's all you can do, and I bet she was as relieved as you to know she was in the clear.'

I give a little nod and look away.

I feel her staring at me. Reading me, like she used to when I was a little girl; when I'd licked all the chocolate off the Hobnobs and put them back in the packet.

'So, come on. Tell your Aunty B what's bothering you.'

'Nothing. There's nothing wrong, really.'

She gives me a look, 'Ava Roberts! I've known you since you were a baby. You don't look like someone overjoyed to be reunited!'

'Oh, I dunno. It's just *complicated*. Everything's happening so fast and then there's the trust issue. I mean Scarlet says all these things, but I can't stop thinking about what she did and...oh, I dunno. Ignore me, I'm just tired.'

'It's natural to be confused, my dear' she says, reaching for my hand. 'Now, this might sound silly, but I find that it never pays to overthink these things. You just have to decide who and what makes you happy. If that's Scarlet, then so be it. Don't beat yourself up with what's happened in the past – that's gone. Finished. Make your decision and grab it.' She pauses for a moment. 'But...'

'Oh great, there's a but!'

'Of course! There's *always* a but! That's what makes life so interesting! *BUT.....*if it's not Scarlet, you need to let her go. Because until you do, you won't let the right one in.'

I sit there, allowing her words to seep in.

'That kinda makes sense.'

'It does? Oh, how wonderful! It's good to know I've learnt something from my four marriages. *Four!* Can you believe it? Two more and I'll be up there with Henry VIII!'

'Ha! Think you'd have to behead a couple first!'

'That can be arranged!' she winks.

I start to pick at my drinks coaster, pulling at the pretty beading.

'So, do you regret it Aunty B – marrying them all, I mean?'

'Hell no! I had some wonderful times with each and every one of them. I don't regret marrying them, dear. In fact, my only regret is *not* marrying the one I really wanted. The man I really loved, I never dared tell. Too afraid of, well, spoiling things, I guess. Or of being rejected. Perhaps both. And you know what, if I could go back, I would tell him. I'd tell him every minute of the day until I was blue in the face!'

'Maybe you still can?'

'Oh, I'm afraid that ship has sailed, dear. Long ago,' she smiles, taking a long sip on her cocktail. 'Anyway. How's your friend Jen?'

'Oh, she's on her way home. Something came up. Why do you ask?'

'No reason dear. No reason. Right, your Aunty B has some serious flirting to do. Why don't you run along and enjoy yourself, hey? Oh, and Ava...'

'Yes?'

'Life's terribly short. It won't be long before your boobs are around your ankles, believe me. So best enjoy the ride. The mistakes and the failures as much as the triumphs. They are all beautiful!'

With that she turns away to make her latest mistake with barman number two (rugged bald type), while I head off feeling a whole lot better. Aunty B's right; overthinking is never good. I just need to relax, not try to figure everything out right away. Tiny steps!

I get one hand on the door when I hear a familiar 'You-hooo!'

Dear Aunty Aggy. What timing!

I try to scurry inside, but alas, no chance. She pounces.

'Hello Ava. Wasn't the wedding just wonderful? Smoky but wonderful.'

'Ha! Yes, it was a pretty special day!'

'Indeed. And more to the point, I was right, wasn't I?' Her face starts to glow with smugness.

'Right about what?' I enquire.

'About the women fighting over you. I mean, one doesn't like to talk out of turn, but there was quite a showdown last night.'

'Sorry, I don't quite follow. What showdown?'

'Why between your throuple friends of course! The two girls you were with yesterday.' She steps in closer. 'Like I said, I don't like to talk out of turn, but I was at the bar minding my own business when the blonde one..'

'Scarlet?'

'Yes, she started laying down the law to the other one, in blue…'

'Jen?'

'Yes, yes, the other one. I mean, one doesn't like to pry, but she was getting most annoyed: telling her that she was interfering in your relationship and that she should keep her nose out of it. And then, the blonde girl…'

'Scarlet!'

'Yes, she got most assertive. Telling the other one that she was standing in the way of your happiness and that you felt the same, and that perhaps it would be best that she left. I mean, it was all very dramatic.' Her words turn into a dull buzz like an annoying mosquito and all I can see is that pink streak of lipstick on her teeth as her mouth opens and closes, opens and closes.

Scarlet told Jen to leave. Surely not? Aunt Aggy must have it wrong.

I stand for a moment, stunned, before turning my back on the harbinger of doom and stepping back into Scarlet's room.

I see her reclining on the bed all tanned and gorgeous.

'Hey, where have you been, beautiful?' she smiles, 'I've missed you!'

She goes to kiss me and I instinctively recoil.

'Oh. What is it now? Have you come to accuse me of another heinous crime? The JFK assassination perhaps? OK. OK. It was me up there on the grassy knoll!' She breaks into laughter. 'I did it! Slap on the cuffs.'

I don't react, taking a slow, deep breath.

'Cut the smart talk, Scarlet. Do you want to tell me what you said to Jen?'

She leans back further on the bed. '*Jen?* What do you mean. When?'

'Last night, before she left? What did you say to her?' I look her straight in her eyes, 'And be warned, Scarlet. I'm not in the mood for half-truths.'

'Err, not much. I just told her that we needed some space, that's all. That we needed a bit of time together.'

'And that was it?'

'Pretty much. Oh, and that she was interfering – by being here, I mean.'

My blood starts to boil, but somehow I manage to remain calm.

'And then you told her to go? Or rather, you told her that *I* wanted her to go.'

'No, not *go!* Not as blatantly as that!' she says a little flummoxed. 'Look, I was scared, Ave. We needed to work through things. Alone.' She starts to make her way down the bed. 'I'm sorry if what I did upset you, OK?'

'Errr, upset me? Of course it upset me! You told my best friend that *I* said she was in the way. *Me!* Bloody hell, you had no right to do that.'

'OK, OK. I stuffed up. Again. But it was for a good reason. I did it for us - because I love you.'

'Well, that's not a good enough reason, Scarlet. End of. You hurt her. You made it look like *I* pushed her away.'

She stares at me as if trying to read my mind and slowly, very slowly, I see her whole demeanour change from one of contrition to one of annoyance. She runs her hand through her hair like she does when she's angry.

'So, what's this really about Ava?'

'Sorry?'

'Why are you so concerned about Jen's feelings in all this? You should be thinking about *us*. That's where your energy should be. Not with your bloody best friend! You know what, I just think it's all a bit strange...'

'What are you talking about? What's strange?'

'Well, you and her! It's just, I dunno. Off. She turns up here in South Africa, *rescues* you with that stupid bloody song, and then, and then..' she starts to stammer and lose her thread.

'Then, what?'

'And then you bloody call out for her!'

I look at her confused. 'Call out for her? What are you talking about? You're not making any sense.'

She glares at me, her eyes narrowing.

'After you got hit by that ball on the beach today. You were spar-ko and I was sitting over you, thinking the worst, and then you opened your eyes and that was the first thing you said. You said *her* name. You called for Jen!'

Her eyes start to well up.

She is in hurt mode now, her mouth opening and closing, saying things she probably shouldn't. Things that are hurting us both. It's like watching someone digging a great big hole that is about to cave in and swallow them up whole.

She suddenly gets up from the bed and steps close to me.

'Do you know what? I wouldn't be surprised if, if…she was in love with you or something!'

'What? That's just…'

'What, crazy? Is it, Ava? Is it really?' She looks to the floor for a moment, 'Or maybe….just maybe, it's you who's in love with her!' she hisses.

'What?'

'Well, are you Ava? Are you in love with her?'

'Scarlet! Stop this!'

'Answer the question, Ava! Just tell me!'

.

.

My mind goes blank. Short-circuits.

I go to contradict her, to tell her she's crazy, that she's got it all wrong, but I can't. I just can't.

CHAPTER THIRTY-THREE - 'O.M.G!'

Around the World in 80 Gays
"Sowing the seeds of change"

(Unpublished entry)

Once you know, you know.

There's no going back, no hitting alt-shift-delete or stuffing the big-bellied genie back into the bottle. It's out there. *It's a thing!*

It's funny how such things magically come into being – like the realisation that you have feelings for someone. *Where on earth did that come from,* you ponder? *How could something so huge, so life altering just appear, like a shoot bursting from the cracked earth miraculously alive.*

The truth is nothing ever 'just' happens. Not really. Like that tiny seed, most of the magic takes place beneath the surface out of sight in the fecund darkness, seemingly without any input.

Of course, we never imagine that it might have been *us* who planted the seed in the first place. That we might have subconsciously brought it into being. Watered it, bathed it in sunshine and then, whoosh, it's there! *New life. New love. A whole new adventure waiting to begin!*

CHAPTER THIRTY-FOUR - 'DO ONE, KITTY!'

'Better a whoops that a what if.'

- Beau Taplin

Flight 456 to London

The secret to happiness is knowing when to leave: the party, the job, the relationship. And when I left that room yesterday, when I walked away from Scarlet and a life I thought I wanted, it felt right. Difficult, but right. It's crazy to think of the months spent missing her. All those sleepless nights yearning to hear her say it was all some big mistake and that it was me, *only me* she loved. Yet when it came down to it, when she finally uttered those words, it was too late. The moment had gone, slipped out the door when nobody was looking.

The rest of the events post-showdown are sketchy.

The packing, the tears, her imploring me to stay; every part of it a blur, aside from Aunty B hugging me until my ribs cracked and Maria insisting I swipe through her new dating profile. #ShortestMarriageEver.

The flight back to London is packed and I find myself ruminating on the events of the past 24 hours, raking them all up again like a big, emotional plough. I sip my shiraz and gaze out of the window, watching the yellow desert give way to ocean and in turn the ocean being obscured by a mass of fluffy cloud. And I can't help but think it's a lot like life.

Things change.

One minute you're all loved up with your person and the next they up and leave, and the landscape is changed forever. A gaping hole is left; the deepest, blackest chasm you could ever imagine. It's terrifying at first, like the nothingness might swallow you whole. But then slowly, very slowly, you start to notice things, wonderful things that were once eclipsed by that person's presence. People start to shine more brightly, so brightly that you wonder how you ever missed them before, and you look about you at the new life springing up in the void. New opportunities, a new career, a whole new love!

Profound stuff, at least that's what my neighbour in 78H tells me. He's a livestock farmer from Petrusburg, a hulk of a man with a chest the size of a whisky barrel. 'I'm Pieter De Klerk, narce to meet you,' he says in the strongest Afrikaans accent and within minutes we are sharing complimentary snacks and photos of his prize-winning bulls. I reciprocate with a few tales of bestie Nandi, which soon leads us onto love of the human variety and the Scarlet/Jen saga.

'Oh ja, ja! I know that feeling very well,' he nods. 'I married *my* bist friend. Ten years this month! Look!' He produces a well-thumbed photo from his wallet. 'There she is! My Mariki. It means little Marie.'

'Aww, how lovely. You fell for your best friend too?'

'From a great height!' he says with a little chuckle. 'Love of my larf, that woman! Love of my larf!'

I smile across at him, heartened by the triumphant bestie love story. 'And where is the lovely Mariki today, may I ask?'

'No idea. She left me.'

'_'

The unexpected plot twist floors me somewhat and I retreat into my seat leaving Pieter to quietly sob into his meal tray. Not the best of omens I have to say and the tale only acts as a stern reminder that there's a lot at stake in all this. It's a risk, a massive risk, like anything in life that really matters. But then, isn't the real risk *not* taking a risk? Not daring to tell someone how you feel? Not daring to see what might be?

It's an unsettling thing realising that you have romantic feelings for your best friend. Knowing that the person with whom you've felt so safe, the person you've entrusted with your deepest, darkest secrets suddenly has the power to hurt you... to reject you.

How did I not see this coming?

Love with a little 'l' turning into love with an f'ing huuuuuge one!

Aunty B explained it best... it's like the whole boiling a frog analogy, she said. 'They don't put them straight into the boiling water, you know. They start off with it nice and cool. Then gradually, very gradually, they turn the heat up so the poor frog doesn't notice. And next thing. Well, I don't need to tell you, do I dear?'

I am the frog in this scenario. Boiled alive in a bestie love soup! My head floods with doubts.

What the hell am I doing? I might be about to ruin everything, bulldoze years of wonderful friendship with a single sentence.

Urgghhh!

The torture is too much so I anaesthetise myself with another glug of wine and check the in-flight map. The little plane is hanging just over Algeria. Four hours to go. Four hours 'til I rock up at Jen's birthday party to embrace my fate. I sink down into my seat, slowly losing consciousness.

*

Bing bong. Crackle crackle. Hisssss.

'Good afternoon everyone. Welcome to London Heathrow. It's 5 pm local time and the temperature is 10 degrees.'

10 degrees!

Instant nipple inversion

I look out at the low grey cloud and sprawling airport buildings. I'm home! Back in my beloved England exactly 80 days since commencement of Operation Scarlet Tennison Detox. I am a woman changed, a woman grown, a woman who needs to shut the hell up and get to this party! I'm one of the first off the plane, thanks to cunning plan of thrusting out my pasta gut and declaring 'I'm pregnant!' to anyone who dares impede my progress. Morally reprehensible, I know.

I turn my phone on.

Finding network, finding network. Connect.

15 new messages. One from Vodafone welcoming me home, another from Cruella announcing some 'fantastico' news and, *flick flick*, heaps about Jen's party. Heaps and heaps! Jen herself is rather subdued. In fact she hardly even reacted to the 'pant-shitting news' (my brother's words) that Marcus has been unveiled as the blog Judas, aside from offering the curt response, 'TWAT.' It's funny, but I'm not the least bit bothered about the whole Marcus

perfidy now. It's like my intense abhorrence of the little toad has been vindicated and more importantly I have bigger fish to fry. Much bigger.

I set my watch to UK time, 1700 hours, sufficient minutage to shower at the airport, slip into party outfit, thus arriving at birthday bash looking downright irresistible. #ReachForTheSkies. Passport control is a cinch and now all that stands between me and agony/ecstasy is luggage pick-up. Carousel 7. *Lucky 7*! Case after case glide past: *not mine, not mine, defo not mine*. And then I see it. My trusty backpack!

Inspects label

False alarm.

Won't be long now.

.

.

Soon be here.

.

.

'Errrr, my bag is *where* exactly, Susan?' I enquire, smashing my head on the lost luggage counter. Operation 'Surprise Jen' has hit an early snag and snooty Susan (*acting assistant manager*) is sorry to inform me of the mix-up aka colossal incompetence of her bum-wipingly useless airline! Long story long: my bag with party outfit, lucky pants and any chance of a happy ever after is presently sunning itself on the paradise island of Madagascar!

'*MADAGASCAR?*' I gasp. '*MADAGASCAR?*'

'Yes. Have you seen the film?'

'Sorry?'

'It's a film you know,' she enthuses, treating me to a few dubious impressions of the main characters. 'Oooh, I do love animation. Do you love animation?'

Err, not as much as I love my bloody luggage, Susan Jenkins!

The conversation is going round and round in circles, rather like carousel 7 on which my bag…Doth. Not. Sit.

I glance at my watch. 6.15 pm!

Still time to turn this wardrobe catastrophe around. I just need to be resourceful – *improvise!* One of the many skills I've picked up on my adventures. I once fashioned an entire outfit from a rusty paperclip and a wet sarong for God's sake. *I can surely handle this.*

I glance down at my current get-up: faded jogging pants (coffee stained), hoodie (wine-splattered) and trainers (dirty white).

Not quite the look I was going for, have to say.

Just 50 minutes to go.

Think Ava, think….

*

Wardour Street, London,

7.45 pm

The taxi door slides back sweeping the glimmering lights of Soho to life. It's like opening Aladdin's cave, bursting with all its glorious nighttime treasures. How I've missed this place! I put one foot onto the street and I instantly feel it, the devastating allure of my presence! Strangers gasp, dogs howl; *I am a rock star. I am legend!* I am wearing the following crumpled items from my hand luggage:

Neon orange fisherman pants. Oversized;
Kid's safari shirt with lion's head;
Clashing sarong (fashioned into boho scarf); and
Kangaroo testicle neckpurse.

Donatella eat your heart out!

Confidence is everything and I glide through the glass doors and past the thick-necked bouncers with such poise that they let me pass unchallenged. Every step attracts another admiring glance, along with the realisation that this is not just some hotchpotch outfit I'm wearing, nor some fashion *faux pas.* This, my friends, is my spin on *Joseph's Amazing Technicolour Dreamcoat!* An outfit fashioned from all my fabulous adventures: the forever friendships, the sexy liaisons, the death-defying encounters with apex predators. Laughter, euphoria, exhilaration, loss, every wonderful emotion and beautiful moment woven into the fabric like an unbreakable thread.

This outfit makes me invincible!

The bar is crowded with lots of merry people knocking back shots like hangovers don't exist. It doesn't take long before I run into a group of friends. 'Ali! TK! SURPRIIIIIISE!' I sing, as they stare back at me blankly. Zero recognition. 'It's meeee! It's AVA!' I repeat, as the cogs slowly start to turn and then, *wham*, I'm descended upon like some returning conquering hero.

'Oh my God! AVAAAAA! You look different,' they grin. I want to tell them they're right. I am different! So different!

I'm remixed, rebooted, re-energised; an all new improved formula!

The reunion is everything: hugs, kisses, more hugs upon more kisses. Coming home is a magnificent thing, like being swooped up in a warm salty wave of love. As delicious as it is, I know I must pull myself away and remain faithful to my mission to find Jen and tell her how I feel. Tell her...*Oh God, I feel sick!*

I neck a complimentary champagne, Dutch courage, and look around the bar. *Where is she?* No sign yet. I slalom through the little groups of well-wishers, 'Hi Suey, hi Alex! Nice hair, Rach!' I call, before I receive a confirmed sighting – Jen was last seen at the smaller cocktail bar in the side room.

I adjust course and wander in, my heart thumping. A quick sweep to the left, then the right, and then...I see her! Standing just feet away with an armful of presents. I quaff champagne number two, touch my butterfly necklace and mutter my rousing battle cry,

'Better a whoops than a what if!'

She doesn't see me at first, far too engrossed in conversation, so I commence my approach, my shaky-kneed approach. Ten steps, nine, eight, seven, and then...

'Avaaaa darlink! You're here!'

Cruella! WTF!

I freeze in my tracks and turn towards her quickly resetting my thunder face.

'Lucrezia. I didn't know you were coming!'

'Wouldn't miss it for the world, darlink!' she grins, giving me a signature air kiss, which for once is more kiss than air. She tilts her head to one side like a cocker spaniel. 'So tell me, how are you feeling, Ava? I've been so worried about you after your showdown with Marcus! To think it was him all along! *Him!* I haven't been as stunned since Britney shaved her head!'

I eye her incredulously.

Cruella the master manipulator shocked? I think not!

In fact, I rather suspect she was privy to the little toad's treachery all along, privy to every duplicitous deed, but I don't go there. I start to inch away but she holds firm, affixed to my side like a limpet.

'Soo, darlink. What do you think about the news?'

'News?'

'The amazing blog news! Didn't you read my text, darlink?'

'Err, not yet! I ...'

Her pupils instantly dilate to the size of serving plates. 'Oh benissimo! I get to tell you *en personne!*' she grins. 'I'm elated to announce that *Around the World in 80 Gays* is number one in Google travel blogs! We did it, Ava! We did it! I knew that the African photoshoot would get us there. We dropped the piece on the socials last night! *It went offfff!* Incredible engagement. Plus possible sponsorship from M&S!'

'Oh! Wow! A lifetime supply of Percy Pigs.'

'And of course, Jennifer is overjoyed. Overjoyed! Always good to leave a project on a high!'

And now she has my attention.

'Sorry, what? *Leave on a high*? Who's leaving?'

'Why Jennifer, darlink! She's been simply sublime – her writing has taken us all the way to the top spot, but now it's time for her to take flight, to sprinkle her magic on a new project!'

'What new project? What are you talking about?'

'Well, it's all very hush hush,' she says, looking around conspiratorially. 'But let's just say it might or might not involve... *Sir Elton!*'

'Nooooo! That's not a good idea.'

'What, Sir Elton? Not a fan of the rocket man, darlink?'

'No, nooo, Jen leaving. It's not a good idea that Jen leaves. She *is* the blog!'

'Oh Ava, Ava. *You* are the blog, darlink. It's your spirit, your essence.' She wraps a snake-like arm round my waist, drawing me closer. 'Be assured, the blog will continue to thrive! In fact, I've already assigned you a fabulous new writer. *Huge* talent, an influencer, massive following!' She promptly thrusts forth a Cruella mini-me: same high quiff, same long painted talons, but younger. Much, much younger. In fact, I don't know whether to shake her hand or burp her.

'Ava Roberts, may I present Ambrosia Quinten-Smythe, your new *80 Gays* writing partner!'

Ambrosia? All I can think of right now is a tin of rice pudding! Rich, white and thick.

She instantly launches herself at me.

'Oh Ava! I am *such* a fan! Like, I just heart the blog! Heart it! And I have so many ideas about how we can amplify it, it's just going to be lit, yah?'

'Oh cool! *Lit!*' I lean into Cruella. 'Ummm, can I be honest, Lucrezia?'

'Of course, daaarlink. What is it your friend Indira says… *speak your truth*! How is she by the way?'

'Dead!' I snap. 'Look, Lucrezia, you can't have this blog without Jen. You just can't! She's the winning ingredient! No offence, Ambrosia.'

'Like, none taken, yah!' she sneers, knocking out a quick tweet to ensure my immediate cancellation. Cruella instantly goes on the charm offensive.

'See! *This* is the fire I told you about, Ambrosia! Ava is such a passionate creature. Can you feel it…can you feel the fire?'

'Yah. I feel it, Lucrezia!' her mini-me enthuses.

'Yah, yah! But really feel it, like, really feel that heat!'

'Yah! I'm feeling it, Lucrezia! I'm soooo feeling it!'

They both have their hands on me at this point, as if performing some ancient healing ritual or exorcising a demon perhaps. I'm just about ready to throw my drink at them, when I feel a tug on my bag.

Another interruption! Really?

'What now?' I snap, spinning round to see a familiar face standing before me. '*JEN!* OMG, Jen! I was just coming to surprise you!'

She lets out a little squeal of delight.

'You're here! I thought you were still in Africa!'

'Ha! Slight change of plan!'

I stand there just staring at her. Overwhelmed. Underprepared.

This is so not how this thing was supposed to go. I'd envisaged the whole scene, planned every single detail. Me striding into the bar to Sia's "Titanium" and then, *Booooom,* I'd see her. The crowds would part and...

'Jennifer daaaarlink. Happy day of birth!' *Air kiss. Air kiss.*

Cruella artfully manoeuvres herself between us.

'Hi Lucrezia,' the birthday girl grins. 'Nice of you to come!'

'Yah, yah! So much to celebrate, Jennifer. So much! I was just regaling Ava with the *fantastico* news re blog! Number one!' she beams, pulling us all in for a quick group selfie. *Snap! Snap!*

'Yes, it's great news, Lucrezia! Amazing!'

'Isn't it darlink? Isn't it? Imagine, the whole world is enchanted by the utterly sublime adventures of Ava Roberts!' She thrusts her arms dramatically into the air. 'It's a triumph: a number one blog, Scarlet and Ava reunited, and a new chapter for you Jennifer. Benissimo!'

I want to stop her right there.

Stop her from spurting all her rubbish, stop her from ruining my moment. The adrenaline rises within and, in a sudden burst of defiance, I reclaim the moment and swoop Jen away to the bar, leaving Cruella mid-sentence and a fair bit confused. #SorryNotSorry.

'Pheww! Safe now,' I smile, promptly ordering two celebratory espresso martinis and commencing what I have come here to do. I get halfway through a sentence when Jen erupts with laughter,

'I just can't believe you're here, Ave! It's such a surprise!'

'Ha! And who doesn't love a surprise? Oh, excuse the outfit by the way. It's a bit of a long story featuring Madagascar.'

'The movie?'

Eye twitch, eye twitch

She looks me up and down, 'I kinda like it you know, very avant garde. So, when did you guys get back?' She starts to peer over my shoulder. 'Is Scarlet here?'

I turn to face her, 'Hey, about Scarlet. I really need to clear the air. I know what she said. That she told you to leave or rather that she told you that *I* wanted you to, which was an out and out lie!'

Her expression changes, 'Well, I did think it was a bit weird.'

'A *bit* weird?' I say, shaking my head. 'How could you even think I'd say something like that?'

'Errr, because she's Scarlet and you're you! I thought you'd fallen under her spell again. Bewitched! Anyway, it was probably for the best. To give you guys some space, I mean.' She pauses for a moment. 'So, how are things going?'

'That's just it. They aren't as much *going* as *gone!*'

'*Gone?*'

'Yes, gone. As in *no more*. I left her there. Well, I left her generally. Basically, we're not back together and it feels great! Honestly, it's the weirdest feeling, Jen. Finally being free of her after all this time.'

She looks puzzled, 'Oh, right? But those photos…on the Insta account?' She starts swiping through her phone. 'Here, look!'

I skim-read the post, "Flying high on love and blogging*"*, accompanied by that stunning aerial shot Andre was practically climaxing over. *Swipe swipe.* Lots of photos of me and Scarlet on the fake beach, fake hugging, fake kissing.

I feel sick to the pit of my stomach.

'But, how? They said they wouldn't use those photos!' I hiss. 'They promised! It was Cruella's idea. She wanted the fairytale ending.' I swipe through the images again. 'Look at them! They're about as fake as that bloody beach!'

'Shit, that *is* fucked up. Even for Lucrezia.'

'Honestly, Jen, I've had enough of this crap – Scarlet, Marcus, Cruella. In fact, I've been doing a lot of thinking since you left and…' I suddenly break off.

This is it. This is the moment I leap from the precipice.

This is the moment I fall or fly!

'Ave? What is it?'

I look into her eyes. 'Jen, I know this is going to sound insane, but I had a realisation – well, more of an epiphany really. When Scarlet was telling me how much she loved me, I realised, well, *she* made me realise…so, I really have her to thank in an odd way…'

'Ava, you're talking gibberish!'

'Oh sorry! What I'm *trying* to say is that I realised it's not Scarlet I want to be with, it's… '

'*JEN!* There you are!' a voice calls.

I spin round to see an athletic looking girl bounding towards us: tall, dark, attractive. She looks familiar, but I can't quite place her. She throws her arms around Jen's neck. And. Kisses. Her.

Heart sinks. Air is sucked from the room

'Sorry to interrupt!' the stranger smiles. 'I need to borrow the birthday girl for a sec! That OK?'

She must she see the abject horror on my face as she swiftly follows up with a conciliatory 'Oh, were you guys having a D&M?'

'No, it's cool,' I reassure. 'Just chatting.'

Jen starts to speak, a little distracted.

'Oh … Natasha, this is Ava by the way.'

The personal trainer, of course!

Her face lights up. 'Oh wow, Ava! *The* Ava! Jen has told me so much about you. So great to meet you at last.'

'Me too!'

'Oh and I love the blog by the way, you guys are doing a great job. Isn't Jen a genius?'

I flash a little smile. I say 'smile', it would better be described as an 'Oscars' smile'. The kind you see plastered across the faces of Academy Award nominees when they don't win. That kind of smile.

It's all feeling a little awkward as Jen touches my hand.

'Sorry, Ave! Do you mind if I run off for a minute? I'll come and grab you later, OK?'

'Yes, of course. You go, birthday girl. This is your night!'

Awkward air punch.

I watch them walk away, Natasha steering Jen over to a group of girls that I don't recognise who let out a massive cheer before handing her an elegantly wrapped gift. Jen breaks into a giant smile while mine floats to the bottom of my martini glass.

Well, bugger me!

Life sure does change quickly.

The desert giving way to the ocean, the ocean…blah blah blah…and here I am engulfed by those dark fluffy clouds and feeling utterly deflated. I stand for a moment. *How did I not factor this in? Natasha, aka hot fitness goddess back on the scene. Why did I think they were no longer a thing?*

Guess the surprise is on me.

I console myself with another cocktail and a shot, and gaze at all the happy faces having a gloriously happy night. This is the last place I want to be right now. Right now I want to be in a dark room, sobbing into my duvet and eating a family box of McNuggets. In want of that, I do the next best thing: retreating into a quiet nook between a wilted pot plant and a grumpy ginger cat, whom I'm told is a furry resident here. She's a funny looking creature with an overfluffed tail and a big, white patch on her face that reminds me of *The Phantom of the Opera*. She greets me with a lopsided scowl.

'Cheer up!' I smile. 'At least you're not in love with your best friend!'

Grumpy cat gives a long evil stare.

'You're right, cat! I really *should* look on the bright side. At least I'll never know the double heartbreak of losing a lover *and* a best friend, like poor farmer Pieter. Now that would be a stinger!'

Grumpy cat continues to stare like she wants to eat my liver, but drunk Ava is not daunted. I inch closer to my ginger confidante.

'And the *really* good news is I didn't humiliate myself, did I? I get to keep my bestie and not ruin a wonderful friendship. Phewwww! And if she's happy with someone else then I'm happy for her. I'll just admire her from afar, secretly pen poems she will never read. Words of love she will never hear. I won't be the first. Shakespeare make a career out of it!'

Grumpy cat is clearly not convinced and promptly delivers a sharp hiss in my direction.

'PAH! I know, I know! I'm bloody gutted.' I whimper, throwing my head in my hands. 'Absolutely. Bloody. Gutted.'

What a night!

Nothing has gone as planned. Not a single thing. I sit for a moment in a depressed alcoholic haze, before I feel a wave of defiance rise up within me, willing me to take back my power. I rise up from my stool.

'I might not be leaving with my girl tonight, but at least I can leave with my dignity!' I declare, looking around the bar for Cruella. 'Right, where is she? I'm going to give that woman a piece of my mind, the conniving cow!'

It doesn't take long to locate her, right across the dancefloor engrossed with her mini-me plus a few randoms who look like they've just tumbled off a catwalk. I wade in, tapping her shoulder.

'Ava, darlink! You must have read my mind. I need you to have a quick powwow with Ambrosia. She has to head shortly; she has a 9 pm with Elon Musk.'

'Sure. I've actually got a few ideas of my own I want to discuss.'

'Oh benissimo. I'm all ears!'

'Well, first off, I think we should change the name of the blog, you know, since we now have our *fairytale ending*!'

She quickly picks up on my thinly veiled sarcasm.

'Riiiiiiight. Change the blog name? Hmm. It's bold, yah. Very bold. But I'm just wondering what we'll lose in brand leverage and recognition. What name were you thinking of?'

'I dunno, how about *Blog off*!'

'Ha! Love the attitude, darlink; just not sure if it's quite right for our demo!'

'No. That's not the new name, that's what I'm saying to you, Lucrezia! *Blog off.* I saw you released those photos, the reunion shots, without my consent and frankly I'm done. No hard feelings, it's been fun – well, some of it anyway – so, yah, have a benissimo night!'

She looks a little taken aback, before erupting with laughter. 'There's that fire again! *That Ava Roberts fire!* Ambrosia, did you hear that? Did you hear what Ava just said?'

Ambrosia starts nodding like her head is on a spring.

'Oh yah, yah! *The fire!*'

I quickly interject, high on champagne and one too many espresso martinis. 'Oh yes, there's a fire alright...and here's a little something to put it out!'

With that, I launch the contents of my shot glass her way, which to be honest is no more than a couple of drops, but a gesture, nevertheless. 'Have a good evening!' I smile, promptly turning on my heels and returning to my bar stool.

I can't believe I did it! I told her where to stick her blog.

What a rush! What an absolute rush!

My heart is still racing when I sidle up to grumpy cat for a well-earned gloat.

'Did you see that? Not such a coward after all, hey?'

I'm just about to launch into another drunken rant when a voice chimes in.

'Are you actually talking to a cat?' I spin round, half-embarrassed.

'*Jen!* Ha! Err, you caught me. Just err, chatting, you know…'

'*Just drunk* more like!' she quips, plonking herself down on the stool next to me. She looks beautiful. Beautiful and happy.

'You having fun, birthday girl?'

'Kind of. Not sure how much I enjoy big birthday parties these days! Stressful!'

'Well, you shouldn't be so popular, should you?' I laugh, passing her a drink. 'Cheers… to the big 3-1!'

'Oh stop! Seems like only yesterday we were partying our lives away at uni.'

'Ha! The glory days! Well, you're looking great on it. As my mum always says, the older you get, the better you get…unless you're a banana!'

She starts to giggle again and I instantly get a warm, fuzzy feeling in my tummy.

'What?'

'Oh nothing, you just make me laugh!' she smiles. 'Sorry about earlier by the way. Getting dragged off. Tash and the girls wanted to give me a gift.'

'It's fine. I'm glad you're getting spoilt. Sadly, I have no such gift to offer. Well, I do but it's on the other side of the world with my luggage!'

We sit for a while, drunk-talking, and I start to think that maybe it's all for the best. I mean, imagine if I had said something. Imagine how awkward it could have been.

'Hey, Ave. What was it you were going to say to me earlier?'

My body instantly tenses.

'Oh, nothing…all good now.' I attempt to change the subject. 'So, Natasha seems great. You look good together – two fitties, looking er, fit!'

'Jeez. How drunk *are* you, Ave? And we're not, by the way.'

'Not fit?'

'No, not together!'

Spurts cocktail down lion head safari top

'Bloody hell! It's not that much of a shock, is it?'

'Hahaha! No, not really,' I smile, dabbing my T-shirt. 'What happened?'

'Oh nothing, really. She's lovely and everything, but I wasn't feeling it. She's dating an Olympian now, that girl over there in grey, see?'

I look over, desperate to stop my mouth erupting into a massive clown-like grin.

'Oh wow, yes.' I say, clocking the fittest woman I've ever seen. 'Look at her shoulders! What's her event, swimming?'

'No. Curling.'

Bahahahahahahaha!

It's a bit of an overenthusiastic laugh, I must confess. A laugh replete with relief and joy. A laugh that's going on a little too long on my part.

'You OK, Ave?' she asks, the tears streaming down her face.

'Never better!'

'So, I imagine Cruella told you the news. I'm on a new project now, but Ambrosia seems really…'

'*Ricey?*'

More laughter.

I take a deep breath and turn into her.

'Jen. Let's get one thing straight. I don't want to do a blog with a teenage influencer named Ambosia, Semolina or even New York cheesecake for that matter! Truth is, I don't want to do a blog with anyone but you.' I lean in further. 'In fact, I've been thinking, we don't even need *80 Gays*. We can do our own blog. Just like you always wanted. Write it *your* way, *your* style. Start afresh!'

'*What?* You'd walk away from all that success, all that…'

'Free strawberry lube? Hell, yes. In fact, I already have. I told Lucrezia to blog off! I even threw my drink over her; well, two drops to be accurate, maybe three. But it's a token nevertheless!'

'I can't believe you did that,' she giggles. 'Wish I'd have been there!'

'Well, it was pretty impressive, I have to say! But that's not the important bit, Jen. The blog was great because it was you and me. The dream team! In fact...' I take a moment to steady myself. 'I reckon everything's better when it's you and me. Life, the blog, everything. And I know this is going to sound weird, but the reason I left Scarlet was because.... because she didn't like my butterfly necklace. Well, that wasn't the only reason. I realised something. Something huge. It's like you said back in Cape Town, about making a choice. Deciding whether you want a Kitty or a Florence, like in *Tipping The Velvet!*'

She lets out a giggle of recognition.

'Oh yes! The Kitty v Florence dilemma. The one who broke your heart versus the new unblemished love. Just a theory I have. I'm yet to publish it in thesis form. So, come on then,' she smiles. 'Who *would* you pick?'

I stare deep into her big green eyes. Not flinching, not looking away, ready to speak my truth.

'Thing is, I wouldn't pick either.'

'Okaaaaaay?'

'No. Thing is.....I'd pick you, Jen! I'd pick you!'

And just like that, it's out there. The genie released from the bottle... big round belly and all.

I wait.

.

More waiting.

.

.

The longer I sit before the stony wall of silence, the more I'm convinced that this might very well be my 'Oops!' moment! My great big...Fuck-off. Oops. Moment! I feel utterly vulnerable, angry that I have just butchered the most wonderful friendship, bludgeoned it to death with one stupid sentence.

The silence is too much and I leap right into it like a kid in a puddle.

'Oh shit, ignore me! I think I'm just tired from the flight and drunk! Sooo drunk!'

'Ava! You can't say something like that and then take it back...'

'No, honestly, Jen!' I insist, shamelessly backtracking. 'You don't need to explain. I'm just a little mixed up with everything. So much has happened, and like I said I'm drunk and talking to a cat, so, yeah. Go figure!'

'Ava! If you'd just stop talking for a moment and let...'

'No, honestly, it's your birthday! Go enjoy yourself. Have a cheese straw, oh the vol-au-vents are...'

She places her hand firmly over my lips. 'Ava. STOP! Please, just stop!'

I instantly fall silent, as she takes my hand in hers. 'Jeez, girl. If you'd let me bloody get a word in edgeways, I'd tell you!'

'Tell me what?'

'I'd tell you...' She pauses again, prolonging the agony. 'I'd tell you that I'd pick you too. I'd pick you a million times over. From the moment you puked in my sink in freshers' week. I'd pick you!'

'You wou-'

Her mouth covers mine, stifling any further protests with the longest, hottest, most glorious kiss. The kind of kiss that makes icecaps melt, birds fall out of the sky and grumpy cats shove their ginger bums in your face.

Jen looks at the cat. I look at the cat. And, as if possessed by the spirit of our heroine Nan Astley, we cheerfully blurt, *'Oh, do one, Kitty!'*

-THE END-

EPILOGUE

Jen and Ava have started their new blog, "The Wild Adventures of Evie and Don". They already have over 150,000 followers.

Lucrezia has been promoted to CEO of Marshall Media USA.

Dawn and Tom got engaged. Cousin Maria is in a three-way and Aunty B checked herself into a sex addiction clinic…for a week. She is now dating a therapist she met there.

Nandi the cow is star of a spin off reality show, "A Mooovable Feast", in which Hannah features as an in-house vet on secondment from Oz.

Sara continues her work in Thailand and was recently awarded a special commendation for humanitarian services to children. She still looks like Rachel Weisz.

And last but not least…

Scarlet is still Scarlet. Ever hopeful she will win Ava back. One day.

*

ABOUT THE AUTHOR

Lisa Frederickson is an award-winning creative director. Born in Norfolk, England, she studied French and English Literature at University College, London and at *L'Institut Britannique* in Paris.

She has previously edited a work of fiction *"Faking It"* by Jade Winters and penned two comedy series. She currently divides her time between Sydney and London, where she works in the TV industry: writing, directing and playing the ukulele. Badly.

ACKNOWLEDGEMENTS

Mark Twain famously said, "Writing is easy, all you have to do is cross out all the wrong words". Well, Mark lied. It's bloody hard! I crossed out words, added in new ones, crossed those out too and I'm not sure whether I ended up with the right ones or the wrong ones, but I did end up with words! A book full of them and hopefully a funny, heart-warming story too.

That said, these words would not have been penned if it were not for some very special people:

Mapa – Forever encouraging, forever loving, forever making tea. You make me proud to be your daughter.

Toni – For your support, endless plot suggestions, love and patience.

My brother, my hero – I wouldn't be me without you. Thanks for agreeing to edit this beast. *We did it!*

Kay – The late addition to the editorial team, who heaved us over the line with her excellent fact-checking and proofreading skills. Hope there aren't any mitsakes(!)

Nat – For allowing me to read to you, often the same bits over and over, and still laughing.

Lisa MC – Thanks for the belief and IKEA meatballs. Both equally delicious.

My amazing college gang, the Sydney Angels, Lon-Whitstable girls and my Foxy Fam, especially Sally-Anne Kerr for the amazing cover design.

And finally, to you, the reader, for buying/borrowing/nicking a copy. I thank you with all my Norfolk heart.

Printed in Great Britain
by Amazon

28137739R00207